M000214181

DIGITAL DIVIDE

Also by K.B. Spangler

A Girl and Her Fed
Rise Up Swearing
The Russians Came Knocking

DIGITAL DIVIDE

K.B. SPANGLER

A GIRL AND HER FED BOOKS
NORTH CAROLINA

Digital Divide is a work of fiction. Names, characters, and events are the creations of the author. Settings are either fictional or have been adapted from locations in and around Washington, D.C. for purposes of storytelling. Any resemblance to actual persons, living or dead, is entirely coincidental. All characters, places, and events are set in the world of A Girl and Her Fed, found online at www.agirlandherfed.com

Copyright © 2012-2013 by K.B. Spangler.
Cover art by Rose Loughran of Red Moon Rising

All rights reserved. No part of this book may be reproduced or distributed in printed or electronic form without permission from the author.

Printed by CreateSpace, an Amazon.com Company
Available from Amazon.com and other retail outlets.

For Brie, Matt, and Gwendy

"The term 'digital divide' initially referred to gaps in access to a computer. When the internet diffused rapidly into society and became a primary type of computing, the term shifted to encompass gaps in not only computer but also internet access . . . while gaps in physical access are being addressed, other gaps seem to widen. One of the factors that appears to be important is the differential possession of digital skills."

Alexander van Deursen and Jan van Dijk,
"Internet Skills and the Digital Divide"

ONE

Three. Days. Three. Days. Three. More. Days.

She loved high heels, how their *tak-tak-tak* against the concrete implied purpose. A woman in heels had places to go, things to do. They kept her company on quiet nights like this, each step an affirmation.

Just. Three. More. Days.

Her shoes used to say *Debt. Debt. Debt. Ninety. Thousand. In. Debt.* Loans, oh God, those hideous student loans, and living off of credit instead of sense. Then came an eternity of paychecks in portions, divvied up and rolled into snowballs thrown against interest. Along the way, and she couldn't remember when, her shoes stopped counting down the money and started counting down the time.

Twelve. Months. Two. Months. Thirty. Days. Ten... Nine...

Such a lame joke, the one where her shoes had been there each step of the way, but every Friday for the past eight years they had carried her to the ATM on her way home from work, telegraphing her progress.

Strange, though, how this ritual had changed. These visits were nothing more than comfort food. She had replaced the weekly receipt with an app which reported her balance in real time, and all of her bills were paid online. She couldn't remember when she had last mailed a check. Her money no longer needed a chaperone: she was a bystander to her own finances as funds moved from her employer's account to her own with happy reliability, then fled to her creditors as they carved it up like a Christmas ham.

These days, everyone might as well be Agents.

She slipped her card into the reader and stepped into the vestibule. The room was cool in the early August evening, and the door closed behind her to seal off the heat and the noise of the city. It was an old bank, done up in worn marble, and the vestibule still had hints of its past life as a teller's office before it had been adapted into an alcove for the ATM.

The screen danced, the bank's animated logo twisting into an ad for loan refinancing until she entered her pin. Welcome, valued customer Maria Griffin. Would you like to apply for low-rate credit card? No? Would you like to be emailed about an exciting new savings account? No? Then please continue.

Her account flashed before her eyes, a very small, very manageable number.

I will never do this again, she thought.

He grabbed her from behind, one arm across her mouth and the other tight at her throat with the knife. She reeled, not at the attack itself but the shock of it. Muggings, yes, practically an annual event in D.C., but not in this familiar, empty room.

She lost sight of the knife as he threw her towards the ATM.

She tried to scream, tried to run, but it burned when she tried to catch her breath. A shoe slipped beneath her and she lost her footing on the floor. Wet? Yes, and slick, and...

Oh God. Red.

Her hands went to her throat and came back red.

TWO

Rachel Peng kept her back to the door so she saw them before they saw her. Most days, Rachel would have stuck it out in silence, but this morning had started off with an emergency trip to the hardware store. The handyman she kept on call would cover over the graffiti (CY-BITCH in neat black letters; she appreciated this tagger's creativity and penmanship), but she had bought a five-gallon drum of paint for this purpose and, in the way of all necessary things, it was nowhere to be found. She knew it would turn up at some point, probably under the bathroom sink or some other place a huge tub of paint had no business being, but she was not in a mood to suffer fools or co-workers with axes to grind.

They rumbled towards the lunch counter, cut young bucks sporting a mix of cheap suits and uniforms, and she had one brief moment to relax when it seemed they'd pass her by. Then Zockinski went red, quick and hot across his core of autumn orange, and she sighed into her sandwich. Game on.

They came at her in a pack, Zockinski at the lead. "Hey, freak."

"Not today, Zocky. Keep on moving."

Rachel had never before said anything with an ounce of personality to Zockinski and he flashed sickly purple-gray, a color she was beginning to associate with doubt. Anger, passion, violence, those were the reds, and stability and peace were the blues. Odd combinations of surface colors showed internal conflict, maybe. She was gradually building an ontology of emotions, but she was self-taught and it was slow going.

Zockinski shifted back to a red-tinted orange and sat down across from her. "Freak," he said again. "Cy-*borg*," he spat, hitting the second syllable too hard to sound like a rational adult. His gang swarmed around the table, hemming her in her booth. They were beginning to pick up Zockinski's hue, red spreading from him through his small crowd like a virus.

Mob mentality is literally contagious, Rachel realized. She reached out to the OACET community server and began recording, just in case.

"Walk away, buddy. Don't make me break out the d-word."

"Been called a douchebag before, freak."

"And I've been called a freak by scarier men than you, Zocky, so that word's lost its teeth. No, I meant 'discrimination.'"

The men instantly ran a fierce dark crimson. These days, cops were taught to avoid committing hate crimes the same way they were once taught how to avoid getting shot.

"Tell me I'm wrong," she said, moving her lunch out of harm's way. "Wait, let's use the legal. Tell me I don't have a case against you, with this…" she gestured at the group, "pinning me down, harassing me.

"Oh," she added before Zockinski could respond. "By the way, you're on camera."

They glanced, almost as one, at the black half-moons mounted behind the register to discourage employees from pilfering the till. When they looked back at Rachel, she was shaking her head and tapping her temple, a sugar-sweet smile wide across her face.

They froze. Everything about them stopped, even their kaleidoscopes of emotions, and Rachel watched as they tried to process something beyond their experience. She had seen this a couple of times before, an internalized struggle to take what was alien and squish it into familiar packaging so it could be safely handled. She didn't think she'd ever fully shake the memory of watching it happen in her own parents.

Two of Zockinski's group spun towards the counter, changing direction like sharks that had scented blood. The others abandoned Zockinski as he fumbled for a way to save face. Hill, his partner, tugged on Zockinski's shoulder to get him to move. Zockinski paused, his surface colors moving through a full spectrum of reds before he finally went a dusky reddish-gray and slid out from the booth. Rachel guessed she had just seen him try and fail to find the perfect comeback.

A lone man, tall and slender, with curious yellows wrapped around a core of ultramarine, came up behind them.

"Goodbye, Zockinski." Rachel said, ripping open her bag of chips. "This never happened."

Zockinski muttered something unintelligible, a threat or thanks, perhaps, Rachel couldn't say. The red had faded from him, so she chose to believe he had thanked her and offered, "I erased the recording." He ignored her and moved towards his friends at the counter.

The tall man slipped into Zockinski's seat. Rachel slid a wrapped sandwich across the table to him.

"You should have done that weeks ago," Raul Santino said, studying his sandwich through wire-rimmed glasses.

"I'm under orders." Rachel rolled her eyes. "Be friendly, be courteous, be an example."

Don't mess it up for the rest of us, was what her boss had meant but hadn't needed to say. She was their first police liaison and she was aware of the weight she carried.

It had been a fast six months since the human mind had gone digital. In point of fact, the cyborgs had been created five years prior, but a joint federal-level handwashing had hidden the Office of Adaptive and Complementary Enhancement Technologies from the general public. The Program had failed, the politicians had said, sadly shaking their heads. Such a tremendous waste of resources. Perhaps we'll try again after technology has caught up with theory.

Except the Program hadn't failed. Patrick Mulcahy, self-appointed head of OACET, had waited until a clear day in early spring when the cherry trees were almost ready to bloom. Then he called a press conference and took a frenzied media corps on a long walk around Washington to discuss how their elected officials had secretly invested in cybernetics. He explained how this particular technology had been sold to Congress as a method of communication for operatives who couldn't carry external equipment into the field. Unfortunately, there was a wrinkle: it seemed the Agents who had received the implant were able to circumvent all electronic security. Passwords, firewalls, airwalls... these meant nothing. If a device could talk to another machine, an Agent could connect to it and take control of it.

Yes, even the nukes. Don't worry. We live here too.

They had stopped at a streetcart for burgers. The media coverage had shown Mulcahy the golden boy, the all-American hero, laughing over a quarter-pounder as he changed the world.

The revelation that the U.S. government secretly employed three hundred and fifty OACET Agents had caused no small damage in Washington. The cyborgs were one thing, their government's decision to sacrifice them another. Mulcahy had gone to the press armed with plenty of evidence to show how certain politicians had panicked and managed the potential OACET scandal through quick, quiet murder. There had been five hundred Agents, once.

Mulcahy and the other members of OACET's administrative team had linked arms with the press and dragged a reluctant Congress into open hearings. The discovery process would probably last for years, but each day a little more information slipped into the news cycle. The Agents were agreeable about letting others carry out the inquiry, as they were more sympathetic if they weren't their own messengers.

Besides, they had better things to do.

Or they had seemed better at the time, Rachel groused into her chips. Mulcahy had approached D.C.'s Metropolitan Police Department and suggested a liaison between their organizations, with Rachel acting as the MPD's first in-house Agent. The police would benefit from a cyborg on staff, and Rachel could put a human face on OACET for the local law. The MPD had jumped at the idea, but it was now brutally obvious that someone high up in management had hitched themselves to the pro-OACET bandwagon without consulting the officers.

Resentment was thick among everyone with boots on the ground except for poor good-natured Santino, who was forced to watch his own promising career collapse under their dead end of a partnership.

"What's on the agenda?" Rachel asked. Mornings were spent doing paperwork filed by officers who claimed their cases had something to do with technology, and thus defaulted to Santino's office. Scut work, all of it, with lost smart phones making up the majority. Afternoons were more interesting, with plenty of time to kill on the shooting range or crawling through the rubble of pawn stores to find stolen electronics.

Santino, engrossed in his footlong turkey sub, wouldn't meet her eyes.

She groaned. "Passwords?"

He nodded. "Sixty-eight of them," he said through a mouthful of sandwich.

She threw up her hands and slumped back in her booth. Passwords were meaningless busy work. When an officer seized a piece of equipment protected by unbreakable encryption software, they sent it to Santino. He would set it up, turn it on, and she'd reset the password to a universal code used by the First District Station of the MPD. It was tedious, made more so by the need to call the office of each judge who had issued the original warrant to ensure the equipment was covered in the search. OACET was too vulnerable to be caught up in accusations of misuse of power.

"Let me guess, they all have to be done by end of shift," she said. Months could go by between password sessions, then suddenly dozens of machines would need to be opened and cleared as quickly as possible. Rachel suspected dickery.

"Actually, no," he said, getting up to refill his soda. "I asked. We've got until Thursday."

Rampant dickery, then. Someone was setting them up for failure, and at end of shift today they'd catch hell for not getting their work done.

Across the restaurant, Zockinski and his pack were huddled

together, food forgotten. Rachel killed time by watching their colors pop and shift; their cores were consistent, but their surface hues were moving towards alignment. Someone, and it looked like Zockinski from the invading autumn orange, was making a persuasive argument.

Most Agents used their implants to interface with technology, but Rachel couldn't care less about that particular ability. Outside of the office, she talked to tech so rarely that she wouldn't give it a second thought if she woke up one morning and machines had gone back to being inert lumps of plastic which chittered and binged. She wouldn't have traded the implant for anything, though. An unexpected side effect of connecting the implant to the audio and visual centers of the brain was the capacity to perceive an almost countless number of frequencies. Information from both force and matter was turned into a sixth sense which wrapped around and through objects, letting her know their qualities more clearly than her eyes ever could. Form, location, even texture and sound, all of these stood out in her mind, allowing her to move through an environment so rich and vivid that she had tried to describe it only once, and badly.

Rachel wasn't sure what she perceived in other people, be it body temperature or energy emissions or the magical residue of unicorn kisses, but whatever it was translated into color. The space a person occupied in her consciousness was defined by a signature hue, overlayered by an ever-changing rainbow which reflected their mood. This rainbow was hard to read (Why would someone flash pink, brown, and green? What did it mean when these colors aligned to match? Did it matter if they clicked into alignment quickly, or if they swirled around in a mess like a child stirring fingerpaints?), but she was getting better at it.

It fascinated her sometimes, those traditional relationships linking mood and color. She wondered whether she perceived someone as blue when they were calm because that was how they appeared to her expanded senses, or whether her mind interpreted something otherwise unknowable as blue because she had been conditioned to think of it as a calming color. Rachel would have loved to stick the implant in her grandmother's head, a woman who kept to the old Chinese tradition of white as the color of death. Would she and *lăo lao* see white at the same time, or would Rachel see black where her grandmother saw white? She had no one to talk to about these things: honestly, she was usually frustrated as much as fascinated.

"You're staring," Santino said as he dropped back into the booth.

She snickered. "Not exactly."

He dropped his voice to just above a whisper. "You're listening in?"

"No. You'd be surprised at how fast the fun of hearing what other people really think about you wears off."

They stood to leave, gathering up their cellophane carnage, when Zockinski and his partner came at them.

"Ah crap. Round two, fight." Santino said. "You better get out of here. They won't bluff off this time."

"Hang on," she said, seeing some blues and greens among the orange. "Let's see what they want."

Jacob Zockinski was a homicide detective and Rachel supposed he fit the part. He wore off-the-rack for plainclothes and was in fair shape. Her frame of reference was different on such things, but she assumed he was decently attractive for a man some years her senior. Matt Hill, his partner, had that rare basketball player's build of tall, whip-thin, and sturdily muscled. He also had the loudest body language of anyone Rachel had ever met. With his height, he might as well have paid for his opinions to be displayed on a billboard. He was there (arms crossed, torso slightly turned towards the door, and standing several steps behind Zockinski) for no other reason than to show support for his partner.

"We'd like your advice," Zockinski said. His hands were deep in his pockets and he appeared casual, but he was flickering that same sickish purple-gray.

"I really don't think you do," Rachel said.

"We have a tech problem," Zockinski spoke over her.

"Somebody should have shown up on film, but didn't. Think she can help us out?" Hill spoke to Santino.

"Work a case with you?" Rachel laughed. "No thanks."

"Look at a tape *for* us. That's what you do," Hill said, glaring at an invisible spot several feet above her head.

"Yup, that's what your tax dollars buy, me sitting on my butt, watching TV. Go find yourself a housewife who kills her afternoons with her soaps. I'm sure there's one or two of them left."

"This would be a big favor to us," Zockinski said through gritted teeth.

"You know what's hard to prove, Raul?" Rachel asked her partner.

"Where to draw the line between harassment and teasing?"

"Indeed! Wafer-thin, especially between colleagues."

"And it's not like someone who hates you would offer to work with you."

"So true. It seems I must be a fragile, overly sensitive woman who can't take a joke."

"I've always thought so."

"I liked her better when she didn't talk," Zockinski said to Santino.

"Yeah, I get that a lot," Rachel said, maneuvering around Hill to dump her trash. "Tell you what, gentlemen, spread the word to leave me alone and all's forgiven."

Hill stepped away, almost dancing sideways to keep her from touching him. "Just come with us. Fifteen minutes."

Rachel leaned towards Santino and stage-whispered: "What do you think? Are we about to be left for dead in a ditch?"

"Nah, but this is a beautiful opportunity. It's not often you get to see an ass-covering unfold," Santino said. He spread his hands, fingers fanning open. "It's like taking the time to watch a flower bloom."

"Almost poetic."

"Quite."

Hill left, utterly done with them. Zockinski, who had invested more of himself in this battle, waited for Rachel to buy her daily cookie and walked back to First District Station with them. Near them. Anyone driving by would have assumed, correctly, they just happened to be traveling in the same direction.

They ended up in a small conference room with a video setup. Hill was waiting with arms crossed, leaning against the painted cinderblock in the far corner.

"This gets a little…" Zockinski paused as he searched for the right word. "Dark."

Santino pulled a chair in front of the monitor. "We assumed. You guys work homicide."

"Yeah," Hill said. "It's almost always boyfriend, husband, ex-husband, or junkie, but this one is bad."

Zockinski went through his pockets and came out with a mechanical pencil. "We weren't kidding when we said we couldn't find someone who should have been on this tape. Okay, so…

He roughed out a diagram on the tabletop. His scratchy gray lines barely stood out against the utilitarian metal. "The bank should have gotten this on three different cameras. There's the usual one inside of the ATM," he said, circling the reference point. "There's one inside the vestibule hallway." Another circle. "And the last one is outside of the building and is pointed at the door." One final circle, off to the side and up.

"It's an old bank, so the vestibule used to be a storage area or something," Hill said. He still kept himself as far away from Rachel as possible but as he spoke, Zockinski drew lines with his finger across the diagram. "It's at the end of a little hallway. There's a window to the street in the hall, but there're none in the room itself. The camera in the vestibule points at the hall, so anyone coming or going? They're caught.

"This is the ATM footage," Hill continued, pointing at the television in the conference room. "It's the angle with the cleanest version of the attack. You can see a glove and part of his mask before he drops back off-screen, but that's all we ever see of him."

Hill picked up the remote and the monitor woke up. A small room with pale walls, pens and deposit slips on a tall slab desk off to the side, a heavily-patterned area rug in the hall to soak up rainy-day liquids. The film quality was excellent. Digital storage was so cheap that security footage had transitioned from still images taken every three seconds to a continuous stream filmed in high resolution.

"Black and white?" Rachel asked. Security systems had evolved ages ago, and she couldn't remember the last time she had seen a monochrome version. This setup was designed for low light scenarios and whoever had purchased it was either cheap or careless, since almost all bank robberies took place during the day.

"Some banks still use it," Hill said, and shrugged. He didn't know why, either. Cops worked with what they were given.

The camera was pointed towards the door. A woman in her late twenties entered the vestibule. She was smiling.

"She looks happy," Santino said.

"She was about to finish paying off ninety grand in loans. She was checking her balance to make sure the payment would go through."

"Oh man. Breaks the heart."

Maria Griffin came towards the camera. Great skin, longish curling hair, some freckles. Certainly not a beauty but still pretty by way of youth and attitude. Nothing about her posture communicated she was aware of another person in the room. Rachel wished she could have read Griffin's mood (if, for no other reason, to see what color was associated with conquering a mountain of debt), but even if it hadn't been in black and white, emotions weren't captured on film.

Then the arm went around her throat, with a fast glimpse of the killer's gloves and his lower jaw under a ski mask. The edge of a knife appeared and Griffin fell towards the camera, holding her throat. Griffin vanished, followed by a cascade of hair and, at the end, one delicate hand low on the marble wall. The hand slid down, leaving a slow wake of black blood against the white marble.

Hill hit pause and the screen froze. It said something about Zockinski and Hill, how they must have seen this tape a couple dozen times but didn't play it down with humor.

"The camera in the hall got this from the knees down," Hill said. "She's alone, and then there's another set of feet, and then you can see her on the ground but she's alone again."

Santino exhaled heavily. "So what can we help you with?"

"Can the cyborg tell anything from the video?"

"The cyborg can tell a woman was murdered," Rachel snapped. Santino flashed an irritated red and Rachel sat on her temper. "What exactly are you looking for?"

"It's just…" Zockinski hesitated, "the room's empty. We have two clear shots of the door, and everyone who used the ATM before her is accounted for. She's the only person there, and nobody followed her in. This guy came out of nowhere. She might as well have been killed by a ghost."

"Is there one of those little access doors for service?" Santino asked, leaning towards the monitor. He was a lifelong fan of the locked room murder mystery, but the reality of that handprint scrubbed the romance from it. "Some of those cover a space big enough to hide a person."

Zockinski shook his head. "It's a newer machine. The entire face pops open. Insurance companies want banks to get rid of the ones with service doors because of, well…" He pointed at the monitor, the smeared handprint.

"And there's no line-of-sight into the room itself?"

"Nope."

Rachel thought aloud. "Business district… There's probably dozens of cameras on that street, right?"

Hill nodded. "We got them in the canvas. They all show Griffin going into the bank, and then nothing until she's found, fourteen minutes later. We went back three hours and everyone going in, went out. We even asked the maintenance guy who restocked the machine around noon, and he said the room was empty when he left."

"There's probably a few other cameras on the street you don't know about, private ones. Nanny cams, mostly, maybe some security systems that wouldn't show up in your records. I'll have to be at the bank to find them."

"Can't you do that from here?" Zockinski asked. Rachel didn't have to check his mood to tell he wanted to kick them to the curb.

"It is just so cute how you people think we're omniscient," Rachel said.

THREE

When they had first been paired as partners, Rachel and Santino had seen no other option than to go out and get completely hammered on straight whiskey. Rum, they agreed, was too popular to be interesting, tequila suffered from delusions of grandeur, and vodka had lost its hearty Russian heritage to peer pressure from vanilla and fruit. But whiskey, good old-fashioned whiskey, still had roots running deep in Tennessee and remembered its sole purpose was to help make awkward social situations bearable.

As it happened, they had more in common than whiskey. Professionally, they couldn't have been more different but they clicked on the important things (him: "Sophia Loren in *Houseboat*." her: "Yes, yes, a million times yes!"). They lurched from bar to bar, finally coming to rest on the front stoop of a local bookstore with a handful of Georgetown students. The students were elated to hear she was with OACET, and they traded her opinions on how cyborgs fit into the U.S. Justice System for bottles of warm beer.

Sometime after the students had shuffled home but before the sun came up, Santino admitted to savage jealousy. At the same time Rachel had a tiny chip implanted in her brain, Santino was finishing up his graduate degree at Cal Tech, developing manual solutions for problems she could now solve with a thought. If he had known what was truly possible, he would have banged on their door until they stuck him in the experiment just to shut him up.

She had very nearly told him then, about what had happened to them during those five years from when they received the implant to the day they went public, but he was still a stranger. He wasn't OACET: he was different, other. Still, with the liquor guiding her, she took a chance. She turned off her implant and sat in the absolute dark. She listened to him talk about his family while the cars rumbled by, and felt comfortable around a normal human being for the first time since she had been one herself.

Anyone else in his position would have lashed out at her, would have taken out their frustrations on the reason they had become a pariah, but Santino had faith. OACET would change the future of law enforcement, he said. He wanted to be part of it, to be one of the first to define how the next generations of technology, law, and society intersected. Even before OACET broke the status quo, Santino had been moving towards that goal. He had left his comfortable Ivory Tower for the Metropolitan Police Department and slogged through four years as a beat cop to get some experience in how things worked, and to gain some perspective towards how things should work. He wrote papers too dense for Rachel to understand and had them published in journals with unpronounceable names. At cocktail parties, the academics peeled Santino off of her arm and rushed him off for questioning; her partner was far more interesting than the MPD's pet cyborg. Sometimes he got mad enough to throw furniture, but he knew—just knew!—things would work out for them in the end.

Now, on their way to the bank, Rachel wondered if he might have been right. He certainly thought he was right; of all of the colors out there, she hadn't expected that smug would come across as hot pink.

"Don't get too excited," she said.

He cocked an eyebrow at her.

"I'm just saying, suppose all of this goes perfectly."

"Do tell."

"We get in there, we find the out that Colonel Mustard did it with the candlestick in the library, and the city throws us a parade."

"With bonuses?"

"Of course. Doubling annually."

"I love me some exponential bonuses."

"Even if all that were to happen..." Rachel said as she reclined her seat and leaned back, arms behind her head. "Plus they give us shiny medals with our names on them..."

"He waits for her to get to the punchline..."

"We still have to do passwords when we get back."

Santino swore and threatened to drive into a passing truck.

When they arrived at the bank, they were directed to a lot cordoned off for the emergency vehicles. They parked beside Zockinski, but he and Hill had already started walking towards the building. Rachel and Santino trailed behind, kid siblings warily dogging contentious older brothers.

When they turned the corner, the street was swarming.

"Why is the bank open?" Rachel asked.

Hill spoke without acknowledging her directly. "The lobby was cleared this morning. They roped off the ATM but the bank didn't want to lose business."

And what a day for business it was, with everyone and their sister overdue to talk to a real human being who, by pure coincidence, worked at the scene. You could share neighborhood gossip online but the thrills weren't as intense. Status updates were poor fare for the ghoul within.

The vestibule was air-conditioned and the chill hit her like a polar blast. Rachel shivered at the smell and wondered if the customers in the bank proper were aware the recirculated air they were breathing was misted in blood. She wanted to reach out and trace the ventilation system back to its source with the hope of bumping into a HEPA filter, but one of the first things she had learned was to never scratch at the thin veneer of sanitation plastered over civilization.

(Poking around her main waterline had changed Rachel's showering habits forever. She paid an outrageous monthly fee to a company who did something with salt and sand to scour each individual water molecule before it touched her body. A real bargain, in her opinion, considering the black tarrish gunk which lined the interior of the city's pipes.)

The room was a classic murder scene, with the first layer of gore covered by a second layer of forensics. Based on the brownish pool and the handprint against the wall, Maria Griffin had fallen several feet away from the ATM. It was easy to read how her body had lain: an inept coroner had dragged the victim's hair through her own still-damp blood when she was removed, leaving an effect across the white marble like brushstrokes through paint.

Zockinski and Hill stood to the side, faces blank, watching them. Santino had put in his time on the force so he wasn't cherry, but she was an unknown. Rachel was in uncharted mood-territory and had no idea what was going on in their heads (what translated to opalescent yellow-green?); she assumed they were waiting to see what she would do, but she couldn't tell if they were impressed at her composure or waiting for her to vomit, swoon, or get the vapors.

"Don't touch anything. *An-y-thing*," Hill said.

"I know. Didn't you check up on me?" Rachel asked, following the blood. The woman had been wearing heels, as large and tiny spots chased each other in a clean pattern until a heavy blotch blurred the tracks. The blood told a story: Griffin had been attacked while she stood at the ATM, had tried to run, had lost her balance…

Hill didn't answer so she took a moment to glance up at him. "I was a Warrant Officer with Army CID. Did three tours in Afghanistan before this," she said, pointing to her head. He flashed an unusual shade of teal but didn't respond.

"Seriously," Rachel said as she returned her attention to the scene. "I used to be a real person and everything."

She squatted on her heels, as far away from the blood as the small room would allow.

"You're supposed to be looking for cameras." Zockinski was getting angry, his surface hue going red again.

"I am. I did," she amended. "They were first on the list. But they aren't the only things out there."

Or in here, she thought. Her sixth sense swept down and

out, moving into the marble to follow the utilities as they carved their way through stone. She poked and prodded from top to bottom, then started laughing when she hit the void.

Clever! She began rolling through different frequencies to test for residue. Agents lacked an olfactory connection so chemicals were generally imperceptible unless they could be detected visually. Same with fingerprints, although those usually showed up when the source was sweaty or greasy, but she could almost always tell when disposable gloves had been used as those left a powder similar to that on moth wings.

Her tongue tapped at the roof of her mouth, ticking like the Predator on the hunt. She hadn't realized she had adopted this little mannerism while she flipped through the spectra until Santino had called her on it a few months ago. It was crazy how quickly new habits were formed.

Dust sparkled and she laughed again. Behind her, Zockinski and Hill were shifting like frightened rainbows, but Santino was gradually building in excitement.

Rachel gestured at her partner. Santino crossed the room and knelt beside her. "As a representative of OACET with no authority at the MPD," she said quietly as his eyes widened, "I'm hands-off from now on."

"No shit," he whispered. They had never invoked this policy before; there had never been a reason. If this case went to trial, she'd be treated the same as a psychic hired by the department to give a grieving mother some hope. Her name would appear as a consultant who had assisted the MPD at their request, and the services she had rendered would be swept under the jargon. The Agents were so new that the judicial process hadn't caught up with their abilities. It was safer to take herself out of an investigation than to risk having the case thrown out in court.

"If I were you," she said, including Zockinski and Hill in the conversation, "I'd check for prints *here* and *here*." She indicated two separate spots placed a few feet apart on a square marble block set on the lowest tier. "After that, I'd press them both at the same time."

The homicide detectives didn't move.

"If you won't, I will," Santino offered.

Hill went looking for Forensics, and Rachel whispered to Santino that there would be no prints since the guy had been wearing gloves, so she was mostly covering the bases, but was also sort of jerking Zockinski and Hill around. Santino approved; he preferred to multitask, too.

Forensics taped the surface and found nothing, but their team hung around to watch as Zockinski pushed on the two locations Rachel had indicated. As Zockinski removed his hands, there was a thin click and one side of the block popped out from the wall. Hill hissed through his teeth as a four-inch thick marble slab swung open on well-oiled hinges.

"Magnets. Big ones," she explained. She looked at Santino, "I should have checked for magnets first. They're easy to find, but they're used in everything so they can throw me off when I'm searching.

"He set it up like the doors on a glass display cabinet," she continued. "Apply a little pressure, and the clasp releases. I guess he stuck two in there to make sure no one kicked it open by accident."

Zockinski hunched down, then dropped down to all fours so he could peer inside a goodly-sized hole. "You could hide in here for a couple of hours, easy…"

Rachel covered her mouth. It was another new habit, one she had picked up from Mulcahy who sometimes didn't want to be caught smiling.

"Whoa!" In his excitement, Zockinski nearly dove headfirst into the hole. Hill grabbed him by his jacket and pulled him back before he could contaminate the scene. Zockinski looked up at Rachel. "A tunnel?"

She nodded. "You guys might want to shut down the bank again. The other end comes out next to the first teller's window on the other side of this wall."

"Well, we'll leave you to it," Santino said, and gripped her shoulder. "Let us know if we have to sign anything." Her partner steered them towards the door. She raised a curious eyebrow at him. "Just go," he whispered.

"Let them have this," he explained on their way back to the car. "They lose face if we stick around and take credit. But you just gave them their biggest lead, and they won't forget it, and it really didn't hurt that you performed freakin' magic in front of the Forensics team!

"We are..." he said as he spun on a heel in a sleek Astaire pirouette, "Golden!"

Several hours later, buried under an avalanche of electronics, they had only unlocked eighteen passwords and she was on the verge of snapping an iPhone in half with her teeth.

"Tarnished gold is still gold," Santino said.

"Stop that."

"I know what you were thinking."

She snorted. "Obviously not. Gold doesn't tarnish."

"Yes, it does."

"You need to stop buying your girlfriend jewelry at the same place you buy bananas."

"They had a sale," he muttered.

On the way back to First District Station, they had wondered why a bank had a secret tunnel. They thought about this for the space of a millisecond, then agreed it had been a remarkably stupid question. Rachel took a moment to search for robberies committed in old D.C. banks over the last century or so, and gave up when the number of results made it unlikely she'd find any information without some hard, targeted digging.

(The problem, as she had explained to Santino during one of their pub crawls, was that they couldn't relate to the seemingly nonsensical nature of electronic data. The information might exist, but there was so much of it that the human mind, augmented or otherwise, would require an eternity to sift through it to find anything useful. Unless they knew how to interact with a specific hierarchical or relational database, the Agents were left to grope around aimlessly in mountains of meaningless code. Santino, who was a programmer in his spare time, had asked how on earth they managed, and Rachel had replied they generally used Google like everyone else.)

She tapped the stack of paperwork in front of her. Warrants, warrants, warrants; searches, seizures, and discoveries... Every item was documented before it reached them but she had to check each by hand a second time before she unlocked the equipment. Rachel certainly wasn't making any friends among the judges' clerks who had processed these warrants once already. When she called for confirmation, she was shunted to hold almost as soon as they recognized her voice.

Oooh, the Bee Gees. She was always grateful that Judge Richards' office had an unwavering anti-Streisand policy. Rachel tapped her pen to the beat.

"'Stayin' Alive?'" Santino's voice came from beneath the table where he was untangling wires.

"Yeah... Wait, how did you know that?" she asked.

There was a knock on the door, followed by the slow emergence of a Krispy Kreme bag and a legal folder through the philodendrons.

"You guys in?"

"Hey, Charley," Rachel said, and went to help the clerk navigate the jungle. The only perk of Santino's new position was a massive private office with southern exposure, and he had covered the walls in plants. She had never seen him tend to them, but they grew at the speed of a tropical rainforest. He adored them and added to the collection almost every other day: she thought the room stunk of ozone, and was nursing a small phobia of falling asleep long enough to be converted to fertilizer.

"Hey, Peng. We heard you were doing passwords today," Charley Brazee said, handing her the folder. She bent her head and shoulder to keep the phone against her ear and flipped the folder open.

"Hah! Confirmation letters," she said to Santino, thumbing through a baker's dozen of notarized documents from Judge Edward's office. "Charley, this is whole hours of time right here.

Thank you!"

The small man smiled. "Time-saver for us, too. We're making copies of these when the warrants are issued so we don't have to drop everything when you call."

Rachel shrugged and nearly lost the phone. "Sorry."

"It's not really a big thing. Ah…" People either avoided her or shotgunned her with questions, there was no middle ground. Charley was a friendly man in his late forties who bribed them with favors for answers. "Why are you on the phone?"

She feigned ignorance and waved the folder at him. "Because not everyone is as amazing as you are, of course."

"No, I mean, why are *you* on a *phone?*"

"I asked her to use it." Santino's head popped up from under the desk, then vanished again. "If I can't hear at least one side of a conversation, I don't know what's on our schedule and I fall behind."

"What he means is he's a shameless eavesdropper."

"I thought I just said that."

Charley leaned against Santino's overstocked bookcase, the only horizontal surface not completely lost under foliage. "So…"

"We can't talk about it," said the underside of the table.

"There might have…" Rachel stopped talking long enough to hear the music change to a different song. *Nope, still on hold.* "There might have been a bank."

"Rachel!"

"What? Charley already knows about the bank."

The clerk nodded. "And the tunnel, and that Peng found it. Edwards is frothing."

"Oh." Rachel winced. "Yeah, he would be."

Judge Edwards was a mainstay on the D.C. judiciary and a fierce opponent of OACET. Several news organizations kept him on retainer as a counterpoint for stories which framed the Agents in a positive light. In his early fifties and with the combination of telegenic features that would inevitably enter politics, Edwards got a lot of airtime. His big thing was attacking what he called "the Forensics God" (and you could hear those capital letters when he spoke), or the idolatry of DNA and other forensic evidence over personal character. He argued in broad strokes that evidence had become so glorified in popular culture that it had become the only thing which mattered to a jury; he claimed that the disposition of the defendant and the testimony of eyewitnesses were now vilified in the courts; he cited case law to prove that the human element of the legal system played a more substantial role in determining guilt than bloodstains or errant hairs. Santino would rage about lies, damned lies, and statistics when the pundits played an Edwards clip.

Rachel, who had served in the Army's version of Internal Affairs, thought the truth was probably somewhere in the middle.

Charley was a newcomer to Edwards' staff. As lowest dog in the pack, Charley had caught the job of managing their warrant clearance. Rachel had made Charley laugh during their first phone conversation, and he had started dropping by Santino's office whenever business took him to First District Station. His core was a smooth bluish-gray which reminded her in turns of the default color at the edges of software windows, or of a little cartoon seal she had loved as a child.

"Well, he's pissed at you but, you know, he's still got those other two cases to keep him busy," Charley said, thumbing through Santino's books.

Santino scooted out from under the table and booted up an ancient personal computer. "No idea why they'd stick encryption on this piece of junk," he complained. "What other cases?"

"You know, the mugging in Ward Six, they got it on tape but there were glitches... Uh, and... And the other one. The guy who got beat all to hell but, on video, he's just drinking coffee..." Charley's voice trailed away as he signed off on the conversation. His surface colors had been tinted with Santino's ultramarine, but those had been immersed by his core of blue-gray and the professional blues of business suits as he found something of interest in Santino's collection.

"Can I borrow these?" he asked, showing Santino the spines of some old college textbooks. Charley seemed to be a habitual Borrower, but it was not yet known if he was also a Returner. Rachel was still waiting for him to drop off a pack of playing cards he had snaked after poker a month ago.

"What glitches?" Rachel prompted, but as Charley started to answer she was abruptly moved from hold into a very loud conversation with the intern manning the phones at Judge Richards' office. Charley and Santino tried their best to ignore her and carry on, but she and this intern shared a seething mutual dislike and spent their off time honing their material. Charley waved to them and bowed out, taking the books and leaving the doughnuts.

FOUR

It wasn't until she was teaching Patrick Mulcahy how to shoot that she realized Charley had told her something important. Mulcahy, towering over her and holding a ridiculously tiny gun, wore a blindfold while she poked him with a stick. (They both suspected the stick served no real purpose, but a sensible person simply did not turn down an opportunity to torment her boss.) Back when she had first realized she could perceive human emotion, she tried her best to explain her world to him. Mulcahy had seized on the possible tactical advantages and asked how difficult it would be for her to teach him how to see as she did.

"Easy! Blind yourself," she had said.

Guilt swept over him. His conversational surface colors had blanched, and even his core hue of cerulean blue went pale. Rachel closed her eyes, embarrassed, but pretended she had meant that he wear a blindfold for several months. Mulcahy thought about it and said while he appreciated the irony of showing up to Senate hearings with his head in a sack, this was also something he couldn't do. But maybe she could teach him how to shoot?

It was tricky, teaching someone how to use a gun when he was already terrifyingly proficient in firearms. Mulcahy had been recruited into OACET from a different kind of agency, one that lacked cybernetics but made up for it in firefights and explosions. After tying a bandanna across his eyes and telling him what they were about to do was mind-bogglingly stupid and potentially lethal, she had put a child's BB pistol in his hand. The colors that flashed across him had gone directly into her ontology; it began with confused oranges and greens, with plenty of good-humored purple as he laughed, the purple growing stronger as he realized she had set him up.

They could have used an adult version but she kept him on the toy gun to push him out of his comfort zone. He was an enormous man with hands the size of dinner plates, and he had to consciously think of how he was holding the gun to use it. Rachel didn't want him to fall back on his training until he had learned to work with his implant to predict a logical path for a bullet.

"So," she had asked on that first day, "why can't real people hit targets on a ricochet, like they do in the movies?"

"Unpredictability," Mulcahy had replied.

Bullets bounced, and they bounced hard. They also deformed spectacularly, especially those designed to go through a person. Only a true idiot would fire at a chunk of metal and expect an intact bullet to change direction on a reliable path. The implant, however, turned them into a new type of idiot, one who was aware that a ricochet would never be as dependable as a straight shot but maybe they could plot a course which minimized the risk.

Hence the BB gun with its steel pellets.

"It's not just about the surface," Rachel had told him. "You want to start by looking into objects. Think of yourself as a universal MRI. You're checking for contrasts. Soft spots, hard spots... If you want to shoot through something, aim for flat soft spots. If you want to plan for a ricochet, pick hard ones with an angled surface.

"And it's all physics," she said. "You're trying to predict inelastic collisions. Some of that energy is lost on contact, but there will always be enough left to keep it moving. So for God's sake, do not fire anything other than a lead bullet directly at something flat and hard, since there are some very good odds that bullet will come right back at you."

The capitol was practically built on a foundation of underground firing ranges. OACET had acquired the lease on an abandoned rifle club for target practice. Rachel had set up peculiarly twisted pieces of industrial scrap around the room, and they took turns pinging them with the BB pistol. Ricochets from the toy gun didn't pack enough punch to knock a fly out of the air, but they were each stung a few times before Mulcahy got the hang of picking surfaces.

"How did you figure this out?" he had asked her after their first lesson.

She had grinned. "I was having a bad day."

It was great fun and they were both fast learners. Early on, their implants had performed most of the calculations needed to knock a bullet off of one course and put it on another. Along with mass, the implant allowed them to process information on the distance to, and the angle of, different objects. Four classes later and in spite of the embarrassingly tiny gun, even Mulcahy had outgrown its help. Practice and slow cultivation of instinct had brought them to a point where they could scan the room and select surfaces without relying on its math.

The trouble was that they now felt as though they had gone as far as they could without upping the stakes. They needed to start using live rounds. As she jabbed him with the stick (too much fun), they weighed out the pros and cons of using their service weapons instead of the pistol. Simulation was fine and all, but Rachel had picked up a box of solid ammunition and they were sure it would unleash a completely different beast.

Sadly, they had more sense.

Mulcahy sat down, still wearing the bandanna over his eyes. He took out his own gun and started idly breaking it down, each piece familiar in his hands. "How'd you find the tunnel?"

She slumped down beside him, the stick flat across her lap. "Scan the north wall. Go deep."

The bandanna turned. Good shooting ranges had thick pine walls layered over concrete to suck up strays. When Rachel looked through her implant, the room lit up with dense metal scattered within the softer wood. Mulcahy, who seldom used his implant to see past the surface, moved into the wood, through the concrete, and recoiled when his mind fell into a nest of rats snug between the cinder blocks.

He bumped her with his shoulder. "Not nice."

She chuckled. "I ran the bank like that. There was a huge void, way too big to be anything other than a service tunnel."

"Fun little mystery."

"Not really. Santino and I talked it over. We thought it had something to do with theft, but as secret passageways go, this one is pretty useless. It just sort of hangs there. Someone added it after the ATM was built, maybe to run ventilation or some extra storage between the two rooms, and it fell off of the blueprints. If it had gone anywhere near the money, that bank would have been robbed like clockwork."

"Still, you were the one who found it. Thanks for that. It might help our reputation on the Hill." Mulcahy rubbed his jaw, a bruise fading from where a popular congressman from Massachusetts had taken a swing at him. Mulcahy had let it land; the media had been there.

"Are we doing okay?" she asked.

Depression and stress, gray as a worn asphalt road, flickered across him so quickly she almost missed it. "It's rough," he admitted. "But we knew going into this the first few years would be the worst."

They sat in silence for a moment. The worst—the absolute worst of the worst—was that they had volunteered for this. Going public had been a choice, and the alternative was so much easier. They could have vanished, with new Social Security numbers and limitless credit in false accounts, drifting at whim and leisure across the planet. Oh, a few of them probably would have been discovered and burned alive as witches, but chances were very good that in some parallel timeline, Rachel's next-door neighbors were a pod of whales off the port side of her yacht instead of an old woman who took a golf club to Rachel's mailbox whenever her cable went out.

Stubborn, vicious Mrs. Wagner, who didn't quite understand what the implant was or did, but still believed Rachel to be the source of every problem she had with technology...

"Scapegoating," she said aloud.

"Hm?"

"I was just thinking. We just got lucky. A decade ago, a locked room murder meant the problem was the room. Today, they assumed the problem was the camera. If I hadn't found that tunnel, they could have dumped this on us. Killer cyborgs from Middle America or whatever, tampering with technology to get away with murder. The press would go ape."

"Heh, you're right. Actually," he said, pulling off the blindfold, "we're lucky you were the one who showed up at that scene. The rest of us would have assumed it was a digital error, too. I know I wouldn't have checked for a hidey-hole."

"Weird, yeah?"

"Yeah. We got lucky. Keep your fingers crossed that this was just a fluke. The last thing we need is to have more violent crimes start disappearing from camera."

She jumped up so quickly the stick went flying.

"Penguin?"

She looked at him, eyes wide. "I need to make a few calls."

Charley claimed to be out to dinner with his wife, but the background noise was very sportsbarish and he got distracted at regular intervals. She prodded him until he coughed up enough information for her to find the rest in the MPD database. Then she called Santino.

"The murder came last," she blurted. She heard a woman gasp and sputter.

"Let me take you off of speaker," he said groggily. *Rachel Peng, Destroyer of Afterglow*, she thought. There were footsteps as he moved to another room. "What?"

"Crimes that don't show up on camera," she said. "Charley tipped us off this afternoon but we weren't paying attention. I went back and checked those cases. There've been two others similar to Griffin's murder. The first was a mugging about three weeks ago. The victim comes out of a convenience store and gets mugged, gets smacked around a little, only he swears the mugger on the store's security footage is not the same man who attacked him. The victim and two witnesses in the store? They say he got jumped from behind by an older white man. But the video shows the assailant as this tall, young black man. I swear to you, Raul, the man on the video looks so much like Hill it's scary. They could be twins.

"And the second case? This one is really strange. This next victim, he's a regular at a local coffee shop. He comes in every night at the same time and buys the same thing. He's so dependable they have his order waiting for him on the counter. Then he goes outside, sits in the same chair, drinks his latte, and goes home. Last week, he got the crap kicked out of him in front of the building. Everybody in the coffee shop told the cops they saw someone walk up and beat on him with a crowbar, but the shop's got an anti-theft camera and it shows him reading a book in his usual chair."

"'S different." Santino's voice cut in and out, and Rachel imagined him rubbing his nose as he woke up. "Griffin's killer was on camera. Those other cases sound like digital manipulation, or maybe a bunch of people got their stories straight before the cops showed up. If anything, her case was more like a... I don't know. A magic trick. Don't pay attention to the man behind the curtain and all that."

"Okay, then where is Griffin's killer on the rest of the security footage? Not during the murder, but when he went into the bank? Or when he left after she was dead? He had to get in and out of that tunnel somehow.

"The techs examined the video from all cases, Santino. Everything's authentic. The time stamps and light sources are solid. Every happy pixel is precisely where it should be. Denmark is knee-deep in dead fish."

He was silent for a few seconds. "You're wrecking my night, you know that."

"And now you get to call Zockinski and Hill. You're welcome."

She updated Mulcahy and begged a ride from him to the convenience store where the first victim had been assaulted. (She would have begged a ride regardless, as he was about to marry into serious money and drove cars that were best photographed when half-naked supermodels were draped over their hoods.) The store was an old gas-and-go in a bad part of town, an option of last resort for those in search of overpriced milk and toilet paper after the bodegas closed for the night. The street seemed all but deserted, but Rachel felt the local element lift their heads and scent the air as Mulcahy's classic Shelby Cobra rumbled up to the curb.

Mulcahy felt it too. "Wait here," he said. He walked around to her door and let her out, his linebacker's silhouette spread wide against the brick of the store in the waning evening light. He cut an iconic figure, his build and his dark blond hair overexposed on every television show and magazine cover in the country. As he waved and drove away, Rachel grinned, remembering a wildlife documentary about an adorable mother hippo and her calf. Mama had hauled the biggest, baddest crocodile in the river out of the water, crushed it into a thin red paste, and went off for a pleasant day to herself at the hippo spa while the surviving crocodiles protected her baby. With luck, some of the smarter ones skulking in the alleys would make sure she didn't have to shoot the stupid ones who assumed small women were easy prey.

"Thanks," she said across the link.

"No problem." His taillights flashed, and he turned the corner and was gone.

After calling Charley, Rachel had found the footage from the convenience store assault on the Sixth District Station police server. The server was protected but Rachel already had permission to retrieve files from First, so had called the evidence room at Sixth and requisitioned a copy of the file for her tablet. She was absolutely certain the elderly officer in charge of the Evidence room had no idea what she had wanted or understood why she wasn't coming in to pick it up, but the paperwork was signed and that was all that mattered. Bureaucracy was an inalienable force of nature; she could march through the front gates of Hell itself if the right paperwork was signed.

Rachel took out her tablet and queued up the video. She froze the image. Top-down, featureless concrete, a curb and the bottom third of a gas pump. The shadows were completely different: then, it was night; now, it was twilight.

She reached out to the security system and cringed when she found multiple cameras. Some Agents were skilled at splitting their perception and could reside in their own minds and electronic devices simultaneously. She was not. Being in several places at once made her nauseated.

Part of Rachel's conscious self merged into the security cameras to watch its physical counterpart in the parking lot below. She was taller and her face was slightly longer than the average Asian woman's, passing nods to her genes from her American father, but her features and her black hair cropped tight in a pixie cut were straight Chinese.

Rachel staggered slowly across the lot, trying not to throw up as she aligned the curb and the gas pump on the screen with her perspective through the cameras. When she found the spot where the assault had occurred, she pulled herself together and pinged the security system proper. *Recent and decent,* she thought, *good for them.* The store might be a shell of its former profit, but its owners had followed the code for security systems. Like the bank, this system also shot in black and white, but she gave them a pass considering the depth of the shadows pooling around her as the sun set.

She ducked into the store and found a bottle of water. The small room reeked of old nachos and pot. The main source of these odors, a lanky kid in his early twenties, gawked at her from his clerk's station behind bulletproof glass.

"You know Mulcahy?" The kid had his face pressed up against the store window as if hoping the old muscle car would suddenly cruise back into view.

"Yeah, I work with him," she said. Celebrity was not the same as acceptance, and she was careful with her words.

The kid studied her and decided she didn't fit his image of an Agent. Apparently she was dressed as a politician's flunky as he asked her, "You're up on the Hill?"

"No, First MPD," she replied, and his conversational colors went flat and retreated to wrap around his core. Now she was on familiar ground. Most of her early practice in reading emotions had come from talking to people who wanted nothing to do with the police.

"Mulcahy's pretty cool," she slid a few bucks through the slot under the glass and twisted open the bottle. "He showed me his gun. I work with the cops so I see guns all day long, but his was different. Don't know what kind it was, though."

The kid seized the bait, and Rachel played dumb for several excruciating minutes as he grabbed every weapon magazine in the store and had her find the one that looked most like Mulcahy's. She picked out a shiny hand cannon at random and he got to tell her why Mulcahy shouldn't be carrying *that,* he should be carrying *this,* because *that* was garbage and *this* was a million times better. From there it was easy to steer the conversation to personal security, and the kid stated with authority how he knew America was messed up thanks to a beatdown in his very own parking lot.

"I know, I heard!" she said, crossing her arms and leaning forward as much as the glass barrier would allow. The kid's eyes strayed south; she was wearing a ballistic vest under her shirt but young men lived in hope. "It's why I'm here. Someone..." she said, glancing over her shoulder as if checking for nefarious villains, "... down at First MPD told me I should come down and check it out. You saw it? You were the one on that night?"

He had and he was. The kid spoke to her breasts and told her a story of two men in his parking lot. The first was minding his own business when the second grabbed him and started pounding away. "But!" he said, leaning close enough to kiss her if the glass hadn't been between them. "You want to know what's weird?"

"Yes!" Rachel said, feigning wide-eyed and eager. She had pinged Zockinski's work phone earlier that afternoon to get its electronic serial number, and had been tracking its movement since she talked to Santino. The police-issued cell had been slowly crawling through the late evening traffic and had finally broken free about two blocks from the store. *Hurry it up, kid.*

"When it was in real life, the mugger was a white guy. But when we watched the tape, it was a black guy.

"Me and my friend, we were here in the store, we saw it happen. Then the guy who got mugged comes in, calls the cops, and he says me and my friend have to watch the video from the security camera right now. Right then, I mean. Like he wanted to go chase the guy down himself.

"So we did, but the guy on the tape is not the right guy. I mean, it's the guy who got mugged but not the guy who…"

Rachel put a palm on the glass to stem the flow of shoddy grammar. It was usually best to hear about an event in the witness's own words but she might have made a terrible mistake. "The victim was assaulted by a white man in the parking lot. Then the victim came into the store, called the police, and requested to view the tape. It was then you saw that the assailant on the tape was a different man than the one who attacked the victim?"

She had strayed too far into police jargon territory. The kid peered at her with mild suspicion. "You sure you're not a cop?"

"I just work with them," she said again. "But the victim was the same person, right? He didn't change?"

"No. Yes. I mean… no, it was the same man. Real life and on the video."

Okay. That's who we're looking for.

"And he wanted to see the tape, you're sure of this?"

"Oh yeah, for sure. Guy said he wouldn't leave until he did."

"When did he leave?"

"After the cops showed up," the kid said. "When they saw the tape, they wanted him to go with them. They said they needed to talk to him down at the station. But he told them he couldn't go, and then he took off."

I'll bet. And since he was the victim, they couldn't hold him.

Zockinski's phone arrived in the parking lot on the other

side of the gas pumps. She peeked through the window to lead
the kid's eyes.

"Hey, the cops who sent me over here just sent some more
of their friends," she said, spreading a thick layer of fudge on
the truth. "Can you do me a favor and tell them the same thing
you just told me? It's been really, really interesting!"

His colors waned slightly but he seemed agreeable. "Sure,
I guess."

Part of Rachel wondered if shameful flirting might go a
long way towards helping bridge relationships between law
enforcement and the community, and the rest of her shouted
that part back down into its little hole. She was still working
this out in her head when she turned the corner and nearly ran
straight into Santino.

"When did you get here?"

He looked surprised. "Right this second. Weren't you
tracking me?"

"No, I was following Zockinski."

He pressed a hand to his heart and gasped.

"Shut up."

"Zockinski looks pissed," he said as the two men got out of
Zockinski's car. From Rachel's point of view, pissed didn't even
begin to cover it. Zockinski's surface colors were churning.
Hill's mood, by contrast, was rigid, that same strange shade of
teal woven within several different grays and a Southwestern
turquoise she had recognized as her own core color only after
seeing it reflected in others. Rachel was familiar with that
weaving effect before and had categorized it as internal conflict,
but the teal was new. If she was being brutally honest with
herself (and if nobody with any fashion sense was listening),
she might admit it was her favorite color.

"What did you say to them?" she asked.

"Nothing. I called Zockinski and told him what you told
me. He made a few observations about my anatomy and the
appropriateness of certain household objects which might
reside therein, and hung up. Then he calls me back a minute

later and says they'll be right over."

Zockinski hung back at the car, but Hill walked straight up to her and held out his hand. Rachel couldn't help but blink at it before she decided it was probably real enough to shake.

"I was with the 7th," he said.

Oh. "Afghanistan?"

He nodded, then turned and went back to join the other detective.

"What was that about?" Santino asked.

Santino, who had never served, would pretend to understand but wouldn't, not really, so Rachel shrugged and headed towards the store. OACET Agents' files were supposed to be sealed but that had never meant anything. Rachel had enlisted in the Army straight out of high school, and had a teenager's talent for being in the wrong place at the right time. Her service record read like the plot of a Michael Bay film. If she had pegged Hill's age correctly, he had probably gone in with the second or third deployments and would know what a record like hers had cost.

Baby steps, she thought as Hill, using Zockinski as cover, furtively wiped his hand against his jeans.

Motion in the store pulled her perspective to front and center as the kid behind the counter windmilled his arms to get her attention. When she met his eyes, he pointed frantically at the two detectives. She slipped back in the store and he opened the door to his glass cage.

"C'mon, get in here!" He tried to grab her arm to pull her into the cage with him, but she brushed him off. He made a second grab and Santino stepped between them.

"It's okay," she told her partner. The kid was bubbling yellow. "He's just scared."

"That's the guy!" The kid stabbed at the glass with his finger. "The guy who mugged the dude!"

Santino made a rolling gesture with his fingers to hurry the kid along. He had no patience for people who were lazy with their nouns.

"That's the guy!" the kid said again as Zockinski and Hill entered the store. The kid abandoned her and shut the door of his cage. "I'm calling the cops!"

"We *are* the…" Santino began, then looked at Rachel. "Could you?"

She rerouted the call before it connected. The letter of the law was hazy about the right to block 911 calls, so she shifted it over to the Coast Guard's main line. The kid stared at the store phone, maybe wondering if he fell within the definition of a maritime emergency, then went into his pockets for his cell.

Rachel tapped on the glass. "It's okay," she said. "They're just here to talk."

"But he's the guy from the tape!" the kid hissed, pointing at Hill.

And then she got it. Rachel remembered her own surprise when she had first viewed the video and learned the assailant was a dead ringer for the detective. This was a violent neighborhood and the clerk probably witnessed ten assaults a month. The typical attack was an inconvenience, like a snowstorm or a flat tire. But a magical assailant he had only seen on film, suddenly living and breathing and walking through his front door?

"We know. You saw it happen, right? So this is *obviously*…" she said, placating the kid by stressing that word as hard as she could. "…a different man. There's a glitch somewhere in your system, and we're just trying to find out why he was on the tape. Go ahead and tell them what you told me."

She must have hit the right notes as the kid plucked up his courage and went back into his story. She sometimes assisted in the translation, but he rambled through it admirably. When he was done, the four of them went back outside.

"Two things," Zockinski said. "This is Ward Six. We're First. We shouldn't be messing around in this District. And we're going off of the word of a guy from a neighborhood where lying to the cops is the norm. There's no proof the man that shows up on tape wasn't the same man who did the mugging."

"That kid was terrified," Rachel said. "He honestly believed

Hill was the assailant."

"Or he's lying. Which of those do you think is more likely?"

Rachel saw their conversational colors withdraw and knew she had lost them. *Hail Mary time,* she thought. "Just watch the video. Watch it from the camera's perspective before you decide," Rachel said.

"Yeah. Tomorrow. It's in evidence," Hill said, and he and Zockinski turned to leave.

"I have a copy here," she said. Santino puffed and braced himself.

"What?" Zockinski rounded on her, furious. "What did you do, cyborg?"

Hill reached over and gave Zockinski a light slap on his arm, and Zockinski reined himself in. "What did you do?" he asked again, quietly.

"I requisitioned a copy," she said as she took her tablet out of her purse and flipped back the cover. "Or I broke into Sixth, grabbed the tape, and burned down the station to cover my tracks. Which of those do you think is more likely? Now, gentlemen, can we just watch the damned show?"

She held out the tablet to Zockinski, who recoiled as though she had handed him a viper. "You are children!" Rachel snapped, and propped the tablet against the hood of a parked car to queue the video.

The angle was terrible. It was fast and done in under a minute, and the back of the assailant's head was the only constant. With every other punch or kick, some cheekbones and jaw got some screen time. It was only towards the end that the assailant swung the victim around and the doppelganger's full face was shown.

"Holy..." breathed Hill. "That's me."

Zockinski snatched her tablet off of the car. "When was this taken?" he asked Hill.

"Two, three months ago? This was from that training seminar when I still had my ankle taped up. Same shirt, same shorts."

"Hang on," Santino said, and moved closer to the monitor. "You mean this guy doesn't just look like you?"

"No," Hill told him as he hit replay. His digital twin attacked the victim and started the assault anew. "This *is* me." He looked around, almost panicked. "This video, it's... I've never been here." He gestured with the tablet, taking in the parking lot, the dark buildings, the old and broken street. "This is me, but it's from a class a while back where we did unarmed combat. I was picked to do the demonstration. They had me subdue..."

"This guy." Hill paused the video. "This guy right here."

The victim on the screen appeared to be in his late twenties and in great physical shape. Rachel had wondered why he hadn't fought back.

"This is a setup," Zockinski said, and glared at Rachel.

"If you don't stop thinking what you're thinking," she growled, "I will kick you so hard you'll be able to pee out of your knees."

"So First MPD holds a training seminar," Santino said, touching her shoulder until she relented. "Was the man on the tape the instructor or an assistant?"

"Assistant," said Hill.

"Hill performs a few takedowns with the assistant. A month after that, the assistant is assaulted here, and the security film shows Hill in place of the assailant. Definitely sounds like a setup."

"No shit," said Zockinski. "When did this happen?"

"Uh..." Rachel checked her notes. "July ninth."

Hill exhaled, relieved. "That's the day my sister got married. There's a hundred witnesses who saw me give a toast at a botanical garden in New York."

"This is really clever," Santino said. He had taken her tablet and was reviewing the video. "You couldn't swap Hill's face over the original without having to render everything separately, and there'd always be a seam between the real and the altered. What I think they did here is take a clean shot of the background and then add the figures over it. They'd have to adjust the lighting but…"

He looked up to three blank faces. "Ah, this is how they make cartoons," he said. "They take a background and then superimpose the action over it."

The detectives turned to Rachel for confirmation. She shook her head. Excepting drunken binges on old *Powerpuff Girls* reruns in her late teens, she hadn't seen a cartoon since she was twelve.

"Don't you know how this stuff works?" asked Zockinski.

"I'm a pretty lousy cyborg," she said.

Santino's expression didn't change but he glazed over with a white opaque film. She had seen this reaction before, always when he had resigned himself to explain something which was, to him, extremely straightforward.

"This is a composite," he said, holding up the tablet. "The footage of the background is real and so is that of the fight. They made it by putting the one over the other. The end result is a fabrication, but they grounded it by adding light sources and shadows. And since it was shot in black and white, they didn't have to worry about color matching."

"Is that possible? You can make a video out of pieces?" Zockinski was completely out of his element.

"Definitely. It's very similar to how they use green screens in movies. A digital forensic specialist can tell you exactly what was done here."

"Do we have one of those at First?" Hill asked Zockinski.

"Yes, but I know where you can find a really good one," Rachel said.

The detectives went gray and cold.

She shrugged. "Fine. Your funeral."

"The tech doesn't matter," Zockinski said. "All we have to do is track down the other man."

"Who? The guy that taught a class to a bunch of cops just to set one up for assault charges?" Santino snorted. "I'm sure he'll be easy to find."

"The cameraman," Rachel said. "Even if he works for the

MPD, talk to him. He needed to get a specific angle to make it seem as though the video was shot from the security cameras, so the cameraman was either in on it or had contact with them."

Hill nodded, his tension easing. Old-fashioned police work was a comfort.

"We can't do anything until we clear this with Ward Six," said Zockinski. "And we have to talk to the Lou first."

"Yeah," Hill said. "That'll be an interesting meeting. 'Hey Lieutenant, want to see something that will put me away for ten to twenty?'"

"God, yeah. What a cock-up this'll be." Zockinski took off without another word. Hill followed, then paused to give her and Santino a cautious wave goodbye.

Baby steps.

FIVE

"Oh hello," Santino said. "Look who's here."

They had decided to check out the coffee store where the second assault had occurred before they called it a night. Santino had driven them back to Ward One along posh tree-lined streets where each person was accompanied by a minimum of two yappy dogs. Rachel was struck by the differences between this neighborhood and that of the gas-and-go, which was just miles away but was worlds apart.

The sun had set, leaving the front wall of the coffee shop a bright bank of windows in the night. Inside, Judge Edwards was standing and addressing a few dozen people. Reporters with handheld cameras made up a third of the group.

"Oh! Oh! Oh!" Rachel, delighted, opened the door and jumped out. Santino yelled something about waiting for him to stop the car first, but he was barely crawling forward and she had never been at one of Edwards' press conferences before. She was sure no Agent had ever attended one in person, and she didn't want to miss the opportunity.

The door to the coffee shop was propped open by a carved wooden owl. Rachel bent down and patted it on its head before she stepped inside. The store was one of those old places formed entirely from dovetailed aesthetics. A small room made tiny by the number of people jammed inside, Rachel moved her sixth sense past them to look at the old brass hardware and hand-cut mosaic tiles of what must have once been the local apothecary. A glass mirror gone smoky with time was stationed behind shelf after shelf of canisters holding exotic teas, and a heavy stone countertop polished by a century of elbows displayed working antique Gaggia brewing equipment worth slightly less than her house. The very air pulsed with the scent of chocolate and freshly ground beans. Rachel had never wanted a cappuccino more in her life.

An eclectic assortment of furniture had been pushed to the side to clear a stage for Edwards. It was not a good location for a press conference, but in Rachel's recent experience, press conferences didn't happen the way they did on television. The crash of reporters clamoring for quotes was great drama but made for a terrible working environment. Large conferences were calm and civilized. The best analogy Rachel had come up with was that of a classroom where the teacher's pet was chosen first, and if they didn't ask the right question then the second-favorite was called, and so on down the pecking order. Geeks, nerds, and hanger-ons rarely made the cut and were forced to compete for interesting sound bites dangled over their heads by the popular networks.

Smaller press conferences were not nearly as friendly. Since the only ones who bothered to show up were the bottom feeders, the rules of the false society did not apply. Most of these conferences were about backpatting and grandstanding instead of news. If something of interest did take place, the networks had found it more cost-effective to purchase clips from their lesser affiliates rather than pay to send the trucks out. Reporters at these lesser conferences knew the only reason they were there was because they weren't important enough to be somewhere else, and they behaved accordingly.

Rachel was sure this particular conference would be of the backpatting-and-grandstanding variety. Edwards was a would-be politician who lacked political strategy. It was a savagely dangerous combination; he knew he had to get his face out there but wasn't quite sure how. Judges were nominated by a commission in the D.C. circuit judiciary and Edwards had earned his nomination from his record as a trial lawyer, but his fledgling platform was nothing more than a mix of his own views and items culled from the headlines.

(She had read his colors several times and wasn't sure if the judge was as vehemently against OACET as he claimed, or if he had accidentally tripped over a topic he could use to distinguish himself as a candidate. She had never caught him lying when he ranted against them, but she still thought it might be the latter since Edwards was awfully comfortable with blending technology with the law when it suited his purpose. The man was a trainwreck, she had told Mulcahy, and her boss had agreed but said the problem with trainwrecks was that people got hurt.)

She entered the store and Edwards' eyes slipped over and past her. Rachel was insulted; she had met him no fewer than four times at various functions. Charley stood at the counter off to the side, hands cupped around a cold drink. He saw her in the crowd and his conversational colors leapt to vivid red, then gray as his face fell. Rachel associated red with strong and sometimes negative emotions and she didn't know what to make of it in Charley. Shame that she had caught him in a lie, maybe.

"Can't be helped, Charley! Work is work."

He glanced down as his phone vibrated. He faded back to his normal bluish-gray as he read her text, and gave her a shy smile.

"They tell us we've entered a new era." Edwards' voice was too big for the store. "One in which technology might have finally outpaced our ability to control it. I say we've not only been living in that brave new world for decades, but we welcomed it with open arms! We are responsible for this lack of control. We are the reason a man was beaten within an inch of his life, right here.

"Because we didn't act.

"We let them build their toys, those almost magical devices which let them spy on our every waking moment, and we didn't say no. We allowed them to take these toys and to put them them into use in law enforcement and the courts. Even if these toys violated the law, the Constitution itself, we created reasons for their use through applying false logic or hiding behind our willful ignorance.

"Friends, we have rationalized away the integrity of our justice system for the sake of convenience and the unattainable goal of complete security. We have been seduced by the idea that we must throw away our values and rebuild ourselves for a changing world each time the opportunity presents itself."

Rachel moved into the crowd. When she had first started developing her sixth sense, she couldn't go anywhere with more than a small smattering of people or she'd have problems processing the madness of human emotion. Now she loved crowds for that very reason. She especially loved crowds with a purpose. Movie theaters, concerts, places where crowds were focused on a single concept… It was beautiful to watch human beings break from their self-centered ruts and come together. Each person was still unique, still kept their same cores, but their conversational colors blended and harmonized within a shared spectrum. This past Fourth of July, Rachel had gone to the fireworks display at the National Mall and hadn't bothered to look up once.

"Friends, newer is not always better. No matter what they tell you, we are not dangling by a thread over obsolescence. My experiences have taught me that an authentic society isn't built on the backs of technology, but is supported by basic human decency. It is time—it is past time!—for us to recognize that innovation is not always a good word. We are the ones who decide what to do with our fancy little toys, whether we want to trade who we are for the sake of innovation. It's long past time that we all take a step back and look at what we've built, and then ask ourselves what we risk if we continue down this path."

He was an excellent public speaker but the crowd was bored to the point of beige; Rachel couldn't shake the feeling she was surrounded by carpet samples. There was no unification of color here, just a mass of people feigning interest. His audience was mostly reporters or entourage, and both groups had heard it all before.

Except…

As she moved among them, she noticed that some of them

were emotionally involved in what the judge was saying. Three men ran strong with Edward's golden teak, with ribbons of jagged, electrified red wrapped around it.

Aw hell, she thought. This was her first time seeing this particular phenomenon but she had a good idea what it meant. It wasn't too much of a jump to assume that the local anti-tech or anti-OACET zealots would rally to Edwards as a leader. She checked them for weapons; all three men were armed, one with a Heckler & Koch MP7 under his suit.

Honest, stark terror shot down her spine. Washington D.C. had some of the toughest gun control laws in the country, and these guys had some serious boundary issues if they were willing to carry concealed to a public event sponsored by a judge.

Rachel called Santino's cell. *"I'm leaving,"* she told him.

"What?" It was always strange to hold a phone conversation in her head. Santino sounded as close as an Agent. "I already parked. I'll be there in a minute."

"I scanned the crowd. There's a disturbingly high gun-to-creep ratio here. And somebody brought their kid and I don't want things to escalate," she added, noting a mother and a young boy playing beginner's Sudoku together in the window seat by the front door. They had the petulant air of persons forced to kill time and Rachel wondered who had dragged them along.

"Wow. Yeah, okay. I'll meet you on …" he said, then paused to check for street signs.

"I'll find you. Get to a bar a couple of blocks away and we'll hole up there until—"

"Agent Peng?"

She swore across their connection as Edwards caught her on her way towards the door. She heard Santino start to run as he promised he'd be right there, and he hung up to call for backup.

"I thought I recognized you," Edwards said, all smiles. "Ladies and gentlemen, it seems we have a representative from OACET with us. Is this a formal visit?"

Rachel smiled back. "No, sir, this is pure coincidence. I just love a good cup of coffee."

She reached out through the link and poked Administration. *"No time to chat,"* she said without waiting to learn who was on duty. *"Send someone to me for damage control at an Edwards event. Possible mob."*

"Why don't you stay and join us? We'd love to hear your thoughts."

"Sorry, but I'm off the record tonight," she said cheerfully, breaking her attention away from the panicked chatter on the other end of the connection.

"Really? You have no opinions about the attack?"

"No comment." This was bordering on harassment. No sensible politician would selectively target someone at a rally. Edwards needed a campaign manager in the worst way. She had a sudden mental image of a sophisticated older woman in a pantsuit floating down from an unseen cloud like Mary Poppins by way of a banner with Vote Edwards! stenciled on its face. Oh, the songs they would sing.

"A man was brutally attacked, right outside this store. They saw it," Edwards said as he swept out an arm. He got a lukewarm response from the baristas. "But since it didn't show up on video, the police say it didn't happen.

"A concussion, four broken ribs, and a collapsed lung, Agent Peng, and the MPD claims it didn't happen? What's wrong with this picture?"

"No comment," Rachel said. Most of the crowd had done the usual sideways leaping thing they did when they learned she was OACET, climbing over themselves like lemmings pushed towards a cliff to avoid touching her. The exceptions were the media, who pressed forward, and the three armed men who swept through the cracks to form a human barrier across her path.

"We're all just here to learn, Agent Peng. Can OACET explain why the tape was in error?"

She ignored him and pushed forward, trying to intimidate

the three men in front of her with a quick sweeping stare. No luck.

"Come on, Agent Peng. Why won't you help us out?"

Edward's small and self-appointed militia wore very nice suits to complement their very expensive haircuts. They had the look of well-fed young lawyers right before they made partner and were allowed to put on weight. Rachel would have been more comfortable if there was just the smallest hint of camouflage or religious iconography somewhere on their persons; being gunned down by yuppies in an upscale coffee house was not a scenario she had played out in her mind and she felt woefully unprepared.

They came at her slowly, three wide, and stopped just out of arm's length. Rachel cut to the side to walk around them. The crowd parted for her but the men moved to block her path to the exit a second time. Edwards' militia couldn't decide what to do. They knew what they wanted to do (turbulent red, with thick streaks of black), but they couldn't find a reason.

Rachel was not about to give it to them. She stopped and stood at parade rest. She kept her voice flat, her body completely still. "Please move."

They stood their ground. The door was open to let in the night air and she was so close to escape she could have chatted with the passersby walking their yappy dogs.

"Please move."

Nothing.

"Judge Edwards, please ask them to move."

The militia split and two of the men flanked her, and she realized the situation was actively dangerous. She should have guessed from the matching haircuts; the men had come to the coffee store as a group. An individual could be persuaded, but a group was unified by a cause.

She hated being a cause.

And Edwards didn't know they were armed.

Edwards laughed. From his perspective, she had allowed herself to stay, to become part of the discussion. Otherwise, she would have shouldered the men aside and vanished into the night.

"You're a federal employee, Agent Peng. If they want to engage you in conversation, that's their right."

It sounded good but Edwards was all but lying. Redress of grievances was not intended to facilitate the wrangling of lone women in coffee shops. Still, nothing would come from arguing law with a judge so she stood her ground. Rachel knew she looked like an idiot, standing motionless and staring off into space, but at least the militia was aware they couldn't touch her without the weight of consequences shifting against them. As long as no physical contact was made, nothing would happen.

Then the man with the personal defense weapon tried to shove her.

He was one of those who had flanked her and she had been watching him and his Heckler & Koch like a hawk, so when he reached out to push her from behind, he fell forward through open air and found her standing a foot to the left.

"Please don't," she said in that same flat voice. She wondered if it would be better to beg in a situation like this, to try and play up her humanity some, or whether that would only make things worse. The Army had emphasized calm and control above all, but they hadn't been exactly on the cutting edge of cyborg public relations.

Oh well. She wasn't much for begging anyhow.

They closed on her. The man who threw the first punch was down in two moves and the others backed off to either side, going pale with anxiety as their buddy gasped like a fish on the floor. To his credit, the judge barked orders into the crowd to try and regain control, but besides herself there wasn't a single person there, militia included, who had come to the press conference to hear what he had to say.

A quick memory, that of Mulcahy telling her she was under no circumstances to ever draw her gun in public ("Never. Not even if—") swam up unbidden. It had been easy to agree in the quiet of his office, several months back before the crazies had started swarming.

The man with the Heckler & Koch was standing between her and Edwards, which gave her a clear path to the door if she was willing to go through his friend to get there. Rachel had no problem with that. They were past the point of no return and she needed to lead these overfed lawyers into the street before the guns came out. She dropped her stance to put the second man on the floor, thinking for a brief moment that once he was out of her way she'd be able to make it outside before anything worse happened.

Then Heckler & Koch lit up white-hot red behind her.

Rachel's conscious mind turned command over to instinct before his right hand made it inside of his suit. She had been on the business end of an automatic weapon before, but never while standing directly in front of a woman and her child: the mother and son playing Sudoku by the entrance hadn't had the good sense to move. She leapt towards them and thought that if she did survive this, if he didn't shoot her cold in the head, if her vest couldn't stop an entire magazine of bullets, if all of the stars in heaven aligned for a miracle, she'd still have banged the hell out of her knees.

With her back towards the man with the PDW, she grabbed the mother and son by the arms and yanked them off of the ledge. She kicked over a small coffee table with a thick granite top and pushed them down on the floor behind it, crushing the three of them into as small a target as possible. Rachel jerked at the sound of screaming, and it was only after the adrenaline stopped pounding in her ears that she realized she hadn't been shot.

Everything slowed back to normal speed. The mother was sobbing. The boy stared up at her. He couldn't have been more than six and had a fresh bloody nose.

"Sorry," she said, releasing them. The boy scuttled backwards on all fours.

Rachel knelt, wincing at the pain in her knees, then looked over towards her partner. Santino's Taser was out, a puff of confetti still falling. The man with the Heckler & Koch was on the ground, his gun several feet away where Santino had kicked it away from his hand. The last man standing from Edwards' little impromptu militia had rushed to the mother and her son, and had gathered them together in a warm familial hug.

Oh for fuck's sake.

Santino helped her up. He was thoroughly shaken, his colors washed out like old clothes. It took Rachel a moment to remember that the last time her partner had committed violence against another human being was in the seventh grade.

"It's okay," she said. "Trust me, he had it coming."

The other man, the one who had thrown the first punch, was on his feet and wobbling towards the door. He ran straight into their backup, two local cops in uniform, who made him stumble back inside and sit down until they could sort out the mess.

"I got here as fast as I could," Santino said, "but Edwards was spitting bile about the police so I had to run around and find the back entrance."

"Smart. Real smart," she said. The arrival of an officer at the moment when the rhetoric was flying hot would have made things worse.

Rachel limped towards the closest upright chair, knees throbbing. *Every damned time.*

She threw a quick glance at Edwards that was full of all of the venom she could produce, then carefully eased herself down into the chair to put him behind her. He looked at her, deep and probing and only slightly curious, and she cursed herself for jumping before the gun was fully out. Rachel and Santino had gone back and forth on the constitutionality of her scanning abilities, what it meant for her to be an officer who could search anyone with a casual glance. They had decided their best course of action was for her to refrain from using all but the most superficial surface scans on private citizens unless she had due cause. From her point of view, scanning the men tonight fell safely within that category, but she could not have a reasonable discussion about self-policing or the nature of her sixth sense with someone like Edwards. Rachel dropped her head into the cradle of her own arms and tried to not think about how she had just given Edwards and his supporters a firsthand example of how OACET blurred the lines of the law.

The cops came over and the evening dissolved into statements. Rachel had dreaded this part, knowing it would end with a call from someone down at First District Station who would use the incident as an excuse to dump her with clean hands. They separated her from her partner, and as they took him aside, Santino gave her the sad *fun while it lasted!* half-smile of lost opportunities.

She had two advantages: everything that had happened in the coffee shop had been filmed in no fewer than five different angles, and the cops had heard about the bank and the magic tunnel. They borrowed a copy of the film from a reporter and she walked them through the scene, changing the timeline slightly but otherwise being as honest as words allowed. *This* was when she tried to leave to keep the situation from escalating. *Here* is when the first man jumped her; *then* she noticed they had guns. *There* was the guy with the Heckler & Koch, reaching inside his suit for his PDW...

The officers were wary, but with less of that flurry of harsh color she had come to expect when talking with the MPD. As she answered their questions, she tried to place what she was feeling. Not belonging, not acceptance but...

Legitimacy? Is legitimate a real emotion?

Eventually her mind circled around the word "credible" and stuck. It might not be her preferred adjective of choice, but she'd take it.

The phone call from headquarters came. Rachel sat, eyes closed, as the senior officer went outside and shut the door behind him to escape the noise. She read his colors through the wall and felt relief.

"There'll be some more questions tomorrow," he warned her when he came back to her table. "But you're cleared to go home tonight."

"Am I still with the MPD?" she asked.

He flashed surprise at her and looked towards the reporters, the guns laid out on a table in plastic bags, the woman and her son.

"Yeah," he said, and walked away.

She gave a quick thumbs-up to Santino a couple of tables over. His surface colors kindled and he jumped back into his debriefing with renewed purpose.

Rachel moved towards the baristas and ordered for herself and her partner. A pretty barista in a starched shirt and dangling silver jewelry shyly thanked Rachel as she slid the china saucers across the old stone counter, charms shaped like hollow stars clinking against the mugs.

She went back to her table and sat alone until Santino joined her. She pushed his coffee towards him and they raised the mugs in toast.

"Tomorrow will suck," he said.

"Like a vacuum," she agreed. The cappuccino was delicious.

The baristas did the math on the upcoming week of free publicity, then declared an open bar and kept the coffee flowing. Lowly news crews called their contacts at the networks and brokered deals big enough to pay a few months' rent. Certain men who had made poor choices were led off in handcuffs. Even Judge Edwards, sitting all the way on the other side of the room where he could ignore Rachel at his convenience, was cracking jokes about the perils of fame.

It was a surprisingly happy atmosphere, Rachel and Santino agreed, and then Josh Glassman swept into the room and everything was brighter.

If Patrick Mulcahy was the professional face of OACET, Josh Glassman was the other side of that coin. Where Mulcahy was aggressively competent, Josh was personable, lovable, everybody's friend. Josh hadn't been appointed the head of OACET's public relations division as much as he had decided the position needed to exist so he could justify his paycheck.

The quintessential charmer, he spent his evenings partying with Washington's elite and dated a string of women so flawlessly perfect they seemed unreal. Many a commentator had questioned whether he was a cyborg at all or just a ringer brought in to beguile the public; he played this up to his advantage in interviews, leading the hosts along and then snapping their assumptions with digital pranks.

He was also one of her dearest friends. There was an unbreakable bond with the Agent who had set you free.

Josh entered like a rock star. Dark sunglasses and brown hair too wild for any government employee framed long features and a smile that promised an excellent night. With the clink of the door against the metal jam, the crowd swung from irritated reds to astonished happy purples, the cops forgiven for not letting them leave. A college kid ran up to ask him for a photo and the floodgates opened in a torrent of patrons waving smartphones.

"*Bad Penguin,*" Josh said when he joined her in the link. "*No anchovy.*"

She covered her mouth and smiled. "*Make this all better, O Mighty Manwhore.*"

He paused in signing autographs to read the room. Josh didn't get bogged down in her nonsense of colors. Like all true athletes, he took the measure of his opponents and adjusted his performance accordingly. "*It already looks good to me,*" he said.

"*Yeah, now it does. Where have you been?*" she asked. "*I sent for backup ages ago.*"

He shrugged through the link and Rachel cringed. She'd never get used to feeling another Agent's physical gestures in her mind. "*We've got to teach you how to use autoscripts,*" he replied. "*I got here right after Santino zapped the nasty gunman, but I've been waiting to see how things played out without me.*"

"*Well, it's all been up and down since I first got here,*" she said. "*And Edwards could shift them again in a heartbeat.*"

"*As you wish,*" Josh said. "*Take Santino and leave as soon as you can. How am I reading?*"

"Crayola pack. Mostly purple, lots of happy yellow, some green, a little gray. Sorry for the stress," she added, noting the gray.

"Stress?" He snorted and it resonated uncomfortably in her mind. *"What you've got here isn't stress. This is a good book and a hot toddy after a long day."*

Josh's core was the rich, honest blue of fresh tattoos as he moved through the crowd, shaking hands and laughing. There was none of the frantic scramble for avoidance that defined her waking hours; you were either made of raw charisma or you weren't, and she wasn't.

Edwards and his small entourage had taken a seat at the other end of the coffee store and Josh moved towards them, arms open. He greeted Edwards with all of the warmth reserved for a long-lost brother and pulled a chair up to the judge's table. The two bowed their heads for a quiet conversation, then Josh scooted his chair back.

"Who wants sound bites?" he shouted. "Everybody is sorry for everything!"

"C'mon, let's go," she whispered to Santino as the reporters stampeded towards the other side of the store. They had nearly reached the door when Edwards called out to her.

"Agent Peng!" The judge's booming shout caused everyone in the room to turn and notice her failed escape.

Rachel promoted the door from inanimate object to criminal mastermind; she had spent far too much time staring at it with some threat or another standing in her way for it to be uninvolved in this disaster of a night. She felt compelled to sneak back in here after hours with the appropriate power tools and lay waste to its painted glass and antique hardware, not for the joy of vandalism but to remind the door of its place in the grand order of things.

And she would steal that owl for good measure.

"Wait here?" she asked Santino, who made the universal gesture for choking the life out of someone.

"Your buddy noticed you were leaving," Josh told her. She

glanced back towards their group where Josh was halfway through a joke, the cute barista with the bracelets on his lap and a bottle of excellent champagne making its way around the table.

*"Trust me, Edwards is **not** my buddy,"* she replied.

"Not him," Josh said. *"The dopey one."*

She looked around his table to notice Charley waving goodbye.

Charley, what the hell? she thought to herself. She could have sworn the man had more sense.

She moved towards the crowd around Edwards' table, and they parted for her like the sea for Moses. Edwards stood and smiled, and walked towards her up the void.

"Thank you so much for what you did here tonight, Agent Peng," the judge said to the reporters.

"You're welcome," she said to the ceiling. *Oooh, pressed tin.*

"Such a world we live in," he said, shaking his head sadly, making eye contact with the good voters watching live from the comfort of their kitchens and bedrooms. "Let's all hope something like this will never happen again."

"From what I experienced tonight, Your Honor, that seems to be entirely up to you."

He laughed her off but flushed an angry red. Ten feet away, so did Santino, although his anger was weak and was overlayed with a strong horrified green.

"For God's sake, Rachel, don't poke the damned bear," Josh nagged through the link.

"But…" she backpedaled, "you're right. We certainly live in interesting times."

"I couldn't agree more," Edwards said, smiling warmly. "And I'd love to hear how you knew that man was reaching for a weapon."

"Well, when you've been cornered like an animal," she said as she smiled back, "if someone goes to grab something from inside of their jacket, you naturally assume the worst."

"Even when he was standing directly behind you?" the

judge said, and she saw Josh mirror her silent sigh. "The police said you told them you scanned those men for weapons, Agent Peng. I think we'd all like to hear more about that."

"Considering how Agent Peng has very recently missed injury, she has no comment at this time." Josh was there, flirting with the folks at home as he pulled the judge back to the table. "Except that she is glad she could prevent anyone from being hurt."

"As are we all." Edwards had to have the last word; Rachel supposed she was lucky he hadn't brought up the boy's bloody nose as his closer.   .

"Scoot, Penguin," Josh said. *"Get out of here. You've done your job, let me do mine."*

She grabbed her partner's arm and they fell into the street.

Santino said he wanted to go home but he was lying through layers of gray, so she said it was only fitting to end the busiest (and perhaps final) day of their partnership over liquor. The search for a good bar became a quest. They were uncomfortable in any place that catered to white-collar professionals, and in that part of town that left a Mexican restaurant staffed exclusively by Koreans. The room was dark, lit only by passing traffic and small potlights stationed over ancient blown-up photographs of Chinese pagodas, black velvet paintings of Pancho Villa, and pyramids made from empty Budweiser cans. The food was delicious and the restaurant was packed.

"I'd pay good money to learn this place's story," Rachel said as their server brought another helping of enchiladas so good they could probably end wars.

"If you ask, they'd probably tell you for free," he said. His core and conversational colors were still washed out, the reluctant khakis of dry riverbeds moving through them.

"You doing okay?"

"Yeah. Well…" he paused. "It's particle physics."

"This'll be good," she said, and held up two fingers for refills on their whiskey. They were already working towards a good stiff tipsy but Santino was trending mawkish, a complete reversal of his usual jovial personality when drunk.

"There's theory, there's reality… Those almost never intersect. Particle physics is mostly theory because you can't do much testing at the subatomic level. So you get all this training in theory, you know what will probably happen if the conditions line up perfectly, but there's no way to prove it. But that's okay, because you're happy working in pure theory anyhow.

"Then someone builds a Hadron collider."

"Or a guy pulls a gun in a crowded room and you have to put him down," she said, finally catching on. Santino's analogies ran heavy on the academia and she was usually a few steps behind his meaning. He wasn't just in a funk about the penalties of tonight or the uncertainty of tomorrow, but that he had drawn a weapon for the first time in the line of duty.

He nodded, staring at his plate.

"He's not dead, Santino. He's a perfectly healthy adult male who took a solid-mass hit from a Taser. He was walking around fifteen minutes after he was hit."

"You know what I'm talking about."

She didn't, actually. Back in the day when she had more youth than sense, her unit used to stun each other to see who'd be buying at the bar that night. Thanks to her almost comically fair skin, Rachel still had the faint scarring of scorch marks on her butt.

"He'll be fine. He's probably at the hospital right now, getting the best checkup of his life on the MPD's nickel. And then he will probably go to jail, or, at the very least, he'll have to sacrifice his trust fund to stay out of it, because he is a stupid man who did a stupid thing."

Her partner didn't answer, swirling the whiskey around and around his tumbler. He shot back the liquor in a single go, then flipped the glass over and started pressing circular patterns into his napkin.

"What?" she asked. Santino tended to show his obsessive-compulsive side when he wasn't sure how to broach a topic.

"So," he said heavily. "You're psychic."

She snorted mid-sip, a tragic mistake. Alcohol shot up her nose and she went into a coughing fit, sinuses burning. Santino reached over and pounded on her back until she managed to choke out a credible threat to punch him if he didn't cut it out.

"Wait, I'm what now?" she said when she could breathe without her eyes watering.

"Psychic. Or clairvoyant, or empathic, or whatever."

"C'mon Rachel, I've worked with you for months," he said when she didn't answer. "For a while I thought you were just good at reading people. That's fine, that's normal for a cop.

"But sometimes... Sometimes you're too quick, like you've read the person before they handed you the book."

Damn.

She reached across the table and lifted an enchilada off of her partner's plate to see if he'd flinch. He stabbed at her hand with his fork and whipped his food back onto his own plate, his colors losing that washed-out khaki.

"Hey!" she complained, absolutely relieved.

"Mine," he said. "It's not my fault you're a bottomless pit for calories. And don't change the subject," he added. "Psychic. Or clairvoyant," he said, pointing his fork. "Talk."

She sighed. "It was the Heckler & Koch guy, right?"

"Yeah. Forget about how you could watch him when he was standing behind you. I know how you did that. But you started moving before he did. It was close, and you could argue to anyone else that he went for his gun first, but I was right there. You had a split-second edge."

"I wasn't thinking," she said, punishing herself in front of him. The whiskey was doing its work; she was too willing to talk about something so private. "He was going to draw in a crowded room... I should have jumped him instead of covering the woman and kid, made it look like I was picking a fight before he got his gun out."

"It's the implant, right?"

"Yeah," she sighed. "You know how I perceive different frequencies, right? Apparently mood has a frequency. It's not mind reading," she added quickly. "I don't pick up, you know, thoughts or anything. I see in color."

"You and ninety-two percent of the population."

"I see emotions in color."

He blinked, dumbstruck, then started laughing.

"I'm serious!"

"That's the stupidest thing I've ever heard. If someone's sad, you can literally see they're feeling blue?"

"Blues are mainly positive." Rachel felt a little sulky. She had held this conversation a hundred different ways in her imagination, but in there he had never laughed at her. "I haven't come across a bad blue. Sad is usually gray, but like a cloudy day gray, not a pavement gray. And you can always see the other colors under the clouds, wanting to get out."

He stared at her. "You're serious."

"You're the one who asked me if I was psychic."

"Well, yeah. But being psychic would be cool," he scoffed. "You're just a mood ring."

"I'm...?" she started to ask, then laughed. "I'm a mood ring!" she gasped as she fell into giggles.

She was a nervous giggler. It always hit after the fact, thank God, but once the stress had passed she buckled in half and hooted like a hyena. Tonight, thanks to the scene at the coffee house and sinuses already abraded from their whiskey bath, she rolled around the table and sputtered in wet, slobbery noise. Santino made a production of daintily eating an enchilada with a knife and fork, ignoring both her and the disdainful sideways glares of their fellow patrons. He waved away the concerns of their server who wondered if, perhaps, the lady might be more comfortable outside? and ordered himself a beer chaser while he waited for her to get herself back under control.

"You could have told me," he said when she was once again upright. "This is the type of thing I want to know."

Rachel did something with her entire upper body that translated loosely to: *Are you kidding me? I'm already a freak.*

He shrugged. *Yeah, and?*

"I thought…" she sighed, "I guess I thought it'd be easier to get to know me if you didn't think I was in your mind the entire time. I'm not," she added, "but it'd still be a barrier."

"Is it something every Agent can do?" he asked.

"Yes. But they don't," she added quickly. "I'm the only one who's developed this skill."

"Why? It seems pretty useful. If you can predict when you're about to have a gun pulled on you, that seems like something you'd want to know."

"There's a…" she hesitated and chose her words around the liquor. "There's a steep learning curve. The others don't think it's worth the time. Honestly, most people don't like us but that doesn't mean they're going to start gunning for us. What happened tonight will probably never happen again."

Santino the scholar stepped up and picked her brain for specifics. (Him: Since you've got an auditory interface, does that mean you could hear emotions, too? Her: No, that's just dumb.) The food and whiskey kept coming, and eventually they reached a level of comfortable saturation where he could ask her the big question: What is it like? and she, for once, could answer.

"The implant… It's different for each of us," she said, deep in her cups. "I think it's based on our personalities. We make it personal. Personalized. Individualized."

"Traits."

"Traits," she agreed. "Me, since I'm…" she caught herself in time. "Since I like to know my environment, I've done nothing but work on perception. You've seen it; I've figured out all kinds of ways to use the implant as an extra sense. One of my friends, Mako? You know Mako. You can't miss Mako! He's this gigantic weightlifter. He's good at blocking. When he gets in your mind and holds you in place, you can't go out-of-body or connect with machines. No one else can do that. I've got another friend who writes and runs hundreds of automation scripts at once, so he's basically a walking complex logic calculator. The guy has so many active scenarios going that he can practically see the future. Mare, she's our organizational specialist…"

"The one with the hair?"

"Mmm, that hair…! She says she inventories her environment. Makes a mental list of everything around her, makes patterns with them… It's like having a photographic memory that can be aligned and processed like a spreadsheet."

"What about Mulcahy?"

She shivered theatrically. "You ever hear how James Garfield could write in Greek with one hand and Latin with the other? Mulcahy does out-of-body better than anyone. He's freaky as shit."

"You are all freaky as shit," he said, and smiled to blunt that edge. Tonight, she found she didn't mind.

Rachel waved the business end of a cocktail sword at him. "Mulcahy has conversations, plural. He can be talking to you in person about, I don't know, carbon trading regulations, and be out-of-body with someone else discussing the proper care and feeding of piranhas.

"I don't like going out-of-body. Splitting yourself in two is… I don't know. There's a wrongness to it. It's really convenient sometimes and I've gone to some amazing places," she said, breaking the plastic sword into small gold bits and plunking them on the ice melting at the bottom of a dead tumbler, "like Paris, and my mom's hometown, but…"

"You went to China?"

"Yeah. I didn't stay too long, just popped in and out. Mom's always on about how quaint and rural it is but there're no farms and they've got a Wal-Mart. I was disappointed to learn I didn't really come from folksy peasant stock."

"You probably did. Wal-Mart hasn't been in China for long."

She nodded as she studied the old photograph of the pagoda hanging across from them. Two women stood in the foreground, posing in unbearably tight dresses and holding fans with limp wrists. Rachel never knew what to make of change.

"So…" he prompted.

"Yeah, okay. So, the implant. We all got the same chip, but

we don't use it in the same way. Each of us, we're adapting the implant to our own lives instead of letting it lead us. I guess we're all… We're building it into ourselves and not the other way around."

"Gotta say," he said, green with envy. "All of that sounds incredibly cool."

"Well…" Rachel looked around the bar, at the endless variations in mood and color and motion that formed the living canvas of crowds. These were a spectrum of inebriation, of lifelong friends and casual acquaintances, of shared futures between sheets or, in the case of one couple blazing fire-red in the corner, the closest bathroom.

"It ain't half bad," she admitted.

SIX

The family who owned the house before her had gotten the newspaper. Rachel had never paid a bill and had called to have the subscription cancelled more times than she could remember, but the hated things were still delivered to the end of her driveway like clockwork. She despised them, the wrapped papers in their clean plastic bags, yet another minor problem that didn't need to be.

She tried to think of it as a form of daily meditation. Every morning Rachel would snatch up that day's edition while muttering profanities so hot and vehement she wouldn't be surprised if it all fell to dust. She channeled every ounce of her repressed anger and frustration into those loathsome little bags, tried to convince herself it was cathartic when the paper smacked against the bottom of the bin. She wanted to make this one small chore empowering, wanted to brush off her hands and walk away, clean and refreshed. Sadly, no amount of magical thinking could change how this routine just ensured she was good and pissed off for the rest of the day, with the added insult of knowing that the entire process would repeat itself the following morning.

The Sunday edition caused her to contemplate murder.

Rachel stood over that day's paper, a hot cup of Earl Grey in her hand, and wondered if she should just leave it where it lay. She imagined what would happen if she allowed them to accumulate. Each morning a new layer would be added to the old, the ones on the bottom yellowing and turned to soggy pulp in their bags...

She would let the delivery service build her a wall, she decided. It would be taller than her house and would bring down property values for miles around, and the stink of mildew would rise to heaven.

"You saved that boy."

Rachel spun, tea sloshing. She hissed and switched the mug to her other hand, shaking the burned one to take the sting out. First Santino, now Mrs. Wagner; Rachel couldn't remember the last time someone had surprised her but she'd been jumped twice in the past twenty-four hours.

"What?"

On occasions calling for liquor and gossip, Rachel had described her next-door neighbor as Dumbledore's evil twin sister. Mrs. Wagner peered at her over with ruddy eyes over half-moon lenses and held up her own newspaper. "You saved that boy."

Reading was inconvenient for Rachel. She used to be able to glance at a front page and take it all in, but she now had to shift her perspective to a frequency which could easily parse text. Her jaw dropped as she saw herself on the front page under the huge bold headline: "Hero Cyborg?"

A question mark, she thought. *They show a picture of me shielding a mom and her kid and they stick on a damned question mark.*

She reached for Wagner's copy and her neighbor scurried away without another word, her paper clenched in a protective ball against her chest. Rachel shifted the frequency on her implant to block out visual data and slowly counted to ten, then shook her own paper out of its plastic sleeve and skimmed the article. It was much ado about nothing. There was a lengthy above-the-fold description of Edwards' press conference, which, in the way of modern news stories, pretended impartiality by presenting two competing but equally outlandish possibilities for why she had been at the coffee shop. On the one hand, OACET Agent Rachel Peng was aware of Edwards' poisonous rhetoric and wanted to forestall any violence by directing the crowd's anger towards herself. On the other, OACET Agent Rachel Peng was aware of Edwards' inspirational nationalism and wanted to destroy his reputation by...

Rachel quit reading before she learned her motive. Anything less than throwing down with Edwards in a Hong Kong cinema-style gun battle, complete with wirework stunts, wouldn't have been worth her effort. She wadded up the paper and chucked it in the general direction of her garbage, then went to get her cell phone.

Her new home was deception incarnate. It trapped the unwary into thinking it was a darling Craftsman revival, not a slumbering leviathan which awoke to demand sacrifices of tax returns and early withdrawals from pension plans. When she had toured the property, she made the classic buyer's mistake of falling in love; she had lived in apartments her entire life and the backyard was huge, almost a quarter of an acre, thick with trees. Having never purchased a house before and hindsight being what it was, Rachel had since realized that she probably should have asked more questions before she had signed away a substantial chunk of her savings (such as: Why are there water stains at waist height in the basement?). She had moved in just before Christmas and had repainted the entire place in mad joy at having of two thousand square feet for her own private playground, then spent the following spring replacing the roof and learning about French drains.

Entire rooms were still bare, waiting for furniture to find its way home from flea markets and malls. The only finished area was the study, which had come with built-in shelves across three walls and now housed her unruly collection of poetry and romance novels: Rachel used to be an avid reader and she couldn't bear to give those old friends away. These surrounded a couch, two matching overstuffed leather chairs that were too expensive to be anything other than an impulse buy, and a heavy plank pine coffee table an old girlfriend's cat had used as a scratching post.

Dead in the center of the table was the pile of that week's hate mail, ready for her to sort and drop off with the unlucky Agents who dissected those language catastrophes for risk assessment. Her purse had landed on top of the heap. It was firm policy to turn off the implants when sleeping and Agents kept cell phones for nights and emergencies. It defeated the purpose of the cell to keep it off, but nine nights out of ten Rachel let it languish at the bottom of her handbag with a bone-dry battery.

She reached out to her carrier to check her messages while she rummaged through her portable trashcan to find her phone and its charger. "You have thirty-nine new messages," the service informed her in its flat, almost-feminine voice. Rachel turned on the phone to confirm, then skipped through the queue to see if anyone she knew had been one of the callers. After the babble had ebbed, she pinged Josh.

He was awake and already at the office. *"Morning, Penguin. You don't sound hung-over **in the slightest.**"*

"Oh I shall destroy you... Josh, I'm up to my armpits in messages from reporters."

"I know, I've been fielding calls all night. Why did you turn your phone off? Mulcahy and I were all set to kick down your front door until you came back online an hour ago."

"Thank you for not," she said. "I was in the shower."

"We figured. Are you decent? I'll pop in."

Rachel searched the study for anything embarrassing. She deemed it spotless; it had been too long since she had gone on a really good date. *"All good, come on over."*

Among the implant's many functions was a remote projection feature which allowed an Agent to create a digitalized visual image and position it in a location of their choosing. Imagination was the only limitation on how these images appeared, or moved, or could be put to practical use. The most common application was a personal avatar for out-of-body communication with other Agents. As long as she was cozy in her own mind and the other Agent was the one talking through an avatar, Rachel greatly preferred these face-to-face interactions to those held via the everpresent link. She was always more comfortable interacting with a person than a disembodied voice resonating within her own head, even if that person was a digital facsimile which manifested in a mind-searing bright green.

Josh, or a perfect copy thereof, appeared in her living room. He was one of those Agents who was skilled in out-of-body projection and wore his chartreuse avatar with all of the mannerisms and quirks of a second skin. His avatar dusted off its pants and dropped heavily in one of her new leather armchairs the same way Josh did when he came over for pizza and beer.

"How much trouble am I in?" Rachel asked.

"What?" Josh looked mortified. "Trouble? Are you kidding? I could kiss you! This is the best press we've had in... Ever, actually. You been on the Internet today? It's nothing but news footage of last night's conference. There's Edwards, firing up a mob, and then there's you, trying to leave, trying to leave, trying to leave... Oops! There's a fanatic with a huge-ass gun. And you do this heroic thing where you leap through the air and turn yourself into a human shield for a sweet young mom and her kid.

"Rachel, I swear, if half of the world didn't want us to be the bad guys, there'd be no question about what you did last night."

"But they do."

Josh paused. "But they do."

"I jumped too early. The gun wasn't out yet."

He cracked his knuckles, a neat trick considering he didn't have any. "No, it's more about how your back was to him, but it's the same outcome. The anti-OACET contingent is saying it was a setup, and we're trying to ruin the judge's credibility. Then there's Edwards. He's starting to ask those questions that aren't really questions about what it means if an Agent can search someone without their knowledge or consent. He's getting a nice bump from this."

Rachel collapsed in her other armchair. There was a smudge of old cheese against the mahogany leather and she wet her thumb to take it off.

She was not looking forward to the next few days. The pundits and scholars made much of how the fear of OACET was always associated with immediate risk, such as wiping out financial records or the ever-popular threat of nuclear annihilation. They carefully noted that the real danger was the lack of checks and balances to restrict how Agents could acquire information about American citizens, law-abiding or otherwise. All of OACET knew her sixth sense was a landmine waiting to go off: "in plain sight" meant something entirely different to Rachel, who violated the Fourth Amendment more times than she could count just by walking to the grocery store. She was their opponents' best example of why OACET shouldn't be. Thus far, the Agents' method of dealing with this had been to hide her unique abilities within the ethical and legal morass caused by those other skills they possessed which also threatened civil rights. It was quite possible that the fallout from the coffee shop fiasco would tear even this flimsy protection away.

"There are two options," Josh said.

"I don't want to hear the second one."

He ignored her. "The first option is perfectly logical and makes you look good. We release some of your service record, the parts which show you've been in similar situations overseas and you have experience in predicting likely outcomes for mob scenarios. The Army will have to back us up on it, so it'll give you some extra credibility.

"We'll also have to tell the public that Agents have some ability to detect metals," he added.

"Yippee. Let's make people think we're irradiating them, too. That'll be jolly good fun."

"We can't help it if they don't understand the science," he said. "We've got to do it. Stack yesterday's bank story with the incident at the coffee shop and it's about to become common knowledge that you can see through solid matter. We've got to try and nip this in the bud before we get sued for causing leukemia or whatever, and if we handle it well enough, they'll be less likely to ask how you knew to jump before the gun came out.

"I'd really like to keep your other skills under wraps," he added. "Mood reading is too close to mind reading for the media to stay on-message. But the timeline works out so we can avoid it. Just remember you scanned them after that one guy shoved you, okay? He gave you cause."

He paused. "The second option…"

"Do." Rachel said as she gave the stain a strong rub. Her thumb squeaked against the grain of the leather. "Not."

"We tell them you're blind."

She looked over at him and met his eyes. It was a meaningless gesture for her but while new habits were formed quickly, old habits died hard. Rachel didn't think she'd ever shake off the unspoken side of conversation; she was sure she didn't want to.

"No," she told him.

It hadn't been easy, those first five years. They all bore scars. Unlike most of the others, hers were physical. Rachel couldn't remember what had driven her out on her apartment's balcony to stare up at the sun until it had set, and then for hours and hours after that, but she hoped it had been her choice and not an involuntary act. She couldn't bear the idea that part of her was so self-destructive that it could override her rational mind.

Josh had been the one who saved her. He had come out to California to help them with the transition. When she failed to check in, he had broken into her apartment and found her, exhausted, dehydrated, and seeping from second-degree sunburns after two straight days of staring up at the sky. He had pulled her back from the ledge and had stayed with her until she came back to herself, screaming.

Her skin had healed but her eyes had weakened until there was nothing left to see but black. Still, Rachel didn't think of herself as a member of the blind community; solar retinopathy, followed by progressive macular degeneration, had locked her into a dark world for all of a month until her implant had provided a substitute. Folk wisdom had it that the other senses become more acute with the onset of sudden blindness, but in Rachel's case it had kickstarted a sixth sense so powerful she preferred it to sight.

She had struggled with blindness. Not so much the changes caused by her loss of sight, but how being classified as disabled would affect her opportunities, her sense of self. Rachel had yet to find the frequency that replicated human vision, but the range of alternatives was so vast her only problem was finding the one which best fit the situation. Unfortunately, rigid clinical definition meant she would always be categorized as blind. If she came out, she'd lose her position at the MPD, or would be held up as an example of how minorities could overcome insurmountable odds, or both. Rachel felt these outcomes were neither fair nor accurate, and she wanted nothing whatsoever to do with disclosure.

Josh knew it, and still he said: "Yes."

"No," she said again.

"Yes. Rachel, it'll come out eventually. If you introduce it on your own terms, you can control it."

"Chinese. Lesbian. Cyborg." She held up a finger for each point. "That's already a lot of baggage to carry, Josh. There's no way in hell I'm attaching another label, especially since I'm not blind."

"A lot of people would disagree with you."

"Yeah, and those people all see the alarm clock when they wake up in the morning. The blind community would flay me alive. I'm not piggybacking on a disability for *good press*." The last two words were hurled like a curse.

"Penguin, this is not just about you. Think about it: you redefine the discussion. It's no longer about how the implant might break civilization apart, it's about what the implant can do to improve it. You would be giving hope to millions of people. And we could really use that kind of publicity right now."

She watched her friend slouch down in her lovely new chair and was glad for his avatar. Emotions weren't carried across projections. Yesterday, Mulcahy had similar body language when he flashed depression, and Rachel wondered what was happening behind the scenes in their administration.

"Are you ordering me to do this?"

He shook his head. "It's your call."

"Go with the Army story," she replied.

He nodded. He knew her well enough to already know her answer; she knew him well enough to understand why he had tried to change her mind.

"All right," he said, standing up to leave. "See you at nine at the coffee store. We've got a press conference planned. Change into a white shirt with a skinny suit. No gun and no vest."

Rachel sighed. When she had started working at the MPD, Josh had taken her shopping for a few outfits which met the public's expectations of clothing worn by attractive women with badges. He had made her promise she would always keep one dry-cleaned and ready to go. She did not like these skinny suits: people with combat experience planned their outfits to reduce risk. Her usual daily attire was made up of jackets a size too large to accommodate her ballistic vest and gun, and shirts that matched her suit to prevent that V-shaped target which came from layering dark fabric over light. The skinny suits made her nervous.

"Hey Josh?"

"Yeah?"

"Dumbledorina?" Rachel took her feet off of her old pine table. "You know, Mrs. Wagner from next door? She talked to me."

"Hm," he said, intrigued. A veteran in the ongoing battle with Mrs. Wagner, it was only Josh's innate charm which carried him safely through enemy lines on pizza nights. "Talked to you or took her golf club to you?"

"Spoke. She was outside when I got the paper. She said I saved the boy."

He looked out the window towards her neighbor's house. "No kidding?"

"No kidding."

"Things might be better than we think," he said. To Rachel, it sounded as though he was talking to himself. A healthy internal monologue was a casualty when going out-of-body.

"Got anything you'd like to tell me?" she asked.

Josh smiled at her, maybe a little sadly. "Keep doing what you're doing, Penguin. We'll let you know if anything changes."

He popped out of existence and Rachel went on the hunt for the much-reviled skinny suits in a house full of empty closets.

She lived within walking distance of the train but the coffee shop wasn't anywhere near a station, so by the time the cab dropped her off she was running late. The place was teeming with reporters. *Now **this**, she thought to herself, is a press conference.* A small podium had been set up at the front of the room, the old brass and stone of the store polished to gleaming. Feds were to the left, with Mulcahy and Josh chatting quietly with representatives from other agencies or various Departments Of The, enjoying the excellent coffee. To the right were the locals. Santino stood with several of the higher-ups from First District Station, and, to her surprise, Zockinski and Hill. Edwards was bright with the yellow-white of eager energy and stood as close to the center of the podium as he dared. A woman with salt-and-pepper hair and a tailored pantsuit was whispering in Edwards' ear, and Rachel grinned. The man was not dumb.

With their attention on the notables at the front of the room, the press ignored Rachel's efforts to squirm around them. She coughed politely, then when that didn't work she went straight to acute pertussis, but when they did finally notice her they didn't trample each other to get out of her way. Instead, they closed in on her and asked for interviews. Heart sinking, Rachel said something happy and harmless and wondered how long it would be before she mourned for the good old days when people tried to spit on her.

Santino adopted a kicked-puppy expression when she passed him to stand with Mulcahy and Josh, but from his colors he had expected it. Surprisingly, the two detectives flashed confusion and Hill cocked his head at her as if to say: *Where on earth are you going?* as she walked away from them, his kinesics set off by that same odd teal.

Josh was slouched against the counter, his slightly rumpled suit a public comment that the previous night had been of far more interest to him than this inconvenience of a press conference. He was buffing his sunglasses on the arm of his shirt; the optical implant made all Agents photophobic and dark glasses were the norm, but Josh had a mild case and wore them mostly for style. She slipped into the niche between him and Mulcahy, and Josh bumped her with his shoulder.

"What's the deal?" she asked, initiating a private three-way link.

"The usual. Bunch of long-winded political wannabes mugging for the cameras," he replied, and dug a thumb at Mulcahy, who took a tiny sip of his coffee and pretended he hadn't heard.

Unless it was unavoidable, Patrick Mulcahy and Josh Glassman never shared the stage at the same event. Theirs was a well-crafted dichotomy. Mulcahy was authority personified. Always calm, always unfailingly polite, Mulcahy did not so much discuss options as state: "This is how things will be," then show how the inevitable would benefit everyone involved. The analogy worming its way around Washington was that working with him was like working with a tidal wave, as there was nothing to do when he came for you but to get out of his path and to appreciate the new topography when he was finished.

Josh was the accessible, approachable one. He was easy to underestimate. Back when they first went public, those seeking to manipulate OACET had targeted Josh until they realized he took a very literal approach to going to bed with his various allies. Or their wives. Or members of their staff, and *their* wives. A combination of Machiavelli and Don Juan, he had ripped entire political teams apart from the inside out and rebuilt them to better align with the purpose of his own agency, all without tipping his hand.

(Once, Rachel had asked Josh how they had developed their public personas. Josh said he and Mulcahy had started with that old political saw: "Who would you rather have a beer with?" and had ended at: "Depends on what you want to get out of the meeting.")

At precisely thirty seconds to nine, Mulcahy put down his coffee. He tapped her on the arm and they walked up to the podium, the rest of the federal delegates following in their wake. Josh stayed behind, flirting with his smitten barista.

Edwards joined them, smiling, but his new campaign manager had firmly muzzled her client and he radiated peace and goodwill. Incite a hate crime? Him? Never.

Mulcahy paused for the press to get themselves in order.

"Thank you for coming," he began. "Last night, there was an incident involving a respected member of the local judiciary and an OACET Agent when three men brought firearms to this public space. Whatever you might have heard, neither Judge Edwards nor Agent Rachel Peng was at fault. Their constitutional right to assemble guaranteed both of them the right to participate in the same space at the same time. The men who assaulted Agent Peng did so of their own free will, and we expect they will experience consequences appropriate for their actions.

"I'd like to address the rumor that this was an attempt by OACET to frame Judge Edwards. Agent Peng came to this location by coincidence. A separate assault had been committed here, a crime very similar to one she was already investigating. A spokesperson from the Metropolitan Police Department will brief you on the details of these events in a moment. Agent Peng stayed to hear Edwards speak, and was then attacked.

"We are aware OACET is controversial," Mulcahy continued, "but conditions which promote violence cannot—"

Rachel didn't catch the rest of that sentence, as *"Whz up?"* flew across her mind.

It was a text from Charley, which surprised her. Rachel wasn't good with scripts, but a friend had given her one that let her automatically dump all unauthorized incoming numbers to her own cell straight to messaging. She had left her phone on, and it was an inconvenient time to realize she must have added Charley's cell to her approval list. She looked around the room and couldn't find his familiar friendly colors, then traced his cell's signal to Edwards' office. *"You stuck at work?"*

"Yes. Want me 2 call?"

"Can't do a conversation now."

There was a long pause as he typed: *"c you on tv."*

Rachel glanced over at the cameras, unsure if Charley had used that particular message to sign off or if he had stated the obvious. Then: *"u guys b careful."*

"Why?" she asked him. *"What's going on?"*

No response.

"Charley? Is there something about Edwards that I should know?"

No response again, and she realized she had been completely out of line.

"I get it. Thanks for the warning."

Long pause, then he replied: *"wish I cld say more"*

"Hey, we all need to eat. Don't risk your job over this."

"thx. gl."

As Mulcahy spoke of community, Rachel watched Edwards standing silently behind him, his colors churning in the whites and yellows of an electric sea.

She was never sure how far she should trust some of her new abilities. Maybe Santino was right when he had called her a mood ring. Maybe she just picked up on body temperature and tricked herself into believing it meant something more. Sometimes she lay awake at night, alone and awash in doubt, absolutely convinced that reading emotions was complete bosh as the complexity of the human experience could not and did not distill itself down into mauve.

Edwards didn't look sinister. He was heady with the same excited rush she saw in teenagers after they hit the adrenaline rides at amusement parks, thrilled to finally be living his dream of standing on the same stage as the big kids. But she wasn't able to shake the fact that he was standing here today because he had painted her up as a target.

She forwarded Charley's message log to Santino's cell so they could go over it at leisure, then pulled her attention back to Mulcahy. Her boss towered over all others in the room while he politely told them how things would be.

"…no place in today's society for discrimination or conflict. We are connected, more so today than ever before. We must decide how to best maintain these connections, and how we want to benefit from them. When we perceive these connections as a threat for no other reason than that they exist, we turn to violence.

"Violence benefits no one. It is not a form of self-expression or communication, as no one person has the right to harm another as part of public discourse. Violence is not now, nor has ever been, an acceptable way to express personal frustration.

"Now," Mulcahy said as he wrapped up the first part of the conference. "I'll turn this over to Chief Sturtevant of the Metropolitan Police Department."

Sturtevant was the Chief of Detectives at First District Station, which in the eyes of its officers put him just one step removed from God. He was not a good public speaker, which in Rachel's opinion meant he was most likely an exceptional cop. He unfolded his notes and read directly from the copy, never bothering to look at his audience.

"We are concerned that last night's incident might be connected to a series of events intended to incriminate both OACET and the MPD, with serious potential consequences for the general public."

Sturtevant paused, not for effect but to control his anger; to Rachel's eyes he was roaring. "Last night, one of my lieutenants ruined my evening when he told me we have a decorated young police detective on tape, savagely beating a civilian."

The bottom feeders in the reporter pool gasped. The others had good connections at the MPD and had been waiting on official confirmation.

"I asked him why this call wasn't coming from the detective's lawyer, and my lieutenant attested that Detective Matt Hill," he gestured towards the detective, who was standing in that old reliable fallback of parade rest, "has an alibi. He was out of the state at his sister's wedding. At the same time he was caught on camera attacking one man, he was giving a toast in front of a hundred witnesses.

"There is no question that the video showing the assault was faked, but digital forensic experts are still picking it apart to see how it was done. Someone was committed to framing one of our officers, and they did a very good job of it.

"Over the past month, two similar crimes have occurred. One took place at this coffee shop. The other involved the murder of a young woman. In all three incidents, the video evidence does not show what really took place."

Fierce muttering from the crowd rose up at this, then slowed as reporters scribbled down possible headlines.

"I don't like doubting my eyes, or the resources we have come to rely on as part of police procedure and community safety. We are appointing a joint task force between OACET and the Metropolitan Police Department. Our organizations will work together to identify the cause of these activities. Then, we will take steps to prevent them from happening again. Whatever our differences, we agree that these two outcomes are beneficial for all parties and must be pursued immediately."

Rachel's eyes widened. On the other side of the podium Santino lit up like a switch had been flipped; news to him too, apparently.

Josh had vanished with the pretty barista sometime during the press conference, so while Sturtevant took questions she reached out to Mulcahy. *"We're doing what now?"*

"You, Santino, and Detectives Zockinski and Hill. All of the MPD has agreed to contribute resources to a task force. They are running scared, since every piece of video evidence they have could be tossed."

"I would have liked to have known about this," she said.

"We finalized the details right before the conference," he

answered. *"Also, I need you to pick two Agents for your team."*

"I have a team?"

"And a pay raise. Congratulations, you're Administration. Find Agents with law enforcement backgrounds and skills which complement police procedure to balance out the MPD side of the task force. And..." he hesitated, then said: *"...try to get Agents who haven't been placed anywhere yet. Mare will tear my head off if I mess up her schedules."*

Rachel agreed across the link. Mare Murphy was a frail Irish waif who barely came up to Mulcahy's chest. She had anxiety disorder and a glorious spill of red hair down past her waist, and was absolutely terrifying. They had all learned early on to never anger an organizational specialist, especially one augmented by a quantum organic computer.

Sturtevant ended the conference before the reporters had finished asking questions, so everyone behind the podium marched out of the coffee shop as a group, the MPD pounding the lead. Rachel was hurrying to catch up to Santino when she saw Edwards reach out from behind to grab her by the arm.

She stopped and turned to face him. "Yes?"

"Agent... I..." the judge paused, caught off-guard. Rachel didn't know why since he had seen her pull that same stunt at least twice the previous night. "I've had some time to think. I just wanted you to know that you have my full support. I'll be perfectly frank: I feel as though I'm being set up, too."

Rachel snorted. She couldn't help it. Edwards' self-important posturing rubbed her the wrong way. That, and she couldn't hear the phrase "perfectly frank" without thinking of really awesome hot dogs. "Thanks."

His edges went red. "I mean it. If last night had ended badly, my future would have gone with it."

Rachel said nothing, allowing Edwards enough time to realize that if last night had ended badly, she wouldn't have had a future either, but he wouldn't have been the one stuck inside an overpriced wooden box.

Edwards flushed red on multiple frequencies. "I didn't..."

he started.

"Yes, you did," she said. Several reporters were following their exchange. "Thank you for your concern."

His campaign manager was all but tugging his sleeve to get his attention but Edwards brushed her off. "Don't quote me out of context," he snapped at the reporters. He pulled Rachel away from the cameras and lowered his voice. "Peng, what happened here last night was actually good luck. If you hadn't shown up, the tampered videos? Those would look like something I did to help my image."

She nodded. "Yes, we already thought of that," she replied, and then added a pinch of sarcasm: "Thank you again."

"Listen," he said, standing over her in a laughable attempt at menace. "A woman is dead, and I won't be railroaded."

"I wanted to confirm our meeting next week," Mulcahy said softly. Quiet as a wolf, he had circled back around Edwards and his campaign manager. Rachel had put a hand up to cover her smile as Mulcahy came in close to the judge's ear and spoke. The nameless woman jumped and squeaked. To anyone else's eyes but hers, Edwards maintained his composure, but his colors scattered like marbles from a broken bag.

"What meeting is this?" the judge asked.

"The one you discussed with Agent Glassman. He let me know you were very concerned about how the public would react to the videos, and he proposed a meeting between our offices."

"Ah… I decided it wasn't necessary," Edwards said. Beside him, his campaign manager was shaking her head frantically. A token gesture of support was one thing, but open collusion with the enemy was hard to downplay on the evening news.

"Really? I thought it was still on the table," Mulcahy replied. "There must be a miscommunication somewhere. Should I call him and make sure?"

Mulcahy was bluffing. Rachel had felt for Josh in the link and knew he was nearby, but neither he nor the pretty barista were to be found. Everyone in OACET had learned to leave

Josh be when he disappeared; Rachel had also learned to never scan the storage closets.

"*My turn*," Mulcahy told her. He put a gentle hand on Edwards' shoulder and steered him aside, waving away the reporters with the other. Mulcahy had made it clear to the press that they would get everything they wanted from him as long as they kept out of his way. The ones who hadn't listened had already crashed and burned, their careers left to rot on that grand battlefield of the fourth estate as an example to their peers.

She shook her head slightly, gladly, and turned to catch up with her partner.

"What was that about?" Santino asked.

"Oh, Edwards is playing the martyr card," she said. "Did you check that chat log I sent you?"

"Yes," he answered. "What did Charley mean? Be careful of what?"

She puffed out her cheeks in a loud sigh. "Honestly?" I think he's trying to warn me about Edwards. He works with the judge, maybe he saw some papers lying around or something."

"Seems strange," Santino said, scrolling through the log again. "That's not much of a warning."

"He's a gossip. He can't help it. They're like locusts when it comes to tasty, tasty information. They don't care about quality or coherency, they just gobble it up and poop it out."

Santino was stunned by her imagery and told her so, and she gave him a small curtsey.

"So, task force?" she prompted.

"Yeah. Who's in charge of that fiasco?" he asked her.

"Oh dear lord, please tell me you know more than I do," she groaned.

"I know we've started to canvas for the man from the gas station," he said. "First MPD took the case from Sixth last night, and they're trying to track him down. They've also gone with your suggestion to talk to the cameraman who filmed Hill during the original self-defense demonstration at First.

"Other than that…" he grinned at her, a tapestry of happiness and smug pink vindication. "All I know is I'm going to hug the snot out of you once we're alone."

Zockinski and Hill were waiting for them outside. Rachel couldn't even begin to make sense of the eclectic prism of their moods so she flat-out gave up and adjusted the implant to exclude the emotional spectrum.

"So," she said, looking up at them, "why you?"

"How many other cops do you get along with?" Zockinski asked.

"Other?" she retorted.

"Folks?" Santino said. "Big picture time. I don't know about you, but I'd like to have a career when all of this is over, and I'm pretty sure Hill doesn't want to end up in jail."

Hill, his arms crossed, nodded in agreement. Rachel had no idea why he had been appointed to the task force when he was one of the victims, but that was the MPD's business, not hers. She imagined one of those scenes straight out of a movie, Hill banging his fists on his superior's desk and shouting: *"Damn it, Lieutenant!"* until the rules shattered around him, but he had probably just called in a favor.

"I guess the first thing to do is to go out to OACET headquarters and pick the other two members of the team," she said to Santino. The detectives' eyes widened and she was glad she had turned off the emotional spectrum; she wasn't sure what colors they were showing but she knew those wouldn't have made her feel any better about the situation. The analog for "lion's den" probably dripped.

"We'll take care of that," Santino said, seeing their expressions, and Rachel let Mulcahy know she was bringing her partner back to their home.

"All right," Zockinski replied. "We'll talk to the cameraman, and then follow up with the guy who got assaulted here last week."

"Shame," Hill said, looking back towards the coffee shop. The reporters had vanished with the elites, and all who were left in the store were the baristas returning the chairs to their usual locations. "You would think this was a safe place."

"Yeah. There's a pattern if you think about it," Santino said. "Gas station, coffee shop, bank... What comes after bank? Hospital? School?"

"Nothing," Zockinski replied. "Nothing comes after bank."

He had a point. They had to stop this now. Not only had the scenes changed but the attacks had escalated. The gas station had been a dry run, followed by an actual assault, followed by a murder. Anything that happened after that would likely be in the realm of multiple homicides.

"Oh, hey," Rachel said, pointing back at the coffee shop. "I never got the chance to examine the security system here."

"We've got a copy of the tape," Hill said. "And the system is recent, good quality."

"You didn't think to look at it last night?" Santino asked her.

She sighed. "Stuff came up."

"Next time, check before you run into a burning building."

"Hey, I'm a little out of practice with people who want to kill me because I'm me."

"Really?" Zockinski didn't realize the quip was out of his mouth before he heard himself say it. He grabbed Hill by the arm and stormed off.

She smirked. "Hey Zockie," she called after him. "I think this is the beginning of a beautiful friendship!" She watched the detective's shoulders jerk back as he bit down on another quick response, and he kept on walking.

"Show the guy some mercy," Santino said.

"Aw, he's old-school," she said as she grinned at her partner. "You've got to chip away at his shell before you can get to his soft chewy center. Where are we parked?"

"Around back. You're driving."

Five minutes later, Rachel reclined in her passenger's seat and let the rhythm of Santino's complaining soothe her. She took her OACET badge from her purse and ran her thumb over its polished surface. The Agents had designed their seal in the vivid chartreuse of their digital projections, and the green eagle with wings displayed over a field of gold binary text was so garish it could be seen at a hundred paces. This was the first time she had looked at it since that day she had reported to the Metropolitan Police Department for duty, then shoved it to the bottom of the bag. It hadn't gotten any less ugly with time.

She stuck it on her belt and hoped it would ride more comfortably once she had changed out of the skinny suit.

SEVEN

The drive to OACET headquarters was too pleasant. Santino's compact hybrid wound its way under the trees crowning Canal Road, its driver perfecting his skills in the distinguished art of annoyance.

"You don't often see mummies in the Palisades. Real honest-to-God Egyptian mummies," he said, the Potomac River rolling past them on their left. "Look, that one's all shambling around, with rags dragging in the dirt and everything."

"Darned undead," Rachel muttered, trying to nap. She had turned the implant off and was enjoying the dappled patchwork of hot summer sun after it had filtered down through leaves and windows and air conditioning.

"Did I ever tell you about the time I learned I was a cat with two heads? Best part? Eighteen lives."

"I'm up, I'm up. For pity's sake, don't tell me their backstories." She turned the implant on and gave herself a few seconds to orient with the highway and local landmarks, then stretched to pop her back.

"I have so much time to come up with them. While driving. Seriously, just once I'd like to be the one who gets in a nap."

"Okay, fine, fun's over," Rachel said as she wagged a finger at him. "I can't drive. So there."

"What do you... oh. Oh." He went yellow and then burnt orange as he put the pieces together; she had reactivated her full spectrum of senses. "Is it the color thing?"

It wasn't the color thing, it was the blind thing, but the difference was close enough for her to ignore. "Yeah. It's safer if I'm not the one behind the wheel. My vision isn't normal."

Santino glared blearily at the road. "You should have told me months ago. This has been bugging me."

"And stifle your creativity? I'm your muse. Your lazy, chauffeured muse," she said, yawning and settling back in the seat.

He imposed payback and forced her to suffer through two stories (a cat in the Industrial Revolution who had an undignified but well-paying job as portable toilet paper, and one who toured the world with Billie Jean King after some major modifications to his intestines) before they turned up the driveway to OACET's temporary headquarters. Rachel cracked the digital lock on the massive iron gate and waved out of her window to the sniper camped out on the roof.

"Hot enough for you, Kit?"

"Bite me," the former Special Forces operative snapped, and sent the sensation of August heat thundering at her through the link. Rachel was instantly drenched in sweat.

"Jeez," she said to Kit, reaching for the climate controls. *"Someone's in a pissy mood."*

"Someone's hot, bored, and tired of the same stupid question. Put your name in the rotation and come up here to do security once in a while, okay?"

Rachel leaned over the vents and tried to pass the feeling of cool circulated air back across the link, but Kit clamped down on her end.

"Don't. It screws with my physiology. Makes being up here twice as bad when my body realizes it's been tricked."

"Okay then," Rachel replied testily, and broke their connection.

"I might have to take a personal day when all of this is over," she said to Santino. "Apparently I've been slacking on my responsibility to develop a tan."

"But we save so much on our energy bills by using you to light the office at night."

"Shut up."

They parked in the visitor lot by the front doors and walked up a flagstone path lined on both sides by ancient hardwoods and immaculate flowerbeds full of fresh annuals. Gardeners poked their heads up like gophers to see who was with her, then dropped back down into the mulch.

"All Agents?" Santino asked.

She nodded. "You're the only visitor today. They say hello."

"Mhmm," he muttered.

"What?"

"It's not that I don't love you guys," Santino said, "and it's not that you don't make me feel welcome. It's that you all give off that Sunday afternoon vibe where a friend has dropped by without calling ahead, and you're happy to see him but you're still a little irritated you had to put on pants."

She gave him that one. Apart from the place being closed on weekends, he had nailed it.

Rachel and Santino dodged the arc of a sprinkler. No one had thought to sneak in sod as a line item on the budget, so the sprawling lawns were mostly dirt with a thin patchwork of sprouting grass. Still, progress was progress, and their temporary offices were becoming more habitable by the day.

Before they dropped the curtain to show humanity the cyborgs in their midst, OACET had been spread out on the East and West Coasts. When Mulcahy had taken over as acting director, he and the other members of OACET's administrative team had launched a tactical clerical strike in which every Agent was brought home to D.C. to regroup. The logistics of the move had been performed as quickly and as quietly as possible. Rachel and the others stationed in California had let the leases lapse on their apartments and had snatched up new ones all the way across the country. They closed down the Los Angeles office on the same day they went public, the doors locked and chairs put up on the tables in advance of Mulcahy's bombshell.

Within hours of that first press conference, Agent Mare Murphy had gone up against Congress and wrangled a sizeable operations fund from their clenched hands. Murphy was OACET's organizational specialist in much the same way that George Marshall had served Franklin Roosevelt, and Congress was still reeling. Murphy had judiciously applied equal measures of carrot and stick: she had guilted Congress to accept their responsibility in the creation of the implant and its Agents, and she pushed them to recognize how the three hundred and fifty active Agents could be of virtually immeasurable service to the good citizens of the United States of America.

And, as Murphy reminded them, the Agents had come forward and exposed the Program not because they had to, but because they felt obligated to do so. Just imagine what could have happened if they had decided to remain in hiding, or had sold their services to the highest bidder! Yes, they were government employees and full disclosure is what they ought to have done, Murphy said, but obligation was a two-way street.

Never let it be said that Agent Murphy couldn't deliver. OACET had been given a permanent headquarters in a decommissioned postal hub (purposefully and perhaps insultingly) close to the U.S. Government Accountability Office. The place was a wreck, the slightest hints of industrial cleaner and anthrax still lingering in the corners. Plans were on the table to gut the building down to its old Aquia Creek sandstone shell and rebuild the interior from scratch, but until construction was complete they were camped out in a property warehouse.

At least, on paper it was a warehouse. In practice, it was a sprawling mansion on the Potomac that had been the scene of a bloodbath between a drug cartel and the DEA at the height of the cocaine craze. The mansion had spent fifteen years languishing on the real estate market before it was repurposed for storage. It was intended as temporary overflow for items seized or recovered by federal authorities when the official storage facilities exceeded capacity, but as anyone with a garage knew, out of sight was out of mind and the clutter had continued to grow. When OACET first moved in, they had opened the front door and found themselves standing in the federal government's junk drawer. There was no rhyme or reason to how items had been crammed into rooms: it was common to find a layer of jewelry on top of birdcages on top of chainsaws. Each item had a little white label listing its origins, but other than that brief nod to ownership the place was essentially orphans piled all the way up to the ceiling.

They knew they were being used. There was no way the mansion could function as their office unless they dug in and scrubbed.

It took them eleven hours.

The organization of one hundred and eighty-three thousand, seven hundred and five objects was the first real task they had handled as a group. They established a map and a database, and fell upon the trove armed with cleaning supplies and RFID tags. They cut a path through the house like a swarm of African ants, picking, sorting, dusting, and cataloging. The only slowdowns occurred when they stumbled across the real treasures, and a cry would go out through the collective for everyone to drop what they were doing and come running (Rachel had sent one out herself when she found an original LP pressing of "Meet the Beatles!" lost amongst too many Captains and Tennilles).

After the cleanup was finished, they had shifted into repair mode. Some of them threw themselves into research and prepared extensive lists of the items, cross-referenced with average resale values, to persuade those agencies which had used the mansion as a dumping ground to come and get their stuff. The outdoorsy types grabbed the landscaping gear and attacked the hedges, the hobby chefs restocked the kitchen, and the engineers went to see what could be done about the pool.

They had made it home. Beautiful, restful, wonderful home. And almost as soon as they discovered this, Mulcahy and his team had kicked them out. Policy was written within the first week which prohibited unauthorized sleepovers; there were too few beds and the stink of chlorine was no substitute for a shower. Then came more policy where overtime had to be approved, followed by even more policy where only the skeleton crew was allowed in on weekends. There was some grumbling; the Agents understood why their Administration was driving them back out into the world, but they didn't have to like it.

Denial, however, turned out to be its own benefit: their time at home was precious. The infighting and squabbles that usually tainted work and family were few, the Agents unwilling to spoil their few hours spent in sanctuary dwelling on petty bullshit. When they were home, they were happy. This protection might fade over time as they reassimilated back into society, but for the time being it was warm and thick around them.

As she and Santino walked up the front steps, Rachel's fingers traced the streaks and pockmarks in the granite columns, scars left from the grand finale of the mansion's heady drug days. Most of the hasty repairs done to domesticate the building for sale had decayed and fallen out over time, but Rachel tried to pick out the remaining putty whenever she could. Their home was wounded but strong, and damned if she wouldn't do her part to call attention to the symbolism.

The silent voices welcomed her as she crossed the threshold. The mahogany doors of the mansion were an arbitrary marker, true, but they had learned to create order when and where they could. The Agents were networked with each other as much as with other forms of tech. Distance wasn't really a barrier between them, not when the others were as far away as a thought, but privacy and personal space were paramount. You offered a greeting, shouted or not, when an Agent came home, and kept them at a distance otherwise. Their presence at the fringes of your mind barely registered until one voice in the crowd was directed at you, and then, like answering a phone, you chose to speak with your friend.

Imposing order on that chaos was critical. They all knew how easy it was to go mad.

She let them know Santino was with her, and there was a scramble to find pants.

A classical double staircase ran up either side of the main hall, framing a regulation-size boxing ring. The ring, along with most of their athletic equipment, had come from a mixed-martial arts chain brought down by tax evasion. The ring was portable and they disassembled it for photo shoots or when they held formal functions, but during normal working hours the first sounds heard upon entering the mansion was the smack of tanned leather on flesh.

Today it was laughter. Dead center of the ring stood the largest man Rachel had ever met in her life. Mako Hill was nearly seven feet of solid muscle, and he laughed and swung clumsily at an opponent slightly more than half his size. He waved at her over the other man's head.

"Hello, tiny Chinese woman!"

"Hello, giant black man!"

Mako leaned over the ropes circling the ring and gave her a quick hug. *"How did you get him to practice?"* Rachel asked, and moved around Mako to face his opponent.

Phil Netz, small and wiry, sniffed derisively. *"He lost a bet, but don't call this practice. I'm sparring with a side of beef that won't fight back."*

Mako lifted his gloved hands, palms up. *"I go out of my way to take the 'fist' out of 'pacifist'."*

Rachel smiled. *"And what happens when you get mugged?"*

"I give up my wallet," he replied, grinning broadly. *"Anyone desperate enough to think I'm a good target for a mugging needs my money more than I do."*

She laughed. Santino suddenly tinged with orange. *Damn,* she thought. Rachel hated it when she made her partner uncomfortable.

"Any bagels left in the kitchen?" she asked aloud.

Mako and Phil both winced. Theirs wasn't true telepathy but whatever they called it, it was easier than speech. Now that they had their own centralized workplace, they had picked up the bad habit of shutting non-cyborgs out of their conversations. Santino had admitted that he could deal with either speech or silence, but outbursts out of context gave him the absolute willies.

"No, but we're making a lunch run in an hour. Hey Raul," Mako said to Santino. "Sorry about that."

"You folks have to get out of your heads," Santino said,

smiling. "It's not healthy."

"You're telling me. I live in this thing!" Mako lightly boxed his own ears, then held out his hands to Rachel. She glanced at Phil, who rolled his eyes and assented to Mako's escape.

"Mulcahy's going to poop kittens if you don't learn how to fight," she said, unlacing the gloves.

"Then the Cyborg King will need to find another lifting partner," Mako replied, "and good luck to him with that."

It was not an idle threat. Mulcahy was a man of reasonable size and strength only when standing next to Mako Hill. After a few drinks, their favorite party game was to hide the guests' cars without bothering with the keys.

"You've got to do something to get your speed up," Phil said to Mako. "My grandmother moves faster than you."

"We could go jogging," Rachel said.

"Jogging? No. This…" Mako said as he made a long gesture with his free hand which started at his head and moved down to encompass his feet, "…was not built to jog. This was built to pick up the couch and see if it goes better under the other window, and then back to where it was because the upholstery looks better in a southerly light."

He sighed dramatically. Mako's wife was heavily pregnant and they were in the last phases of frenzied preparation. His arms were flecked with pastel paint and crisped marks from a soldering iron. His wife, Carlota, was also an Agent, and they were childproofing their home by building and installing various devices that responded to their implants. Mako admitted they might have gone a little overboard: when Carlota's parents came over to visit, they couldn't use the toilet without help.

He cocked his head to the side. "Ah," Mako sighed. "Pregnancy craving. Apparently I am to go and fetch a pickle milkshake."

"Ugh," Santino grimaced. "Really?"

"No, she wants pizza. But pickle milkshakes are funnier." Mako slowly navigated the ropes and dropped to the ground. Behind him, Phil threw in the towel and muttered that he was not going to be held responsible when Mulcahy found out.

As Mako waved and headed towards the bath they had set aside as a makeshift locker room, Rachel caught a glimpse of her friend from the side. She had spent the past twenty-four hours staring at various angles of Matt Hill's face, and when Mako turned sideways there were enough genetics in his profile for her to make the connection.

"Hill…" she said under her breath.

"Hm?" Santino glanced towards her.

"Mako's last name is Hill… Hey Mako!" Rachel called out. "You got any family in D.C.?"

"Maybe. Can't say for sure. We're not really talking these days." He shrugged like an apologetic mountain as he walked away. "Why?"

"Just an idea," she said. *"I'll tell you about it when I know more."*

"Sure."

"Coincidence," Santino said.

"It'd explain why Matt Hill was targeted. If he's got family in OACET, that's the link we're looking for."

"The link you're looking for. I have no delusions the world actually does revolve around me."

She snorted. "Don't make me break out the Scully."

"Hill is probably one of the most common surnames in the country."

Rachel flipped her hair and affected the trademark sarcastic eyebrow. "Mulder, what you are proposing is simply impossible. You cannot expect me to believe it."

Santino pushed back the tails of an imaginary trenchcoat. "But Scully, you're up to your armpits in an alien cadaver. How much more proof do you need?"

"There are many documented cases of human beings having six hearts and fifteen legs, Mulder. Olympic athletes, for example. Aliens are silly and you are silly for believing in them, because everyone with good sense knows they don't exist, which includes myself, despite the fact I am covered in gooey, sticky evidence."

"Perhaps it is but another excuse to remove your clothing and cultivate sexual tension."

"I concur. Excuse me, for a moment. I will return in a flowing robe, holding an oversized glass of wine, and will be promptly attacked by the nameless abomination hiding in my apartment. Exit, stage left."

They bowed. Phil golf-clapped politely through his gloves. "Nicely done," he said, "but, context-wise, shouldn't Santino be playing the skeptic?"

Santino shook his head. "She can't do Mulder."

"I can't. I just can't," Rachel sighed. "Something about his inflection eludes me. It's a combination of a native Philadelphian and constant hay fever... I can't get it right."

Phil snorted.

"Okay. In all honesty," Santino said, "I'll admit we shouldn't rule out the possibility. Yeah, this could be about OACET. There's a clear association between OACET and technology in everybody's minds these days.

"But!" He cut Rachel off before she could speak. "You have to admit you guys are a little defensive, maybe a little over-protective. Everything we've got so far is circumstantial. I'm not saying that you don't have enemies, but I think you should be sure that this is *because* of your enemies. If you go looking for a fight, you'll probably find it, even if you start it yourselves."

"Rachel, let's not go looking for that fight."

"He's right," Phil said.

"Don't you start."

The small Agent sighed in golds, then said aloud, "I hear you're looking for a couple of spares."

"Oh, hive minds," Santino grumbled. "What don't you know?"

"Why you haven't asked me yet," Phil said. "Former U.S. Marshal, specialization in tactical operations?"

Rachel leaned towards Phil from the other side of the ropes. "You're on the short list," she grinned.

"Don't you dare pun me, woman," Phil said. "You're better than that and I'm taller than you."

She laughed. "You're one of my first choices, but I just can't start cherrypicking my friends."

"Get one friend and one qualified asshole," Phil said. "That way you do right by everyone."

"Man has a point," Santino said. He liked Phil. The lively Agent had an artistic streak, and he and Santino had gone to more than a few gallery shows together. From what they told her, they had the most fun when the art was dreadful: somewhere under the coleus plants in Santino's office was an oil painting of a dewy-eyed duck Santino claimed he couldn't live without.

"I was thinking maybe Jason Atran," Rachel said.

Phil grimaced. "He'd do. Until he's accidentally strangled in the line of duty, that is."

"Have I met him?" Santino asked Rachel.

"No." She shook her head. "You'd remember." She looked around for Jason in the link and found him in his office in an upstairs bedroom.

"So?" Phil asked, bumping his gloves together.

"Give me an hour," she said to the other Agent. "No promises."

"Works for me," Phil said. "Happy hunting." Shadow-boxing, he moved back to the center of the ring and put out an open call for a new opponent.

Rachel and Santino meandered around the precarious stacks of junk and through the kitchen to reach the back staircase. Santino had been to the mansion countless times since they had been partnered, but he had never gone down into its bowels. Today, Rachel led him through a landfill of utmost quality. Some rooms, like the parlor full of pinball machines and classic arcade games, were devoted to larger items, but the high-traffic areas were mostly given over to boxes marked in black scribbled print. This forest of cardboard closed around them and sometimes moaned like the wind in the trees, the complaints of careful packing settling slightly under its own weight.

The two of them headed down a wide wooden staircase decorated in panels carved with ferns and the occasional lion head, stopping for a fast chat when they passed the Agents who had their offices on the landings. In a building where unoccupied square footage was already at a premium, three hundred and fifty people just barely fit. You made do wherever you could cram a desk, and tried to keep the power and networking cables out of the walkways.

Santino was stunned by the spectacle. He stopped to touch the fragile glass shade of a vintage Tiffany lamp propped up against a used toaster oven. "You guys work in the Hoarder Barbie Dreamhouse."

"Not yet. It's depressingly urine-free in here. We're looking into adopting at least sixty cats."

Despite the size of her partner's private jungle, Rachel hadn't been given a desk over at First MPD. Her office was in the billiards hall in the mansion's basement. She shared the area with thirty other Agents, and they had brought in some modular walls to partition off sections and create the illusion of personal space. The cubicle farm made the place look like any other government agency, albeit one with fluted ceilings and elephant tusks crossed over the doors. The tchotchkes at each desk were also the norm for young professionals, but a visitor with an eye for antiques might notice the posters from World War II were perhaps a little too authentic, the Batman and Star Wars action figures a little too mint. The rules were that you could do whatever you wanted as long as the items never left the grounds and were kept in the same condition as you found them.

Most of the Agents who worked in Rachel's sector weren't at their desks and the room was dark and peaceful. Santino was a curiosity so they took a few minutes to make the rounds and say hello to those few Agents who were in, then headed towards Rachel's station in the back corner.

She turned on her desk light, causing pinpoints of reflected brilliance to splash across the cheap fabric partitions. Santino gasped. Rachel had a magpie's love of sparklies and had filled her cubicle with jewelry and unset gems. He gaped at the dragon's hoard that covered her workspace. "Holy crap," he said softly, as if to not disturb it. "How much is all this stuff worth?"

"Forty-point-two million," she replied automatically. "Here, catch."

Santino jumped and his colors blanched from anxiety as she threw a diamond the size of a chicken egg at him. He juggled frantically for a few seconds, then got it under control and cradled it against his body. "Rachel!"

"It's a diamond," she laughed. "If you had dropped it, I'd be more worried about the floor."

He held it up to the light, and prisms fell across the rest of the gems. "It's gorgeous. How much does something like this cost?"

"It can't be sold, so it's got no value," Rachel said. "That's a known conflict diamond. Most of these are, too..." she swept a hand across the surface of the desk and the gems rolled over her fingers like water. "Otherwise this'd all be worth ten, twenty times as much. They'll never go to auction. The feds unloaded them here because this place has good security and they don't know what else to do with them."

Santino put down the diamond and wiped his hands together. "And you're okay with having them around?"

"I like things that seem beautiful until you learn their stories," she said.

"Somebody was a Goth in high school."

She chuckled. "Maybe a little bit."

"Do you have a favorite?"

Rachel turned her sixth sense on the pile to find a particular resonance. She pushed through the stones and pulled out a round pink sapphire the size of her pinkie nail. "Here."

"Really?" Santino was skeptical. "What did you do, pick the smallest one?"

"Almost. It's not conflict, and I can afford it when it goes up for sale."

"What's its price?"

She shrugged. "Lots. Bunches. I've spent the last five years living cheap, though, so I'm due for a splurge."

"Why do you want to waste your money on something like this?"

Because we'll leave here someday. Because I need to carry a part of this place with me forever. Because I have to.

"It's a girl thing," she said, and pointed to an ornate dining room set stacked high with banker's boxes and loose pottery. Santino unearthed one of the chairs and dragged it over to her desk, then straddled it so his chin rested comfortably on the padded backrest.

Rachel had taken an especial liking to a golden crown set with emeralds which she referred to as her "Thinking Tiara" and wore when she typed, but out of deference to her partner's well-practiced skills in mockery she left it perched atop her old stuffed teddy bear. She groped under her desk for her keyboard. When she had started cultivating her hoard, she had screwed a high metal rail around the edges of her desk to keep the stones from falling. It served its purpose but her desk had become a wicked snare of carpal tunnel, and was all but useless for those who wanted to keep their wrists. Rachel loathed those stupid undermount sliding keyboard trays but she had installed one at the same time she had put up the rail. The company of millions of dollars in gems was a once-in-a-lifetime experience, and she would gladly suffer the indignity of poor ergonomic design to enjoy it.

She woke up her monitors and started pulling potentials from the Agent roster. The candidate pool was surprisingly small. When Rachel thought of federal agencies, she went straight to law enforcement or military, but the list was dominated with unpronounceable acronyms which usually led back to the sciences or public policy.

"How about Mako?" Rachel asked. "Says here he was with ASCR. That sounds Air Force-ish."

"Really?" Santino perked. "How did I not know that about him?"

"Let's see… ASCR. …" Rachel called up her search on the second screen. "Advanced Scientific Computing Research. Not military. What do they do?"

"Pretty awesome stuff. New ways to apply mathematics and computer technologies, mostly. I thought about applying there for a while during grad school."

"Never get you and Mako drunk together in the same room at the same time. Check."

He took the high ground and ignored her. "There's that Jason Atran guy's name again," he said, pointing at the list of candidates. "Drug Enforcement Agency?"

Rachel chewed her lower lip. "Yeah. Damn, damn, damn," she grumbled. "We're going to have to go with him. He and Zockinski are going to end up stabbing each other."

"Is he really that bad?"

"No, he's that good," she replied. "He was the poster boy at the DEA until he was picked up by OACET. I mean, not to brag, we were all selected for the Program because we had the skills and the talent, but Jason has the ego to go along with it.

"And he's antisocial with a persecution complex," she added, knowing her partner would diagnose Jason within seconds without her help. The Agent was one of those who didn't try to hide how badly he'd been damaged. "It's a terrible combination. You just want to slap the smug smile off of his face, but if you did that, you'd be proving him right."

"Okay," Santino said. "Let's go with someone else."

"Well, he's also a digital forensics expert. He's the one I mentioned back at the gas station."

"Oh."

"Yep," she said.

"There are hundreds of you cyborgs. There's nobody else from law enforcement with that specialty?"

She shook her head. "Doesn't appear to be."

He thought about it. "If you get Jason, can I please have

Phil?"

"I don't actually want Jason," she muttered, scrolling through the list to see if someone better was available.

"Why do you type?" he asked.

"What?" The change of topic threw her off. She looked up, not sure what he had meant.

Santino pointed at the monitor, where the cursor flew back and forth, seemingly by magic. "You navigate the screen with the implant, right? So why can't you do the same thing when you type? Seems like using a keyboard would slow you down."

"Oh. Yeah. Well, I could, but I'd be typing what I thought instead of filtering content when I entered it manually."

"That's my point."

"Don't think about the Stay Puft Marshmallow Man," she said.

"Ah."

"I can autotype but it's not worth it. It's not natural. You have to concentrate, remember to format and punctuate… Editing's a bitch! It's all conscious, very purposeful. The end product reads like a robot wrote it. Your body has to be involved if you want any feeling in your words."

Her partner scrambled for the notebook where he jotted down her observations of how she and the other cyborgs balanced their human and technological sides. He referred to the notebook as his eventual bestseller; Rachel referred to it as kindling followed by a lengthy argument. "Want me to leave out that line about editing being a bitch?" he asked.

"Would you?" she sighed, then stood up. "Come on, let's go talk to Jason. If you don't want to run him down with a car after the interview, he's on the team."

They checked the cuffs of their clothing for hitchhiking gems, and she took him on a shortcut through an enclosed veranda. They crossed the length of the house in the August mid-day heat, then reentered through the servants' quarters. As the cool of the building returned, a woman in her late twenties spun into the hallway in front of them in her stocking feet and a vintage Funkadelic tee over torn denim shorts, eyes closed and singing along to an old Cameo song only she could hear.

"Zia!"

Zia froze, balanced on her toes like a deer that had scented the hunters. She blushed furiously. *"Hey Rachel,"* she replied, embarrassed, and then she opened her eyes and saw Santino.

Beside her, Santino surged bright red. Rachel was shocked, not by his sudden lust—with long blond hair and perfect curves, Zia set the standard for the California dime—but from the shift in Santino's smooth ultramarine core. She had assumed core colors were forever unchanging but his had lightened to cobalt as it seized a thick strand of Zia's pure honey rose and merged it into itself. Her partner had fallen wildly in love at first sight.

And, as the other woman's core took in Santino's blue and deepened slightly towards violet, she saw Zia had done the same.

Oh for fuck's sake, Rachel thought as she buried her face in her hands.

She quickly introduced Raul Santino, police officer and professional computer nerd with First MPD, to Zia Hallahan, cyborg and professional physics nerd formerly of NASA, then fled to the safety of the nearest bathroom as Santino began the slow and awkward process of remembering he already lived with his girlfriend. Rachel set her implant to straight reading mode and grabbed a recent copy of *Vogue* from the pile of magazines beside the toilet. She cleared some space from the top of the vanity and settled down for a long wait, reminding herself that the star-crossed courtship on the other side of the door was None Of Her Business.

She was bending down the corners on those pages with the most appealing fall fashions when Zia screamed.

Rachel burst through the door and saw Santino with blood streaming down his left arm and his Taser held at the ready in his right. Her partner had been backed into a corner and was using a stack of old carousel horses for cover, shouting warnings at the man menacing him with an antique straight razor.

"SHAWN!" Rachel lashed out with both her voice and her mind. *"He's with me! I brought him here!"*

The man with the razor gibbered through the link, and Rachel felt the entire mansion drop what they were doing and come running.

She walked slowly towards Shawn, hands outstretched and open. Shawn had forgotten his clothes again, and Santino couldn't tear his eyes away from the heavy white scars on his wrists. The Agent lashed out towards her partner with the razor and found Rachel in his way.

"Rachel!" Santino called out.

"It's okay," she told him. "Shawn?" She had fully reactivated her implant and the naked man roiled in colors and patterns that were beyond sense.

"get him out GET HIM OUT he hurt Zia"

"He's a guest, Shawn," Rachel said aloud. She spoke slowly and carefully, as if talking to a child. "He's not going to hurt you, and he didn't hurt Zia. He's putting the Taser away now, see?"

Behind her, Santino shot her a look of pure confusion, then holstered his stun gun and wrapped the tail of his shirt around the gash on his arm.

Shawn, wild-eyed and face drawn so tight he seemed fifty instead of thirty, stared at Zia.

"he touched her he hurt her"

"No Shawn, he didn't hurt Zia. Look at her, Shawn. Zia is fine." The Army had trained her to use names like a hammer in cases like these, to drive home, again and again, the fact that the person on the other end of the name was a living human being. She had yet to see this tactic work and doubted today would be the first time.

"he touched her he hurt her HE DOESN'T BELONG"

"He's our guest," she said again. "Is this how we treat guests?"

Shawn exploded in reds and screamed through the link.

Wrong tactic, moron, she berated herself. She felt Mulcahy thundering down the stairs and knew she had to wrap this up before he got there. Shawn hated the man and would certainly go after him with the razor, and that would not end well for Shawn.

Rachel pretended to notice the weapon for the first time. "Oh my God," she said. "Is that… property?"

Shawn saw the fresh blood coating the old blade. *"nooooooooo,"* he keened, and the entire collective winced.

"Shawn, it's against the rules to damage property. You have to leave it as you found it! You know that! You broke the rules!"

"nooooo no no no no no…" The Agent turned gray and his hands went limp, the razor falling to the stone floor. *"I didn't break them I didn't break them I didn't break…"*

Zia caught him before he collapsed, and he buried his head against her chest and wailed aloud. The blond woman stared at Rachel in horror, wide-eyed and open-mouthed, as though she had just caught Rachel assaulting a baby.

Rachel felt awful. *Nothing like winning a fight by twisting the knife in the trauma,* she thought sadly. She bent down to scoop up the razor as Mulcahy turned the corner and walked into their little hallway, calm and collected, looking for all the world as though he hadn't run a mansion-sized obstacle course at a dead sprint.

Shawn, weeping uncontrollably in Zia's arms, was too far gone to notice his arrival.

"Take him back to his room," Mulcahy said to Zia.

"You can't leave her alone with him!" Santino shouted. Both Shawn and Zia ignored him. Santino's heart broke a little as Zia carefully guided his assailant through a set of double doors without a backwards glance.

"How did he get out?" Mulcahy asked Rachel.

"I have no idea," she said. "I was in the bathroom when I heard Zia scream."

"He's supposed to be on lockdown when we have visitors."

She glared up at him. *"Don't put this on me. I gave you advance warning I was bringing Santino here. Talk to Shawn's babysitters."*

Mulcahy turned to her partner, who was oozing blood and holding onto a gaily-painted horse as though it were a lifeline. *"What about him?"*

"I'll take care of it."

"Rachel—"

"I'll take care of it."

He looked at her partner and measured the outcomes. Then: *"Watch what you tell him."*

"Always."

"Back to work," Mulcahy sent out on the public band, and Rachel saw them fade away on the other side of the walls. He pushed through the double doors and was gone.

"Let me see," she said. Santino stared at her as if she had grown an extra head; he was yellows and grays throughout. "C'mere, let me see that arm."

"Rachel, what the hell just happened?"

"First things first," she said. "You're losing a lot of blood." Santino took a deep breath and some of the yellow faded, and he hauled himself out from behind the wooden horses.

He peeled the end of his shirt from the wound and she hissed. "Damn, he got you good."

"He came out of nowhere. I barely got my arm up in time. I think he was trying to kill me."

"You're going to need stitches," she said. It was something of an understatement; Santino had used his left arm as a shield and the wound ran on a long diagonal across the leading edge of his forearm. Shawn had missed anything vital but he had cut Santino deep enough to nick the bone. "We can do it here in the med center, or someone else can drive you to a hospital.

"We've got some primo painkillers," she said, grinning a bit to coax a laugh from him.

He wasn't buying. "That man, he's an Agent." When she didn't answer, he tried again. "He spoke to you without talking, Rachel. You might not think that's obvious, but it is."

She rewrapped his wound with his shirt to keep it covered. "Yeah," she said. "Yeah, Shawn's an Agent."

Santino was fuming. "And?"

"And you never should have bumped into him. He's our dark, dirty secret. We think he gave his caregivers the slip."

"What's wrong with him? The implant?"

She shook her head. "No. But adapting to the implant pushed him over the edge. The five years between when we got it and when we went public...

"Well," Rachel paused to measure her words, "they needed to give us better mental health care to help with the transition. Some of us never came all the way through it."

"He can do everything the rest of you can? Interface with machines the way you do?"

"Him and two others just like him," she said quietly.

"My God," he whispered.

"Which is why we keep them chained up in the basement," she said gently. "Figuratively speaking, of course. They have free run of the place except when visitors are here. But we can't leave them unsupervised and we can't tell anyone outside of OACET about them."

"Insane cyborgs," he said. "That's the scariest thing I've ever heard."

She nodded. "If it got out that some of us were unbalanced, it'd be open season. We couldn't protect them, and it'd probably be a good excuse to take us all down with them. You know, just to be sure.

"I'm trusting you with this," she said, meeting his eyes with her useless ones.

He looked away. "What did Mulcahy say to you?"

"I told him I'd take care of you."

"Like..." Santino turned his right hand into a gun and cocked it with his thumb. "...take care of me?"

"Jeez, you and the movies! No, like giving you the option to decide what to do, dumbass. If Mulcahy gets involved, you do as he says, no alternatives. This way, you still have a choice."

"I'm not going to break down and crumble because of him," he said.

"It's sweet how you can still believe that," she said.

He was silent for a moment. "How big of a risk are they?"

"Shawn and the others?" Rachel realized she was standing at parade rest and forced herself to slouch. "I don't think they're a risk at all, not unless something triggers them."

"Be honest, Rachel," he said, staring at the stain slowly spreading up his shirt. "What happens if I keep quiet and they set off the nukes? I couldn't live with that. I need to know if they're a risk. Do they want revenge or... or what?"

"No," she said. "They don't think in those terms. All they want is to be safe."

Santino suddenly slumped forward. Rachel grabbed him by his uninjured arm as he steadied himself against the horse.

"We need to get you stitched up," she said.

"I want a cookie," he mumbled. He saw her confused expression and said, "You know, you get a cookie? For donating blood?"

"Oh thank God, you still think you're funny," she said, helping him climb out of his protective pile of wooden animals. "You'll be fine."

She took him through the double doors and into the catacombs.

"What. The. Hell." Santino gasped. "Rachel, what... Am I hallucinating?"

"I wish you were," she sighed. During the mansion's tenure as a drug den, the main hallway connecting lowest level of the mansion had been remodeled after the municipal Ossuary under Paris, complete with faux skulls. The catacombs were a main reason the property had failed to sell, prospective buyers making it as far as the basement before discovering they were to purchase a graveyard which required plastic ghosts. "We have no idea what they were thinking," she said. "Cocaine was involved, that's for sure. Beyond that, it's anyone's guess."

The walls of the catacombs were covered in boxes stacked four deep and eight tall, with a path barely an arm's length across to allow passage between rooms. The Agents had tried to insulate themselves from poor taste but there was little they could do about the ceiling, which stared down at them with hollow eyes and grinned.

They made slow progress and walked single-file, Rachel at the lead. Santino, understandably gun-shy, jumped at every noise. She told him she had her implant set at full scanning mode and that she'd know if someone was lurking in a cardboard foxhole, but he was still shaking and she wasn't sure how much confidence he had in cyborgs right now.

"His wrists," Santino said softly.

"Yeah," she replied. She meant it to be an answer, and hoped he wouldn't ask.

"That scarring… it was all ragged. Like… bite marks."

"There were more than three of us who couldn't adapt," Rachel said. "Shawn and the other two? They were the ones who lived."

"How could someone do that to themselves?" he asked. "It's crazy."

Rachel glanced up at the smiling skulls with their empty sockets and wished she knew the answer.

EIGHT

"Should I be worried this place is better equipped than an emergency room?"

"Shhh." Jenny Davies was no longer used to working with patients who needed to vocalize. She was remembering old skills as she stitched the gash on his arm closed. "If you're going to talk, turn your head away from the injury. Saliva is a bacteria engine."

The Agents had set up their medical center in the wine cellar. The catacomb theme had been carried into this room. Santino had turned down Percocet in favor of codeine so he wouldn't be completely useless for the rest of the day, but he was still having problems focusing. He jumped between critiquing the fake bones and complimenting the physician on her surgical technique as she repaired the gash across his forearm.

Santino reached out with his good hand and poked the nub of a femur positioned upwards to form a cradle for a thirty-year-old merlot. "Both too much and too little planning went into this design," he said.

Davies grabbed him by his shoulder to stabilize his injured arm. The petite brunette was loads of fun at parties but she brooked no nonsense on her table. "If you don't stop moving, I will have Rachel tie you down."

"I got me truckloads of rope," Rachel agreed, sitting off to the side and away from Davies' surgical stage. She had gone back to the bathroom for the fashion magazine. Winter was coming, and she wasn't about to spend another year freezing in the thin piece of cloth that had passed for her coat back in California.

"All right, all right," he muttered. "Why are you down here in a wine cellar?"

"It's quiet, it had built-in refrigeration, and it keeps us amused. Those skulls are hilarious anatomy fails."

"What were you?" he asked.

"What do you mean?" Davies asked, tying off the suture. She had removed her sunglasses to focus on the knots and the strain of a headache was starting to pull her eyes tight.

"Before the implant. What were you? You're too young to have been a doctor."

"Aw, thanks. Flattery will get you more drugs," Davies smiled. "But I am a doctor. Graduated from Harvard Med with honors. Medical research was my calling, though. I was at the National Institutes of Health for about a year before I got picked to join OACET.

"All of our medical team used to be in health and human sciences," she added, snipping the line. "Now, I'm going to clean the site again before I cover it. It'll be disgusting; you've been warned."

Rachel, who had already set her implant to exclude most visuals, moved in her chair so the magazine hid the action on the table, and wondered if she should ask her therapist why she was fine with gore anywhere but inside of a doctor's office.

"You think you'll go back to research?" Santino asked, watching closely as Davies dabbed the drying blood and tissue from his arm.

The physician shrugged and applied some topical disinfectant. "Probably not. My education and training are five years out of date, and that's an eternity in science. Even if they were willing to put up with the security risks, my old team wouldn't want me. It's not the end of the world. Now I get to study cyborgs, and that's a groundbreaking field.

"Besides," she said quietly, "everybody is trying to cure cancer. They don't need me."

There was a light tapping on the door and Zia let herself into the wine cellar. She was holding a small bundle of folded clothing and stopped when she saw Santino. He leapt up and started towards her, deaf to Davies' protests as the roll of sterile gauze she was wrapping around his arm was yanked from her hands. He managed a few steps before he started to wobble from a combination of blood loss and head rush.

"Sit down, idiot," Rachel said as she stuck out her foot and nudged him back towards his seat.

Her partner slowly lowered himself back on to his stool. Davies removed the contaminated gauze and started rewrapping from a clean roll.

"What's all this, then?" Davies asked via a closed link.

"Inevitable tragedy," Rachel replied. *"Or true love straight out of a fairy tale. Maybe both."*

"Rachel said you needed some clothes." Zia said. She was staring openly at Santino. Davies had cut off his bloodied shirt to treat him, and he had a swimmer's lean muscular build.

"Don't let him tell you I've never done anything for him," Rachel told Davies. The physician laughed, but quickly covered her mouth in a Mulcahyism. Neither Santino nor Zia noticed.

"How are you?" Zia seemed to have a problem finding words. Rachel wondered exactly what had happened between them while she was in the bathroom, and why Shawn had become so angry, so quickly. She knew firsthand that anyone who had met Zia nursed a small crush, but maybe Shawn had seen something more than small talk.

"It's fine, I'm okay," he said, and moved his arm to prove it. The gauze jumped out of Davies' grip again and she swore as she grabbed for it.

"Rachel told me about Shawn. I'm…" Santino glanced away, then back to Zia. "I'm sorry there's a Shawn."

Zia looked as though she couldn't decide whether to smile or cry.

"We are invisible," Davies said to Rachel.

"Yeah," she replied. She hadn't guessed that her small effort to patch things over would lead to live theater. *"Finish taping him up so I can take him out of here. I'm sure this is a perfect moment for them, but it's just embarrassing for anyone else."*

Davies wrapped the ends of the gauze and gave Santino a

bottle of water from a box stored at the bottom of the white wine fridge. "Drink this," she told him, "and eat something with protein."

"We have sandwiches!" Zia, unsure how to put things right, hurled the promise of food.

"They are adorable," Davies said. *"But you shouldn't encourage them. If you do, he's just going to get hurt. She can't have an honest relationship with anyone outside of the Program."*

"Hello, medieval!"

"Be realistic, Rachel. He doesn't belong here. Zia knows that."

So did Rachel. And even if a miracle happened and Santino and Zia made it work, some of the other Agents would resent him, or at the very least would remind Santino every waking hour that his life hung in the balance of how he treated her. Six months into it and the coupling was starting to stabilize, the madcap roulette of attraction finally winding down. The spares were many and mostly male; with nearly twice as many men as women in OACET, the math of traditional relationships didn't play out. Mild panic was setting in among the unattached, Rachel among them. She hadn't clicked with any of the other women in the Program and was beginning to wonder how a monogamist such as herself would deal with a lifetime of superficial one-night stands.

"He'd be good for her," she sent back.

"You can't seriously believe that. You work with him, but so what? It's not as though you trust him."

And suddenly Rachel realized she did trust him. The shock of it hit her so hard it must have been physical, as Davies felt it through their link.

"Oh," Davies said. On the other side of her table, Zia's long hair fell around Santino like a golden curtain as she stood over him, lightly touching his injured arm while they spoke in hushed voices about that mildest of all topics, childhood pets. It didn't change Davies' mind, but Rachel knew that the other Agents regarded her as a very accurate judge of character. And so Davies gave the highest blessing she could: *"At least she'll be*

safe."

"Lunch!" Rachel clapped loudly, and Santino and Zia broke apart as though caught *in flagrante delicto* and not discussing long-dead guppies. "Zia, thanks for the shirt. Santino? Put it on, or I swear I'll find a stapler."

Rachel fled the med center, forcing her partner to chase after her in a cloud of fabric and apologies. Through a screen of plastic bones and cardboard, she watched as Zia started after them but was called back by Davies. *Girl talk,* Rachel thought, and wondered what Davies would say.

They walked in silence for a few minutes, moving down the long central hall of the catacombs. The Agents had set up this hallway like a subway tunnel, with alcoves in the stacks every thirty feet to prevent collisions between those passing in different directions. These offshoots were deeper than they were wide, and when they had first moved in, the ossuary's bare smiles would peek out at them as they walked by. The others had told Rachel it was astonishingly creepy to see these glimpses out of the corners of their eyes and she believed them; she always did a superstitious scan for wayward serial killers whenever she came down to the catacombs. Someone had gotten fed up with it and had hung sheets and mismatched curtains over the exposed sections, which went a long way towards muting the feeling of living in a haunted house. Still, the ceiling leered, and the medical team had been known to mess with the others; sometimes the fabric was pulled tight across the skulls and strategically-placed LEDs flared in the sockets, and then it was all over but the shouting.

"What were you?" he finally asked.

It was not what she had expected. She had thought he would move towards something different, something about either Shawn or Zia, and told him so.

"Please don't change the subject," he said, and pulled her into an alcove where they had some room to breathe. "You were military police in the Army before you got recruited, I know that. But you weren't just a cop, were you?"

She looked away. Across the path was a maple coffee table standing strong on tall bun feet. Rachel made an idle mental note to come back and check its provenance; if it wasn't an antique priced up in the stratosphere, it would be a perfect replacement for her ugly pine beast.

He waited.

She relented. "Right before I left I was a Special Agent in Criminal Investigation Command."

"That's an achievement, right?"

She kept her attention on the table. "It was a big deal at the time. I was the youngest ever to qualify."

"And what did you plan to do after that?"

"It's not important," she said. "That's all over now."

"Humor me," he said, stepping towards her. Rachel reactivated the full capacity of her implant and he was suddenly stark blue and yellow in front of her, intent on an answer. "I'm starting to put things together."

Man's too smart for his own good, Rachel thought, but the lies didn't come as easily as they usually did. Damned epiphanies, tripping up her style. *Well, fine. Let's try the truth.*

"After that, I planned to leave CID and go to West Point, then serve as a career officer as high as I could go. But the Senator I found to write my letter of recommendation to the Academy?" She blanked out the visual spectrum and closed her eyes, and there was Senator Hanlon seated across from her at a restaurant so far out of her league she would have been tossed out with the trash if she had gone there alone. The man in her memory smiled at her with tiger's teeth. "He said he could offer me something better than a General's star, and the next thing I knew, I'm in OACET."

"The Army won't take you back?

It was still dark around her but she laughed so fast and hard it went white. "Right. Cyborgs who can get into any computer, anywhere in the world? Me and the other Agents who used to be military? Our former COs have been throwing so many incentives to get us to come back that it'd be suicide to consider it. They'd run us down until there'd be nothing left."

"Zia was going to Mars," he said, and she flipped her implant on to see him staring back towards the medical center.

"What?"

"She's an astrophysicist. She said she wanted to be on the first team to Mars. And Davies wanted to cure cancer, you were on your way to becoming a general... What was Mulcahy supposed to do?"

"Things we'd never, ever hear about," she replied, then added, "Unless he failed."

He was silent for a moment, his conversational blues slowly fading towards gray. There were small bursts of iridescence as he rode his codeine buzz, but the dominant movement was a thin line of red fury undulating around his feet like a snake. The red wasn't quite sure where it belonged so it kept churning along the floor, but it was growing thicker and more solid by the moment.

"Is it like that for all of you?" he finally asked. "You had these amazing plans and now you're stuck here?"

"I honestly can't say," she said. "Most of us don't talk about the past." She felt comfortable using the truth to cover the lie; the company that sold the implant to Congress had proposed a top-down acceptance model in which the next generation of leaders would pioneer the technology. Every single member of OACET had been at the top of their game when their lives had come to a screeching halt.

"What about Shawn? Do you know his story?"

"Yeah. He was FBI. Josh Glassman used to work with him. He said Shawn was..." And in her mind, there was Josh in her living room again, but this time he was drunk and ranting how his old friend had been *exceptional, gifted, intelligent,* and then: *ruined.* "He said Shawn was a good agent and a great guy."

"Jesus," Santino breathed. The red was growing thicker, more solid, and moving up his legs.

"Hey, it's okay," she said. "We got a bad deal but we're putting things right."

"How do you put something like this right?"

We don't goddamned know! nearly made it past her lips, but she managed to catch and change it to the OACET Administration's mantra before it broke free. "It'll work out. We just need some time."

Well. I'm one of them now, aren't I? Rachel growled at herself. *Get a little bump in the salary and suddenly the manure they've been spreading makes sense.*

"Why didn't you tell me about this?" He seemed calm but the red was still growing, still looking for a place to go, and she was thinking it might be looking for her. Nothing like learning your friendship is riddled with lies of omission, or that your partner got you stabbed, or being asked to side with a bunch of freaks against your own kind because the crazy razor-wielding assailant used to be a really *nice* guy!

"I couldn't," she said. "I'm sorry for..." she swept out a hand back towards the med center and hoped he understood she meant everything from the lies to the stabbing to accidentally introducing him to the girl of his dreams when he already had one. "When we went public, we decided that we could either be people or problems, and if we wanted to be people, we'd have to manage all of our problems in-house. We're not forcing anyone else to clean our dirty laundry."

He stared at her as though she had slapped him. The red was looping ever higher, covering him like armor.

"Dirty laundry?" he snarled. "I don't think so. They fucked you guys, Rachel!"

"Maybe a little," she said, bringing both of her hands together in a ring to depict an asshole the size of a grapefruit.

He laughed. He couldn't help it; red anger fractured under a blast of purple humor and the scattershot glow of the codeine. Then: "Goddamn it, Rachel, don't you realize what they did to you?"

Oh, just wait until you find out about the bad stuff, she sighed to herself.

"Every minute of the day," she told him, grinning.

He took a breath and leaned against a polka-dotted bedspread, then jumped forward as he felt the bones press against his back.

"Can we get out of here?" he asked.

"Back to First District Station?"

"No, just not…" Santino angled both hands at the catacomb walls, then winced. "I thought the anesthetic was supposed to last an hour," he said, rubbing his injury gently through his shirt.

"Come on. Let's find you some food before you start getting nauseous."

They went through the double doors and up into the light, and Santino tried not to look at the freshly-mopped spot on the floor near the tangle of carousel horses. The room stunk of bleach.

"Out of curiosity, why did you bring me down here?"

"Hm?"

"Seems like when you have a Shawn, and when you know he doesn't like outsiders…"

"What, you think you're the first non-Agent to ever go downstairs? It's a property warehouse. There's always somebody dropping in to inspect their junk."

Santino's conversational colors went bright purple.

"Shut up, you know what I mean. When we have visitors, Shawn and the others are sealed in an old panic room. There's movies, video games… It's a pretty awesome man cave. They never notice anyone else has been here.

"The thing is," she said, finally catching hold of a nagging stray thought. "You're the first person he's seen outside of the Program for almost a year, but he's not a violent man. I don't know how he slipped his guardians. I have no idea where he got the razor. Anything smaller than a breadbox has either been adopted or is still packed, and nobody has admitted they left a razor out."

"Would they?"

"What?" It took her a moment to catch his meaning. "Yeah,

they would. We don't lie to each other."

"Yes, you do. People lie. It's human nature. I've lied to you eighty times today."

"Agents don't. It's not that we can't: it's that we don't. Network three hundred and fifty people together and you've created three hundred and fifty fact-checkers. At best, a major lie puts us six degrees from embarrassment and forced apologies."

They retraced their steps, winding back up the stairs and the forest of boxes. Those Agents they passed demurred to Santino, their colors flickering yellow as they fled.

"They're scared of me?" he whispered.

Rachel shrugged. "Knowledge is power," she whispered back. "You could shut us down, force us to go into hiding, all of the things that keep us up at night. They're waiting to see what you decide."

"What? I've already decided." Santino tried to catch the attention of a woman across the solarium, and she fled out the side door into the topiary. "Can you promise me they aren't a threat? Shawn and the others?"

"Yeah, I can. But I would have said the same thing before Shawn attacked you," she said. "What I do know is that this will never happen again. Mulcahy's already locked it down."

His colors did that weaving thing as he weighed a hundred outcomes. "You'd really go into hiding?"

She nodded. "Got my tropical paradise picked out and everything."

"God," he groaned. "Fine. Let them know I'll keep your secret."

She hugged him. Neither of them were big on casual hugs, but sometimes the friendly pat on the back wouldn't do. "Thank you," she said against his chest.

"If Shawn starts the apocalypse, I'm going to be so pissed at you."

She let go and grinned up at him. "If it makes you feel better, we'll probably die in the first wave of bombing anyhow."

"Oh, sudden annihilation," he sighed. "One of the many

advantages to living in D.C."

They entered the empty kitchen. Like all good kitchens, it was the heart of their home and was usually thrumming with life. The room had escaped the heavy hand of renovation and had kept its classic cafeteria galley design, with worn oak floors and copper pots hanging from the crossbeams. The industrial-sized fridge was stocked with ice cream and beer, and a shopping list written in forty different hands curled down its front. Plastic bags from a favorite catering company covered the worn butcher block of an island stationed between the two counters. OACET was an army which marched on its stomach.

Rachel dug through the bags until she found a chicken salad sandwich which was still reasonably cold, and slid it across the island to Santino. She was rummaging through the rest to find something for herself when Phil came in.

"I've been drafted," Phil said, helping himself to one of Rachel's discards.

"That does not live up to its labeling as roast beef," she warned.

He took a cautious bite and agreed. "Strangest-looking pastrami I've ever seen."

"Drafted for what?" Santino asked.

"To see if you're going to bring us down," Rachel said. "I already told them but noooo…" She rolled her eyes. "Apparently this is serious enough to require confirmation."

"Hey," Phil mumbled around a mouthful of mystery meat, "we're terrified. No offense, we all think you're great," he said to Santino, "but you've got to understand we're basically huddling together for warmth in our house of cards. We're slowly reinforcing it with concrete but there's no way we can withstand a direct hit."

"Doesn't it bother any of you that you're putting a hell of a lot of pressure on me?" Santino asked. "I feel like I'm responsible for the survival of an entire civilization."

"At least it's a small one," Phil said. "So the guilt shouldn't be too bad if you wipe us off of the planet."

"Dick."

"Yup." Phil was relaxed in greens and blues, trusting in Santino.

Rachel closed her eyes and rested against the counter. A summer thunderstorm had crept in while they were down in the catacombs, and the rain pounding on the skylights kept time to Phil and Santino's bickering. The house was getting back to normal (*coming back online,* said that part of her brain she loved to drown in whiskey), and green avatars began to float through the kitchen to see if it was safe for their human forms to follow. Rachel waved them off, asking the collective for a few moments of peace, and the kitchen was theirs again.

"Have you tried to get them professional help?" Santino asked.

"Shawn and the others? No. This is one of those there-but-for-the-grace-of things," Phil said. "Even if they could get better therapy somewhere else—and I sincerely doubt that, since our psychologists are pretty much the only ones in the world who have experience working with cyborgs—I don't know if we could leave them with anyone outside of OACET."

"How hard was it, going public?" Santino asked as he went to the fridge for a soda. He snapped the tab and took a large swallow to chase the codeine in his system with a Tylenol. Rachel had been watching a small but intense spot of red in his conversational colors hovering over his left arm, its center burning bright white and traveling the length of his stitches. The spot pulsed along with his heart and grew stronger as the local anesthetic wore off. It was morbidly fascinating; this was her first time tracking injury progression, and her growing curiosity was keeping pace with her partner's level of pain.

"Toughest thing we've ever done," Phil replied. "The only good part is that now we're together as a group. If we didn't have each other, we wouldn't have made it this far."

"You know," Santino said as he poked through the sandwiches in search of more chicken salad, "it might not be so rough if you guys were open about your problems. I'm appalled—seriously appalled!—that you guys feel as though you have to hide people in your basement like it's the nineteenth century and they're your mentally-ill cousins or something."

"And he's already forgotten how he nearly pissed himself when he found out about them," Jason Atran said, pushing open the swinging kitchen door. With dark hair over dark eyes, Jason had the polished features of a European male model and dressed to match. He positioned himself directly across from Santino and leaned back against the counter: there was ample space in the rambling kitchen, but Jason was there for no other reason than confrontation, flowing in reds and jealous greens.

"Did you tell him to come down here?" Rachel asked Phil, who shook his head.

"I don't think so. I haven't spoken to him in weeks," the small man replied. *"This probably got grapevined."*

"Outside voices, remember?" Jason said to them, quick to notice the glassy stare that marked Agents chatting via a private link. "We have a guest."

"Thanks." Santino smiled at Jason but his colors were ramping up to red as he picked up on Jason's antagonism. Rachel would have been worried if Jason had come in and thrown a punch at Santino, but her partner was a seasoned gladiator on the verbal battlefield. The Agent didn't stand a chance.

"Heard you met Zia," Jason said. "Tight little lay, isn't she?"

Rachel was struck dumb. The comment was beyond the pale, even in their home where civility was so lax it was barely an afterthought.

"Did Zia and Jason have a thing?" Rachel asked Phil, who was so mortified he was blushing pink from head to toe.

"Not recently," he answered. *"Maybe back in the early days, but who knows? Can you remember everyone you were with those first couple of months?"*

She couldn't. It had been a carnal madhouse. They had all agreed to forgive, forget, and dig up the past only if the tests failed to come back clean.

"Agent Atran, right?" Santino extended his right hand. It

hung out in space until the Agent shook it to make it go away. "I thought so. You've got something of a reputation.

"But I have to be honest, man," Santino said as he sighed and shook his head. "This interview is not going well."

Jason blinked. "What?"

"You probably heard? Someone's murdering people out there. We're putting together a team to help catch him, and your name kept coming up as a top pick. It'd be me, Rachel, two MPD officers, and two other Agents. We thought one of them would be you, but you come in here insulting Agent Hallahan?"

"Technically, that was a compliment," Jason said with a thin, angry smirk.

"Technically, I don't care," Santino said. "It was rude and unprofessional. You really think I want someone who is rude or unprofessional on my team?" He was furious but smiling kindly, bubbles of cheery springtime yellow moving in and out of his reds. Rachel saw traces of Zia's violet core within the yellow: he was defending Zia and was happy to do it, she realized, and Rachel was suddenly fiercely proud of her friend.

"Your team?" Jason was building momentum when Santino held up his injured arm. He wasn't done shutting Jason down.

"Mine and Rachel's. It's our call who joins, and I'm sure as hell not working with someone who doesn't have any respect for his teammates. Or..." and Santino let the word hang long enough for Jason to fill in the void with whatever word he wanted before he added: "co-workers.

"So," Santino continued, and she saw he had borrowed this particular smile from her own toolkit, "we'll go, and you'll stay here and do... What is it you do again?"

Jason didn't answer, so Phil chimed in. "Data entry."

"Oh," Santino said, rounding the word with scorn. "Exciting. Well, we're about to head back over to First District Station. Be sure to let me know how data entry works out for you." He clapped Jason on the shoulder and turned away, stalling to grab one last sandwich for the road.

"What do you want, an apology?" Jason was running gray,

his best opportunity to get back in the field snatched out of his grasp.

"Couldn't hurt," Santino said. "Or,"—and he was suddenly much, much taller. Rachel was envious; she lacked the physical presence to loom—"You recognize the next time you go after Zia, I'll have to do something about it."

"I want her to marry him and have beautiful nerdbabies," Phil said.

"He didn't know she was alive an hour ago," she replied. *"Give them some time to get around to the nerdbabies."*

Jason relented. "Fine."

"You done here?" Rachel asked. "Because the odds of me making a good alpha male joke are low."

"Oh, you'd do the best you could," Phil said. "You can't help that you have no sense of humor."

NINE

"This is sick," Phil whispered.

The cameraman was in his late thirties and running gray; Rachel had read him as clinically depressed. She and Santino would have to break out the whiskey and that damned notebook of his to pin down the ethics of interrogation via the emotional spectrum, but, Phil's opinion aside, this new technique seemed to fit comfortably in her old bag of tricks.

On the other side of one-way mirror, two men strutted and postured around a third. Zockinski had taken Jason into the interrogation room, saying that if they had to keep the freaks around, they might as well get some use out of them. The detective had tapped Jason for the chore because, in Zockinski's words, "he looks like he should look," but Jason also acted like he should act, and the two of them were slowly stripping the real story from the cameraman's bones.

"Tell me about the money," Jason said. He leaned forward as the older man pushed his chair away, their movements so perfectly aligned they might as well have been choreographed.

"I already told you, they offered me money. I didn't take it!" Chris Burman couldn't take his eyes off of the Agent, who was so happy to be back in action and tormenting another human being that he practically glowed.

"Is he lying?" Jason asked.

"Yes," Rachel replied. Lies were easy to spot; skittish dimples puckered the surface colors of the speaker across their shoulders. Santino had exaggerated; he was almost unfailingly honest and lied to her maybe a dozen times a day, tops.

"And if I go through your accounts?" Jason dropped his voice conspiratorially. "Are you sure I won't find anything?"

"Do you have a warrant? You can't do that without a

warrant!" The cameraman jumped, then threw a panicked look at Zockinski. "Can he do that?"

Zockinski spread his hands wide. "Buddy, you've heard about them. They can do anything."

"Phenomenal," Phil growled into his milkshake. "They're doing Good Cop, Cyborg Cop. I've always wanted to visit the Supreme Court." He was no longer complaining to her through the link; Phil needed some sort of public record, even if it would only exist among the four observers.

"Don't worry about it," Hill said from the other end of the room. He was pressed up against the mirror while he watched his partner work. "We do this with racists."

"What?"

"You play off of their hate. They don't think as quick, as clean, when they're talking to someone they hate."

"I can't believe you let yourself get used like that," Phil muttered.

Hill laughed without humor. "Nine times out of ten, Zockinski's the bad guy. You wouldn't believe the hate that's out there for white cops. Everybody already thinks Zockinski's there to put them away, doesn't matter whether they're innocent or not."

"But we're not threatening that guy in there with loss of due process," Phil snapped. "You're basically waving technological witchcraft at him like a loaded gun!" The small Agent had been with Special Operations and knew eight ways to blow up the room with a bag of potato chips, but his job stopped when the cuffs went on the suspect. He had never been part of an active interrogation and was disgusted to learn where the others drew the line. For them, an interrogation with a third-tier suspect like Burman was usually a waste of time, so they had to find ways to keep themselves engaged (Creativity was key. Rachel had once started an interview with a coulrophobe by reading him the first three chapters of Stephen King's *IT*. Poor little George, swept beneath the street... Her suspect had broken like a twig.).

"What's-his-name, Jason?" Hill nodded towards the mirror. "Is he going to pull those accounts?"

"Nope," Rachel said, working on the last dregs of her chocolate shake. "Not unless you get him a warrant."

"Then we've got his back," Hill said.

"This isn't about what you do," Phil said, tapping a closed fist, slow but hard, against the cinderblocks beneath the glass. "It's about what we do... This guy? This guy will never trust us. Never. And he's gonna go home and tell all of his friends that an Agent threatened to wreck his financials, and his story will be blogged and Tweeted and..."

Phil trailed off, forehead pressed against the glass. Hill looked at the small Agent, really looked at him, and Hill's wall of warm browns and golds softened around the edges with a gentle wine red. She had seen that hue at funerals and nowhere else. Sympathy? Pity?

Who knew?

On the other side of the glass, Chris Burman was having a very bad day. He had been filming a local high school team's football practice when he was hauled off of the field by two uniformed officers. During the early stages of the interview, he had described himself as a freelance cinematographer who picked up odd jobs wherever he could. He claimed he was friendly with a staff sergeant at First MPD who passed work his way; this staff sergeant had thrown his so-called buddy under the bus by saying he only requested Burman when his first choice in audio-visual guys couldn't make it.

The cameraman was close to frantic. "Okay! Okay, listen," Burman said, spreading his hands wide on the table and rubbing it with the balls of his hands. "I didn't help anyone. I came in, shot some training videos, and got paid. That's it."

"He's obsessive-compulsive," Rachel said, following Burman's movements.

Santino, sitting in the room's only chair with his paper cup pressed against his injured arm to chill it, perked at this. Rachel had observed the same type of tactile grounding behavior in him when he wasn't watching his own body language. He stood and crossed the room to watch Burman trace small spirals on the tabletop. "Yeah, he is. Tell them to put something on the table in front of him. Make it messy."

Hill's hand was moving towards the wire in his ear when Jason roughly shoved a stack of papers at Burman with the tough guy line of burying Burman under the evidence. The papers slid out of their pile and cascaded towards the cameraman, who restacked them and placed Jason's pen at the top like a mint on a pillow.

"Perfect," Santino said. "How much do you think a guy like this makes in a year?"

"I couldn't say," Rachel shrugged. "I'd be very surprised if he breaks forty-k."

"Yeah…" her partner mused as Burman sheltered the stack of paper in a cradle of his arms, protecting it from Jason and Zockinski. "Control freak, probably broke or close to it… I'll bet you the next round of drinks this guy made a one-time payment to a credit card around the same time he shot the video. Not a lot of money, probably a couple hundred bucks. He wouldn't get more than that for a digital copy of the film and a weird camera angle."

She smiled. There was no way Santino could have gotten that from hands laid on a desk. "You're on," she said, and sent Jason the bait over the link.

In the interview room, Jason leaned forward and whispered something about debt and money and suspiciously-timed payments to Burman, whose grays faded as his head slumped forward. Caught. Resigned. Done.

"Aw, damn," Rachel sighed. Santino would no doubt order something from a fancy bottle and request for it to be served in an unreasonably large and fancy tumbler.

Jason and Zockinski knew Burman was theirs. They stopped circling and sat down on the opposite side of the table, all cheery yellows and self-satisfied blues for a job well done.

The cameraman, broken, started to talk.

"A man came up to me a few weeks before I shot the video. He said his name was John Glazer." Burman opened his wallet and slid a crisp white business card across the table to Zockinski. "He said he worked for Internal Affairs and he needed to get evidence against some cops on the force."

The television mounted high on the wall in the interview room burst into life without warning. Zockinski had known it was coming and his colors barely shifted towards the reds at all, but Burman's collapsed into terror as the screen froze on the face of the man who had sparred with Hill the day the original video had been taken. Jason leaned towards him and hissed: "Is that Glazer?"

Burman shut his eyes and nodded. Glazer was young and good-looking, but even from a distance it was obvious he had a savage edge to him.

"And you believed him when he said he was investigating corruption?" Zockinski asked.

"Yes."

"Rachel?"

"He's lying."

Zockinski took the cue from the Agent and waited.

Burman's chin dropped to his chest. "I might have thought something was up," he admitted. "He told me he was after this one cop, Hill, and he said he'd pay for the tape of Hill beating him. But it had to be just right, no mistakes. I thought…"

His gray edges flushed red in shame.

Aw man, Rachel thought.

Zockinski didn't need her help. He caught on before the rest of them. "You thought he wanted porn."

"Not porn, but…" Burman said with a hurried glance at the mirror, perhaps sensing Hill's fury boiling behind the glass. "Everybody's got kinks, you know?"

"How often did you work for him?"

"Just that one time."

"Rachel?"

"True."

"How did he pay you?"

"Cash. Two hundred bucks."

Santino reached out and bumped her shoulder with an I-told-you-so fist. She rolled her eyes and pretended to pout.

"Did he say anything else?"

Burman cradled the stack of papers within his arms. "He said he might have some more work for me at the beginning of October. Um… October 7th. He was really specific about that date."

"What kind of work?"

"He didn't say. He told me to keep his card on me until then. He, uh, Glazer said his phone wasn't listed and calling the number on his card was the only way I could reach him."

Zockinski picked up the little white card and started to ask Burman something else when Jason leaned over and snatched it out of his hand.

"Hey!"

The Agent ignored Zockinski. Jason turned the card over, then held it up to the light, suspicion and curiosity painting his conversational colors. Burman scooted his chair to the side as Jason got up and smacked the business card flat against the one-way mirror. Rachel switched her implant to reading mode and made out Glazer's name and number an instant before Jason flipped the card to reveal a silver-black pattern covering the reverse side.

"Ping this," he said.

"Whoa!" Rachel reached out and pressed her fingers to the glass, as if touching the paper might confirm what her implant had told her. She turned to Santino and Hill. "It's got an RFID tag printed on it."

"No kidding? Man, what a pretty thing." Santino smiled at the card; her partner loved new technologies. "I had heard they had developed a specialized ink for printed tags, but I didn't know it had made it to commercial use."

"I don't think that's commercial. Somebody download a reader app," Phil said as he left the room to collect the card from Jason.

Hill, silent, sat in uncertain yellows.

"Radio-frequency identification," Rachel explained. "Most people compare RFID to barcodes. It's a self-contained data profile. The profile stores information, and when you activate the tag with an RFID reader, the tag sends the information to the reader."

Hill nodded. *Not confused-yellow,* Rachel corrected herself. *That's an oh-right-I'm-surrounded-by-freaks yellow.* She needed to make a chart.

"I know," he said. "Store security, anti-shoplifting…"

"They're everywhere," Phil said as he shut the door behind him, holding Glazer's business card lightly by its edges. "If you've got three credit cards on you, you're also carrying at least two tags. They're even in security badges." He lifted the MPD visitor's pass clipped to his lapel and let it drop.

Santino ran his phone over the card in Phil's hand. "You can't read this?"

"No," Phil said "Not us. One of the other Agents might have written an RFID reader script but nobody here has it. When I ping it, I get a bunch of meaningless data."

The phone chirped. "It's an address," Santino said. "405 East Dalton…"

He stopped, his colors fading to a dull orange-red with a thin gray shiver across them. He turned and knocked on the glass to get Jason and Zockinski's attention.

"What?" Rachel asked as he handed her the card and his phone, then retreated to his chair as the last two members of their small task force joined them.

"The bank where Maria Griffin was murdered?" Santino leaned back and closed his eyes. "That's its address. There's also the number of a safe deposit box."

Confirmation, she thought wearily as gray flittered across the room. They were finally past the point where coincidence could be explained away by anything other than willful rationalization. She'd still sit on her suspicions that the crimes were targeted at OACET, but there was no longer any doubt they were connected.

Zockinski left to start the paperwork required to keep Chris Burman in lockup for seventy-two hours; they agreed the cameraman was nothing more than a delivery vehicle to move Glazer's card from Point A to Point B, but they didn't want to lose him on the off-chance he was an exceptional actor.

Nor, they realized after extensive discussion, could they agree that the MPD was Point B. They could safely assume Burman was to hold on to the card until someone came to collect it in the early days of October, (and, as Jason pointed out, this implied there would be a reason someone would come to collect from Burman), but this chore did not necessarily default to the police.

And Santino, who found it best to err on the side of first-generation equipment failure, proposed that if Burman had been set up to deliver the card to the MPD, he would not be the only one.

"There's a design flaw in paper RFID tags." Santino held up the card in its new protective evidence bag. "They're not in commercial use because the tags are made from electromagnetic ink, where the ink is the transistor. Burman gets the card wet, or keeps it in the middle of a stack of cards with magnetic stripes? There's no telling whether it would still work after a few months of pocket abuse. It's amazing it lasted this long. You can bet Glazer knows that. There are other messenger boys out there, folks."

Rachel concurred. Her usual method for storing business cards was to chuck them in her purse and then watch them fall like tattered snowflakes when she upended the whole thing into the garbage eight months later. If Burman committed pocket abuse, she perpetrated handbag genocide; she could have been a messenger herself and would never know it, the card passing unnoticed from hand to purse to trash.

Zockinski stayed behind to deal with the paperwork as the others set out for the bank. Hill drove, the detective's sickly green-and-yellow conversational colors pulling him down. Rachel would have sympathized with the detective, stuck in a clown car crammed full of nerdcops and Agents, if he hadn't brought their number up to five and, as the smallest member of the group, she was thus relegated to riding bitch on the pillion.

The bank was different, hollow. The lobby was almost surgically spotless, even after an afternoon of foot traffic wet from the summer storms and filthy from the streets. But Maria Griffin's last moments still lingered; customers could be counted on the fingers of one hand and the tellers huddled together for warmth. All ghoulish proclivities from the previous afternoon had disappeared, replaced with some fear, maybe a little embarrassment and shame, for sharing the same space as a murder.

The bank manager was apologetic: they had missed him.

"No," Hill said, annoyed. He was cramped tight in the manager's shopworn Knoll chair and was not about to work on puzzles. "We're not here to see anyone. We have a warrant to search a safe deposit box."

The manager had a frenetic chipmunky air about him, fast and nervous movements sharpened by the sideways glances he kept sneaking at Rachel. *Find your own secret tunnels,* she thought, and the next time he looked at her, she winked. He went yellow and did his best to pretend the only other people in the room with him were Santino and Hill.

Yes," he said, sliding the warrant back across the table to Hill. "But this box? The owner emptied its contents yesterday afternoon."

"And you know this off the top of your head?" Jason asked. A good question, considering the manager had been swarmed under by cops, Forensics, and specialized sanitation for the better part of the day. If this was the level of customer service he offered, Rachel would change banks on the spot. She'd be sure to ask the manager for help in filling out the forms...

"He said you'd be coming."

Rachel could almost feel the temperature in the manager's

office plummet; everyone's conversational colors had gone white with shock.

"Who did?" Jason made a grab-hand motion at her and she gave him her tablet. He called up the best image they had of their suspect. "Was it this man?"

"Yes, yes," the manager said. He went into the top drawer of his desk and pulled out a file. He pushed the file towards Hill. "Jonathan Glazer. He signed a consent form. No one has ever done that before, signed a form to let the police have access to his personal information or..."

"I don't think you need that warrant," the manager said. "I'll honor one, of course, but I don't know if you need it. Glazer brought the form in with him, and had our notary sign and seal it. He said it allows my bank to give you full access to his account information, personal data, whatever you need."

"We've got his home address," Hill said. He had put on gloves and was carefully turning through the few pages in the thin file. "Let me get Forensics in here to go over the box." He spread the pages out on the bank manager's desk and left the room to call his partner.

Rachel flipped her implant to reading mode and browsed the file over Santino's shoulder. The notarized consent form, the usual contract from the bank which outlined terms of use, and a fingerprint card with ten squares covered in black made up the sum of the documents.

"You printed him?" she asked the manager.

"It's our policy when we sign a lease for the largest boxes," the manager said to Santino. "After 9-11."

Bingo. Most days, the reason for doing anything and everything could be summed up by those two numbers.

She had no confidence in the fingerprints and leaned over the ten-card from the file to run a quick scan. "Faked," she said. "There's synthetic oils mixed in with the semi-inkless ink." Santino lifted an eyebrow at her, and she shrugged. "Hey, I don't make up the product names."

"I'm sorry, Agent," the bank manager's eyes had found a

happy place somewhere in the vicinity of her left ear. Maybe he was a lobe man. "But you're wrong. I took these prints myself."

"Nope," she said. "There's barely any squalene in those. No squalene, no fingerprint. Glazer was wearing reproductions of someone else's prints."

The bank manager fell silent and went green in resignation. Rachel was grateful. She wasn't sure she was up to an organic chemistry lesson more specific than how squalene was part of what made those squiggly patterns show up on clean glass, or to explain how a good set of fake fingerprints could provide better impressions than natural fingertips. An authentic print was like pornography; she knew it when she saw it, and explanations were a fumbling mess.

She handed the card over to Jason, whose eyes still worked in the usual way. He took the card to a side table to scan it and send the data through IAFIS, the national fingerprint database. It was a cursory search, and one that would never enter the formal record. Jason's visual scan was as accurate as anything they would perform in the lab, but Agents were not yet classified as part of the official process used to enter data into evidence. Much like how smartphones which captured latent fingerprints still required cross-confirmation for validation, Jason would flag the first search as OACET-enabled, and the task force would later run the same scan all over again when they got back to First District Station. But most fake fingerprints were made from models and Glazer seemed to enjoy hiding his clues in plain sight: Rachel had a gnawing suspicion that these prints would point them towards another body.

Phil removed his sunglasses and rubbed the bridge of his nose. "If Glazer made you notarize a consent form and gave you permission to turn over his information to the police," he said to the manager, "you must have thought that was strange. Why didn't you call the MPD?"

"It wasn't their business," the manager apologized to his desk blotter, then looked to Santino for help. "You have to understand, this wasn't the strangest request I've ever gotten.

I've been told to honor wills written to people's pets! If I called the police whenever a customer does or says something unusual, you'd block my calls."

Phil conceded the point.

Rachel asked the manager if he had actually followed through with those wills. *Really, **really** good customer service,* she thought as he told Santino a charming anecdote about a parakeet who now owned a car.

Hill returned and said they were cleared to go to Glazer's apartment. As they stood up and gathered their things, the manager asked if they wanted to see the security footage from the vault before they left.

Their colors rose in a silent orange-red cloud, and Santino, politely, said yes, that would be helpful, thank you.

"Almost an hour in that shitty little office..." Jason fumed as the manager's assistant set up the equipment. *"...and he had Glazer on tape the entire time."*

"We're watching it now, Jason. No harm, no foul." Phil was making a point of responding to all statements as if they had been spoken aloud. He meant it to be a polite gesture but it was perhaps not coming across as intended, especially as Jason kept setting him up to sound slightly unhinged. The bank manager was starting to panic.

The video launched. Monochrome footage again, and Rachel took the opportunity to ask: "Your entire security system is in black and white?"

"Yes," the manager said, tapping the fast-forward button, his eyes firmly on the screen. The tape showed the interior of the vault. Its heavy steel door was left open during business hours, the room secured by thick shatterproof glass. Behind this glass, digital people hurried about the lobby, the occasional child cupping their hands and peeking in at four times normal speed.

"It seems like a new system. Why did you decide against color?"

The brick and brown of walls built themselves around him.

"It's more than adequate for our needs."

Translation: We got a good deal on it. She decided her money was safer where it was, stellar customer service be damned.

"Our policy is that customers can use the vault in privacy," the manager said. "We go with the customer into the vault, make sure they have what they need, and we secure the glass door behind us when we leave. They have the option of closing the steel door, but most people don't," he pointed to the door, nearly twenty inches thick. "I think they've seen too many movies about getting locked in. We've taken precautions to make sure that doesn't happen, but…" he shrugged.

In the video, a woman in business attire escorted a man past the glass barrier. It was John Glazer, but a different John Glazer from the one who had sparred with Hill; the long hair had been cut and he wore a full three-piece suit in the August heat. She doubted the kid from the convenience store could have picked him out of a lineup. She was sure Glazer was playing another role here, but perhaps one closer to his true self, and so she asked Hill: "Military?"

"Yeah," he squinted at the tiny man on the monitor. The details were hard to make out, but not his movements; this version of Glazer was a precision instrument.

"Wait, wait. I want to see that again," Jason said, and the video reversed and resumed to show Glazer glide up to the glass.

The bank manager stood up and walked straight out of his own office.

"There, in the background. Just a second after Glazer shuts himself in the vault," the Agent said, and pointed. "Riiiiight… There."

Two men walked past the glass door, accompanied by the manager himself. Rachel blinked her implant off and on, hoping it had malfunctioned.

"Aw hell," Phil whispered.

Nope, she thought, *not a malfunction,* and waited for the explosion.

"Play that back again!" Santino shouted, and Jason did.

On the screen, the Glazer from yesterday afternoon closed the glass door of the vault right as Hill and Zockinski entered and exited the camera frame on the other side.

Hill crossed his arms and said nothing; red with anger, yellow with self-rebuke, his colors twisted violently while his body tensed.

"How long were you in the bank after Rachel and I left?" Santino asked.

"To clear the bank and process the tunnel?" Hill said. "Hours."

"But there are customers," Santino pointed at the screen. "If you cleared the bank again, this must have happened before then..."

Timeline again, she thought. *It's all about the timeline.* Glazer must have jumped into action the instant he heard... what? Her best guess was that he had been watching the MPD process Griffin's murder, just in case they stumbled over the hidden tunnel when they searched the room. When it had been found ahead of schedule, whatever had been left in the safe deposit box was suddenly yanked out of its proper chronology.

She felt a little flush of pride. *I think I just screwed up a killer's master plan.*

Glazer was staring directly at Rachel. He had locked on to the security camera when the banker left him alone in the vault. Then he turned away from the camera to swing the steel door shut behind her. After the heavy metal door had closed, Glazer took off his suit jacket and went to his knees to pull out one of the lowest and largest boxes in the vault. Using his jacket as a shield, he blocked the camera's view of the contents of the safe deposit box as he transferred them to an oversized leather briefcase.

Then Glazer stood and moved to the work station in the middle of the room. He laid a piece of stock copy paper on it, folded it in half, and applied a Sharpie marker in swift, aggressive strokes.

When he held it up to the camera, two lines of black print stood bold against the white.

HELLO OACET

YOU'RE EARLY

TEN

Everyone knew the task force was the bureaucratic equivalent of a bunch of gaily-painted wooden ducks. Their small group was a show of faith and strength and unity, of the good guys coming together in force to prove to the public that the threat was external and easily managed. Their role as decoys explained why Hill was permitted to work his own case, why Edwards was the pen behind the warrants, and why Rachel was not buried under preparations to testify against three men with matching haircuts. Due process was not ignored, but public affairs was the pretty younger sister in this whole mess and everyone paid her court first.

Just past the camera's range was a veritable armada of the Metropolitan Police Department's best officers. These officers were the ones doing their grunt work, the ones who dredged through stacks of video evidence dating from the time of the gas station assault through the present day to try to find anything hinky, who returned to canvas the scenes of the three known crimes with fresh eyes, or any of the other countless thankless tasks that went into the unglamorous side of policing.

This set the members of the task force to quaking. Cops had long memories. When Glazer went down, the task force would get the credit, but if they hadn't earned it? Well. If the task force was truly nothing but a sham, if those behind the scenes were the ones who built the case, then Santino, Zockinski, and Hill would be forever punished through all of those myriad and subtle rites of workplace torture, and the Agents would be shown no quarter until they severed ties.

So they must succeed. Not only that, but they must succeed as quickly as possible, and without help if they could avoid it.

No pressure.

And then there was the nagging doubt at the back of Rachel's mind, telling her that maybe they were already succeeding too quickly, and maybe that was a very bad thing.

Back at the bank, she had felt a rush of righteous vindication when Glazer had held up his snide little sign, but that was crushed beneath the surge of hate and adrenaline and the overwhelming urge to stick her thumbs in his eyes until her nails scraped the back of his sockets. She had left the building as quickly as possible, instinct driving her to look up at the sun and remind herself of consequences. As she had passed the vestibule where Maria Griffin had fallen, her rage rose anew when it hit her that a woman had been killed because someone was in a snit about something as small as her implant.

"What?" Rachel asked her partner. Santino, dusky purple with concern, had been watching her closely since she had kicked open the door of the bank manager's office and left the rest of them behind to finish up.

He dropped back a few steps and they fell behind the group. Glazer's apartment building was three blocks away from any semblance of parking and they were hoofing it. The narrow streets were barely wide enough for a car and the neighborhood was slipping into decay, but it was just a matter of time before it would be demolished to make room for high-end condos: location, location, location, with glimpses of the white of the Washington Monument through the alley straightaways.

Santino scouted the street. "Is he here?"

Rachel snorted. "I'd have mentioned." She had run the local public spaces for someone of Glazer's height and weight and had come up empty, but you never knew who was lurking behind the blinds of someone's private residence. Caution paid all, and she was keeping a weather eye out for sudden movement behind them, or in the windows of the apartments above.

Then he said: "Tell me."

"Glazer's a planner; he knew to get in and out of the bank the second I found that tunnel. And he's committed. Have Jason tell you exactly how Glazer made those videos. Prepping those would have taken him more labor than I've ever sunk into a single project in my entire life."

"Yeah?"

"I know planners. OACET's ruled by planners. You realize our administration debated for six months to decide how we should come out? They made this master plan here," she said, sketching a space in the air with her hands, "but they had a hundred other plans branching off of it, just in case the main one fell through. Contingency plans *everywhere*, Santino!" She scattered that space with a flit of her fingers. "The goal stayed the same, but every day they adapted the strategy.

"Glazer's not going to change his goals." Rachel pointed her face upwards to hold on to the heat of the sun. "All we'll do is force him to work around us."

"Ah, then we're fine," he said, hinting at humor. "Everyone's always telling us that we're good for nothing but getting in the way."

"This isn't funny."

"Since when do you find me funny?" Santino was doing his best to keep things normal. He was hurting but was able to hide it. No one outside of OACET knew he had been injured, although Hill kept telling him he shouldn't go out drinking with the girls if he couldn't keep up with the men the next day.

He could pull it off with anyone else but her. Only Rachel saw how the pain had bloomed out from the wound to cover his entire lower arm and tint the rest of his conversational colors in red. She knew that scarlet bloom would haunt her until he healed, so she played along and they talked about basketball until they caught up with the rest of the team at the corner of Glazer's building.

"What's the scope of the warrant?" Phil asked.

"So broad we could hide a corpse with it," Santino answered. He was exaggerating but not by much. With Edwards behind the pen, the task force was cashing the judicial equivalent of signed blank checks.

They picked up the key from a superintendent who asked

them when he could start cleaning out the apartment, then threw them out of his office when Zockinski told him Glazer was still nothing but a suspect.

Glazer's apartment was several flights up. There was no elevator. Brown streaks of water damage chased each other down the drywall, and Rachel saw the glaze of rat urine peppering the stairs.

"Nice." Hill pointed at a sprig of exposed wires where a lamp had been torn away.

"They're live," Rachel said, noting the glow, and Santino took out his cell to put in a fast call to the fire department.

They found the right floor and the right door. As Zockinski went to open it, Rachel idly scanned the room behind it. The apartment had that empty feeling of nobody home, but she swept the corners for men wielding machetes.

Then: "Holy crap!"

She body-checked the older man before he could touch the key to the knob.

"Bomb!" Rachel shouted, pushing the group down the corridor at a run. "Back! Get back, get back!"

They took shelter in the stairwell, and half the group fell into the chaos of *whats?* while the others collapsed into the *how?* Zockinski and Hill tried to brush her off until the other three bullied them into accepting that yes, if she could find a hidden tunnel, she could find a hidden bomb.

"There's a table in the west bedroom," she said when the adrenaline rush had subsided. "It's got some hardware on it... Could be radio equipment, but I don't think so. It looks very..." She stopped herself before she gave voice to the amorphous "explody."

"Shit." Santino went for his phone again. "I'm calling SWAT."

"No, wait. Let me check it out before you cause a riot," Phil said. He removed his sunglasses and covered his eyes with his free hand. Rachel saw his vibrant green avatar appear in Glazer's apartment and walk quickly towards the table.

"Ugh," the Phil in the stairwell snarled. "She's right. These are chemical bombs. Nasty pieces of work, too."

"What is he doing?" Zockinski asked Santino.

"He's in there," Rachel said, pointing up the stairs. "Just..." She waved a weak hand and let it fall. Describing the same thing over and over to the neophytes exhausted her. "It's a thing we can do."

"What!? Is he going to set them off?" Zockinski moved towards Phil, but Jason laid a strong arm across his path.

"Come on, think, man! Why would he set anything off when we're standing ten feet away?"

"I couldn't even if I wanted to," Phil said. "These aren't digital. They're analog... basically clockwork! Nobody builds like this anymore."

He shook his head savagely as he came back to his own body. "Four devices," he said, sliding on his dark glasses. "All inert. Right now they're nothing but framework. The explosives are situated but there's no trigger or chemicals. And that explosive payload is too small to be the main source of any damage. They're harmless."

Hill, who had arrived at the MPD by way of U.S. Special Forces, grimaced. "You're thinking ventilation systems."

Phil nodded. "There're only four of them but it's summer, and the air conditioning is on. You get a strong aerosol agent, set off all four in a medium-sized building at night... Yeah, you could definitely wipe out everyone in there."

"But they're inert? You're sure?" Jason was moving towards a strong electric blue.

"Don't even think about it," she said to him.

"Anyone else would have found those bombs after they went in."

"We're not everyone else!" she said, a little too loudly. The detectives went yellow and she took a breath. "Boy Wonder here still wants to check out the apartment."

"No," Hill said. "We do this right. We call Sturtevant and let him know we need the bomb squad."

"Hang on, the... Agent Atran's right. We don't know what's

in there," Zockinski said as he rapped the stairwell wall with a thick knuckle. "I'm sure as hell not going to call the Chief of Detectives and look like an asshole when the bomb squad doesn't find anything."

"And that's different from you normally looking like an asshole, how?" Rachel unsnapped her handbag to look for an aspirin, Tylenol, a travel-sized bottle of chloroform, anything that could muzzle Zockinski short of actually muzzling Zockinski.

"We're not calling Sturtevant," he said, flushing red.

"Your boxers have cute little Scottie dogs on them," she snapped, and his mouth dropped open. "You really want to keep making me prove what I can do? Because you've been at it all day and I'm running low on examples."

"We don't need to get anyone else involved," Jason said. "Phil is the bomb squad. He dismantles them and we go back to First ahead of the game."

"If you think I'm going in there without gear, you're fucking crazy," Phil retorted. "Guys who play with chemical weapons get their chuckles from making people die in agony, and I don't even want to know what guys who build clockwork bombs are like. I'm not going in an apartment that might be booby-trapped to all hell."

Santino came back into the stairwell and shouted over Jason and Phil to let them know he had put in a call to Sturtevant to get the ball rolling on bomb disposal. The Chief of Detectives had said they could expect backup within five minutes, but because of the unprecedented nature of their report, Sturtevant wasn't sure who'd be showing up.

(The nexus of federal and local law enforcement agencies, political leaders, national landmarks, and global financial institutions all situated in or around Washington meant that bomb threats were subjected to a Gordian knot of bureaucracy. Sturtevant would call someone at the Department of Homeland Security, who would determine if the site of the bomb was especially prominent or of strategic import; if not, it got bumped back to the MPD's in-house Homeland Security Bureau, who would call someone on their Special Operations Division, who would call someone in the Tactics Patrol Branch, who would then contact the Explosive Ordinance Disposal Section, which would then activate a tactical team to respond to the threat. And sometimes even when the police were handling the situation, a federal tactical unit might still tag along for the ride. The entire process was needlessly complicated at every level: Rachel's orientation packet at First District Station had contained a checklist on how to document a bomb threat, with items such as "If a bomb threat is received by email, do not delete the message" and "Remember to ask the caller his/her name," but the contact information of persons or agencies who would act on this information was conspicuously missing. When she asked her orientation officer about the process for submitting a completed bomb threat checklist, he said she should give it to her superior officer at the MPD, and when she said she didn't have one, he had shrugged and advised her to wing it. Rachel had politely excused herself and rushed to the bathroom to laugh herself numb.)

In Washington, as in most cities, the building's manager was responsible for deciding when it was necessary to evacuate private property in the event of a bomb. The superintendent laughed at the suggestion but said if they needed him, he'd be at the deli down the street. Their small group returned to the stairwell and killed time wondering if the bomb squad could move fast enough to be in and gone from the apartment before Glazer got back. Jason and Zockinski nursed the fantasy of setting a trap and capturing the enemy as he returned home from a day of nefarious deeds, none the wiser until the disembodied voice read him his rights from the darkness. The rest of the task force sat back in silence and let them play imaginary superheroes until the team from the MPD arrived.

With the exception of a chiseled-jaw behemoth they kept around to swing the battering ram, the members of the unit were built to a man like Phil Netz. Their sergeant, a stoic man named Andrews, was well past the age of wanting to be the first one through the broken door and had let himself get away with a slight paunch, but he had retained the same wiry frame and lightning-fast movements as Phil and the rest of his squad. He identified the small Agent as kin on sight; a long-lost SWAT-team cousin, perhaps, or some other professional relation remembered from a chance meeting at the annual convention.

Phil borrowed a rubber band from Rachel's voluminous purse and tied his shock of wild blond hair into a rough ponytail as he and the sergeant talked shop. At least half of the sergeant's questions were designed to test the Agent, and their conversational colors moved up and down the spectrum until they aligned near a companionable forest green.

That was when Phil told her they had decided to send her in.

Explosives had never been her thing: she was usually called to investigate the scene after they had done theirs, so she was understandably wary about two thin walls separating her from four of them, inert or not. But she nodded and smiled, chest out, hands crossed firmly above her butt, as Phil had her go out-of-body into the apartment and send back what she saw to her tablet so he could talk the Tactics team through the scene. Her avatar looked up, down, north, south, east, west, and walked through the apartment as directed while Santino steadied her physical self in the hallway.

Rachel thought that if she didn't already know Glazer was a borderline sociopath, his apartment would have been the tipoff. The tight space was packed with enough couches, chairs, and audio-visual equipment to qualify as a franchise of OACET's headquarters. She found it easier to walk her avatar through the furniture rather than find a way around it, but Phil kept her on the path of most resistance so she could mimic Glazer's movements.

"Do you always need two Agents for this?" Sergeant Andrews asked, tablet in hand.

"No." Phil scratched his chin as he made a rough sketch

of the apartment on the back of a receipt. "I could go in there instead of her, but it'd be harder for me to talk you through what she's doing…" he said, tapping the tablet with his pen, "… at the same time. This is new to you, and being in two places at once is hard on me. Hey, Rachel, three meters to the left? What's that silver thing under the armchair?"

"Empty can of Budweiser."

"You sure it's empty?"

Her avatar crouched low to peer through the hole, and her body said, "Yup."

Andrews reminded Rachel to keep her distance from it, just in case; chemical bombs were sneaky little weasels.

"Doesn't matter," Phil shook his head. "Rachel's… Ah, the Rachel in the apartment… She's a projection. She can't physically connect with anything."

"And if something in there goes off?"

"Don't worry. She's perfectly safe."

Two walls, she thought. *Crumbling pressboard between us and oblivion.* She wondered what might happen if she was blown to bits while part of her mind was out-of-body, if ghosts might be what was left of those who had atrocious timing when they took a mental walkabout.

"We're done," Phil said. "Rachel, come on back."

She dropped her avatar and drew herself together, and the colors of the crowd came up around her. The sergeant had brought six men, all of whom were burying their excited yellows and purples under a blue so dark it matched their uniforms.

"You coming in with us?" Andrews asked Phil.

He shook his head. "No gear."

"Then you're in luck. Officer McCall has the sniffles," the sergeant said, and the man closest to Phil in size went gray. "McCall, let the Agent borrow your equipment."

Phil changed clothes right there in the hallway with an officer who would have gladly burned Phil's suit and sauntered home stark naked if his commander hadn't been watching.

"Door or window?" Andrews asked Phil.

"If this is up to me? Neither," Phil answered. "Glazer does chemical weapons. I don't trust chemical guys. They love to trap entry points, and there are plenty of cavities between us and his living room. I wouldn't put it past him to fill them with something nasty."

He tapped the wall beside him. "Rachel, find a way to get us in there."

"Sorry," he sent over the link. *"I know I'm asking you to run a lot of data, but..."*

"Yeah, yeah, you're in the middle of a job interview, I get it," she said in a fake sulk, and he coughed to cover a chuckle.

Rachel flipped through the most likely frequencies and found nothing, but it was the luck of an itchy nose which caused her to find the device tucked behind the door jamb. She turned her head to lean into her thumbnail, and what she thought was a reinforced door catch turned into a long tube attached to a metal rectangle the size of a pack of cigarettes.

"What the heck is...?" Rachel knelt and ran her hands over the wall to see if her fingers could feel what her implant couldn't quite see, but she found no bumps or nulls in the plaster. Whatever the device was, it had been installed from the inside of Glazer's apartment.

"What the heck is what?" Jason dropped down beside her, and she looped him into her field of sight in the link.

"Stop," Jason whispered and pressed his thumbs to his temples. "Stopstop*stop!*"

"Oh, sorry," she muttered as she broke off the visuals. Most of the time she could pass her perspective to the other Agents with no ill effects, but every so often she plunged them straight into a Stygian hellscape.

Jason scraped the top of his tongue against his upper teeth. *"I think I tasted that."*

"Santino? Phil? I've got something. It's not another bomb, but... I don't know. I've never seen anything like it before." She grabbed her tablet from the floor and handed it to her partner, then connected her tablet to a user-friendly version of the same image she had sent to Jason, gussied up to appear as similar to a plain old X-ray film as she could make it.

"This main box? I think this is an RFID scanner," Santino said. "But the rest of it..."

"This part is photoelectric..."

"... memory card here..."

"I don't think this thing has its own power source! It's hooked into the building's grid."

The bomb squad gathered around them and their sergeant went straight to the only question that truly mattered: "Will it blow up?"

"No." Santino was sure. "It's surveillance equipment, but we're not sure what kind."

"Is it connected to another device?" Andrews asked.

All three Agents and Santino shook their heads. "It's not hardwired into anything other than the building's power supply, and we can suppress any wireless signals it puts out," Phil told Andrews.

The sergeant's conversational colors brightened. "You can do that?"

Phil pretended surprise. "Suppress the wireless? Yeah, of course."

Andrews, who worked with men's lives on his conscience, went blue in relief.

Rachel switched to the other side of the door and found a clean void between the studs with nothing on the opposite side of the wall. Phil took out a pocket saw with a wicked curve to its blade. The building predated current construction codes and was made with the cheapest materials available; Phil sliced through the thin firewall in seconds. He removed a square panel the size of two large loaves of bread, and was up and through the hole in a blink.

"Clear!" he shouted, and the members of the D.C. tactical unit followed him in, their broad-shouldered giant complaining bitterly.

The bombs were disassembled and their component pieces

brought out in specialized padded bags for delivery to Forensics, then the tactical unit ran the room. Their methods were slower than Rachel's sixth sense but were as thorough, right up until the walls got in their way.

"Rachel, Jason? Can you come here?"

After the bomb squad had entered Glazer's apartment, Santino and Hill had gone downstairs to stake out the doors on the slim chance that Glazer hadn't abandoned his apartment. No one expected Glazer to show, but Santino was looking for an excuse to sit down and Hill was spoiling for a fight. Everyone reminded Hill of the minor issue that the man who had set him up would probably recognize him, but Hill was confident the blind corners of the back entrance would allow him ample opportunity to properly introduce himself to Glazer.

When Hill had insisted on leaving, Zockinski had insisted on staying. He was vocal about keeping someone from the MPD on hand to babysit the Agents at all times; apparently Sergeant Andrews was so friendly with Phil that he couldn't be trusted. Zockinski and the rest of the task force had spread out across the hall and busied themselves with the minutiae of documentation and police procedure as they waited for the bomb squad to finish. When Phil called out, Rachel and Jason's heads came up in synchronous motion; the officers went orange, and poor Officer McCall nearly fled for home in Phil's nice new suit.

Jason got up without a word but Rachel muttered a quick explanation to keep Zockinski in the loop. She hoisted herself through the hole to join up with the Agents on the other side, and came through to find Jason and Phil staring up at an off-brand fire alarm positioned directly over the door.

"Did it insult your sister?" she asked.

"Ping it," Phil said.

Rachel did. A motion sensor and a pinpoint camera the size of her little finger were tucked into the alarm's usual hardware.

"Well. That's certainly.... something."

Phil showed her a similar alarm cradled in the crook of

his arm, its plastic case cracked open to show the guts within. He was dissecting the alarm piece by piece, dropping each component in his gloved hand as he plucked them from its body. "There's one in each room. Apartments, even dumps like this, have a centralized alert and fire suppression system. I didn't even notice these until somebody on the tactical team realized they shouldn't be here. I pinged one to check if it was another bomb or just extra personal safety, and got the same thing as this," he said, slowly rolling the fragments around his palm like a prospector panning for gold.

Both Rachel and Phil had missed the alarms, but there was no blame. The devices blended into the digital ecosystem. Alarm systems, cell phones, thermostats, security cameras, all the rest of those little electronic things, these were the insects of the modern world. They were everywhere, droning away in a monotonous mechanical buzz, important within their own specific ecological niches but generally ignored by everyone and everything else. It was beyond an Agent's capacity to recognize each individual device—kick over a rotten log and you disturbed a nest of water meters—so these were shoved into the background, white noise across the mind. It was only when they flew straight in your face that an Agent remembered: *Oh, yes. Those.* and then only just long enough to wave them away.

Behind them, Zockinski's face appeared at the hole in the wall. Phil, nice guy that he was, brought the rest of the task force over to him and explained the oddity.

"Cameras?" Zockinski looked at the alarm over the door, then back at Rachel. "I thought you could find cameras."

"Usually," she said. "But these are retaining data, not talking to a separate storage device. Point-and-clicks are harder to locate unless we're paying attention." When she searched for cameras, she usually checked for movement, the flash in the underbrush of information scurrying from one point to another. If the machine hunkered down and kept quiet, her mind would usually pass over it without noticing it was there.

"Did you get the thing out of the wall yet?" Zockinski asked Phil.

"No," Phil said, glancing towards the spot where Glazer had stashed the RFID scanner. A stack of electronics and audio-visual equipment had been piled in front of it. The bomb squad was carefully, cautiously moving these away from the site to give Phil enough room to apply his wicked little saw.

Something had been nagging at Rachel since she had gone out-of-body to walk Glazer's apartment. She moved about the living room in her own body, testing if the flow of the room was as halting and awkward as it had seemed when she was in her avatar.

It was. She shuffled around a chair to the kitchen, then to the back bedroom where the burned-out husk of a computer tower had been left for Forensics. Rachel kept one eye on Glazer's oversized television as she moved from room to room. An opinionated Chinese traditionalist for a grandmother and a neoclassicist architect for a mother had convinced her that feng shui was the snake oil of interior design, but the layout of Glazer's apartment room was both physically and psychically offensive. Rachel could almost hear her entire matrilineal line call shenanigans.

"Gentlemen, I'm about to go girly on you," Rachel warned.

"Duly noted," Phil said.

"How would you arrange your furniture in here?"

They looked at her, then at the room, then back towards her, and their conversational colors ended somewhere in the yellows as they tried to guess what she wanted.

She tried again. "Where would you put that TV?"

Glazer's television set was ninety inches of pure high-definition plasma magnificence, and all three men agreed the only logical answer was to put it in the trunk of Zockinski's van as quickly as possible.

"Santino would get this," she muttered. "Okay, sports fans, it's the third quarter and you're watching the game while building your doomsday device in the office. Why is the TV on that wall…" she pointed to where the bomb squad was untangling cords, "… when you could see it from your workshop if it were over there?"

"Oh." Jason went yellow and gray in turns. "Camouflage?"

She nodded. "I think so. That's a lot of crap piled in front that RFID reader for no good reason."

"You don't buy a TV that expensive for no good reason," Zockinski countered.

"It's a prop," Rachel said. She watched as the bomb unit removed the gigantic set from its cradle on the wall. Maybe she could pull some strings to get it shipped to OACET for storage. They were using an ancient projection TV from the Eighties in their community rec room. "Glazer used it as a screen to hide the scanner."

Yeah, the guy's definitely a planner, she thought to herself. Glazer would have ditched his apartment around the same time he cleaned out the safe deposit box, but that machine had been built into the wall long before that. The AV system had been purchased to conceal the RFID scanner rather than for Monday night football. Glazer might have plastered over the device six days or six months ago, but whenever it was, he had anticipated that someone with the ability to detect hidden electronics would be standing in his living room.

Sergeant Andrews signaled to Phil that they were ready to start cutting, and the Agent left to join them. Rachel and the others scooted behind the kitchen cabinets. Those, at least, were solid wood lacquered over in fifty years of cooking residue; she felt the cabinets made much better cover than pressboard.

The bomb unit severed the device from the building's power supply and Andrews declared it good and dead. The Agents and Zockinski gathered around the hole to poke at it *in situ*; Rachel looped a finger under the remaining drywall between the device and the door jamb and started to rip it away, allowing the others to see it from her perspective. Once the wall had been removed, the exposed device seemed almost menacing. A hollow metal tube the diameter of a quarter ran from a hole drilled in the frame of the jamb to a dust cover slightly smaller than a pack of cards, giving the impression of a tiny tank capable of blowing planets loose from orbit.

Phil tapped the rectangular dust cover with a pen. "RFID reader," he said, then ran the pen up the length of the tube. "Um…"

"I know what this is," Zockinski hit on the answer. "It's an identification system. You said this was supposed to be camouflaged?"

Rachel nodded.

"Most RFID readers have to be within a couple of inches of a card to access the tag," he said. "This…" he pointed at the tube, "is a directional antenna. Glazer could hide the reader behind the AV system and amplify its signal to get clean scans off of any tag in a wallet."

Rachel and the bomb unit cleared the door for Phil, who cautiously opened it and moved under the lintel. He positioned himself next to the antenna. The tube was angled upwards and hit slightly above his hip; it was pointed directly at wallet-height for a man of average size.

"He's right. Add this to the cameras in the fake fire alarms, and you'd be able to tell anyone who comes through that door. The reader gets the RFID tag on a security badge or a credit card, and the camera takes a picture of the person's face for confirmation."

"After," Jason said. "This wouldn't have helped him until after he got back and checked the, uh… How was he storing this?"

Nobody knew. With the exception of the hidden cameras, nothing in the apartment was capable of writing data. Despite his stunning AV system, Glazer didn't own so much as a gaming console.

"Probably that smoking crater where a computer used to be," Rachel said as she nodded towards the back bedroom.

"Think we'll get anything useful off of it?" Jason asked.

Rachel looked through the wall to where the melted plastics

and metals had congealed in runny pools across Glazer's worn oak desk. "Probably not."

Sergeant Andrews came over and said he was throwing them out. "Sorry folks," he said. "The room's clean so Forensics wants to move in. We need to leave."

Rachel felt for Andrews. In times of a bomb scare, the bomb unit took priority over any other department—safety first!—but were then swept aside the moment they signed off on the site, all but ignored until the next time a suspicious suitcase reared its cheap vinyl head.

Phil dumped the pieces of the butchered alarm in an evidence bag and handed it to Zockinski to sign into evidence, then hung back to switch clothes with Officer McCall.

Rachel turned into the stairwell to go pick up Santino. Before she had turned down the first landing, she heard Andrews ask Phil: "That trick she did at the bank, and the one where she found the thing in the wall. Can you do that?"

"No." Rachel watched through the wall as Phil shook his head. "But I can learn."

"Get on that," the sergeant said, and clapped Phil on his arm. "And come talk to me after this is over."

She pumped her fist and practically skipped down the stairs.

Rachel found Santino sitting in an alcove of a neighboring building, sheltered from the late afternoon sun by a concrete overhang. He was toying with a nap and sighed when he saw her: time to go back to work.

"Smells like hobo pee in here," she said

"Why are you so sure it's from hoboes?" he asked, and she laughed. "You find anything interesting?"

"Oh, bombs, hidden cameras, the usual," she said, and rooted her stance to help him up. "His computer was slag. Looks like a small heat grenade went off inside of it."

"That's probably what happened," Santino grabbed her outstretched hand in his and let her haul him to his feet. "If he's done making videos, he doesn't need it."

"Did Glazer come back?"

"Yes," he said. "We had lunch. Good guy, if you can get past the supervillainy. Tell me about the hidden cameras?"

She did, and was adding Zockinski's passion for RFID scanners as a footnote when he said, "Hold on. Did it look handmade?"

Rachel shrugged. "I guess. I'm no expert, but it didn't look like something he bought off of the shelf."

He brightened in blues and smiled. "I need to see it. I think I know how to find him."

ELEVEN

The First District Station might as well have been governed by bells. When the First District Police had outgrown their old precinct house, the city had commandeered an entire elementary school as a replacement. Unlike OACET's gentle coddling of their property warehouse, First MPD was not trying to reclaim the old school from ruin, and the contractors had reached a compromise between form and function. Any space large enough to seat more than ten people still looked exactly like a classroom, and the urinals were higher up on the walls but the bathrooms still remembered the begging screams of swirlies. These perfunctory renovations had stopped at the doors, with changes to the exterior perpetually scheduled but never begun. Every time she clocked in, Rachel could almost hear her mother sigh; in a city with some of the most beautiful architecture in America, Rachel spent her days in a building the twin to good old Eastwood High back in Texas. Go Mustangs.

The task force had been given a large meeting room off of what must have been the old cafeteria; when Rachel scanned the walls, she found grease embedded so deep within the concrete that sandblasting hadn't been able to remove it. The room was situated on a corner and the two walls facing the hallways were nothing but glass, the blinds pulled high to put them on perpetual display to the rest of the station.

Wrinkled suits and ketchup stains, she thought. *Now at Macy's.*

She missed the privacy of Santino's office and its lush tropical forest, but her partner worked fast; three orchids and a fern had appeared in the windows of their new glass fishbowl, and an eight-foot buffet table had been set up in front of those to hold their new computers. Almost every penny of the task force's budget had been dumped into those machines, Santino's logic being that if they were asked to go up against someone as tech-savvy as Glazer, they should at least have access to the same type of tools.

Her partner had grudgingly left the tech setup to Jason and had vanished into the Internet. Santino had dissected the device taken from the wall of Glazer's apartment and had photographed every square inch in a resolution so high his phone screamed for mercy. Typing one-handed on his laptop, he was falling on the mercy of the maker communities, which, he said, was bound to end in some form of highly educational drama.

"Could he identify Glazer?"

Zockinski shook his head and wet a finger to turn the page. The cops who had interviewed the victim from the coffee shop had dropped off three sets of notes. There was the original report compiled back when they had thought the assault was an isolated incident, the notes from a new interview done this morning after they had recognized his assault might be connected to Griffin's death, and the third made after Glazer was identified and the officers went back to use Glazer's name and photo as memory prompts. It had yielded three sets of nothing. "He's never seen Glazer. Didn't even get a clear view of who hit him. But the witnesses…" Zockinski paused as he skimmed the text. "…were shown two photos of Glazer and IDed him.

"At the time of the assault, he wore his hair short, like he did in the bank," Zockinski added. "Maybe he's got a good day job somewhere."

Rachel made a little tic on her notepad to denote a possible point in the timeline. Her notepad was full of little tics and minor facts, trivial details gleaned from the casework that might add up to all or nothing. The battalion of officers serving as their support staff kept giving them new reports, and she and the detectives were all but suffocating in paper. Somewhere in those stacks might be some evidence that the victim from the coffee shop was connected to Glazer, but so far he seemed a dead end, someone chosen by Glazer for no other reason than his flawless predictability. She gnawed on the fact that someone who had his life so tightly knit together could be exploited for it. Even if he healed past the point of scars, the person he had been was probably gone.

She really hated Glazer.

Rachel flipped through the stack of papers until she found the witness statement from the source of Glazer's fake fingerprints. An elementary school teacher in Virginia had received a coupon for a free manicure from a local salon. Part of the service was a hand bath in a semi-liquid substance the teacher had described as "different, but nice." The salon had closed down back in February following an ICE raid, its employees deported or lost in the wind.

Planners. At least the teacher was alive and unharmed; Rachel was glad to have called that one wrong.

This was the waiting phase, where no one really expected to discover the smoking gun in the paperwork but they couldn't in good conscience sit around doing nothing while they waited for the evidence guys to uncover something they could use. She had felt the odd one out on the techie side of the room, so she had dragged her chair over to where Zockinski and Hill were delving through reports. They hadn't yet figured out how to get rid of her (she had followed them when they had attempted a strategic coffee run, smiling at them like a happy shark), so they had eventually given up and started passing her files.

She sighed and complained at the right times, but deep down, she was dancing.

Rachel had gone ahead and outlined her theory of plans within plans to the detectives, who agreed with her but said it didn't matter. The bottom line was a woman was dead and a man might never walk again, and so what if Glazer had been forced to deviate? As long as they caught him, his plans weren't any of their goddamned business.

To which she had replied: "Since when do we ignore

motive?" and held up a little doodle she'd scribbled on a scrap of paper. *HELLO OACET, YOU'RE EARLY* in overlabored ballpoint, surrounded by a daisy chain and bunnies.

They had returned to the files to look for any connections between the victims and OACET, between the victims and technology, between the victims and... Nothing. But if they had been profiled for predictability, then nothing was to be expected.

Jason had inadvertently hit on Glazer's victimology in an impromptu lecture on the way back to the Station. The videos, Jason had said, were extremely well-done because Glazer had micromanaged the events leading up to them. He had profiled people who loved routine as that allowed him to build scenarios that hadn't occurred around events that did. "But none of this matters, now" Jason said as he finished. "He's done making videos. Getting the right setup to do this level of digital manipulation is a labor of love, but he fragged his box. He wouldn't have done that if still he needed it."

First store, then coffee shop, then bank... Rachel slapped her pen against the back of her hand as she tried to see what they were missing. *HELLO OACET, YOU'RE EARLY.*

It was ten at night. Frustration was setting in. Both Zockinski and Hill were running orange, a little bit of gray sneaking around their edges.

"Can we guess why Glazer would have an RFID scanner in his apartment? Maybe we can backtrack or..." *Order some more food,* she thought, staring wistfully at the empty pizza boxes in the corner. All three Agents were starving.

"Easiest way to ID someone," Zockinski said. Hill went slightly puce, a color Rachel associated with a sigh, but didn't look up from the report on his desk.

"Yeah, we know it's an ID system, but why was it there? Why would he want to know who was in his apartment?"

"If he knew law enforcement would be there, he wanted the names of people involved in his case," Zockinski said.

"That's a lot of assumptions," she said, counting on her

fingers as she listed them off. "That the cops would find his place, that they'd be carrying RFID tags, that he'd still have a computer there to store data..."

"And that they wouldn't have one of these," Zockinski took out his well-worn wallet and smirked at her, smug in pinks. "Bet you can't see through this."

"American Express, Sam's Club membership, transit card, Visa debit, and Discover," she said, and his face and colors fell. Hill laughed without looking up.

"Nice Faraday cage," she said, pointing at his wallet. "It'll block most RFID readers, but..." she said as she tapped her head and winked at the big detective. "...this ain't something you can buy off of eBay."

Zockinski said nothing as he turned away and buried his wallet back in his pocket, but he had started to pick up a furious red.

Oh hell. Rachel suddenly remembered how Hill had no problem following the discussion on RFID tags back when they were interviewing Burman. That, along with Hill's refusal to engage in the current conversation, said plenty about Zockinski: the man was a privacy bug. Hill had probably listened to his partner complain about technological violations of personal privacy so often he could recite them from memory. *No wonder Zockinski can't stand OACET,* she thought. *We're a worst fear realized.*

Before she could smooth over her mistake, Jason dropped himself on top of her files.

"Rachel's wrong. Faraday cages are a gimmick," Jason said, nudging aside a few loose pages and letting them slide out of order. "They might distort signals, but they can't block signals unless they're grounded. Glazer's was a low-to-high frequency reader, and if he rigged up a signal boost to read a tag from five feet away, you can bet that thing'll also bust through your wallet. "

"Pull up a seat, Jason," she said in a tone that meant: Move. He ignored her, so she said the same thing over the link, and he lunged for the nearest chair to get her out of his head.

Before he could reach it, the dry sound of Styrofoam sliding across the floor made the whole room shiver. Jason changed course and scrambled to get the packing materials from the new computers out of the path of the door, and Phil snuck in around the mess, apologizing.

"Hey, Santino?" Phil was carrying a small box which gave off the soft sounds of small metallic collisions when he tilted it. "There's something you should see."

He placed the box on the table and pulled out four long metal pins, wrapped with springs and set with a circular disk on the one end. Each was slightly different, with pieces of indiscriminate origin cobbled together to form similar wholes, and each was about the size of his palm. He put them down one by one, and they rolled with the slope of the table in a fixed circle.

"Fuzes?" Hill asked, and raised an eyebrow to ask permission.

Phil nodded, and Hill picked one up with careful fingers. "I've been breaking down the four bombs with the tactics unit," Phil said. "Sergeant Andrews brought in a specialist in military antiques to see if they have a historical antecedent. They seem to be custom, but he's getting a second opinion just in case it's obscure.

"So far," he continued, "there's nothing to link the bombs to any parts suppliers. They're definitely handmade. Glazer could have gotten most of the pieces from hardware stores, old clocks, scrap bins... none of the individual components are especially unique. But look at this."

He grabbed one of the fuzes by the long pin and flipped it over. "See that pattern on the back?"

"A star?" Rachel peered at it from her vantage point behind Zockinski, who quickly stepped to the side to make room for her at the table.

"Could be a star, could be a funky icon or initials," Phil said. "But it's on all of these. And it's not an accidental tool mark.

Glazer etched the design into the brass."

"Hang on," Santino said, his thumb flying across his phone's screen. "The reader has that same mark. It wasn't etched, though. It was done in flux so I thought it was castoff from a sloppy solder." He handed his phone to Hill, then turned to the bin where the innards of the RFID reader had been tagged and bagged to locate the original.

Rachel plucked the image from his phone and held it clear in her mind, then joined Phil and Jason in the link to explore its nooks and crannies.

"Not a star," she said. *"More like a W in a fancy script."*

"Or one with an E across it," Jason said, and took the image from her to flip it sideways. Part of the pattern started to glow in OACET green. *"See how the bars intersect?"*

"You're right," Phil twisted the image again to test the alignment, and Rachel felt the feathered notion of motion sickness catch in her throat.

"Guys." Rachel held up her hands in surrender and dropped out of the link. She flipped her notepad over, and on the cardboard back she drew the W, then the E, and made sure to round the letters so they matched those on the metal.

The MPD officers dropped into to vivid reds and yellows as they realized they were after a madman courteous enough to sign his work.

"Are the prints in for Glazer's place?" Zockinski asked Hill. Glazer had done a thorough job wiping down his apartment, but the forensics team had ripped the place apart and had put together full sets from three different people. No one ever thought to clean the lip on the underside of the toilet tank lid.

The tall man shook his head. "Not yet. If they belong to someone with a different name, these could be his initials."

Santino burned bright blue as he scuffed his chair across the linoleum and grabbed his laptop. "It's definitely his signature," he muttered. "Some maker out there knows him."

"Maker?" Zockinski asked.

"There's a huge subculture of do-it-yourselfers out there,"

Santino said as he hunted and pecked at the keyboard with his right hand. "The active ones—the really good ones—they keep tabs on each other."

"If they know Glazer," Zockinski said as he picked up a fuze and ran his little finger over the etching, "why do you think they'll help you catch him?"

"Makers aren't crazed anarchists." Santino grinned without looking up. "They're hobbyists. If they know him, they'll come forward. And if he's ever posted his craft online, someone out there will know him."

One of Santino's many pet theories was that makers, especially tech junkies, were a cross between archivists and anthropologists, and had appointed themselves the record-keepers of the digital landscape. The tech junkies loved to track inventions originating off of the grid, as independents often created new technologies that were of greater interest to them than what they considered to be mass-produced trash. Glazer's little RFID scanner was distinctive, and Santino was betting that a device so complex could not spring forth fully-formed from the brow of someone unfamiliar with technology. When he had uploaded the images of the scanner to makers' communities, Santino had put out the online equivalent of an Internet-wide Amber Alert.

Now, with the signature from the fuzes, Santino hoped to draw in those makers from outside of the tech subset. "We just got lucky," Santino said as he updated his earlier posts with images of Phil's fuzes. "Analog and digital widens the field of people who might know him."

"How long will this take?" Hill asked. Behind him, Jason rolled his eyes.

"*Watch yourself,*" she told him.

"*...morons who don't understand how the new world works...*" Jason muttered in her head.

"*Or, persons with different abilities,*" she said, nudging him towards the Agents' version of political correctness. She wasn't sure whether Hill had a particular specialty or was just a darned solid cop, but out of all of the men in the room, he was the one she'd pick to stand beside her in a bar fight. She had met less reliable rocks.

Santino sent the last request off into cyberspace and slumped back in his seat. "If Glazer was an active maker, then we'll know his history in ten minutes," he said to Hill. "But I think it will take longer. Glazer probably stopped contributing to the community when he started to plan out his perfect crime. He needed to put some distance between his name and his product. Still, if he ever posted anything, someone will remember it. This handmade hardware is so unique it might as well be made out of his DNA. Someone out there knows him. Nerds are like elephants: we never forget."

There was a knock on the door and Chief Sturtevant leaned in. "You're over your twelve," he said. Shift policies were structured to prevent officer fatigue, which set in after twelve hours; Rachel pinged the closest computer for the time and realized she had been trapped in her damned skinny suit for almost fourteen. "You're off the clock. Go home."

He shut the door and walked away, and Rachel promptly forgot about him until she realized Zockinski and Hill were packing up.

"You're leaving?" Rachel found it hard to believe the two detectives kept the cop's version of banker's hours.

"I've got kids," Zockinski said as he grabbed his suit coat from the rack and disappeared.

"Like hell he does," she said to Hill.

"Twins," the large man said before he followed his partner into the hallway. "Two little girls. See you at six."

"Did you know Zockinski's got kids?" Rachel asked Santino. She was almost indignant; Zockinski should not be allowed to break out of the box she had made for him.

Santino nodded. "They're adorable. His wife is smoking hot, too."

"That's just not right," Rachel muttered.

"How are we going to handle transportation?" Phil asked

Santino. Her partner had their only car and one usable arm.

"Give me another ten minutes here to wrap up," he said. "Some replies are starting to come in, and I want to manage my logoff."

"Okay," Phil said, and left with Jason to grab a snack from the vending machine in the hall.

What do you want? Phil asked her.

Anything king-sized, Rachel replied. *If there aren't any left, snack cakes.* The prepackaged pastries tasted like gummed flour but they packed the most calories per punch. She could ride one of those until she got home and could make herself a proper meal.

She grabbed a chair and scooted in close to Santino. He was playing a puzzle game.

"Hard at work, I see?"

"I think I might stay here a while," he said. "You guys can borrow my car tonight. I'll find a ride." He hadn't mentioned Zia once, not since his run-in with Jason, but while he had carried some gray with him ever since they had left OACET headquarters, a joyous yellow spun into the same thread as Zia's violet core was woven into it. The yellow and violet threaded through him meant she was always on his mind, but he had treated her as a taboo subject whenever Rachel had pressed him on it. Now the yellows and violets were fading, and the gray was heavily tinted with drooping oranges and the deep amber that Rachel associated with Santino's live-in girlfriend.

"Want to talk about it?"

"Why bother? You're Super Emotions Girl." Browns rose up around him like the mess in a clogged sink. "You were there. You saw everything."

"And this is why I didn't tell you what I can do." Rachel caught herself and softened her words before she came across as snappish. It had not been an easy day for him and she didn't need to make it worse.

He hauled himself back out from under his grays. "Sorry," he muttered.

Sorry. She hated that word; she lost track of how many times she said it, or heard it said, in a single day. *Sorry, sorry, sorry,* lives punctuated by regret.

"Don't be sorry," she told him. "Just don't do it. Now," she said as he lost some of the petulant browns, "want to talk about it?"

"Sure. I'm planning to go home, get in a huge argument, and knock on your door at four in the morning to crash on your couch. This is all your fault, by the way, so I'm staying with you for a few weeks."

Rachel chewed the inside of her lip to keep herself from calling him names. "Don't you think that's a little... extreme?" she asked. "You just met Zia."

"I'm not breaking up with Maggie." Santino took off his glasses and rubbed his eyes. "But I'm not going to be dishonest to a woman I've been with for years, and she is going to throw my ass out cold when I tell her about Zia."

"Good lord, you move fast. I was in that bathroom for all of five minutes."

He laughed quietly. "Nothing happened, but would you want to spend the rest of your life with someone if they had doubts?"

He paused and reached out with a gentle finger to touch the nearest orchid. "Love at first sight is a joke, Rachel," he said. "It's how we whitewash the same pheromone rush we got when we were kids. I'd be so... God! It'd be evil of me if I let my dick call the shots on this. I'll go home, Maggie'll be pissed for a while, and then when she gets over it, we can talk it out."

Santino put his glasses back on and turned back to the computer. Rachel rested a hand on his shoulder in sympathy and then walked back to her files. *Poor guy,* she thought. She didn't know if this was good or bad timing on Fate's part, as he had been days away from dragging Rachel with him to help him pick out a ring. Maggie made him happy, and Rachel had liked her those few times Santino had dragged them both to dinner.

But Santino—practical, logical Santino, who no doubt believed every word he had said to the core of his very soul—had nonetheless been lying when he said there was no such thing as love at first sight.

(And Rachel, whose only furnished room enshrined that ideal in books she could no longer read, wrapped herself in the unexpected joy at how, for those few lucky people, there might actually be some real magic left in the world.)

There was a quiet knock on the door and Rachel looked up to see Charley Brazee struggle with the knob, arms full of banker's boxes. His colors were off, his friendly blue-gray core hidden under purples and grays locked in mortal combat. She jumped up to help and he gratefully dropped the uppermost box into her arms.

"Jeez, Charley, is there gold in these?" Rachel's sore knees throbbed under the new weight.

"Maybe. If they help you, then yes. These are some of our notes on the court proceedings where the MPD has processed video evidence over the last six months. Edwards had me go through them all last night and pick out the ones that might be relevant."

"Oh, Charley," Rachel said, wincing. "We've got a full team doing that same thing here."

His colors didn't change but he rounded his shoulders and started rubbing his hands together. *Stress,* Rachel noted, the kinesthetic message unmistakable.

"I knew it," he sighed. "Edwards has me doing busywork. I'm so behind on everything…" He pulled himself straight, as if he had made a difficult decision. "Can you help me get another box out of my car?"

"Yeah, sure," she said, and kept the conversation light and fluffy as they walked to the parking garage. It didn't seem to help; Charley went deeper into his shell until even prattling on about OACET couldn't draw him out.

The city had decided the solution to First MPD's perennial parking shortage was an adjacent garage, but they hadn't quite understood the problem when they approved the project. Zoning prevented the garage from being taller than the building itself, and the available surface area was smaller than the lot of a small car dealership. The result was a narrow concrete iceberg, with six floors of the garage hidden beneath the ground and the uppermost two cresting to merge with the back of the school.

A total of two doors connected the old building to the new garage; First District Station was a protected space, and access was tightly controlled. She took Charley on the least-traveled of those two routes, past the break room and down a hallway with paired rooms used for interrogations. This corridor had been designed to facilitate for prisoner transport and ended in a small room with steel doors and bulletproof windows on both sides, a rodeo chute to secure the felons before entering or leaving the building. Both the interior and exterior doors swung open for them as Rachel and Charley walked down the hall: in Rachel's opinion, one of the major perks of being a cyborg was never having to dither with the digital locks.

Charley, who usually loved it when she showed off for him, didn't so much as crack a smile. Rachel was unable to get a clean read from him. His movements were tight and he spent too much time picking what he wanted to say, looking at everything from the fluorescent lights to the scuffs on the glossy floor to avoid meeting her eyes. His conversational colors were a swirling blend of happy purples and the gray of stress: the man was his own house divided.

He had parked three floors down. Rachel didn't like tight city spaces, especially at night, and Charley kept crowding her towards the cars. She kept the center of the garage on her left as they descended, and every few steps she'd take a breath to remind herself that the void between the levels let in the relative coolness of the August night air.

There was one box on the passenger's seat of his car. It was the size of a shoebox, much smaller than the two he had lugged into her temporary office. Rachel knew a setup when she saw one. "What's on your mind, Charley?"

He paused and leaned against the car, but his happy purple popped. "If I give you some information," he said, "can you promise it won't get back to me?"

She reached out to the OACET community server and began recording.

"I don't know how that would work," she said, glancing up at First District Station. "I think you need to talk to an officer. Let me get Santino out here."

"I'd rather you handle it," he said. "I've been thinking about this and... If I don't do it, people could get hurt. I *have* to do this.

"But I can't lose my job, Rachel," he said in a rush. "It's a bad economy, and if I'm burned as a law clerk, I'm too old to start all over again."

Lie, she noted as the dimples emerged. *That's not what's bothering you.*

"Charley, are you in trouble?"

The dimples disappeared and reappeared as he spoke, truth and lies blended together. "No, not right now. But if things keep going the way they are... Listen," he said, fumbling inside of his suit, "Please. Your case? This was in Edwards' office. I need you to handle it, or people could get hurt."

He handed her a wrinkled sheet of paper. Rachel flipped her implant to reading mode and made out the name of a bank and the first few digits of a routing number before she hastily crumpled it up.

Charley went red. "Hey!"

"It's okay, I'll keep it safe," she said, digging around in her purse for a plastic evidence bag. "But I can't look at it until I have a warrant." She wasn't one of those Agents who found themselves performing unconscious data retrieval searches, but there was a first time for everything. She didn't want to read Charley's note and suddenly find herself squirreled up in a bank's database, her grubby little synapse-fingers ripping through its files.

He looked towards the stationhouse. "Don't get a warrant,

even if you use a different judge. Edwards will be watching...
He says he's scared of OACET." Charley pointed to the crumpled
wad in its little plastic baggie. "I've seen your suspect. And that
account? It's a payoff from..." Charley's voice trailed off as he
noticed the security cameras above his head.

"Tell me about the money, Charley." *Shades of early Shawn,*
she thought as she worked with calm words and stressed
Charley's name to ground him. "If it's so important, tell me.
Then I'll find a way to do this legally, okay?"

He tried to pull her into the shadow of a minivan, but she
stood firm. "I don't know if you can. There's someone high up
in the government involved in this," he said, relenting. Before,
the dimples in his colors came and went as he spoke; now, they
were gone. Charley was finally telling the absolute truth. "But
that's all I'll—"

"Senator Hanlon," she cut him off. "It's Senator Hanlon."

Charley went white in shock, then replaced it with a happy
yellow. "How did you know?" he whispered.

*"Get out here **now**,"* she sent to Phil and Jason.

"Come back inside with me. Fill out a report with Santino,"
she said, knowing it was a lost cause. "You'll be treated as a
whistleblower, you'll be protected. You have my word," she
lied. She felt terrible about misleading him but there was no
such thing as a confidential informant. Like chupacabras, they
existed purely in fiction and in human interest stories on the
evening news.

He was shaking his head before she had finished. "You
know that never works," he said, and pushed himself off of the
minivan. "I need to go. Don't tell anybody I gave you that, okay?
Promise me you'll look into it yourself."

"You realize you're asking me to break the law," she said.

"I know," he said, nodding nervously. "Check out those
numbers and you'll see why. But you didn't get them from me,
remember? Anywhere else. Just not from me."

"Charley..." Rachel closed her eyes tight, but he still stared
at her, pleading. "I can't. And I won't. You have to file a report

or give me something I can use to get a warrant."

"Listen to me!" He grabbed her lower arm with a doughy hand, then looked past her to where Phil and Jason were sprinting down the pavement towards them. "Forget it," he said, dropping her arm as though it had burned him. "I tried."

"Charley," she said, dodging his car door as he slid into the driver's seat, "if it's important, you know you have to talk to me. That's why you came here tonight!"

"Lots of things are important, Rachel," he said. "Right now, it's important I don't get caught with you."

He threw the shoebox at her and ended with a hard: "Good luck." He pulled out into the travel lane as the other Agents arrived, shading his face with his hand to hide his profile from two men he saw as strangers.

"Who's that?" Phil asked.

"A law clerk in Edward's office. He's sort of a friend. He gave me this," she said, and held up the baggie. *"He claims it's information that incriminates Edwards, and..."*

She paused and crushed the paper tight in her fist. *"And he told me that Senator Hanlon is involved."*

The two men dropped into reds and blacks. Jason grabbed at her, but she saw it coming and his hand closed on empty air.

"Give it to me."

"I need your lighter," she told him.

"Rachel, wait," Phil said. *"Think about this."*

She pressed the wad tight between both hands. *"No. If I do, I'll talk myself into doing something we'll all regret. This isn't evidence, it's hearsay."*

Jason came straight at her like a prizefighter. *"Give it to me."*

*"He was **lying**, Jason. Our entire conversation, right up until I mentioned Hanlon, he was lying."*

"What did he say?" Phil asked, putting a hand on Jason's shoulder. Jason shrugged it off and started pacing.

"Here," she said, and passed them the location of the file. "I taped it."

The rule was that emotions couldn't be captured on film; the exception was when she was the one doing the filming. As they watched the video, she talked them through Charley's moods, how he shifted between truth and lie. "He was showing a lot of stress, and most of his lines seemed scripted," she explained. "My best guess is that he was coerced to try and set me up. Whoever's twisting his arm wants me to incriminate myself.

"And Jason?" Rachel pointed up to where the security camera tracked them from its chickenwire nest. "You don't pull a Woodward in a police station parking garage."

He handed her his lighter.

They watched Charley's note, now forever unread, burn down to a slurry of plastic and ash beneath the watchful glass eye of First MPD.

As they walked back towards the station, they were joined by two very confused officers who were sent to learn why the cyborgs were setting fires in the parking garage. Phil told them he had lost a bar bet with a local law clerk, and offered to treat them to vending machine cuisine to make up for their inconvenience.

"The bank account. Do you think that was real?" Jason said to her as they ripped into stale cupcakes. Across the table, Phil was entertaining the officers with the saga of the bomb scare at Glazer's apartment. Like every good fish story, the bombs had grown in size and threat; they were lucky the city was still standing.

The calories hit her bloodstream and her body twitched itself awake. *"Yeah, I do,"* she replied. The cupcakes were gone in two bites each and she tossed the wrappers in the bin to keep herself from licking the frosting off of them. *"And probably at least one large cash transaction went through it. Deposit or payment, doesn't matter. It'll lead straight back to Edwards in some way."*

"Is the judge involved?

She shrugged across the link before she realized it. *"Sorry,"* she said as he flinched. *"I don't know. If you asked me that an hour ago, I'd have said yes."*

"And now?" Phil asked. He had been relieved of storytelling duties and was nodding in the right places as an officer told one of her own.

"My gut says Edwards is being set up as a sacrifice. He could be innocent, he could be complicit, but I don't think he's the brains behind this. He's too..." Rachel thought back to Edwards during that morning's press conference, how he had shimmered with energy on the podium. She leaned forward and rested her chin on the lid of Charley's shoebox. *"He's too eager. He's a little kid who wants to be famous, but I don't think he'd set up a murder."*

"Hanlon would," Jason said, and started to pick up reds. *"We already know that for a fact. If Hanlon was the one getting his hands dirty, would Edwards help him?"*

"If Hanlon lied to him to bring him on his team? Yes, Edwards would definitely help him. Edwards would get to run for office with the support of a beloved Senator. It'd be his dream come true."

Rachel paused, then added: *"But if Hanlon was honest with him? I just don't know."*

Phil bid goodnight to the officers and got up to leave, and Rachel and Jason followed him out of the room. *"Why be honest with someone if you're setting him up? Rachel..."* Phil paused and looked at her. *"Your friend, Charley? What if he wasn't lying, and Hanlon and Edwards are working together?"*

She said, very quietly so they wouldn't feel her anger: *"Then we put another name on the list."*

TWELVE

The sun wasn't up but Mulcahy was waiting for her just outside of her front door. She looked around for a classic muscle car and came up empty.

"I'm walking you to work," he said.

Rachel assumed he meant First District Station. OACET headquarters was twenty miles away, and they both had busy days ahead of them. "Okie-dokie."

She went back inside and taped a note to the coffee pot to let Santino know she had left early but would be running late. Sometime after two in the morning, her partner had shown up on her doorstep with a hockey duffle stuffed with clothes. He had gone straight to the inflatable air mattress she had set up in one of the empty rooms without saying a word. Rachel saw that he had come back downstairs and used the kitchen countertop as his dumping ground for his workday debris: his badge, belt, wallet, and Taser were strewn out between the sink and the fridge, and when she took a quick peek in the freezer she found his gun hidden behind the ice tray.

Buy a gun safe, she added to her mental list of things to do. She kept hers in the nightstand beside her bed, but the guest room didn't have a stick of furniture. A few nights in the freezer wouldn't corrode Santino's service weapon, but it looked as though her partner might be staying with her for longer than that.

It stopped her cold, realizing this would be the first time in years she would share her private space with anyone for longer than a night. Rachel looked towards the staircase and caught herself before she scanned her own house to see if Santino was up and moving. She rubbed the stress from her hands and made herself walk away from the imprint he had already left on her kitchen, the jacket he had tossed over the newel post on his way up to bed, his shoes on the mat by the door.

She darted outside to find Mrs. Wagner stalking across their conjoined front lawns towards Rachel's front porch, golf club held parallel to the ground like a samurai sword.

Mulcahy, bemused in golds and purples, asked: *"Does she do nothing but watch your house?"*

"I think she sleeps when I'm at work. Come on." Rachel took off in the other direction, the morning dew on the grass soaking her pant cuffs as the large man followed in her wake. Behind them, Mrs. Wagner went red with rage as her targets escaped at the speed of a brisk walk.

She and Mulcahy passed the first few blocks in small talk. She needled him with questions about his upcoming nuptials to see if she could get his colors to shift, but he seemed genuinely enthusiastic about his starring role in a wedding that would rival any held at Westminster Abbey. He was not, however, familiar with organza; with a perfectly straight face, she told him he should call the flower shop as quickly as possible to set up the order while it was still in season.

They detoured through a small public park which catered to soccer moms by day and junkies by night; with dawn barely touching the bottom of the clouds, they had the place to themselves. Mulcahy steered them towards a footbridge which passed over a puddle and a clump of weeds, the rain from yesterday's storms already drained from the channel. He stopped in the middle of the bridge and leaned on the railing.

"How many surveillance devices are on us?" he asked.

"Right now? Is this a test?"

He shook his head. "This is a meeting."

She flipped to frequencies which let her pick out audio, then video, and mostly for giggles she ran a few to cover some of the less common spectra (she didn't expect to find anything in those but Mulcahy loved to throw ringers).

"Fourteen," she answered. It was a pittance; fourteen signals aimed directly at the park was practically nothing. They were within spitting distance of Pennsylvania Avenue, and there was so much electronic chatter the hairs on her arms twitched.

"You're tracking them?" Mulcahy asked. When she nodded, he grinned. "Watch this."

He lifted his chin and closed his eyes. Rachel had no idea what he was doing until the signals started to fade and a gray fog rose up around them. The signals waved in and out, like losing a favorite radio station as your car drove out of range, then vanished entirely.

"Here," Mulcahy said, and she looked up to see him kneeling beside her and holding a pack of tissues. She didn't remember sitting down. Or crying; her face was wet.

"Shit," she said, wiping her eyes with the flat of her hand, careful to avoid smearing her makeup. "Sorry. I thought I was done with the blackouts."

"It's my fault," he shook his head. "I should have let you know what was coming. It hit me hard the first time, too."

She took one of his hands with both of hers, and he lifted her up like a kitten. "Look," he said, smiling.

They stood at the center of an opaque silvery-gray bubble, the edges of which sealed away the pervasive digital world. Rachel could still perceive those same fourteen signals if she went looking for them, but their pressure was blocked from this sanctuary of Mulcahy's making. Nor could she feel the timers on the traffic lights, the Wi-Fi blanketing the park, the chatter of cell phones in the cars driving by... The digital ecosystem was silent.

The sphere around them was centered on Mulcahy, whose conversational colors nearly matched his cerulean core. This was probably as close as he came to being at peace.

She understood. It felt as though she had stepped from the water and could move without its weight.

In their secret selves, every Agent wondered when they would end up like Shawn. It seemed inevitable; they could never escape from the pervasive presence of mechanical things. It was possible to narrow the scope of what was perceived to the immediate area, but even that left dozens—sometimes hundreds, sometimes *thousands!*—of devices. These formed an unrelenting pressure on the mind which could be ignored but never avoided. The only real relief was to turn off the implant. For Rachel, for the others, this was not an option; they might go insane as quickly without the implant as with it. There was no going back.

Then, suddenly, sanctuary. Control without the clamor. Little wonder she had fainted.

Things were… fuzzy in the sphere. She was having difficulty seeing Mulcahy as anything but his colors, and when she looked down, her torso and legs were fit together like a jagged jigsaw. Their feet, the ground beneath them, these were barely visible at all.

She reached out, halfway expecting to feel the edges of the bubble as her fingers vanished into the gray, but they fell through empty air. Rachel pushed her arm forward and found the more of her body that extended past the edge, the greater the pressure of the oppressive chattering things. She stopped before she moved her face beyond the barrier, sure that they would surge over her in force when her head and its blended circuitry were exposed.

"Is this yours?" she asked. It seemed the sort of thing he would discover.

"No," he said, his eyes closed. He let the railing do the work of holding him upright as he drank in the silence. "Danny in Accounting figured this out, can you believe it?"

Danny in Accounting… Danny in Accounting… There were several Dannys in OACET, and she tried to place his face among those Agents in other departments before she realized her mind had gone out through the collective to locate him. She backpedaled quickly before the many Dannys felt her and thought she was trying to call. "The link is still active?"

Mulcahy nodded, and the railing gave a slight creak in protest as he shifted his weight. "We can't even keep ourselves out," he said with a trace of fierce red pride.

He pushed himself off of the railing. "I have to drop the barrier. Ready?"

Rachel took a deep breath and nodded, steadying herself for the rush of the shrieking things. Instead, as the gray slowly faded and the details of the park returned, they crept back like beaten dogs and slunk around the edges of sense. She closed her eyes and exhaled in relief.

"Danny found it when he was looking for a way to block the paparazzi."

Oh. That Danny in Accounting. Josh and Mulcahy were merely movie-star handsome. Danny in Accounting had stepped straight off of the pedestal of a Renaissance sculptor. The man couldn't take out the trash without ending up on the cover of a magazine, and Mulcahy's standing agreement with the press to leave OACET alone was ignored by those bottom-feeders who thought that holding a camera gave them the right to use it. Someday there would be an object lesson so profound it would pass into press corps legend.

"I can't maintain it for long," he said. "I'm still training the autoscript. But in a few weeks, it'll be an independent program. I still have to test if it blocks traditional film photography, but streaming digital is cut off at the barrier."

"Nice." Rachel flipped off her visuals and felt her way through the digital ecosystem. It was muffled, as though she had slammed the window shut to block out the summer screech of the cicadas. She wondered what her implant had learned while the sphere was active. "Can you do anything about the gray?"

Mulcahy's blue took on a streak of yellow. "Gray?"

"Yeah. The bubble..." and she trailed off as she realized Mulcahy's field of vision didn't stop at the barrier.

"Listen," she said, and cocked her head as if checking the time. "Today's going to be a bear and I need to get to First District Station."

"Rachel."

She waited. She was not about to lie to him, and she definitely didn't want to deal with his guilt when she told him that since his new program blocked digital frequencies, it also blocked some of the media she used to see.

He must have guessed; his colors went pale.

"I need some time to play around with it," she said through the link. *"I was able to see, just not as well as usual. It's just a matter of finding the right spectrum. Don't worry about it."*

She started walking, and he fell in a few steps behind her.

"Rachel."

"Hey, look. Geese."

He relented and they made their way across the park.

"Have you learned how to move your autoscripts yet?" Mulcahy asked.

Rachel shook her head, slightly annoyed. Mulcahy hadn't shown up on her doorstep by accident but she had assumed this meeting would be about Glazer and the case, the facts she reported to him carried back to OACET for dissection and analysis, their plans within plans adjusted to cover all possible new scenarios. She was wrong. Apparently this was a strategy meeting and her performance review, all rolled up in a brisk morning walk.

"Please make that a priority. I'd like everyone in the Program to have at least some of your capacity. And maybe they'd have some feedback or advice that would help you, too."

Doubtful, she thought to herself, then glanced at Mulcahy to check if she had accidentally sent that through the link. If she had, he chose to ignore it.

"You've been keeping up with your therapy?"

"You know I have," she said, and kicked a rock at a trash can. She regretted it as soon as her foot moved, acting the petulant child in front of her boss.

"You ran out of the bank yesterday."

Rachel kept her back straight and bit down on her first response. She'd take it out on Jason later. It had to have been him; Phil would run tattletale to Mulcahy only if she posed a risk. Jason had probably called Administration the instant she had burned Charley's note in the parking lot to catch them up how poorly she was managing OACET's affairs at the MPD. "It won't happen again," she said.

"Good. Also," he added, and smiled tightly, "kindly remind Jason Atran that even if I were to pull you, he would not be the one to take your place."

"One might say he's a whiner."

"One might."

Pigeons mobbed their feet as they cut through the thick of the park. Somewhere high over her head, Mulcahy hummed a few bars from Tom Lehrer.

"Life is skittles and life is beer?"

He grinned; she had caught the reference. "Not the nicest song out there. Reminds me…" he said, and tossed an audacious pigeon off of his shoe, "tell me about Zockinski."

"He's bumping chests with Jason," she said. "But in the rah-rah manly-man way. Zockinski is still keeping him at arm's length, but I think that's more because of what we are rather than who Jason is. You should probably ask Phil; that's not my culture."

It wasn't. Every day she had been in the military, she was thankful for those women who had come before her, the ones who had marched through thirty years of hell so she merely had to slog through waist-deep heck.

"I meant his wallet."

Oh crap, she thought. She had meant to tell Mulcahy about this herself. She had filed her daily report last night but had left this little bit of information out; Jason had struck again.

"Yeah. High-end RFID blocker."

"What's your opinion?" Mulcahy asked over the link.

"I don't think he's a technophobe," she replied. They left the relative peace of the park and blended back into the tangle of the city's streets. *"Maybe he's just a privacy buff. Either way, it explains why he went after me for six months straight."*

"Do you see him as a potential problem?"

She shook her head. *"I would have before all of this, but now? Not if we bring down Glazer before anything else happens.*

We do that and OACET will have made his career. He'll be ours for life."

Alliances were her priority. Her role in OACET's plans within plans was to entrench herself within routine police work: she was to make allies while simultaneously proving that the MPD benefitted from having an Agent on staff. It was a long-term strategy designed to play out over years, but as of two days ago, Glazer's campaign had launched Rachel ahead of schedule. While the MPD officers on the task force were concerned that their careers might hinge on Glazer's arrest, Rachel was terrified that OACET's ground game might be ruined if she fumbled.

"Good." Mulcahy's conversational colors dropped some of the cool grays and shifted towards a more peaceful shade of blue. *"And Detective Hill?"*

"He had an actual conversation with Phil yesterday, said he and Zockinski would defend Jason if they had to. His mood was pretty stable. He's started to overcome that instinctive aversion to us, too. I like him." Rachel realized with mild surprise. *"Did you look into a connection between him and Mako?"*

He nodded at a passerby who recognized them. *"Yes. Cousins, but as far as I can tell they haven't seen each other since they were kids. Detective Hill's family moved to New York when they were both about ten and their families lost touch."*

She knew it. Rachel nearly clapped her hands in delight. *"Did you talk to Mako yet?"*

"No. Carlota's almost ready to go into labor and they don't need any extra stress right now. But I did put extra security on them in case they're a target."

They passed a bakery and were buying doughnuts before they realized it. Doughnuts were an undignified pastry, she told him, lacking the stateliness of muffins, or the secret shame of cinnamon buns who at least tried to live the lie they weren't really cake. Mulcahy went purple and laughed into a napkin.

They left the bakery and made their way through the usual small crowd that gathered when Mulcahy could be viewed through the safety of a window. Someone shouted something venomous at him from the other side of the street. The Agents ignored her and kept walking.

"Did you know it would be this bad?" Rachel took the chance; she had always been afraid to ask. He had told them they should prepare for war but at the time she had felt this was mostly rhetoric. She had changed her opinion almost immediately after they went public. Rachel still felt he couldn't have predicted how they would be treated; no one in their right mind would willingly turn themselves into a public target for this much hate.

"Yeah. It'll pass."

"You don't honestly believe that," she replied, watching the red swell among those who noticed them. *"We're the new monsters."*

"I do believe it," he said. *"Monsters don't exist. We want them to, because enemies are convenient, but sustaining a delusion takes a lot of effort. It's easier to forget. In 1826, my great-great-grandfather was beaten to death for the crime of being Irish. Forty years ago, you wouldn't have been allowed anywhere near West Point.*

"It's a process." He sounded almost wistful; Rachel doubted he would have said any of this outside of the link. *"It's slow, it's hard, and yeah, the odds are against us. I can't even tell you how glad I am you're the only one who's almost been shot..."*

She coughed politely around a huge bite of her third doughnut.

He grinned, then gestured towards the street. The foot traffic was aggressive; Washington woke ready for battle. He took in the people around them, the rooftops, the windows covered with slitted blinds. *"There's nothing we can do about a sniper,"* he said, *"or cyanide, or a speeding car. But we are protected from discrimination, and we can work within the system to prove ourselves. In the long run, our best defense is to change public opinion, to show them we're still just people."*

"I know the party line," she said.

*"But I need you to **believe**,"* he answered in hard steel blues.

"*We have to be committed to more than lip service if we ever want to be seen as anything other than monsters.*"

She turned her face away but he was still there in her mind. "*I know it's hard,*" he said, understanding but not quite sympathetic. "*Next year, it'll be easier for us. We'll get a huge sympathy bump around March.*"

God! March! Rachel thought to herself. *It's so soon.*

OACET had always planned to allow the full details of what had happened to them during their five years off of the grid to be disclosed, but only after the public had plenty of time to recognize the cyborgs were not going to reduce the planet to a smoking crater, or render the credit ratings of their enemies to digitized dust. It seemed as though their Administration had decided the public was ready. Sometime during the next few months, a certain member of the press who had been friendly (but not fawning) to OACET would trip over a small piece of evidence that would point her in the direction of the story of the century.

And then the poop would really hit the fan.

He put a reassuring hand on her shoulder. They did not have what one might call a hugging relationship, but even if Mulcahy hadn't heard her, he had picked up on her panic.

"*I want to tell Santino,*" she said in a rush. "*I don't want him to find out through the news.*"

"*No.*" He removed his hand. "*Everyone has friends outside of the Program. Santino won't be the only one who'll be hurt at having been kept in the dark. We maintain control over this, no exceptions.*"

"*Like we keep control over Shawn, no exceptions?*"

"*That couldn't be helped,*" Mulcahy said as he looked out over the street. "*You handled it well, by the way.*"

"*But if Santino can be trusted with Shawn—*"

"*No,*" he said. It was quiet and final.

They walked a block in silence. Lulls in conversation were always awkward with other Agents. You could still feel them rattling around in your head, waiting. She groped around for a safe topic to get him to drop those hard and distant blues. *"Did you learn who let Shawn out, or how he found the razor?"*

"I have a good idea," he said. His expression, his posture, his presence in her mind hadn't changed, but he was instantly bleeding cold in reds and grays. Rumor had it that Mulcahy had searched and had come up empty but she hadn't expected this type of response; he was balanced on the edge of serious violence. Rachel was almost ten feet away before she knew she was moving.

He stopped and drew his anger back into his core, his conversational colors draining until there was little left; it was always guilt with him. Rachel took a quick breath, then calmly stepped back beside him and pretended she hadn't nearly mown down a regiment of passing accountants to get out of arm's reach.

"Sorry, Penguin," he said. *"I forgot."*

*"Have **you** been keeping up with your therapy?"* Rachel asked.

He nodded. *"I'm sorry,"* he said again. *"The Shawn incident is… It's a sore spot for me."*

They walked in silence until they turned down M Street and the First District Station came into view.

"Rachel," Mulcahy began, then stopped and pulled her out of the way of the foot traffic. *"What you're doing with the MPD, there's no way I can tell you how important it is for us. Thank you."*

"Thank me when all of this is over." Rachel looked towards the sturdy brick building. *"I can't promise I'll get this guy, and there's probably a lot of people hoping I fail."*

"Well, we Irish have a saying," he said. "May those who love us, love us. And those who don't love us, may God turn their hearts. And if He doesn't turn their hearts, may He turn their ankles so we'll know them by their limping."

Rachel laughed. She had read the abridged version on a bumper sticker a long time ago and preferred his full-length one. *"And if you're wrong and nothing ever really changes?"*

"Aim for their ankles."

She smiled and looked towards First District Station a second time, and when she turned back he was gone. Rachel could pick him out of the crowd by his core colors but the rest of him had blended into the morning masses. Quite a trick, considering. She sent him a quick wave, and Mulcahy waved back before he vanished into the day's chores.

She barged into the temporary office in the fishbowl and sat down in the same chair she had occupied yesterday, an old Army trick of validating her place in time as well as space. Santino and Jason were late. Phil said hello and the detectives each gave her a nod, and they all busied themselves in the forensics reports that had come in during the night.

Santino crawled into work ten minutes after she arrived, the sleeves on his dress shirt pushed up just enough to reveal the edge of a fresh bandage. When Zockinski pressed him for details on the asskicking, Santino said he had broken up with his girlfriend and left it at that. (Rumors of Santino's breakup coincided with Zockinski's trip to the bathroom, new opinions forming throughout the precinct of the nerd cop who dated women wild enough to wield knives.) It also gave Santino a much-needed reprieve; as they waited for Jason to saunter in on his own schedule, Santino commandeered the couch, put his jacket over his face, and dropped into a dead sleep.

Rachel and Phil left to get coffee. The break room was one of the busiest places in the building but it cleared out as soon as they walked through the door. Rachel yanked the coffee machine's cord from the outlet and dragged the machine over to the sink. No one else bothered to clean it properly and she refused to let herself suffer through coffee that tasted of soap.

"Is it always like this?" Phil asked as the officers stampeded out the door. He poured himself a cup from the pot before she emptied it. For him, coffee was coffee.

She nodded as she dumped yesterday's grinds in the trash. *"Yeah, but it's gotten worse now that there are three of us. You and Jason reminded them I was here."*

"It's pretty unbearable. This is almost Old Testament-style shunning."

"Oh, we'll survive," she replied. *"You know how it goes. Repress, ignore, endure."*

He popped in sickly yellows and grays. *"Rachel, no!"*

"Hey, those are coping skills now," she said, and pointed him towards the cupboard with the supplies. *"They've let me get through months of aggressive hazing."*

"Coping skills?" Coffee shook over the lip of his cup. *"No... No! I **won't** live that way again."*

"Calm down," she told him. *"It was supposed to be a joke. I can't help that I've got no sense of humor, remember?"*

Phil didn't reply, his colors ratcheting up from anxiety to agitation as he looked past her to the officers in the hall, so Rachel pulled out the juicy gossip as she lathered up the coffee pot. *"Speaking of coping, somebody's finally found a way to block digital feeds. Mulcahy showed me on the way to work. It's like sealing yourself in a bubble, shuts them out completely."*

"Really?" Phil seized the change of subject like a lifeline. *"Show me?"*

"I can't." She shook her head. *"He had an autoscript."*

"Oh."

She was awful with autoscripts. Phil had given her the one which allowed her to set parameters for incoming callers, so he had been deeper in her head than almost anyone else and was intimately aware they scared the everloving shit out of her.

The Agents had found themselves in the unenviable position of living with awkward words. The term "autoscript" had been stolen from programmers and hobbled by Agents to describe an aspect of their relationship with their implants. The implant was a dynamic device and was designed to evolve with its user over time, changing itself to complement its user as they navigated their environment together. With practice, Agents could eliminate the tedious process of imposing conscious control over the implant, and their shared experiences would become second nature to both.

Agents could not avoid creating autoscripts any more than someone tossed out and left to survive on the frozen tundra could avoid learning how to find food, water, and shelter. Rachel was aware she was constantly writing autoscripts herself. She and Mulcahy had created one together as they experimented with BB gun physics, and each day it was easier to find the frequency she needed for a specific task without running the full gamut.

She did not, however, know where her brain shelved the damned things.

An autoscript could be passed from one Agent to another to help them shortcut the adaptation process. A foreign autoscript would have to be handled and reshaped through use before it fit snugly into the recipient's repertoire, but giving an Agent an autoscript cut down on the time it would take to develop one from scratch: someone had used the analogy that passing an autoscript to a friend was the equivalent of handing them a preprogrammed GPS and a gas card before they set off on a cross-country trip.

Rachel knew if she could just figure out where she kept her scripts, she could give all of OACET a strong head start on learning how to see via the unseen. But finding them was the first problem. Even if she tripped over an autoscript lying around in her own head, she would have no idea how to pass it to another Agent. She barely understood what to do with those foreign autoscripts she had received; since her implant had become fully active, Rachel had accepted a grand total of two. She had practically bludgeoned these small and harmless scripts to force them to behave, smacking them around until they crept off to pack with her own native scripts somewhere in the back of her mind.

She hadn't seen those foreign scripts since they had come to her, but they worked like magic charms. Autoscripts made life easier, and she knew she should join in the fun of passing them around with the other Agents, like siblings who pooled their baseball cards. But to get an autoscript from one Agent to another, the walls had to come down, and she was happy with her walls where they were.

"Give me a few weeks and I'll get a copy to you," she sighed. *"Direct orders from Mulcahy. He told me to get my ass to school."*

"Autoscripts?" Phil guessed.

She nodded and watched the water swirl around and around the glass pot as she rinsed it. It was hypnotic; she had problems understanding water.

"They just take a little practice," he said. *"I'll bet if you accept a few more, you'll get the hang of them."*

"Do you ever..." Rachel tipped her chin up towards the fluorescent lights, the working man's substitute for the sun. *"Do you ever wonder what will happen if the implant reaches capacity? Just... you know... fills up so we're left flopping on the linoleum like tuna..."*

He laughed out loud. *"I don't think that's how it works."*

"How do you know?" She turned her back on him and prepped an extra cup for Santino.

"Because I do. Mine grows with me. You're asking if we ever run out of brain cells to store memories."

Cup, cream, sugar, done, and she wouldn't let herself look at Phil. *"Who says we don't? We know next to nothing about how the human brain works, and we went cramming all sorts of garbage into it."* Unbidden came a memory of early childhood and the unforgettable sensation of shoving a crayon up her nose as far as it would go.

Phil chuckled as he rubbed his own nose to take the sting of preschool out of it. *"I think this is one of those things you have to take on faith."*

"Faith?" She gave a dark laugh. *"No."*

Phil poked her with his free hand.

"Fine." Rachel finished setting up the machine and got a fresh pot brewing, then unbuttoned her left shirt sleeve and pushed it up her forearm. Physical contact had to be involved for the transfer. No one knew why, the educated guess being that the implant was itself partially organic and maybe biology

had to be involved with the process.

Phil took her wrist, his fingers resting against her pulse. *"Are you sure you're okay with this?"*

"Of course!" She smiled brightly.

"You're not," he said aloud, and pulled his hand away. "It's okay. Maybe after work."

"When we're exhausted from a full day of mind games with a wacko killer? No. Come on," she said, and snapped her fingers twice, quick. "Show me. I promise I'll pay attention this time."

Rachel hadn't bothered to track how those two foreign autoscripts had come to her. Josh had given her the first script in his own inimitable way, grabbing her face and shouting: "My mind to your mind! My thoughts to your thoughts!" By the time she was done laughing, the new script was lodged comfortably in her cellular chemistry.

Phil had introduced her to the wrist technique when he had passed her the second script. When she had realized his technique was more intrusive than Josh's, Rachel had retreated to the Agent's equivalent of closing her eyes and thinking of England: she had flipped off visuals and used the implant to stream acid rock directly into her auditory processes until the transfer was done.

"Don't go gray on my account," she said, seeing Phil's conversational colors fall. *"If I have to learn, I have to learn."*

She held out her left hand. Phil paused, then moved to find her pulse again.

"What script do you want?" he asked.

"Surprise me."

It all happened in the mind; there was no physical sensation beyond the pressure of an unfamiliar hand on her arm. Then came a nagging thought, but instead of pressing out, like the drive to go clean the toilet or pick up milk at the store, it pushed in. Rachel tried to follow the new autoscript as it took on form and function, and watched it as it leapt the barrier she had put up to preserve a small part of her mind from the voices of the link.

Damn, she thought. All of this time her autoscripts had been hiding out in the one part of herself she thought was still her own. Nothing was sacred.

And then, just as she thought she had discovered where she stored them, the new autoscript stopped being separate from her and vanished.

"I lost it," she said. "I saw it come in and then it was gone."

"Run it and check to see if it took," Phil said as he removed his hand. "That's a baby script, absolute basic level. It's a locator for any Agent within a specific radius. I had it set to a thousand feet when I passed it to you, so just do a search for me and see who else pops up."

"Sure." Rachel dropped her connection to Phil, then searched for his GPS as if he wasn't standing beside her. Phil's position came up, along with Jason's, one block south.

"Jason's almost here," she said, amazed.

Phil smiled. "Train it a little and you'll know exactly where everyone is without having to do an individual search. It's really handy. I think you're probably the only Agent left who didn't have a copy."

"Yeah, I think Josh was nagging me about this script last night. Thanks."

"No problem. Do you think you can pass it back to me?"

She leaned back and closed her eyes (*oh, habits*), and searched for anything alien or new. "No," she said as she shook her head. "It's gone."

"It's not," he said. "But I don't know how to help you find it. Mine are… They're just *there.* I can put a finger on them without trying."

Rachel moved to the coffee machine and started pouring. *"Mulcahy wants me to package up all of my perception scripts."*

"Man, I'll help in any way I can with that. To do what you can do?" Phil whistled dramatically and held out his cup for a top-off. *"That'd be incredible. Would guarantee a place for me with Andrews and the bomb unit, too."*

"Want to explore?"

"*Hell yes,*" he said. He grinned and put his mug down. "*Link me in.*"

She did, and Phil shut his eyes as the building shifted from concrete and metal to a chromatic spectrum. Level after level of mass and void and mass again, with people throughout, each painted in a chaos of color and texture… "I don't know how you understand any of this," Phil said, smiling. "It's unreal."

"Practice, practice, practice," she replied. "*Can you see how I'm doing it?*"

"*Nope. I can't follow your process.*" He opened his eyes, then squeezed them shut again as information from two sets of visual stimuli broke within him. He groaned and dropped from their link. "Whoa. That's… That's too much."

He staggered over to a chair and put his head on the table while his senses realigned.

"You okay?"

"Remind me to wear a blindfold next time," he said into the cave of his arms. He sat up and blinked furiously. "Why is everything green? That's definitely not right."

"Your mind is playing tricks on you. Give it a second."

"*Yeah, there it goes. I wonder,*" he said, "*you ever think maybe the reason you can't find your perception scripts is because they're part of you?*"

She had. Every autoscript became native, but hers had been formed by trial and fire and nearly breaking her nose on every wall in her old California apartment. Autoscripts were by their nature supplemental; her perception scripts were unique. No one else in the Program had written scripts to replace something they had lost.

"*I should still be able to find the others,*" she said. "*Even the one you just passed to me is gone.*"

"*Maybe you should practice with Jason.*"

She stared at Phil in open disgust.

Phil shrugged. "*I know, I know, but you might resist his scripts, and they'd be easier to track.*"

I'd rather swallow broken glass. She wasn't sure if she had intended for Phil to pick up on that thought, but he smiled into his coffee anyway.

"*Just an idea,*" Phil said. "*Or maybe we can try with a more complex script next time. It might take longer to disappear.*"

"*Let's do that instead.*" Rachel turned them towards their office, where they joined up with Jason in the hallway and entered as a group. Zockinski gave Jason a half-handed wave. Rachel went over to the couch and poked Santino's legs with her shoe until he growled and moved so she had space to sit down, and then she poked him with her elbow until he lurched upright.

"How much sleep did you get?" she asked in a perky cheerleader's voice.

Santino glared at her with bleary eyes. "Five minutes less than I could have had."

She held out his coffee and he purred something about eternal gratitude as he cupped it in stiff hands.

"Did you check the forums?" Rachel asked. The previous evening, she had followed him around the Internet as he had prodded the maker community to action. She had periodically visited his posts to check if new replies had come in: if so, whether they contained any information good enough to justify waking up the task force. They had, and they hadn't. The replies were nothing short of paranoid rambling and she wanted Santino's opinion before she wrote the whole thing off as a false lead. "And don't bother lying. The answer's no."

"Then why bother asking?" Santino reached into his briefcase and pulled out his laptop.

"Because I'm reminding you how you're a cop and this is your job and I think you should take a look at what they posted. They claim to have some info on our guy."

His colors brightened as he came fully awake. "No kidding?"

"Yeah, but it's all... Ah, look for yourself."

Santino loaded the forums and scrolled down. His original posts had exploded, the words *liar* or *fraud* peppering each response. "Eric Witcham? That's not possible."

"I saw his name come up on a few threads," she said. She hadn't bothered to read the messages in detail once they were dragged down by the surreal. "Who's Eric Witcham?"

"A dead man," Santino replied.

"Yes, thank you. I noticed that. But why do they think he's back?" She stuck her fingers out straight and let her eyes roll back as her head drooped to the side. "We're chasing zombies?"

"Wouldn't that be fun? No, Glazer's plagiarizing Witcham's signature. The tech community is pissed. Witcham was a legend.

"Hey guys," he called out to the others, who were still poking through the reports from Forensics. "We've got some feedback on the signature.

"Okay," he said, skimming a biography of Witcham at lightning speed while he spoke. "Here's the abridged version. Glazer is using a maker's mark unique to a man named Eric Witcham. We would have gotten responses last night as soon as I put up the posts, but Witcham hadn't been active since 2001 and he died in 2004, so anyone who isn't a community veteran wouldn't know of him. When he was active, he was the leading authority in pretty much everything related to tech. He gave lectures, he wrote textbooks, you name it. His specialty was encryption and he did a lot of work in biological enhancement…"

Santino looked up from his laptop to where Rachel sat, Phil and Jason standing behind her. "Guys, some of his research was used to build your implants. He was working on the first-generation tech right before he disappeared."

Another OACET connection, Rachel thought. *Glazer did his homework.*

Then an idea niggled at her, and she did a quick search. *"Guess who his employer was,"* she said to Phil and Jason.

She wasn't sure if one or both answered: *"Hanlon Technologies,"* but Phil bled white and Jason tore open in reds.

"Add it to the list, guys," she told them. *"It's got nothing to do with the here-and-now."*

"And there's no doubt he's dead?" Zockinski asked. "We still haven't found the assailant from the gas station, the older man."

"Um... No, Witcham is definitely dead," Santino found the right link and scrolled down through the news report on Witcham's death. "Murdered, actually. They found him in the trunk of a junked car. He had been killed about six months before, so they had to ID the body through DNA and dental."

"Is Glazer is his son?" Rachel hadn't seen any mention of family in Witcham's obituary, but it was worth asking.

"I don't think so," Santino said. "There's always the chance, but he never married and there's no record he had any children. It's more likely that Glazer worked with him, or maybe was a student of his when Witcham was still teaching."

"Or Glazer just admired Witcham's work and plagiarized his signature," Rachel said. The detectives agreed with her—they only considered zebras after every horse had been shot—but Hill still went to update Sturtevant and to assign a few officers to track down any possible relationship between Witcham and a man who would now be in his early thirties.

"So, dead end, literally," Santino said, and pushed his laptop aside. "I guess we've learned Glazer knows his history, but that gets us nowhere. Did Forensics find anything?"

"No," Zockinski rifled through the stack of files and threw one to Santino. "Of the three sets of prints from his apartment, one belongs to his superintendent and the other two are unknowns. I'm thinking his prints and DNA aren't in the system."

"Strange," Rachel said, reading over Zockinski's shoulder from her place on the couch. "Hill and I would have sworn Glazer was military."

"Nope," Zockinski said. "He's not in their databases."

The huddle broke and they fell back to their tasks. It was a repeat of the previous evening; after the run on the bank and Glazer's apartment, they had nothing to do but wait for something to break. They had been counting on Forensics finding something they could use as a new starting point, but the tests that were already back had yielded nothing.

Still…

The flutter of motion through the walls drew her attention first, followed by a quick change of colors which jumped from person to person. Bad news moved almost preternaturally fast and she saw it seep into the building, those outside of their office shifting from the colors of early morning boredom into the oranges and reds as fast as spoken words.

Rachel realized she had cocked her head to the side as though she could hear the growing anxiety. Her partner was watching her. "What?" Santino whispered.

"Something's wrong," she replied.

She found Hill in the mess, plowing through a group of people who flashed panic and anxiety, each of them crowding him with questions until he managed to break away.

She had the door open for him when arrived.

He stared down at her, then looked over her head at the rest of the team. "We need to go."

THIRTEEN

She was glad the dinosaurs were dead. Not because of the teeth or the tonnage, but for the selfish joy she stole from their bones. Rachel checked to make sure the security guard was busy with Zockinski and she leaned out over the glass partition to stroke the spine of the closest skeleton. Her fingers lightly brushed the pebbly-cool surface; stone, but not stone, and somehow still alive in the way of all inanimate wonder. Rachel flipped the frequencies on her implant to read the plaque *(Camptosaurus, herbivore)*, and looked around the room to see if she could manhandle the Tyrannosaur before getting caught.

Sadly, no. A child too young to have wandered off from her school group watched her with a scowl.

"...n't do hat," the girl said. She was in the final stages of finding her new front teeth, but some of her consonants were still missing.

"Shh," Rachel whispered conspiratorially. "I'm a cop."

"Sill sln't do hat."

Kid would change her mind if I let her pet the T-rex, Rachel muttered to herself. She flipped open her suit jacket to put her badge on display and walked the girl over to a gang of children wearing matching shirts which branded them as property of the Essex County school system. She passed the girl off to a harried teacher's aide and told the woman in dark terms that she was to keep her students in sight at all times. There was a thinly veiled *or else!* in there, and Rachel made sure the aide saw her badge and its hallmark stamp of OACET green before she stalked off. Sometimes it was good to be a monster.

She turned back to her post and caught Zockinski sneaking a soft pat on the thigh of the Triceratops. He was warm blues over golds, his colors almost reverent, and Rachel thought maybe it wasn't a fluke that he had ended up with her in the Hall of Paleontology.

The call had come in to First District Station at seven in the morning, the man from the Department of Homeland Security claiming that someone had hacked the Smithsonian. The same nineteen images kept rotating through the security system, he said, locations from the Institution's nineteen core museums and parks. Each image had two names written beneath them in an elegant copperplate script, set off in a decorative frame. The images formed a list of people and places; most of those on the list were cops, but the members of the task force had been included. Detective Hill and Phil Netz were sent to stalk the Renwick Gallery, while Santino and Jason Atran were given an especially picturesque location on the Castle grounds.

And she and Zockinski had pulled the dinosaurs.

There was no evidence whatsoever to connect the hijacking of the security system to Glazer, but the Metropolitan Police Department was done coddling coincidence. The gut reaction had been to interpret the images as an overt threat and to shut the Smithsonian down for the day, but saner heads had prevailed and had decided there was no reason to take anything other than precautionary action. The museums would remain open, and security would be increased. Including those thirty-eight persons named in each of those nineteen rotating images.

Chief Sturtevant had raged: the task force had been moving so quickly that this was most likely a delaying tactic designed to buy Glazer some time. Sturtevant had said, loudly, he wouldn't allow his team to waste an entire day standing around waiting for Glazer to make the next move, that Zockinski, Hill, and the rest would be put to better use following known trails than standing around, genitalia in hand, waiting for the unknown.

He had been overruled.

Thirty-five personnel from First MPD and three Agents had marched with slow and measured steps to their designated locations. They weren't alone. The parks and museums were crawling with cops in plainclothes. Attendance among younger and middle-aged males was up, the janitorial service was ridiculously overstaffed, and tourists were ushered into groups with guides who stammered and had to consult their notes.

Hours of this.

Her early morning had disappeared into mid-afternoon, but apart from the feeling that someone had chained her in place, Rachel was enjoying herself. As far as stakeouts went, the Museum of Natural History was a far cry above the typical parked car or seedy diner. She had told herself she needed to visit the Smithsonian at least once a week since moving to D.C., but it had never popped on her to-do list. She needed to come back when she wasn't working, maybe take some time to appreciate the collections and the building's gliding lines of architecture without worrying about whether she was lined up in a sniper's telescopic sight.

And working with Zockinski had been astonishingly pleasant. The first few hours were like standing in barbed wire, as they didn't so much as move for fear of getting cut. After that, boredom and the ever-present swarms of students had blunted their edges. It was impossible for Rachel to maintain an active snit among the dinosaurs, as wave after wave of children swept into the hall in a prismatic riot, followed by a crash of emotion breaking over them as they saw the raw stuff of dreams.

Or nightmares: some of the younger ones plunged into terror. Rachel and Zockinski had made a game out of picking those kids who would break down in tears. They had played for money until they realized nothing was changing hands; they were each too good at reading the crowd. When he asked, she had straight-up lied about being trained by the Army to read microexpressions, and Zockinski eventually let slip that he had worked as a guide in this very hall during his college summer breaks.

He came back towards her and they made the rounds again. Ten times an hour they walked the circumference of the room, checking for anything new or out of place. Rachel had run so many deep scans she was familiar with the gobs of chewed gum shoved into almost every available cranny, some so old they were practically fossils themselves.

"They're shutting this place down soon," Zockinski said as they crested the stairs and resumed their vantage point on the balcony.

"The Smithsonian?" she scoffed. "I don't think so."

He shook his head. "This exhibit. Some rich guy gave them thirty-five million to fix up the dinosaur hall."

She whistled. "That's a lot of new dinosaurs."

"No new ones. They already have the best in the world," Zockinski said, looking down at the Triceratops. "They're just going to repair the hall and update the displays. Place'll be closed for five years."

Rachel leaned on the rail and watched the field trip kids rocket up and down the aisles, shrieking at a decibel that would have made James Joyce hastily rewrite his definition of God. Some of those kids would be headed to high school when the hall reopened, she realized. And there would be a good part of an entire generation who would miss out on this experience completely, five years of disappointed field trippers who would come to the museum only to find a barrier of painted plywood between them and the lost world.

Five years was an eternity.

Five years could change everything…

Zockinski was still talking. Rachel shook off her malaise and asked, "Sorry, what?"

"I said this used to be called the Hall of Extinct Monsters."

Rachel smiled and made a note to tell Mulcahy. "I love that. It's poetry."

"But it wasn't accurate," he said. "They've remodeled the hall a couple of times to make sure it all keeps up with the science, and they've always changed the name. They keep the same dinosaurs, but those're changed too, put in new poses or on new stands.

"You used to be able to walk under that," he said, and pointed at the gigantic skeleton of the Diplodocus. "Back before they remodeled the hall in the Sixties." The sauropod stretched the length of the room, blocked off from the tourists except for the skull suspended sixteen feet above the ground. It dangled like a low-hanging fruit and the bolder children would leap up to grab it, then squeal when they crashed back down to earth.

"What's it like?" she asked. He looked down at her in curious yellows. "Oh come on, you know you've done it. After hours, no guards..."

He didn't blush but his conversational colors did, and she chuckled. "Okay, not quite what I meant but yay for you. Did she complain about the fake rocks?"

"They never did," he said. "It was a really good job. *Summer* job," he clarified as she burst out laughing.

Their rapport was fragile and they were going out of their way to avoid carrying topics with any weight. Cyborgs were taboo, as were politics. They had mainly stuck to work: good stories were currency in law enforcement, and everyone banked away their best for situations like this. She wove some tales from her ongoing war with Mrs. Wagner into the mix—her neighbor was universally relatable; as far as Rachel knew, every street in America had a slightly racist, extremely homophobic gossip who kept her nose pressed against the window—and Zockinski retaliated with the tale of his epic battle with his homeowner's association when he tried to build a tree house for his daughters.

"Rachel?"

She sighed quietly. "One sec," she told Zockinski. "I've got a call." She turned away and tried to miss the change in his colors that came up whenever he remembered what she was, and joined Phil in the link. *"What's up?"*

"There's a courier coming towards us. Jason says he sees one, too. How about you?"

"Hang on." She glanced at the hall and saw nothing. *"Not yet. Let me go long-range."*

"The guys say something's happening," she said to Zockinski, and expanded her sixth sense to take in the first floor of the museum and the street. The surge of new information crashed into her and she grabbed on to the balcony's railing to keep her balance; she had misjudged the size of the building and had pulled too much, too quickly. "We're looking for a courier service. Wait…" she said, as a distinctive brown truck pulled up to the curb. "South entrance."

Zockinski radioed the undercover crew and every adult in the room was suddenly preoccupied with little plaques and large skeletons.

The courier was in his early twenties and resentful. He walked into the hall and searched the faces until he located Rachel and Zockinski. He stomped up the stairs when he realized they wouldn't come down from the balcony to meet him.

"Here," the courier said, jabbing the corner of a rigid cardboard envelope into Zockinski's gut.

"Hill's always saying how some people can't tell I'm a cop," Zockinski said to Rachel.

"Seems pretty clear to me," she said, and smiled at the courier.

The courier blanched; assaulting an officer was a law writ wide.

The handwritten note on the package still smelled faintly of permanent marker. It read: OPEN IMMEDIATELY.

And in smaller print below: NOT A BOMB.

"Don't you hate those weeks where your life revolves around whether things are, or are not, bombs?" Rachel asked Zockinski as she waved over an undercover officer posing as a security guard. She set the officer on the courier with due prejudice. One did not shoot the messenger, but one certainly did lock him up in a small room and ask him pointed questions.

She took the envelope from Zockinski and flipped it over a few times in her hands, looking for a way in that wouldn't disturb evidence trapped in the sticky bits.

Zockinski told her to wait. "We have to call Forensics," he said, and took out his cell.

She glared at him and pulled her badge off of her belt. Someone had added a slight hook to the crest and it served dual purpose as a letter opener. She threaded the leading edge under the flap on the envelope and ripped it open.

"Hey!"

"Oops," Rachel said. "I'm not of your police community and am unfamiliar with your strange, alien ways. It's just a few pieces of paper," she added. "No electronics, no unusual chemicals or dust." She ignored her bruised knees and knelt on the thin carpet to shake the contents from the cardboard package.

"Wait," Zockinski took a plastic grocery bag out of his coat pocket and spread it flat across the ground. "We're going to catch hell for this."

"Sometimes dirt is just dirt," Rachel muttered. In her soldier's heart, she agreed with Edwards; the Forensics God demanded too much from its followers. "This is more likely to be time-sensitive than anything else."

She carefully tapped the back of the envelope so the stack of paper slid onto the plastic. A couple of cards, covered in black dots slightly smaller than dimes...

Zockinski, father of two young girls, went white.

"Call Hill," she said, giving Zockinski a task before his fears rose up and pulled him under. "Tell him to give the package to Phil. If Phil says it's clean, have them open it right away."

She reached out to her partner. *"Santino?"* Rachel asked when he answered the phone. *"The National Child ID Program. Does it apply to D.C. or just the states?"*

"D.C.'s included," he replied. "Why?"

"Trying to narrow the search," she said. *"Have you opened your package?"*

"No, are you nuts? We've got Forensics on the way."

Rachel stretched her mind across the distance between them. Her implant and her sixth sense might be infinite but her mind was not; the Castle grounds were directly across from the Museum of Natural History and were at the very edge of her ability to make sense out of raw data.

"Walk towards me and hold up the package," she said. *"I need to scan it before you open it."*

"Forensics is five minutes away."

"And they're bringing an hour of tests. Santino... Ours had ten-cards." She closed her eyes but couldn't look away from the happy comic strip characters spot-printed around ten individual boxes, each box with a black dot in the center.

The pieces of the conversation clicked. "Kids' fingerprints," he said in a dead voice, and she heard the sound of ripping, with Jason shouting in the background.

"Don't! Let me scan—" Rachel began, but Santino cut her off.

"Ours too. Rachel... I have three cards here. Three kids."

"Right now it's an implied threat," she said. *"It might be a distraction. These children might be sitting in a math test as we speak. Turn the scene over to the security detail and meet us back at District Station as soon as you can. Tell Jason to coordinate with Phil; I need to calm down Zockinski."*

The detective was off in the corner, a riot of fear in yellows and grays. He had his phone pressed to his ear as he left a quiet message.

She walked over to him as he hung up. "Your daughters," she said. "Where are they supposed to be?"

"With my wife," he looked down to where the security staff was herding a mob of protesting children from the hall. "They've got morning kindergarten... They should be home but she's not picking up."

Rachel lowered her voice. "I can check on them," she said, and he flared a different sort of yellow, uncertain but hopeful. "You give me your wife's phone number, and I can go to her cell." She pulled her tablet from her bag. "Or I can go straight to your house if you tell me your address. You can use me as your eyes, like we did at Glazer's apartment yesterday. You tell me know where to go and what to look for, and we'll see if your family is safe."

She took a step away from him; she didn't recognize the sudden burst of red, and reds outside of passion were never good. "But if I do this, even if you give me permission, this'll be a huge violation, you understand? There's no guarantee that I won't pop in on your wife when she's cooking, driving..." She let the ideas dangle and hoped he understood. Rachel was the ultimate Peeping Tom and he would be turning her loose on his family.

He did. He closed his eyes and weighed his choices. "Five minutes," he finally said.

She nodded and shoved the tablet back in her purse, willing to wait if he was. They slipped the cards back into their envelope, bundled it up in Zockinski's plastic bag, and left at a run.

They caught up with Hill on the old dry lawn of the Mall and traded their sedan to an officer with a conveniently-parked patrol car. Hill drove them back to First District Station, siren blaring, while Zockinski sat in the passenger's seat and divided his calls between Sturtevant's line and his wife's voice mail.

The details were starting to trickle in and a pattern was emerging. The team back at the MPD had tracked down some of the names on the fingerprint cards, but the children they belonged to could not be easily located. Hill asked why, and Zockinski said those children were supposed to be on a field trip but the parents and teachers chaperoning them weren't answering their phones.

They stopped talking.

Hill dropped Zockinski at the front doors and they parked five floors down in the garage. The smell was rank; the ventilation system never seemed to penetrate the lowest parts of this concrete well. They kept close to the center of the garage as they hurried upwards, the void created by the split levels their only source of fresh air.

"This place is too new to be so poorly designed," Rachel said, mostly to herself.

Hill heard her. "Lowest bidder."

They reached the security doors and Hill stepped to the

side, waiting. It took her a moment to realize he wanted her to open the digital locks.

"You're kidding," she said.

He shrugged.

"You realize I can't win with you guys," she said. "I'm the biggest freak on the planet, right up until you have to grope around for your keys."

Hill went mustard yellow in surprise. He gave Rachel the same curious probing look he had used on Phil the day before in the interview room, a trace of that wine red coursing through the yellow, then took out his ID card and opened the door for her.

"Thanks," she said, stepping into the chute. She popped the lock on the second door and returned the favor.

Zockinski had acted as their vanguard, delivering theirs and Hill's packages to Sturtevant. The older detective was finishing a phone call in the hall, relief washing over him in blues.

"They're fine," Zockinski said as he hung up, then laughed. "They went to get ice cream and she forgot her cell, can you believe it?"

"Of all the days," Hill said, almost smiling.

"What's so funny?" Rachel asked.

"My wife's a diabetic," Zockinski said, then shook his head and chuckled. "Doesn't keep anything sweet in the house. The girls have to wear her down for weeks before she gives in."

Sturtevant and a handful of other high-rankers were waiting for them in the task force's glass fishbowl. They entered the office and Rachel saw the six bureau chiefs were wearing Sturtevant's core colors over a layer of reds. She would have loved to have been an out-of-body fly on the wall when Sturtevant tore the MPD's administration apart for letting half of their finest officers loiter around the Smithsonian while their suspect snapped children up off of the street.

Rachel picked a quiet corner and fell straight into parade rest. The cards and envelopes that had come in with Zockinski were waiting for Forensics in two clean Tupperware bins. She noticed a stack of identical containers off to the side and realized each of the teams sent into the field had gotten the same type of package.

Her new autoscript put Phil and Jason in the same car as Santino's cell, barely half a block away and closing fast. The adrenaline rush was starting to fade and doubt was stealing its way in, helped along by the six bureau chiefs sneaking quick and angry glances at her. Someone was always at fault in cases like these, and it was easy to hang the outsiders. In fact, now that she thought about it, it was amazing it hadn't happened before now. *Hello OACET, you're early...*

Hill tapped her on the shoulder and pointed her towards the empty chairs on the other side of the room.

"The handwriting on the packages matches samples from Glazer's apartment," Sturtevant said to her and Hill as they found their seats. "We're willing to bet he's our guy. If we're wrong, you're gonna be another day behind, but..." the Chief stared daggers at his counterparts as he spoke, "...that's not your fault. We all agree these missing kids are the priority."

Rachel closed her mind against the image of dull red brushstrokes across white marble. Dead was dead and children were children, but Maria Griffin deserved better.

"We don't know much right now, but what we do know is that the kids named on these cards are missing," Sturtevant said, and tapped the side of the closest bin. "They were on a field trip from a school in Virginia. Guess where they were headed."

This might as well have been a rhetorical question. Another batch of kids had been robbed of their chance to see the dinosaurs.

"The principal sent us their itinerary," Sturtevant continued. "They were supposed to start at the Castle, then split up into groups to cover other parts of the Smithsonian. We're still checking the ten-cards from the other teams, but they all seem to be enrolled at the same school. The principal can't find the buses, the drivers, any of the chaperones..."

He paused. "Worst-case scenario is a hundred people are

missing. That's a little more than the maximum capacity for two buses. The principal thinks it's probably less than that, and he's getting us the full list."

"GPS?" Rachel asked.

"Not working. Their school district invested in embedded GPS and vehicle diagnostics for their fleet, but these two buses aren't on the grid anymore.

"And," he continued with a fresh surge of red, "kidnapping is a federal crime, so we've just lost jurisdiction."

He looked at Rachel when he said this, a piercing bright blue filtering through his anger and pointing directly at her. She had seen this phenomenon before, always when Mulcahy or Josh were hoping the person they speaking about was smart enough to sift through their words to find the hidden meaning.

She nodded, very slightly, to let him know she understood, and his red faded at the edges.

"The FBI is on their way." Sturtevant rose and walked towards the door. "They're going to want everything we have on Glazer, so pack it up and put a bow on it. They're taking control, but they're still our next-door neighbors so we need to stay friendly."

He left to meet the FBI at the front door, most of First MPD's bureau chiefs dogging his heels. Two stayed behind to start boxing up the case files, but Rachel drove them out by crowding them and asking, over and over again, if they were *sure* she couldn't help? They fled as Santino and the other Agents entered, awkwardly pretending Phil and Jason didn't exist while still trying to use the door at the same time.

Rachel held out a Tupperware container and Santino placed an envelope identical to hers into it, holding the open end by its corners as he carefully laid it flat on the bottom of the bin.

"Hope you didn't pamper it the whole ride home," she said. "This is a forensics dead end."

He shrugged, sick purples and grays as she placed his bin next to hers. "Data is data."

Hill clipped his phone back to his belt. "The others'll be

here soon," he said, and began spreading the bins out across the table. "Everybody got the same package."

"Fine," Zockinski said. "Let's turn this over to the FBI and get out of here. The paperwork'll keep until tomorrow."

"God, what a quitter," Rachel said.

He looked at her, annoyed. "We're done. This went federal."

"Thing is," she said, grinning at him and making a fast circle with her finger which encompassed Phil, Jason, and herself, "so did we."

Santino brightened. "The charter."

She nodded. "They can't keep us out."

Long before anyone underwent brain surgery, the OACET charter was written in such a way so the cyborgs wouldn't be limited by jurisdiction. As the Program was designed to cross the boundaries between federal agencies, its charter granted Agents the authority to go wherever they wanted, to intrude in those affairs which caught their interest, so long as they perceived a valid need. It was the type of back-door political shenanigans that, like OACET itself, should never have been approved.

Rachel did her best to pretend this part of their charter didn't exist. Better to follow her agreement with the MPD and take herself out of an investigation than force herself into it and risk a jury tossing the case. Those few other Agents working alongside law enforcement followed similar policies, and anyone outside of OACET was generally unaware an Agent could seize a case on a whim.

But Sturtevant had known. At least, that's what Rachel was betting on. She hoped she had read him correctly: it would be awkward if she pulled rank on the FBI when he had meant instead that Rachel should pass the case to the Feds and take the rest of the week off.

"We're back in the game?" Hill asked.

"We were never out of it," she told him. "The FBI'll just try to convince us we can't play in their court."

The other teams started to trickle in, dropping their

packages in the bins before leaving for the break room or clustering in groups to gossip. Rachel moved to her makeshift desk and started shoving the untidy but well-organized files into neat and abhorrently chaotic stacks for the FBI.

Zockinski came towards her, his autumn orange caught under a prism of reds, grays, and a thin but beautiful blue. He leaned towards her. "About what you said before," he whispered. "What you offered to do for my family…"

She shook her head. "Don't mention it," she replied softly. "I mean it—don't mention it. The only reason I brought it up was because we didn't know if Glazer had your kids. It's something I'd never do otherwise, and I feel filthy for suggesting it, so do me a favor and let's pretend it never happened."

Rachel turned her back on him and stormed off to the ladies' room, making a show of rubbing her upper arms as she left. Behind her, his reds faded and the blue running through him bloomed, and she quickly scratched her nose to hide her smile before remembering he wouldn't be able to see it as she walked away.

She felt awful for playing Zockinski so soon after they had found some common ground, but she had been sent to First District Station to make allies, not friends.

The suggestion to pop in on his family hadn't bothered her. Rachel's internal compass pointed somewhere other than due north, but the planners at OACET had told her that her purpose at the MPD was to show through word and deed that Agents were governed by integrity. She was absolutely fine with this: she knew the value of order, and that was a good enough reason to throw her full weight behind the law. (Better than most, actually. She had no idea how seemingly rational people could claim to have a strong moral code and still go about their average workaday lives; everything was a contradiction if you picked at it.) Rachel followed the letter of the law so closely she was a blight among law clerks and officers alike, and was happy to do so as long as this guaranteed they would each swear up, down, and sideways that she was such an outstanding example of good conduct they had considered drowning her in the sink.

But she also couldn't ignore the value of a co-conspirator. Zockinski had been there at Glazer's apartment and had seen her search for things unseen; if his kids had been taken and she hadn't made the offer, he would have never forgiven her. That Rachel would ask him—quietly, secretly—if he wanted her to do this thing that wasn't technically illegal or unethical but was still certainly both would do more to bind Zockinski to her than if she had stood idly by.

Ah well, she sighed to herself. It wasn't as though Zockinski would ever find out.

When she retraced her steps to the task force office, she found the windows jammed in black and blue suits. The FBI had arrived. Apparently they had decided to hold the briefing in the fishbowl instead of one of the conference rooms. Rachel took this as a compliment; she had arranged the visuals and the timeline covering most of the back wall herself. If you cannot bring the presentation of the crime scenes to Muhammad…

She walked in and took the vacant folding chair next to Jason, nodding pleasantly at the FBI agent seated on her other side. He looked up from his phone and quickly appraised her with a little bit of lusty red, then recognized her and went vividly gray.

The door snapped open and a woman in her early fifties and her hair in a shoulder-length brunette bob walked in, Sturtevant and the rest of First MPD's bureau chiefs following close behind.

Everybody told themselves they could command a room by entering it. Rachel, who routinely bumped elbows with politicians and generals, had met a grand total of four people who could do this without trying; one of them had walked her to work that morning. The rest were con artists. Heavy steps, quick movements, words just a little too precise, these were tricks they used to set themselves apart from the rabble. Special agent-in-charge Charlotte Gallagher's technique was to enter a room and say her name as she cleared the threshold, as if she were getting something essential out of the way so they could then focus on the trivial.

Gallagher wore her confidence like armor and had likely earned it; the FBI wouldn't have trusted this case to green wood. She was exceptionally polite but her message was clear: kidnapping was a federal crime, and kidnapping on such a large scale demanded an immediate response. "What we have here is not as much an investigation," she told them, "as a rescue mission."

Rachel pulled up Gallagher's service record and skimmed it while Gallagher gave a status report. Rachel could have delivered the exact same speech herself, as no progress had been made on locating their best suspect, no progress had been made on locating the buses, and approximately sixty children and twenty adults had gone missing, names coming soon.

It was unnerving to realize the FBI knew nothing more than the MPD. All of those resources and Glazer was still a cypher.

Then Gallagher segued into the standard FBI boilerplate about how the Metropolitan Police Department was a valuable asset and they would still play a large role in the investigation, but as this had evolved into a mass kidnapping and there was no proof the victims had ever crossed the D.C. city lines? Well, Gallagher was sure the members of the MPD understood this phase of the case was now out of their jurisdiction.

Liar. The dimples were there; Gallagher knew. Rachel looked to Sturtevant, who caught her eye and nodded.

Okay then, she thought.

Gallagher wound down her quick speech by assigning tasks and setting check-in times for updates, then ended with the perfunctory: "Does anybody have any questions?"

"I'm assuming you want my team to drive separately?" Rachel asked. On the far side of Jason, Santino went smug pink. "We'll stay out of your way as much as we can."

Gallagher tinged orange in annoyance, but to her credit she didn't play dumb. "Agent Peng, I trust my men, and I try to keep a bare minimum of personnel in the field. Do you really think your presence will be necessary?"

Has been so far, Rachel thought, but instead she repeated, "We'll make sure we stay out of your way."

Then Gallagher made the mistake of trying to stare her down.

Rachel waited, smiling politely.

She had no problem maintaining the illusion of social eye contact. The brief passing glance, the brush of eyes during casual conversation, these little moments of humanity were easily preserved via the visual frequencies of her implant. But she was careful to keep all contact short because the longer it went on, the more the other person began to suspect that something about Rachel was... *off.* And that's when their colors usually wrapped tight around them like a shield, because everyone knew that the eyes were the windows to the soul and... well... that meant...

(Her windows might be broken but her soul was just fine, thank you very much.)

Rachel had an entire arsenal of her own tricks, and most of those were much more fun than a staring contest. But this particular trick was the most effective. So Rachel sat, legs crossed daintily at the expense of her bruised and screaming knees, as the woman's strong blues started to flicker and run orange.

Oh, little alpha dog, Rachel thought, smiling kindly at her. *Don't waste your time barking at me.*

Rachel stood up and Gallagher stepped backwards, then recovered as she realized the Agent wasn't coming at her but was walking towards the door. Rachel opened it in time for the young officer who had been sprinting down the hallway to come in without breaking her stride. The officer searched for Sturtevant in the crowd, then sidestepped Gallagher to hand him a packet of papers.

Chief Sturtevant flipped through the stack. "We've got their names," he said. "There are a total of seventy-two missing. Eighteen adults, the rest are kids. And..."

He flipped to the last page, skimmed it, and said: "And the Virginia State Police found the abandoned buses about a half-hour south of D.C. The vehicles are empty, but they left one teacher behind as a witness."

Sturtevant glanced up at the young officer, annoyed. "Never bury the lede."

FOURTEEN

Two school buses had been driven straight off of the road and into one of Virginia's over-ripened corn fields. Coupled with the corn, the ridge between the field and the road had done a fair job of hiding the buses from sight; then again, anyone driving past would have seen the neat cluster of yellow and assumed nothing out of the ordinary. *Howdy kids, come to see the cows?*

The rural highway was narrow and Hill parked as far off to the side as possible without rolling the SUV into the ditch. On the high side of the vehicle, Rachel tried to push the door open and found gravity working against her. She gave the door a hard shove and caught it with her foot, then lowered herself down.

It was hot, it was humid, it was nasty. *August in the South,* Rachel mused, her mind roaming across the nearby field and through the yellow buses. School started early here, the students locked away from the summer heat. She followed the edge of the road to where the vehicles had left it, both buses driven down into a ditch and across two bundles of railroad ties before going up and over the crest of the hill. The lash straps holding the railroad ties had been cut apart and scattered across the field to slow down any who followed; these were engulfed by the FBI's forensics team and would not be put into practical use again. On the far side of the ditch, her long-legged partner held out his good hand and helped her jump across the worst of it; blown trash and scraps of tires, and for a brief moment she found herself weightless over the husk of what might have once been a deer.

They staggered up the trail through the broken brush. The buses were parked side by side, a normal, routine sight except for the corn and the crows. They were far enough away so the people swarming around them seemed child-sized; Santino went purple-gray as he gave a silent sigh.

A lone figure was sitting in the back of an ambulance, surrounded by a tight knot of FBI and paramedics. Rachel pushed a fast scan through the crowd. The witness was a young woman, slightly heavy and extremely pretty. Her features and her core colors were somehow familiar, and she sat motionless as Gallagher leaned towards her and tried to coax a response.

Good luck with that, Rachel thought. The witness's surface colors were flat and layered between whites and grays. Shock, maybe, definitely some sort of trauma. Gallagher pressed the witness's hands around a bottle of water, encouraging her to drink... Rachel stumbled over a small hillock and she yanked her sixth sense away from the ambulance to focus on the knobby path.

Their small group hung back at the edges and watched. Gallagher's team was efficient. Their SAC had been right when she had said extra bodies would get in the way. Every few minutes, the team from First MPD was forced to shuffle to the side as the space they had occupied was repurposed by the FBI.

"Why are we here, again?" Jason's fingers drummed against his upper arms.

"We're helping," Rachel replied.

"Ah."

There was just enough of a breeze to blow the heat around. The mosquitoes struck like clockwork, and the ticks took a particular liking to Zockinski's ankles. They had passed the point of feeling awkward when Gallagher left the ambulance and crossed the field towards them.

"Agent Peng? Do you have any experience as an interviewer?"

"Army CID," Rachel said dryly. She hated it when people pretended they hadn't been briefed.

Gallagher feigned surprise. "Oh? Good. Could I borrow you for a moment?"

The SAC started walking back towards the ambulance,

and Rachel looped Phil and Jason into her perspective as she fell into step beside her. "I'd like to send you in to talk to the witness," she said. "Her name is Ellen Lewis, she's a teacher from Culpeper County. She's been mostly unresponsive, but…" Gallagher paused. "Someone mentioned there were Agents here."

Rachel stopped dead. "Listen," she said. "If you want to use me as a scare tactic, that's fine. But not with a victim, okay?"

"No." Gallagher shook her head. "She overheard my team talking. When they brought up OACET, she showed interest, wanted to know who was here."

"Huh," Rachel scanned the ambulance again. The surface colors of the witness—*Ellen Lewis,* she corrected herself—was slightly brighter, the whites and grays less pronounced. "We've got our fair share of fanatics and groupies," Rachel said. "Maybe she's one of those."

"It's possible," Gallagher said. "I'm willing to try anything right now. You're a woman, you're her age… Try to be her friend, get her to feel safe. Be sure to remember what she says to you. We need information, and we need it as soon as possible."

Rachel took her tablet out of her purse and passed it to the older woman. "I'll do you one better," she said. "You can sit in."

They arrived at the ambulance. Rachel opened the rear door and hopped up on the gate. The paramedics in the cab up front had pulled the privacy curtains for Gallagher's interview, but every so often the fabric would bump and rustle as they checked in on their patient. The motor was running and the relative coolness of the air-conditioned interior felt as though she had entered a small little world within the greater one of the field.

Ellen Lewis was curled upright in a tight ball on the paramedics' bench, staring down at the floor. Rachel bounced her hands on the low portable stretcher to make sure it wouldn't fold up beneath her, then sat facing Lewis.

"Hey," Rachel said. "I'm Agent Peng."

Lewis had lost her last hour to the FBI's Special Agents, so she made no distinction for Rachel's title. The woman's eyes barely flicked towards Rachel before she lost interest. Her gaze fell, but touched on the green and gold badge at Rachel's hip on the way down. "OACET?" Lewis asked, focusing on Rachel for the first time.

Rachel nodded. Lewis leaned forward, then collapsed on the floor before Rachel could catch her. Lewis grabbed Rachel around her legs, sobbing into her lap.

"Ellen, right?" Rachel tried to detangle herself from the weeping woman. Ellen Lewis had lit up like Christmas when she had realized Rachel was an Agent, a warm rose glow interwoven with a hair-thin strand of that same odd teal. It was a definite improvement over the usual shirking terror but certainly no less visceral, and Rachel had no idea what it meant.

"My brother," Ellen Lewis sniffed and dabbed her eyes with her shirt cuff. "Can you call him? My phone's gone."

"Your bro—*Graham?*" Rachel felt exceptionally slow; the woman was a plump feminine version of her fraternal twin. "You're Graham's sister?"

The schoolteacher nodded, and Rachel pushed down her own surprise as she reached out through the link. Graham was working back at the mansion. He dropped everything and ran for the nearest unoccupied room when Rachel told him his sister had come within an inch of being abducted.

"Do you know what we can do?" Rachel asked.

Lewis nodded again. "Graham's told me everything."

Doubtful, Rachel thought. Mulcahy would be wearing a new Graham-skin jacket if he had. "He's finding a private place where he can talk," Rachel said. "Can you answer some questions until he gets here?"

"Yeah," Lewis sniffed, then started sobbing into Rachel's pants again.

Rachel helped Lewis back to her seat, giving Gallagher a subtle wave out of the ambulance's back window. Gallagher flashed an uncertain yellow as the screen of the borrowed tablet turned on, framing Ellen Lewis's face. Several yards away from

Gallagher's team, Santino waved his own cell at Rachel; she split the feed in two to bring him in on the interview.

"Can you tell me what happened?" Rachel pressed again as she searched her voluminous purse. She found an almost-clean stack of paper napkins and passed them to Lewis, who took them gratefully.

Lewis nodded. "Field trip day," she said thickly. "I teach fourth grade. We were supposed to go to the Smithsonian. You know, see the dinosaurs."

Rachel smiled.

"So… It was chaos. Field trip day is always chaos. It's almost two hours to get into the city, so we left early. The driver said the GPS rerouted him," Lewis said into a napkin. "I was sitting up front so we were talking. We were going up Highway 29 like usual, then the GPS just took us off of the map. It said there was a major accident ahead so the driver followed the alternate route.

"We got out here," Lewis pointed towards the highway, close but unseen over the ridge. "There was a police car blocking the road."

"Agent Peng, does this… uh… does this go both ways?" Gallagher had traded the tablet for Santino's phone. Her voice in Rachel's head was halting.

"*Yes,*" Rachel replied.

"Okay… Okay, good. Ask her if it was state or local."

"Do you remember what type of police car it was?" Rachel couldn't recall where Graham had worked prior to OACET. She hoped he had been with law enforcement; no one made a distinction beyond the generic Police! unless they had some frame of reference.

Ellen Lewis shook her head.

"Do you remember colors? Silver, blue, brown…?"

"Silver," Lewis said. "Silver and blue."

"State," said Gallagher, and a member of her team peeled off to call the Virginia State Police and ask if they had had any vehicles stolen recently.

Graham's chartreuse avatar appeared in the ambulance, and he nodded when Rachel asked him to wait until they finished the interview. He sat beside his sister, pained when his hand passed through hers. Behind them, Rachel saw Gallagher and her team jump at the sudden appearance of a bright green stranger who only showed up on their screens, and Jason moved from her group to theirs to explain.

"So after you found the road was blocked, what happened?"

"An officer came on the bus," Lewis said, and a storm of grays and oranges rolled over her; the woman didn't want to revisit this part. "I remember thinking he was really good-looking," she whispered.

"That's the first thing most people notice about this guy," Rachel encouraged her.

Lewis nodded, staring down at the pressed rubber floor of the ambulance. "Then he took out a gun," she said softly. "He had us drive off of the road. The other bus was already here. Nobody knew what to think. He told us where to park and had us all get off of the bus... the kids were crying. One of the parents is a pro hockey player, thinks he's a real hard-ass. I was scared to death he was going to try something, but he just kept his hands on his daughter's shoulders the entire time, like he was going to wrap her up if things got bad. All of her friends were hanging on him... it was so sweet and sad...

"The man had them all get on the truck," Lewis said, and those outside the ambulance watching the interview brightened at the new information.

"This truck, we don't know anything about it. Can you describe it?" Rachel asked.

Lewis shook her head. "Normal shipping truck," she said. "Huge... I think they're called semis, the ones that haul those big freight trailers. You see them all the time on the highway."

"Was there a trailer on this truck, or was it just the cab and engine?"

"An orange trailer. That's where he took the kids. That's where he took everyone," she corrected herself. "He took the parents and the other teachers, too."

"Okay, you're doing really good," Rachel said. "This is important. Did you see what happened when he put them on the truck?"

"Yes," Lewis nodded quickly. "Yes, he said I was his witness. He told me to watch. The other man stood at the back of the truck—"

Gallagher shouted in Rachel's head.

"Could you tell me about this other man?" Rachel asked. "This is very helpful. We didn't know there was anyone else involved."

Lewis shrugged. "I can't, I'm sorry. He wore a mask and he never said anything."

"Height, weight, race…?"

"Short, a little overweight, I guess. I didn't see any skin so that's all I know… He wore black gloves and one of those black stocking masks that covers your entire face but you can see through it."

"Okay, good," Rachel said. "Thank you. What else was he wearing?"

"Um… Jeans and a shirt? I'm sorry, I wasn't really looking at him. The other man was doing all of the talking."

"What happened then?"

"They loaded everybody up. There were already a lot of people from the school in there, kids and adults. The other bus on the trip was about fifteen minutes ahead of us because we got separated when we had to stop for a train. The rest of us got on the truck, and he made them sit with their backs to the wall. Then he went back to the road—"

"You said them," Rachel interrupted. "What did he make you do?"

"They had me sit on the edge of the truck with my back to the open door." Lewis paused. "Everybody looked at me. They were angry with me, like I was blocking their escape…"

"You know you weren't," Rachel said. "That's survivor's guilt talking. Don't listen to it."

"The men were at the back of the truck." Lewis pressed her face into the napkins and sobbed. "I could have run, tried to get help..."

"And you would have been shot," Rachel replied. "You did the right thing. Don't let the guilt talk you out of it."

Lewis nodded, but there was no heart in it. Her brother reached out and his hand passed through his sister's shoulder; avatars offered no comfort, except for other Agents.

"We're almost done. What happened after everyone was on the truck?"

"I don't know what happened to them," Lewis said. "They put me back on the bus and tied me up with... I don't know. Those plastic strips that hold shoes together at Target."

"Zip ties," Rachel said.

"Yeah. Like those, only bigger. I tried to get out of them, but they cut up my wrists." She held up her hands to show the light bandages. "After that, I heard the truck drive off. Then nothing for... I don't know how long it was."

"You've been out there pretty much the entire day," Rachel said. "The FBI probably has a change of clothes if you want it." Nobody would be so crass as to call attention to the faint smell of urine, but Rachel was sure it was weighing on the schoolteacher's mind. "One last thing, though. Can you think of any reason they'd take everyone else but leave you behind?"

"The bright green man sitting beside her?"

"Boys?" It sounded like Jason's voice but she hadn't been paying attention. *"Let me work."*

"I don't know why they picked me," Lewis said, shaking her head.

"It's almost funny," she added as an afterthought. "But this is twice in two days I've been part of something illegal without, you know, meaning to."

"What do you mean?"

"Yesterday I got a call from the police. They told me someone had rented a safe deposit box using my fingerprints. Weird, right?"

Dead silence from the task force and the FBI; then from outside of the ambulance came Santino's sharp: "Son of a **bitch!**"

"Okay," Rachel said. "We'll definitely look into that."

There was a knock on the door and Phil let himself into the ambulance. "Hey, Graham," he nodded at the disembodied Agent, then placed a plastic bag of unisex clothes next to Ellen. "Sorry to meet you under these circumstances," Phil said to her. "Are you doing okay?"

Ellen Lewis was far from okay, but she nodded and tried to smile.

"All right," Rachel scanned the ambulance, taking stock of the storage compartments. "I'm going to update the FBI. Phil will stay with you," she said, and put an assuring hand on Ellen's shoulder when the woman bloomed with anxiety. "He's an Agent, too. He'll be your intermediary with your brother.

"And keep drinking, all right?" Rachel opened a lower compartment and found Ellen another bottle of water. "You're lucky you didn't broil alive."

Rachel hopped down from the ambulance and shut the door to keep the cool air in, leaving Phil and his phone to facilitate conversation between the Lewis twins. Gallagher was waiting outside for her. They stepped around the ambulance to stand in its shade.

This time, the SAC had no problem meeting Rachel's eyes. "We usually have to run a full AV system if we want to sit in on a private interview," Gallagher told her.

Rachel shrugged. "Hopefully the connection went through. It's pretty new to me, so I'm still working out the kinks."

Gallagher nodded. "It did. I've got BOLO alerts on the police car and the truck, and I've put out notice for possible satellite tracking. Since we've narrowed the time frame, we might be able to get an image of the truck."

Satellites. Rachel glanced skyward. Some of the others enjoyed the occasional out-of-body excursion to orbit, but she had never gone herself. Space was well beyond the range she imposed on the world of chattering things, and it was far enough away so she had never heard one as it passed overhead. She wondered how hard it would be to reach out and ping one, wondered if it might be necessary to catch Glazer.

Wondered if Glazer, with all his technological prowess, could hack a satellite.

"What are you thinking?" Gallagher's colors had shifted, a trace of Rachel's own Southwestern turquoise core showing. Rachel hid a grin behind a hand; the SAC's opinion of Rachel had changed during her interview with Ellen Lewis.

"Just whether we should trust any information we get, unless there's a human being involved. All of the data we've gotten from Glazer has been corrupted. He likes to play games but there was more than one reason for leaving Lewis: we can believe what she says. She's a lead that finally goes somewhere real."

Gallagher's conversational colors shifted heavily towards Rachel's core in agreement. "Good point. Thank you for your help, Agent Peng."

Rachel knew a dismissal when she heard one. She headed back to her small group, still standing apart from the others.

Santino was livid. "This is our fault," he said, pacing. "We've known every single thing Glazer's done so far had been micromanaged. We should have dug into the teacher's background, or…

"None of you guys knew her?" Santino rounded on Rachel and Jason.

"Maybe?" Rachel threw up her hands. "Graham's a drinking buddy. I knew he had a twin sister but I've never met her."

"Name three hundred and fifty people you work with," Jason said. "Then name all of their siblings. Or tell me if they know someone else's siblings."

Santino snorted in disgust but didn't respond.

"Besides, most of us aren't that close with our families," Rachel added. "There's probably a lot of people out there who don't even realize they've got relatives in OACET." She said it just to see Hill's reaction, but his colors didn't change. *Man has no idea,* she thought. *Mako, too, probably.*

Hurry up and wait. Their moment of usefulness had passed, and they were back on the sidelines until another came around. Rachel was used to it. Hill, too. The others chafed and paced. When the satellite images of Glazer's truck came in, Rachel pushed Jason's credentials as a digital expert on Gallagher until the SAC took him off of Rachel's hands. She breathed a silent sigh of relief as Jason and his angry energy went to join the FBI.

Fifteen minutes later, he called to her over the link. *"They're leaving."* She watched as Jason, still cloistered with the feds, accompanied Gallagher and most of her team as they started to clear out of the field. *"They can't do anything more here."*

"Stick with them," she told him. *"See how far you can get before they drop you. Phil?"*

"Coming," the small Agent said. The ambulance door opened and he dropped lightly to the ground. *"Ellen's calmed down. I think she'll be fine. The FBI's bringing her back to D.C. for a formal interview."*

"What about Graham?"

"He'll get a ride to the Hoover Building and meet her there," Phil said, then added: *"I gave Ellen my phone."*

"Good thinking," she replied. Phil had LoJacked their witness. As long as Ellen kept Phil's phone on her, Graham could find his sister anywhere.

They set out across the field, retracing their path through the beaten grass. Jason was waiting for them by the road as the FBI drove away; no space for the Agent. His colors were damp and lonely. Rachel pushed aside his resemblance to a dumped family pet before it provoked a laugh.

The drive was quiet. Rachel turned off the emotional spectrum. Everyone was keeping their thoughts to themselves, and those were harshly gray. She was almost drowsing when their SUV shifted, Zockinski jumping two lanes of traffic to keep up with the sudden change in direction of the FBI's caravan.

"Dinner?" Jason reached out to her through the link. He

sounded hungry, and Rachel idly wondered if it was actually possible for a person to sound hungry or if her own moods were piggybacking on his.

"Ready to eat?" She poked Phil.

He sighed. *"Always."*

Rachel thought back over her day. She hadn't eaten anything other than the occasional snack since she and Zockinski had gorged themselves on overpriced museum croissants. There had been some sneaking off to the side in the cornfield, but nobody had enjoyed a proper bathroom break in hours.

They pulled off at a wreck of a strip mall with more empty stores than customers, a Subway and a McDonald's the last remaining signs of commerce. Gallagher gave everybody a firm thirty minutes, to be cut short without notice. Most of the FBI started walking towards the sandwich shop, but some headed towards the fast food restaurant at the other end of the parking lot. The group from First District Station broke up, the police moving towards the American equivalent of health food, while the cyborgs pled the need for coffee that hadn't been boiled in the same pot since noon and gravitated towards the calories.

It was an old McDonald's and hadn't yet been renovated into a polished plastic café. This one had an agricultural theme, with farm hand tools nailed to the walls and a row of stationary saddles where the stools should be. Rachel ran her fingertips over one of these on her way to the counter; hard leather, shiny from decades of dropped fries and jeans. It'd be gone soon, plowed under when the building was razed to the ground, the old broken character of the place turned into so many pieces of brick. She had read the cost analysis of what it took to renovate old buildings and bring them up to code, and there was a definite logic in starting from scratch, but it seemed wasteful in a different way.

They got their meals, found a table far away from those few from the FBI, and soaked in the grease.

"This is going to kill me," Phil complained.

He was not referring to the cholesterol. Rachel patted her

purse. *"Energy bars,"* she said. *"I brought enough for all of us. Just snack when you take a bathroom break."*

Jason snorted around a huge bite of his burger. *"Men don't have to piss fifty times a day. That'd be almost as suspicious as eating all the damned time."*

They stopped talking to concentrate on their food. When the last of her fried chicken sandwich was gone, Rachel drew a breath and slouched forward, sated. *"Think we can get away with shakes?"* She balled up the last paper wrapper and dropped it on her tray. *"I'm not sure when we'll get another chance to eat. The kids, Glazer, those RFID readers... I don't see us getting another meal in tonight."*

"Oh yeah," Jason said, and put down his third burger. *"Rachel? I forgot. Here."*

He reached out and grabbed her nearest wrist.

"What's up?" Rachel started to ask, and then she felt the new autoscript worm its way into her mind. She yanked her hand away from him and barely stopped herself before it completed the arc towards his face.

"Asshole!" she hissed aloud.

"Rachel! What..." Phil, engrossed in his food, had turned at the exact moment to see her nearly punch Jason. It took him a moment to guess what had happened. Rachel, furious, rubbing her wrist; Jason, annoyed and self-righteous... Phil's colors drained out of him. "Jason, you didn't!"

"It's the same RFID reader script I gave you this morning," Jason glared at Phil, then back at Rachel. "Grow up," he said to her.

She had to keep herself from clawing at her own skin. "I didn't ask for this."

He shrugged and picked up his burger. *"Like we asked for any of this."*

The restaurant muttered in data. Little plastic tags hidden in boxes chirped names, dates, and locations at her. Machines kept shouting their batch numbers. Down the hall, a copier kept telling her it was overdue for servicing, and every computer, each credit card, and the security badges worn by the FBI three tables down chimed like hollow clocks. It was worse than the usual clamor of the digital ecosystem. This was not a passive environment; these devices wanted to talk to her.

She pressed her fists against her temples. "How do you shut it off?"

"It's already off," Jason said, shaking his head. "The script doesn't activate unless you've scanned an RFID tag."

She nearly went to hit him again, but closed her eyes and grabbed the edge of the table instead. Her fingernails skidded across the old laminate. *"I'm almost never **not** scanning, idiot."*

Jason slowly lowered his hands, the self-righteous blues fading. "Oh shit, Rachel. I didn't think."

"Yeah, I got that," she said.

"Rachel, I—"

"Quiet." She cut him off and put her hands over her ears as she wrestled with frequencies. The majority of RFID tags around them were the cheap disposable kind and she could weed those out by dropping the microwave and radio bands from her environment scans, but those on the copier and food machines were more complex and broadcast their own signals. She had heard all of these before but they were just more of the ever-present white noise; now, they spoke, crickets and locusts that begged her for restocking or to change their ink. "How do you get rid of the active tags?"

"Oh God, Rachel, I don't think you can," Phil said, deeply gray. "I just ignore them."

"Shit. I can't do that," she whispered, and gave up and shut down all radio. The room lost detail and depth as she shut away those familiar frequencies, but the passive tags were silenced.

The active tags howled on.

"You will fix this," Rachel snarled at Jason. His expression was fuzzy but she knew that was her own fault. "I'm not giving up radio or microwave. They're my staples. Can I delete the script, or overwrite it, or what?"

They didn't know; no one had tried to eliminate an

autoscript before. Phil put a general call out through the link for advice, and Jason flinched when Josh responded with a harsh: *"He did **what?!?**"*

"Rachel?" Jason pleaded as the collective beat him down. *"I am so sorry."*

"I know," she said. The emotional spectrum was not carried by radio frequencies: Jason was miserable. *"But you fucking ask first. Always."*

Across the room, the FBI suddenly burst into bright colors.

"Oh, what now?" Rachel asked the others. They didn't know, and she could barely make out the outlines of the Special Agents as they stood and frantically gathered their trash. She sighed and flipped on radio frequencies. The FBI bloomed into high definition and the RFID tags on their badges and credit cards welcomed her back. Outside, Gallagher and her team were driving towards them across the parking lot, multiple cars in a quick-moving line as they came to pick up their missing members. She could track each of them by the name and credentials in their wallets.

Maybe this wasn't so bad. Maybe the radio signals were just another layer of data within her already-saturated environment. She had taught herself to see through walls and to stay sane in the midst of the emotional maelstrom around her; maybe she could learn how to use these, too.

Ah crap, Rachel thought, picking Santino and the others out of a car at the rear of their pack. She had been so preoccupied with the RFID data that she hadn't noticed how the men from First MPD were running red again.

"I think they got a lead," Rachel said. "It's not good."

Gallagher entered the restaurant and came towards them. Rachel assumed the woman was headed towards her own team members, but she stepped past them to reach the Agents, a large piece of paper in her hand. Before Rachel could scan it, Gallagher wordlessly slid the photo across the table. Rachel flipped to reading mode, then blinked her implant off and on as she took a closer look at the satellite image.

"You're kidding," Rachel said.

FIFTEEN

The Portsmouth Marine Terminal had wharfs sized for battleships and encompassed more than two hundred acres of open land. Their guide, an office administrator whose job responsibilities had suddenly veered into the grim, drove a glorified golf cart through truck-sized dirt roads lined with the steel shells of shipping containers stacked five, six, seven tall above their heads. It was a different version of OACET headquarters and its forest of groaning cardboard, remade in rusting steel on a giant's scale.

"How many of these are here?" Rachel shouted to their driver, and pointed to the containers.

He glazed over in annoyance; everyone who came to Portsmouth must have asked him that same question. "We don't know. We've got an inventory for everything sent here after 1986, but this port's been around for almost a century and they've been using these FEUs since the 1950s."

"FEUs?"

"Forty-foot equivalent units. It's cheaper to build new ones than ship them back and reuse them, so once they're emptied, they're usually dumped. We've got another yard for the twenty-foot units. And we're state-owned, but a private shipping company leased another three hundred acres from us, so when they get overflow they've got the option to dump.

"It gets pretty bad," he admitted. "The state shut us down for containerized cargo a few years back to give us a chance to manage the surplus. As soon as we finished clearing one yard out, they went and dumped another fifty thousand units right back on it. All combined... I don't know. High end? There might be almost a quarter of a million FEUs on site."

They sped through the yard, the utility cart bumping along

the bare earth. The ground was as dead as if it were paved; Rachel was no engineer but she assumed no matter how thick the concrete pad, it would still sustain damage from the weight and the movement of the freight. Cheaper to leave it as they had found it, and pray to keep the rain away.

The yard was the equivalent of an archeological dig site for the Agents. Shipping containers were part of the digital ecosystem, the tracking devices embedded within falling into various stages of decay. Newer containers with RFID tags were layered atop three generations of radio receiver units and ancient data buses. Those old systems were mostly long dead, their power supplies drained dry decades ago, but every once and a while Rachel had caught a flicker of movement in the lowest layers, a twitch of energy like a run-down rabbit trying to drag itself out of the road.

It was shockingly sad. She wished she could turn off everything other than straight visuals and ignore the slow rot around them, but there was a chance they might drive past the container with the kids. Rachel was running a continuous scan at the very limits of her abilities, but this had accomplished nothing other than showing her how the container yard was freakishly, terrifyingly enormous. The scope of the place was beyond her comprehension. The very fact the yard existed seemed somehow unfair, as though the human race had no right to make something of this size.

Rachel glanced behind her to where the other members of the task force rattled around in the rear of the cart. To a man they kept a stoic face, but each was moving in greens and curious yellows. A crane swung directly overhead, another container dangling in midair. Santino glowed. He caught Rachel's eye and the thumb on his good hand flew across the screen of his cell.

"If I wasn't so pissed off right now, this would all be so damned cool."

She grinned at him, then turned back to watch the dust clouds sheer off the windshield.

Their cart was the tail on a convoy moving towards

the last place Glazer's truck had been spotted. A private communications satellite had been perfectly positioned to follow Glazer's semi as it moved past the Terminal gate, through the security checkpoint, down the main road, into the graveyard, and disappear. The security checkpoint registered one semi entering at that time; then, thirty minutes later, the same truck leaving minus its payload. Glazer's bill of lading had put his cargo as Virginia soybeans bound for China, but it had never arrived at the docks.

Glazer had slipped a purloined letter into the stack.

They hadn't fully appreciated what Glazer had done until they entered the container graveyard. The satellite images had distorted the problem; what had seemed on paper a matter of finding one misplaced container among many was now the equivalent of finding a single Lego at Legoland.

Rachel stepped from the utility cart, the sole of her boot hard against the ground. In the cart closest to her, a technician opened up a crate with a portable sonar array. He stared at it, then at the metal hulls around them, and went gray. Sonar was useless here.

An FBI helicopter flew low. Rachel flipped through a few frequencies and caught the resonance streaming from it as they scanned the nearby containers, deploying thermal imaging across the graveyard.

Good luck with that, she thought. She had tried it herself before abandoning those frequencies. August in acres of baking metal made for poor resolution, and she was sure Glazer hadn't stuck those kids into a standard shipping container. Based on what Ellen Lewis had told them, Glazer had modified it in some way. Even if the FBI's thermal imaging hit on Glazer's container, he had probably shielded the interior to compensate for the temperature. Rachel was hoping this meant air conditioning; she was holding on to the belief that Glazer might have a reason to kidnap nearly a hundred people and keep them alive.

Like brushstrokes in paint, her subconscious whispered, and tossed her the memory of dried blood against a white marble floor. Rachel ignored it and paced towards Gallagher's team, grouped together in the center of a rough crossroads.

Jason followed closely, always a step or two behind her but making himself available. He was still trying to atone for what he had done at the restaurant. Rachel knew the main reason for his remorse was the group ass-kicking he had received from the entire collective, but you had to start somewhere.

She was loath to admit it, but this new autoscript was phenomenally useful. *Homeland Security, Department of Transportation, Customs and Border Protection, Virginia state police... and U.S. Navy?* Rachel had taken a page from Glazer's playbook and was pinging the RFID tags in the security badges to get an accurate head count. She did a quick search to learn why the military had dropped in, and found the shipping yard was within spitting distance of the naval base at Craney Island.

Add these newcomers to Special Agent Gallagher and staff, and you got an especially fragrant potpourri of state and federal law enforcement.

Or... witnesses.

Rachel stumbled as she finally realized what Glazer had done. Jason grabbed her shoulder to catch her. As his fingers brushed the skin on her neck, her fear jumped across to him. He recoiled as if struck.

"Stop!" Rachel ordered as his hand flew to his gun. *"Get your shit together right now."*

She grabbed his arm through his suit coat and forced him over to the side of the nearest container. Jason faced the side of the truck and started whispering in French. Rachel didn't speak the language but she knew a prayer when she heard one.

Rachel leaned against the side of the truck and pretended they had stopped so she could shake a stone from her boot. Phil came up beside them and joined her and Jason in the link.

"What's wrong?" Phil asked.

"Look around," she said. *"Do you see what's happening?"*

Jason rose up past his emotions and saw what she meant almost immediately. Phil, who in spite of the last five years still failed to appreciate how horrible people could be to each other, didn't understand the problem until Jason told him: *"It's a trap. For* **us**.*"*

"How is this a..." Phil, trained to see the threat in the inanimate, instinctively looked towards the heavy machines swinging high overhead, then back down to the near-infinite rows of shipping containers. Last came the humans, small and fragile in comparison, walking in staggered rows around him. His colors fled as he caught on, and his voice was small in her head. *"Rachel, all of those kids..."*

"I'm taking the lead," she told them. *"You can beat me down later, but here, now? It's us against them, and you're standing with me."*

Jason agreed without a second's hesitation. Phil, who had broken into a run and was already a hundred feet down the road, stopped to stare back at her.

"I won't let it get to a point where the kids are at risk," she promised him. *"Glazer only thinks he's got us in a Catch-22. You can't profile somebody unless you can get in their heads, and nobody gets in our heads but us."*

Phil almost laughed.

Rachel pushed herself off of the truck and walked towards where the others had gathered, kicking up dust with each step. The small group of who's-whos had reached the central hub of the shipping station. She knew she was on display as she marched up the road, Jason at her side. They met up with Phil and formed the most meager of phalanxes, three abreast.

When they reached the center hub, she drew them off to the side. *"With luck,"* she told the others, *"they won't even consider us as an option. They usually see us as a liability, not a possible solution."*

"You've been flaunting your X-ray powers all week," Jason retorted. *"It'll be a miracle if they don't."*

She ignored him and pretended he wasn't absolutely right.

Twenty feet away, the clash of bureaucracies was heating up. Gallagher held her own against those others fighting for control of the scene; under the circumstances, every agency represented had some claim over the shipping yard, and they all wanted the credit for the rescue. But, as the children were still missing, seizing claim and credit might boomerang in the worst possible way. Rachel watched the core and conversational colors sweep over the group in grayish-reds; the search parties had already gone out, the first reports coming back to their supervisors, no news, no trace, no small voices calling out for help. This was a Herculean task, a quarter of a million units to search, winnowed down to perhaps fifty thousand if geography and timeline were applied, and they could not summon enough manpower to cut the burden.

The three cyborgs slowly maneuvered themselves under the cover of the team from First MPD. Santino, Zockinski, and Hill were all big men; Jason hid himself by sitting on the far side of one of the carts, and Rachel and Phil had never been so glad to be small.

"When do we stop this?" Phil asked. *"If we can help, we have to stop this."*

Rachel couldn't answer.

The helicopter made another pass, flying so low its rotors whipped the dirt and trash on the ground into small cyclones. She watched it as traveled overhead, still spreading its useless thermal imaging across the shipping yard. Jason's avatar popped into view next to its tail.

"Jason," Rachel said, straightening. *"You are a genius."*

"Hm?" His avatar vanished from the sky and he turned to look at her. *"I wanted to read the serial numbers."*

"Hey! Hey!" A man with sunglasses and a shaved head pointed towards the task force. "What about the cyborgs? Can't they see through walls?"

The heady reds and oranges lightened, with bits of green-blue hope spotting them across the torso. A solution; a good one. Let the freaks try, and then negotiate credit or blame based on outcome.

The team from First MPD was mobbed. The crowd was

calm and polite, but swimming in demands; the Agents would not be allowed to say no.

Rachel held up her hands for silence. "Sure, she said. "Of course we'll help. Just tell us what to do."

The man with the shaved head was aggressive and insistent, and didn't bother to identify himself until Zockinski and Hill blocked him.

"Bryce Knudson, Homeland Security," he said to Zockinski. To Rachel, he demanded: "Go. You can see into the containers. Start looking for the kids."

"Right," Rachel agreed. "Good idea. We can definitely do that. Let me check one thing first." She turned to Gallagher and asked, "What does the warrant cover?"

The conversational colors of Knudson and the rest plunged into sooty gray. *Hope dashed,* she thought. Not only monsters, but child killers, too, and Rachel turned her body towards the ships so they couldn't see her face.

"Well?" Rachel asked, comfortable in parade rest.

"There are provisions for a general external search," Gallagher said, and pointed to the helicopter. "They're doing thermal imaging. Would that cover it?"

"I've been doing thermal scans myself and haven't found anything." Rachel shook her head. "What about a direct search? Say we start on one end of the yard and go into each container?"

"How?" Knudson asked.

"It's a thing we can do," she replied, her new default response for questions she didn't want to bother with. "We can cover a lot of ground, definitely faster than opening each container. But does the warrant cover individual entry?"

"No," Gallagher said. It was almost a sigh.

"Can you expand the warrant?" Rachel asked.

The SAC shook her head. "Not on this scope, no."

"Hey!" Rachel singled out the worker who had driven her in on the utility cart. "Who owns these? Does Portsmouth Marine Terminal have the authority to open any container?"

"It depends?" He looked around, wide-eyed at suddenly

being the center of attention. "If they're abandoned, yeah. But if they're full and waiting for transport, no. We have shippers sign a dock warrant when they store the FEUs, but we don't hold those, the consignee does."

Rachel looked at Knudson. "Homeland's got authority for yard-wide searches, right?"

"NINs first," he said. "Then, if there's cause, we can open to confirm contents."

"Technically, we'd count as non-intrusive inspection technologies. We would not be physically present in the container." Rachel raised her voice to carry through the crowd. "Can you guarantee that Homeland will protect us if there is a legal challenge?"

"Start looking," Knudson replied. "I'll make some calls."

"No," she said coldly. The man's shoulders were thick with dimples. "Get a judge to sign off on this first. I need to see that we're covered by the warrant. Then we're completely at your disposal."

"There are kids out there," Knudson moved towards her, a little too quickly. His chest bumped into Hill's outstretched arm. The man from Homeland backed down. "Kids," he said again, more quietly. "Just get out there."

"If I heard you correctly," Rachel said, "you're asking us to break the law. We will not participate in that."

Anger was building. *Thank God these people are professionals,* she thought. They might want to tear her limb from limb, but at least they'd do it in effigy. Rather than attacking, they started to turn away: one solution didn't work; time to find another.

The helicopter made another pass. She tipped her head skyward to call attention to it.

"But," Rachel said. "I have an alternative."

Within the space of ten minutes, nearly two hundred Agents had joined them, green avatars spread out across the sky. Rachel had put the call out through the link for volunteers to help in the search for Glazer's missing container. Even Mulcahy, sitting in Senate hearings back in D.C., had stepped out-of-body to help.

Rachel organized them into a traditional grid pattern with two Agents per sight line, half traveling north and the other half traveling west. She told herself this was no different than a good old-fashioned ground search, where visibility was directed down instead of out; still, the other members of law enforcement grumbled. Most had left to run their own searches, leaving only Gallagher and her team to mingle with those from OACET and First MPD.

"You're looking for one container," Rachel shouted through the link, and sent the cleanest satellite images of the truck and the shipping yard to the Agents. *"Check the numbers and iconography, compare those with notable dents, scratches, and other markings. All of these FEUs look alike, so if you find one that you think is a match, note the location, then compare what you see to the satellite images on the grid before you call it in.*

"We're looking for something new," she told them. *"An FEU that wasn't there before. Glazer's good at manipulating digital images, so cross-reference everything and run anything you find past Jason to make sure it's authentic. Got it?"*

They did. The Agents moved forward in pairs, the first serving as advance scouts, the second reviewing and comparing. Communication through the link was a flurry of false positives, with Rachel, Phil, and Jason throwing new images up on tablets and cells as quickly as they came in. These slowed as the excitement wore off and the Agents above started to work in earnest, crossing over each other's lines and circling back when they reached the edge of the yard.

"Hey! Hey!" Phil, surrounded by taller men, held up his tablet over their heads while he shouted. She picked the image off of it and sent it around her group. "I think we've found it! It's close!" Phil shouted. "Two rows over."

"That's it," Zockinski said as he compared Phil's find to the satellite image of Glazer's FEU. "Same color, same markings."

"Agent Peng?" Gallagher tapped her on the shoulder. "You have confirmation. The FBI will be opening that container, no matter what."

Rachel nodded. *"The warrant covers this one,"* she told Mulcahy, and threw her mind towards the swarm of avatars gathering around the container. Two rows over, maybe, but a single row on this scale could be measured in football fields. She grabbed at Santino's good arm to steady herself as she pushed herself past her limit.

Mulcahy's avatar stepped through the metal doors at the same moment her scan went through its walls.

"Oh, Penguin," he whispered to her across the link.

"I know."

She dropped her scan. "Alive," Rachel said to Gallagher. "I don't know if they're unharmed, but they're all definitely alive, kids and adults."

Everyone in earshot went blue in relief.

The fitter members of the FBI were already running. The team from First MPD joined them. Rachel felt each step in her knees as she moved across the hard-packed earth. She fell behind, motioning Santino and the others to keep going when they waited for her to catch up.

A service cart piled under with Gallagher and the rest of her squad slowed down, letting her grab a roll bar and swing herself up. Rachel clung to the side of the cart, feet slipping from the wheel well as they bounced down the track. They turned down one alley, two...

She let herself drop off when the cart slowed. The orange FEU was at ground level, with other units piled neatly all around. Rachel marveled at how fast Glazer had moved. They had assumed that wherever his container ended up, time constraints would have put it on the top of the stack. The unit was surrounded by law enforcement of all stripes on the ground, Agents in the air. Most of the green avatars were half-in, half-out of the container, trying to console children who had no way of knowing they were there.

Rachel limped over to meet Santino. She had expected to see the First MPD's task force shunted off to the side again, but they had a spot close to the doors. Everyone was bright with anticipation but they parted for her, some nodding in steady blues and greens.

Well, she thought, and then the men on the doors determined the container was safe to open, followed by the shouted: "FBI! We're coming in!"

Then nothing but the screaming yellow terror of children.

Rescued. It should have been a happy moment, but the seventy-two people trapped in the FEU reacted as though a gun had gone off in the doorway; the last police officer they had seen was the one who locked them in. The adults gathered the students to them as they all wept and cowered, waiting for the next blow to land.

Rachel staggered backwards and dropped the emotional spectrum before she blacked out. She returned to the service cart and sat in its wide back seat as the screams stopped, teachers and parents realizing that it was over, the students slowly transferring their trust from one group to the other.

Mulcahy's avatar met her at the cart. "Nice job, Penguin," he said. His hand on her shoulder was air, but she couldn't help but throw a weak smile back at him.

Gallagher took charge. The team from First MPD was allowed to stay and the paramedics were allowed to enter, but the others were escorted past the perimeter of yellow crime scene tape that appeared like magic wherever Gallagher pointed. (Rachel gave a cheery wave to Knudson as he left; the man from Homeland Security pretended he hadn't seen her.) Gallagher broke the students into smaller groups and tasked FBI, police, and Agents alike to take their names and call their families, then sent the students off to a local hospital in an assembly line of ambulances.

"Please make friends with Special Agent Gallagher," Mulcahy told her, and she nodded.

Things slowed down considerably after that. Mulcahy and the other out-of-body Agents left, and Rachel let the rest happen without her. She stretched out in the back seat of the utility cart and tried to keep to her old Army habit of napping when she wasn't needed, but when she flipped off her implant, the memory of the rush of emotions from the group trapped in the truck kept circling through her thoughts.

Enough of that. Rachel turned on her implant and swung herself out of the cart. She made her way over to where Santino was finishing up with his last group of kids. He saw her coming and whispered something to a small boy, who turned a shy violet with curious yellow sparks.

"What would you like to say to Agent Peng?" Santino prompted.

The boy blinked up at her. "'anks."

"'ur 'elcome," she said. He rolled his eyes at her and ran back to his classmates.

"Keep trying," Santino said, and dusted off his pants as he stood. "You never know. Someday, somewhere, someone might find you funny."

"I can dream." Rachel glanced towards Glazer's FEU. The FBI had covered it from top to bottom in plastic sheeting to preserve the evidence. "Be right back," she muttered, her subconscious prodding her to move.

She walked up to the crime scene tape and ran a scan through the container. Her scan pinged off of hardware. Machines, none of them digital, all with industry-hard edges and wrapped in insulation. The insulation continued up and around the sides, keeping the temperature in and shielding the interior. Rachel had scanned so many containers that day that she would almost categorize this FEU as a refrigerated unit, but one with a custom design; some of the more common radio and microwave frequencies bounced off at the first layer. She felt a little like Superman trying to see through lead.

Gallagher spotted her. The SAC shook hands one final time with the adults, then came over to join her. "You can go in if you'd like," the other woman said. "Just stay near the doors."

"No need." Rachel tapped her head. Gallagher's forensic team was carefully ripping the place apart with tweezers and she didn't want to muck up their efforts. "What have they told you about the modifications?"

"It's been fitted with lights, an air conditioner, and a carbon dioxide scrubber. They were gas-powered and the tank was getting low. There was probably enough fuel for another hour."

At least they weren't sitting in the heat and the dark, Rachel thought, and said: "So we still don't know if he was trying to kill them."

Gallagher was a mild orange; she couldn't answer. "It might have been for ransom, it might have been for torture. I hate dealing with psychopaths. They only make sense to themselves."

"Amen," Rachel agreed, although the distinction between a psychopath and a terrorist shifted heavily towards the latter in Glazer's case. Psychopaths didn't need a reason. There was motive here, they just had to find it. "You're a profiler?"

"No," Gallagher replied. "Violent crime specialist. Also, kidnappings."

Rachel decided not to argue. Gallagher knew her psychopaths.

"I'm going in," Gallagher said, and pointed at the shipping container. "You're welcome to come."

Rachel nodded and held up the yellow tape so Gallagher could duck underneath. They kept to the walkway designated by the forensics team, marked off at the sides by lengths of heavy-duty climbing rope. Rachel prodded it with her toe and looked at Gallagher.

"Doesn't leave any fibers," the SAC explained. "Cheap hardware store rope sheds like a cat."

A metal sheet had been laid across the entrance of the container as a ramp to reduce the amount of dust tracked in. It rang hollow under their feet as they crossed. Rachel had expected the interior of the container to stink, but there was a small chemical toilet bolted to the floor at the rear of the unit.

She and Gallagher stopped in front of a box full of empty water bottles, each tagged in its own individual plastic evidence baggie. Beside that box was another with wrappers from prepackaged lunch snacks.

"Oh hell," Rachel muttered. She was glad Gallagher had talked her into coming inside; with everything laid out in front of them, it was plain that Glazer had meant to keep the victims alive.

"He knew they'd be rescued before the fuel ran out," Gallagher had reached the same conclusion.

"One hour is a brutally tight window."

Gallagher nodded.

"I know how this is going to sound," Rachel began. "And please don't think this is anything other than establishing a timeline..."

"No," the other woman said, anticipating what Rachel was about to ask. "Realistically speaking, we would not have found them in an hour without your help."

"But you still would have found them."

"Yes. We had dog teams en route. The dogs would have had to walk up and down every aisle because there's no trail, but they would have hit on the scent."

Rachel sighed and threw her sixth sense across the shipping yard. She could not get over the scope of the place. The FBI would have needed dozens of dog teams, but they probably would have located the trailer before the kids got too hungry or thirsty. And the sun would be going down soon, so they wouldn't have been baked alive when the fuel ran out...

Planners. It had been a timed exercise for OACET, with the victims as incentive.

"What do we do about this?" Gallagher asked.

Rachel chuckled dryly. "I have no idea."

Gallagher's phone vibrated. "Excuse me," she said, and stepped outside the trailer.

Rachel began exploring. She didn't expect to find anything new, but she had just been proven wrong and was willing to let her sixth sense go in favor of walking the scene. She hadn't gone more than ten feet into the container when Gallagher lit up yellow-white with excitement. The SAC said something to the FBI agents closest to her, and they scrambled towards the service vehicles.

She reached out to Jason. *"Good news?"*

"I don't know. Something's happened," he replied, *"but they're keeping it close."*

She left to find Santino. He was standing by the crime scene tape with Phil, Zockinski, and Hill. "What's going on with them?" Santino called out to her.

"I don't know. They didn't tell me," she said. As the news spread, each member of the FBI turned brilliant yellow-white with excitement. "It's good, whatever it is."

"We've caught him!" Jason said across the link.

"Caught who?" Rachel said aloud. "Caught Glazer?"

The officers stopped. "What?" Zockinski demanded. "They caught him? How?"

She shushed him to listen to Jason.

"His truck. It broke down just outside of the shipping yard. A security worker found him before he could ditch it and run, and his ID didn't check out. Rachel, we drove past him when we came in."

She repeated this to her team, then turned as Gallagher waved towards the group from First MPD.

"Agent Peng," Gallagher called as she stepped aboard a cart. "Meet us by the Railroad Avenue Entrance."

Easier said than done. The road looped halfway around the port, and the service vehicles vanished along with the FBI. Phil and Rachel pointed the group towards Jason's signal and they started walking. Ten minutes later, an empty service cart bumped down the road towards them; Gallagher had sent someone back to pick them up.

They reached a secondary gate to the shipping yard. Just outside the perimeter, the cab of a semi truck had skidded off of the road, leaving deep marks gouged into the hot pavement in arcs, the tracks of a seriously broken axle. The asphalt was summer-soft, but the damage proved that Glazer had been going at a decent speed when his truck gave out.

"Damn," Hill whistled, using his foot to test the depth of the ruts.

"I know," Santino said. "Glazer's lucky the cab didn't roll."

Lucky? Rachel pushed a scan through the crowd. She couldn't find Glazer at first, and then when she did, she shuddered.

She no longer noticed faces. Faces were irrelevant, a second-rate identification system that couldn't compare to the nuanced individuality of core colors. She supplemented core colors with physical markers such as height, weight, and body language, including general facial gestures. The detail-oriented spectrum she saved for the environment. Buildings and spaces didn't broadcast who or what they were; she had to go search those out on her own.

Rachel didn't expect to have to search for Glazer's face. She thought he'd pop out of the cluster of law enforcement on his own, his core colors insidiously dark or his conversational colors raging. Instead, he blended perfectly into the other excited professionals and she had to cross-reference his face with that of the Glazer from the video to make sure the figure that had all the hallmarks of a man under arrest was actually him.

It was. Glazer's core was an almost-warm sandalwood. His conversational colors were slightly gray but this minor anxiety was woven into uniform-dark blues, with a goodly hint of purple. He was surrounded by cops, handcuffed, locked in the back of a sedan with wire mesh across the windows, and exactly where he wanted to be.

And he found all of this to be funny.

"Shit," Rachel said.

Gallagher overheard. The SAC looked from Rachel to Glazer and back again, and raised an eyebrow in question.

"This isn't right," Rachel said to her. "You know this isn't right. A guy like this doesn't get caught because of equipment failure."

Gallagher's eyes traveled back to Glazer, but she said

nothing.

"Ted Bundy was caught during a traffic stop," Zockinski said.

"And Ed Kemper had a body in the trunk when he was pulled over for a busted tail light, and he got away clean," Rachel said. "Bundy's not the norm."

"Randy Kraft."

"Stop listing serial killers! Glazer's smarter than your average bear-strangler. Look," Rachel said, and pointed to the security guard who had apprehended Glazer. "Small guy, getting on in years… Glazer's already a murderer, remember? What kept him from putting a knife in one puny old man and stashing the body somewhere in the yard? And how does a guy who can manipulate tech like Glazer does get caught by a bad ID?"

"What are you saying?" Gallagher asked. Rachel's own turquoise core moved throughout Gallagher's conversational colors; Gallagher already agreed with her, but was letting Rachel take the risk.

"I'm saying he plays the long game." Rachel nodded towards the truck and its broken axle. "And so far, anything that's seemed like a coincidence with him hasn't been one."

"He wanted to be caught?"

Darned skippy, Rachel thought, but shrugged. "Who knows what someone like him wants? I just think we shouldn't assume we were lucky enough to bag a criminal mastermind because he forgot to get his front end checked."

"Good point. We know he works with explosives." Gallagher waved her team away from Glazer's cab, then started running. They all followed, not stopping until they were five hundred feet away and secure behind the husk of an old FEU. The sedan carrying Glazer pulled in behind them. Glazer had gone to a rich purple; he thought this was hilarious.

"Do we need to get a bomb squad in here, or can you check it?" Gallagher asked Rachel.

Rachel looked to Phil, who nodded and took off his

sunglasses to go out-of-body.

"What's he doing?" Gallagher pressed.

"It's a thing we can…" Rachel began, almost automatically, but caught herself. Gallagher knew the basics by now. The SAC wanted useful information. "He's checking the truck from a safe distance," she amended.

"Are you doing that, too?"

"Nope," Rachel said as she peered through the side of the cab. "I can't tell a carburetor from a fan belt from a battery. Matter of fact, I don't even know what a carburetor is. Whole thing could be a bomb and I'd never know until it went off."

"And Agent Netz?"

"I grew up in an auto shop," Phil replied for her, his eyes covered by one hand, sunglasses dangling by an ear stem in the other. "I know what belongs and what doesn't."

"Really?" Rachel hadn't known.

"Yeah, it's how I ended up with the bomb squad," Phil said. *"I'm good with machines. Can I piggyback on your scan and make sure he didn't stick something inside the fuel tank?"*

"Yep." Rachel looped him into her scan and let Phil explore the interiors of various compartments on the truck. *"After this is over, you're definitely getting lessons."*

"Thanks," he said. *"I have no idea what I'm looking at."*

"All clear," he said aloud.

"Um…"

"Mostly no idea," he clarified. *"There're no bombs."*

"Good. Take his rig down to Quantico." Gallagher said to her team. She pointed at the cab, then at Glazer. "Him, too."

The small group from First MPD exchanged sad smiles. They knew they'd never put their hands on Glazer once the FBI had gotten involved. Still…

Rachel caught the fluttering shutters of digital cameras at a distance. *"How long has the media been here?"*

"They just arrived," Jason answered. *"Gallagher made a call to a friend in the press after the kids were taken to the hospital."*

Excellent, Rachel thought to herself. This was the type of press that OACET badly needed. She threw a scan through the gathering crowd and her new autoscript fed her data: name, rank, and the media's equivalent of a service number made a tidy list in her head. At the periphery was Bryce Knudson, her new friend from Homeland Security, his head tucked in close to a network reporter. She sent a quick note to Josh to be ready for possible damage control.

Hill tapped her in the shoulder. Rachel glanced back at him, and he nodded towards the service carts.

"Yeah," she agreed. They were done here.

They made sure to pass the sedan on their way to the carts. Rachel kissed her fingers and pressed them against the glass of the rear window as they passed.

Behind it, Glazer smiled at her.

SIXTEEN

Left took them towards the Palisades, right took them back towards the city and its dense fringe of suburbs. Rachel slumped forward over her knees. "I just want to go home," she said, and Santino nodded and started to turn right.

"No." She leaned over and touched the wheel. "Sorry, no. Not my house."

They were both exhausted. Sturtevant had kept them late; the media was pressing First MPD for details on the kidnapping and he had none to give until he debriefed his team. She and Santino were interrogated as though they were suspects themselves. They were separated and asked the same questions over and over again until the words lost all meaning. Then came the paperwork, both digital and hard copy. They would still be filling out forms in triplicate but for Santino's overloud sigh that at least he and Rachel were on overtime. The Chief of Detectives had thrown them out; time-and-a-half was sacrosanct.

Santino began to turn onto the parkway automatically, then realized where Rachel wanted to go. Zia's new violet surged within him, mixed with yellow apprehension. "I don't know if they'll want to see me."

She rested her forehead against the window. "After Shawn," she said, feeling the coolness of the glass against her skin, "there's nowhere else on earth you're more welcome."

Rachel turned off her implant and they drove in silence until they arrived at the mansion. The grounds were lit by reproduction gas lamps and straggling fireflies. Half the usual number of cars were in the lot, as most of the Agents had already gone home for the day. Santino parked beside a third-generation Plymouth Barracuda; Mulcahy was working late.

The front doors were kept locked after dark so Rachel took them around the back to the solarium. Like the kitchen, this room had been kept relatively free of mess. The solarium was a peaceful place, especially at night when the windows were open to the sound of crickets. Stained glass ran up to the ceiling and melded with the roof, wrought iron defining the edges. The Agents had layered every stray rug in the mansion to hide the floor, which had been remodeled in a glossy golden walnut parquet around the same time the skulls had gone in; the carpets were firm enough to walk on but soft enough for sleeping, and she and Santino carefully stepped over those Agents scheduled to come on for the graveyard shift.

"Penguin?" Josh, backlit by the glow cast by a crystal chandelier two rooms over, greeted her from the arched solarium door. She stepped over the last of the slumbering cyborgs and dropped gratefully into his hug. His chin brushed against her ear and her mood jumped to him; Josh closed his eyes tight against it.

"Rough day?"

"The worst," she sighed.

"But you got the kids back," he said, and looped an arm around Santino's shoulders. "You guys are heroes."

"Off-duty heroes," Santino clarified.

"Right," Josh said, and steered them towards the kitchen and its not-so-secret stash of liquor.

Someone had forgotten to turn the air conditioner down for the night and the kitchen was almost unpleasantly cold. The dishwasher was going. Rachel positioned her barstool so she could rest her back against the escaping steam. Josh went on a half-hearted search for shot glasses before he gave up and pulled down some pewter beer steins from a rack on the wall. A bottle of whiskey vanished into these before Josh slid their steins to them down the old butcher block counters like a bartender in a Western saloon.

"Want to talk about it?" Josh asked.

"No," she and Santino replied.

Rachel drank almost half a hand of whiskey before it calmed her down enough so she could feel it. Seated across from her, Santino set down his own empty stein and let himself collapse backward along the length of the island. "You know what I never want to see again?" he said, absently reaching for a copper saucepan dangling just out of reach.

"Truck filled with kids?" Josh was matching Santino drink for drink. Moods didn't lose their intensity when they jumped from Agent to Agent. The way Josh felt now, he might as well have been standing beside them when the doors had opened.

"They were so scared, Josh..." Rachel said, and slumped forward to rest her cheek against the slightly sticky wood of the island. "That truck was a furnace of yellow..." Santino and Josh exchanged wry grins. "Shut up. Walk a mile in my head and see how you describe it."

"Eh, furnace of yellow works for me," Santino said as he tilted his head towards her. "Everybody always says you can smell fear but damned if today wasn't the first time I've ever actually experienced it. That truck reeked."

Josh held up the bottle for refills and they waved him off, unwilling to get real and truly drunk until the events of the day had faded.

"Well," Josh said, "the important thing is that you feel really, really shitty."

"Yes," Rachel muttered. "Thanks."

"Yeah, but if anyone had turned up dead, you'd be wrecked."

"Egads, man," Santino smiled. "Why aren't you writing greeting cards?"

"I've been known to dabble in Hallmark on the side. Cyborgery doesn't pay as much as you'd think."

"Hey..." Rachel said, remembering. She peeled herself off of the countertop and pushed herself back against the dishwasher. "Mulcahy said I got a raise. How much, and when does it kick in?"

The conversation moved towards money, or the perpetual lack thereof. Agents had a generous salary for civil servants but any real profit went to those personable few who were also marketable properties. Josh was one of these, but he also enjoyed his life as a party boy, and his advances and royalties went out almost as fast as they came in. He and Santino got in a pleasant argument about whether it was better to save for retirement or live for the day; Santino was proud of his pension, while Josh had been known to rent out entire restaurants to impress his dates.

They were still arguing when Phil and Jason found them in the kitchen. They had both felt the pull of home. The five of them were soon sprawled across the wide planks of the oak floor, mostly laughing, sometimes falling silent before the others drew them back.

They turned to idle games and stories of pretty women. Santino had found a pack of cards and he and Jason built thin houses over Rachel's boots. She and Josh took a drunk's delight in letting them get four rows high before pretending to sneeze.

Phil stared off into space with the glazed expression of a man trying to see through walls. He had received a copy of the target practice autoscript from Mulcahy, and was working to strip the calibrations and calculations from it until only the ability to look through objects was left. Until Rachel could successfully package up her own scripts, this was the only perception script available, and Phil wanted a head start in case Sergeant Andrews came knocking.

She was comfortably tipsy, almost dozing. Josh's shoulder made for a hard pillow but he was warm. When he laughed, she felt it through the side of her head; his conversational colors were quietly blue, pushing and blending with the others' colors. *Ripples where the water meets,* she thought, and Josh glanced down and grinned at her.

"Sorry."

"Don't be. You're the sweetest little drunk poet."

Phil's head came up. His colors dimmed as he looked at the black hallway leading to the kitchen, then towards Santino. "Uh…" he started.

Josh was suddenly standing, comfortably casual as he moved towards the door. "Santino? Someone's here for you."

Rachel reached out and recognized the approaching Agents by their colors before they came into view. She swung herself up on her bare feet. "Come on," she said, tugging on her partner's sleeve. "It's Shawn. It'll be fine," she reassured him when Santino fluttered yellow. "He's…"

She stopped before she said "okay"—Shawn was still anything but.

He led his caretakers into the kitchen. Shawn had found an old suit which fit him perfectly except for the slightly too-long shirt sleeves, which covered a third of his hands and were cuffed tight with carved ivory cabochons. Rachel hadn't seen him fully clothed in ages; so strange, how she hadn't noticed how thin Shawn had gotten until he was dressed. He seemed half-starved and exhausted, drained, but he came up to Santino with steady steps.

"Blue…" he said in a voice gone to seed. The Agents went white in surprise; Shawn was one of the mutes. "The blue is everywhere, little men with wings.

"This is not me," Shawn croaked.

"This is *Not. Me!*" Shawn said again, almost shouting, and banged on his own chest with a fist to keep time with his words.

He reached out towards Santino. His caretakers scurried to block but Rachel told them to back off; Shawn's colors had never been so stable.

He put his hands flat against Santino's chest and leaned in close. "Sometimes I can almost see myself," he whispered. "After that I'm …" And Rachel and the others were knocked back and forth on Shawn's internal roller coaster, the car buckling up the high track right before the big drop.

"Shawn? Remember to talk," Rachel said, more to stop her sudden motion sickness than anything else.

He nodded, shaggy hair flying. He stepped back from Santino and covered his mouth. Through his mesh of thin fingers, Shawn apologized.

Her partner had been as much an observer as the rest of them, heartsick in grays. He sat down at the island and slid the bar stool to his right out towards Shawn.

"You play poker?"

The wight in the old suit smiled.

The cards were swept up from the floor and Santino dealt them in.

At first, they played for Shawn. Santino lost hand after hand, Shawn laughing wildly, until he realized the Agent was going out-of-body to spy on his cards. Their small group grew as others working the night shift wandered in, drawn by the noise and the inevitable arrival of pizza.

When they ran out of chairs in the kitchen, they moved to the game room. Nights in the game room were like sneaking into an arcade after closing, the walls crawling with light cast from the cabinet consoles. A large tournament-style card table was submerged under cardboard, and the Agents quickly cleared away the boxes and replaced them with candles.

They never played cards. When things were fresh and new, they had trained themselves out of the idea of it; cheating was too easy and bluffing too hard. With Santino dealing like a Vegas pro, they studied the table, their hands, each other, with trepidation.

And then, like stars winking out, they started to drop from the link.

Rachel knew better than anyone how their implants had become part of them. Turn them off to play a game? Such a simple solution, and one beyond their imagining; you woke up in a cold sweat over the nightmare of the accident which took your eyes, your hands, your mind... You did not see the loss of such things as solutions.

She played the first few hands but she quickly bowed out to let a newcomer take her spot. Rachel could not drop out of the link herself, not without losing her sight, but flipping between reading and interpersonal frequencies was bringing on a headache. She found some pillows and a ratty handknit afghan, and curled up on top of a bumper pool table with her whiskey, cozy amongst the boxes.

"Rachel?" Phil called from the kitchen, several rooms away. *"Do me a favor and hold up some fingers."*

"How many?"

"Surprise me.

She hunkered down in her nest of cardboard to make sure she was hidden and waved.

"All five. Again?"

Bunny ears.

"Two. Again?"

Rachel held up her other hand.

"Seven."

"You've got it!"

Phil's happy mental whoop was so loud it resonated throughout the collective.

Happy, she thought, watching the blues and purples mingle. Lovely rich reds floated through the mix; she might have to change her assumptions about reds in her ontology. Everyone at the table wanted to be there, even Santino.

Especially Santino.

Home.

Shawn's voice kept failing but he pushed on through the dust. He told a riddle. It wasn't very good, and Santino told him so, and Shawn laughed and laughed.

Rachel wrapped her afghan around her shoulders and jumped off of her table, wavering slightly from the whiskey as she headed to the bathroom. She rounded the corner and crashed straight into Josh: she had done her own version of dropping out of the link without realizing it, shutting down her range to encompass only those within the same room.

Josh held a finger to his lips before she could speak and she realized he wasn't alone. He stood in front of Mulcahy, whose face was hidden behind his arm against the wall. Josh pulled Mulcahy away and gently pushed the larger man down the hallway, quickly, quietly, so the others wouldn't see their unbreakable leader weeping with relief.

"Mulcahy says you can tell him," Josh said to her as they disappeared into the dark.

"Santino?" She looked into the game room, where her partner was talking to one of the gardeners about the care and feeding of African violets. *"How much can I tell him?"*

A pause, then: *"Everything."*

SEVENTEEN

They left the mansion a few hours later, the last of the whiskey buzz burned off by exhaustion. Rachel wanted nothing more than to fall into her own bed, but she had Santino turn off the road at a supermarket. This was a good enough place as any; she had never felt comfortable in parking lots, especially at night. They were about as removed from reality as you could get, sodium lights beating down on dead pavement, half-dead bushes mounded in wasted soil, the cars staking claim to chipped painted lines.

Santino asked her what she needed to buy at this time of night, and Rachel tucked her feet up against the dashboard and started talking.

It was, oh, close to seven years ago when she had been recruited for OACET. She had been about to apply to West Point to pursue her officer's candidacy. She wanted to go career military all the way, as high as she could before the glass ceiling kicked in, and then she'd fight to break through that. Secretary of Defense had such a nice ring to it...

But September 11th had been a couple of years before that, and the phrase "connect the dots" would never mean the same thing again. Even when she was out in the field, there were rumors of a pilot program designed to bring together the best and the brightest from the federal government, to connect those many disparate agencies and departments and organizations and the labyrinthic tangle of bureaucracies in a way that transcended self-interest.

A program that would allow the country's government to finally work.

Who wouldn't want to be a part of that?

She had been told she would return to the Army once the

orientation was over, that her career path would be straight and true thanks to her participation in this program. She would be changed, but in the best ways possible. She would be able to speak with forces trapped behind enemy lines, or, if necessary, could go in herself and never be cut off from home.

(And if you peeled back the flowery language to see the rot beneath, those departments with the three-letter-names could not *wait* to get their hands on the cyborgs! Imagine the potential. The out-of-body feature alone had them salivating.)

There was a long selection process. There were countless tests, screenings, drills… The dropout rate was immense. Twenty-five was the top age for candidates, so the competition was energetic and savage. Eventually, the candidates were narrowed down to an even five hundred.

The surgery was successful. The technology was experimental but safe. Not a single person was lost on the table.

For the first few weeks, they lived as though they had discovered magic; they saw the world through fairy-tale eyes. The link was everything. It was impossible to know how alone you were, to appreciate how bitterly isolated you were as a living thing, until that fell away in the collective. Every moment was perfect, like those idyllic nights with a new lover where you get lost in the conversation, the connection, adoring every part of their aspect while you were in turn adored.

It got old pretty damned quick.

They received no helpful advice from those who claimed to know how the implant worked. There were no instructions on how to keep the others in the link out of your own head, and you couldn't stop yourself from reaching out them when you thought of their name, their job, the brand of their favorite shoes.

(They had already started calling themselves Agents, and were inventing new words as fast as they could. Not being able to describe what they were experiencing to those who supervised their transition was an unexpected and overwhelming barrier: for the first time they realized that, despite all assurances to the contrary, they were no longer normal.)

And then there was the personal digital assistant. It was an interface built into the implant and was cued to the Agents' emotional status. When an Agent experienced any form of stress, good or bad, the PDA was automatically activated. It was like their avatars, a bright glowing green thing hanging in mid-air. Someone who was either very political or very shortsighted had programmed it to resemble a cartoonish caricature of George W. Bush, and it yammered at them in his voice as it floated at the periphery of their field of vision.

Like all PDAs, theirs was buggy beyond belief. Direct, simple questions were answered in riddles or not at all. It tended to ask them how they were feeling, over and over again, like an insecure junior high school girl terrified of losing a new boyfriend. It wouldn't deactivate until they gave it a satisfactory answer, and there was no way to tell what answer would finally shut it off on any given day. At first, most of them believed this meant the PDA was a direct interface with a psychotherapist, and they treated long sessions where they couldn't get it to deactivate as if they were receiving advice from a shrink. When they finally recognized its advice was never helpful, often harmful, they started screaming at it, this thing only they could see.

The medication came next. Obviously, their new tribe of cyborgs met with doctors on a very regular basis. Obviously, they complained to those doctors about the constant stress of never being alone in their own heads. Obviously, they demanded these doctors get rid of this thing that fed off of their stress so the Agents might have a fighting chance to get themselves together. Instead, they got pills. Prozac and Zoloft at first, then lithium with a small chaser of Thorazine. These came with assurances that the PDA was being retooled, but it would take some time to get rid of it entirely: later, when their assurances were no longer believed, the doctors started added sleeping pills.

This was when they had started dying. Not physically—

although that was when the suicides had begun—but the life bled out of them all the same. The more resilient among them compartmentalized their minds and bricked off their inner selves from the PDA and the drugs. They trained themselves to ignore their own emotions; the negative reinforcement of the PDA made this a fast process. Those who couldn't make themselves detach retreated to those time-honored coping strategies of addiction and abuse.

They were slowly abandoned.

Those doctors who had been so conscientious for the first few months vanished, replaced by a lone harried psychiatric resident who made them fill out a Myers-Briggs questionnaire twice a year and was otherwise there only to update the prescriptions. The politicians and officials who had cosseted them like beloved children disappeared into their respective bureaucracies. OACET's budget was cut to shreds. No one returned their calls.

They stopped talking to their families, their friends. Making idle conversation with the clerk at the local convenience store was an effort. Easier to shut down completely, to go through the motions of the day on routine alone. They even shuttered out the other Agents: they might not be able to stay out of each others' minds, but they could train themselves out of accidentally triggering the connection. No physical interaction, no reaching out with questions, or jokes, or conversation, No love, no sex, no new experiences of any kind. They maintained, but they did not live.

Five years of this.

Five lost years.

Mulcahy pulled them out of it. He was sketchy on the details—he had been recovering himself and said much of what he went through was missing or fuzzy—but his soon-to-be fiancée had somehow deactivated his PDA. With that gone, Mulcahy had been able to rebuild himself, and, as was his wont, rose up and laid waste to their keepers.

Josh had been the first one Mulcahy had set free. A heavy,

clunky phrase, but an accurate one: the flawed PDA, the constant emotional exhaustion and eventual detachment, the complete lack of support?

All intentional.

They learned their destruction had been designed from the start. The implants required a biological component to function, and no amount of tinkering with monkeys yielded the same results as when the implant was set in a human host. Someone wanted the technology but not the minds attached to it, so they created a secondary level of programming through which the hosts were gradually beaten down, their personalities eliminated. Their implants were only partially activated during this phase: the cyborgs had some of the capacity of full activation, but all interaction with technology and other Agents had been routed through the purposefully-buggy PDA. The antidepressants and sleep aids had been increased until the Agents were barely self-aware. The goal was to break down the Agents until there was nothing left, until they were shells of human beings, good for nothing but obeying a strong, guiding voice. At that time, the PDA would have been removed and their implants fully activated, and those who wanted access to the implant's abilities without accepting its risks would finally have their army of living weapons.

Poor Congress! They had been sold a bill of goods when they had signed off on OACET. With a handful of exceptions, they were innocent of this scheme, convinced by its designers they were dumping hundreds of millions of dollars into cutting-edge technology when instead they were funding the living deaths of their best and brightest.

But perhaps not so innocent. Some of them had supported the winnowing. Five hundred Agents at the beginning, their number gradually cut down, and down, and down again...

And Santino knew the rest of the story, or most of the important parts at any rate, so Rachel stopped talking, pressed her face against her knees, and tried to pretend she was alone in the car.

"We're all a little fucked up," she said into her knees after he had sat in silence for longer than she thought was possible.

"I got that," he said.

A few minutes later, he asked: "So Shawn is…?"

"A casualty. Mulcahy turned off the inhibitor and brought his implant to full activation, but it didn't help. He never came all the way out of it. It… cracked Shawn and some of the others. They had held themselves together for so long, and then they were free, and it turns out they couldn't handle it. They broke. Some of them killed themselves, and the ones that didn't are locked up in our basement. Mulcahy's been beating himself up about it ever since."

She had her implant turned down to basic light sensitivity, so when she peeked out at him she had to raise her head to see what he was doing. He was staring straight up at the sky. Another summer storm was coming in; lightning lined the clouds, barely noticeable above the halos of the sodium lights.

He must have seen her move in his periphery, but kept staring at the coming storm. "You don't seem fucked up."

"Me-you, or all-of-us-you?"

"Both, I guess. But you definitely don't seem fucked up."

She dragged her feet off of his dashboard and wiped off the dirt with her sleeve. Wasted effort. He'd steal her Windex and do a thorough job in the middle of the night.

"I'm a best-case scenario. It feels like all of my problems stopped when Josh activated me. I see a therapist but I'm not depressed. I can sleep at night. I drink too much but I can blame you for that," she tried, and was rewarded with his little grin.

"Why haven't you told anyone this?"

Rachel leaned back against the headrest and sighed. Outside, the first beads of rain appeared against the glass. "Plans. Strategy. Brainwashing has such a negative connotation, don't you think? We figured it'd be hard enough for the public to deal with us—the idea of us!—without implying we're waiting to go all Manchurian Candidate.

"And if we did let this out," she said, "it'd be polarizing.

There'd be two camps: those who think we're about to snap and wipe out the planet, or those who'd pity us and treat us like convalescents. We wanted to prove we're neither, first."

"First?"

"This'll come out," she said. "There's no way to hide this forever. But we figured we could buy ourselves some time, show the world we're stable before they get more ammunition to use against us.

"It's another reason to protect Shawn and the others," she added. "They'd be used as ammo, too. You know how people are: 'If three cyborgs went nuts, who's to say they all won't go nuts? Better to shoot first and set fire to them later... Anyone remember to bring the shovel and the tombstones?' Etcetera, etcetera, and etcetera."

"So you're telling me this because I know about Shawn?"

She shook her head. "Because of what you did *for* Shawn. Tonight," she said, waving off his next question. "You saw him. Smiling, laughing... Interacting. We had written him off, but now... I don't know. He was trying to pull himself out of it. He might come back."

"I should get stabbed more often."

"Don't tempt fate. We've still got those two others down in the skull cellar."

A moth the size of her fist landed on the windshield. They watched as its wings pumped slowly, then it flew back into the night to escape the rain and was gone.

"Why aren't you freaking out about this?" Rachel asked.

He blinked. "I am. Can't you see that?"

"Turned the emotional spectrum off. Couldn't handle it."

"Ah." He was silent for a moment, then said, "Back in college, a friend told me she had been raped."

"Jesus."

"Yeah. And I did what I thought a good friend should do. I lost my shit and demanded she go to the police so they could destroy the guy."

"Bet that ended well."

"It was the last time she spoke to me." Santino shifted around in his car seat so his gun wasn't digging into his back. "It took me a few years to recognize how I had made it about what I wanted, not what she needed. Believe me, I really want to hurt somebody for you, but that's not what you need."

"I don't like the comparison."

He shrugged. "I can't help what you don't like."

It was one of those conversations that moved in fits and starts. The heavy stuff had been thrown into the open and they were trying to pick up the pieces, gently, carefully, wary of the exposed edges. Outside, the storm was growing; rain slapped against the car and lightning cut across the sky. Santino flinched as a bolt shot down, grounding itself on the bent rooftop rods of the strip mall across the street.

"It's right overhead," he said.

"Yeah." Rachel had her implant set to close proximity and she barely noticed the lightning. She ran a loose scan through the storm. "It's moving fast. It'll be out to sea in a few minutes."

Another bolt of lightning crackled, bright and strong enough to shake the car.

They watched the storm in silence.

"I have a cousin-in-law who's blind," he finally said.

She stuck her feet back up on the dashboard and buried her head in her knees again.

"I don't want to have this conversation," she said.

"Just this one time, I promise."

"Fine," she said into her knees.

"How long? I'm assuming it wasn't congenital."

Rachel shook her head slightly. Her suit pants smelled of alcohol and dirt. "There was an... accident right before we went public," she whispered. "How did you know?"

"Just a guess. You might want to start wearing sunglasses, or covering your eyes when you go out-of-body," he said. "You're the only Agent who doesn't."

"But how did you know?"

"Little things, like not reacting to lightning." Santino said.

"You don't turn the lights on when you go into a room, you never meet anyone's eyes for longer than a few seconds. I finally put it all together after you explained why you never drive."

"Oh, wait," he said, and she could hear him laughing at her. "No, it was probably that day when you put on a blindfold and still beat me during target practice."

"You're a terrible shot," she said, and came up out of her knees.

"You put on a blindfold. And beat me. At target practice."

"Comment stands."

He started the car and splashed through the new puddles dotting the old parking lot. They pulled into the sparse midnight traffic. After a few blocks, she said, "I don't talk about it. Even with the others in OACET, I don't talk about it."

"I didn't say anything."

"I'm just clearing this up." Rachel flipped her implant back to the full spectrum and his colors, worried yellows and oranges, flooded through her mind. "I don't want to be 'the blind one,' okay? That label doesn't come off. And it's not accurate anyhow, because I am *not* blind. I see better than anyone else on earth."

"Done."

"Thank you."

"But my cousin-in-law?"

"What happened to done?" Rachel sighed.

"You're just lucky I don't like him. Otherwise I'd be on the phone with him in a red second."

"Oh for fuck's sake, Santino!"

"I'm just saying."

"You done?"

"Done. But…"

Rachel slumped sideways and let her head slide down the window, her short hair making quiet squeaks as it slipped against the glass.

"But," he said again. "This'll get out, too, and there'll be a lot of people who will be furious you didn't share this with them."

"It's my decision," she said, pointing a finger at his nose.

"No argument," he said. "This won't leave my lips, I swear."

Santino pulled into her driveway. The porch lights were on. The tagger had been back; fresh black spray paint glittered against her garage door. (RO-BITCH this time, and still neatly done, but the term was too close to its predecessor to award additional points for creativity.) They trudged up her walk to the front door and Mrs. Wagner's bedroom light went on as Rachel fought with the lock.

"Wonder what she's thinking about you bringing home a man," Santino mused.

"She's probably just relieved you're not a woman. One of these days I'm going to show up with a goat," Rachel said, and threw her shoulder against the door to pop it open. Humid nights were the worst; everything in the old house stuck. "Maybe a chicken. I haven't decided. Some kind of livestock."

"How progressive."

"If it's to be non-stop war with her, I'm going to have fun with it," Rachel said.

"Think she's the one who does the graffiti?"

She hadn't considered that. It might explain the tidy workmanship.

They went straight to the kitchen. Santino unloaded his service weapon, opened the freezer door, and stashed it behind the ice bin. He held up the magazine in question.

"The flour canister is empty," she said. "Where'd you keep it last night?"

He took the lid off of the largest of a matched pottery set and dropped the magazine inside. Rachel winced slightly as the edge of the metal rang on the ceramic. "Took it to bed with me," he said. "You sure you want both pieces in the same room?"

"No one will break in. Tagging the garage door is about as close as anyone wants to get to the neighborhood boogeyman."

"That's grim."

"That's realistic," she said as she hopped up on the counter. "You still want to be one of us?"

He opened the fridge and passed her a hard cider.

"Hypothetically speaking? Do I have to be grandfathered into the brainwashing, or can I join up now and miss it?"

"Brainwashing is included. It's a package deal," she said.

"Tough call." He took a long drink. "Yeah. Yeah, I think I'd still have joined you."

She gaped at him and nearly dropped her cider. "You are insane. It's been nothing but misery for the last five years!"

"Well, yeah, but you need to remember that I'm more objective than you are."

If her bottle wasn't fresh, she would have thrown it at him. Santino held up a hand to mollify her and continued. "I'm an outsider looking in. I can sympathize, but I don't really understand, so it's easy for me to say that it was worth it. I'm not just looking at what you can do, I'm also looking at the technology. The biggest concern about OACET is who should control it, who has the right to hold all of that power. The universal assumption is that it shouldn't be you, as if you guys needed handlers or something to keep you in check. But even though everybody always talks about what happens when technology gets into the wrong hands, it sounds like it started out in the wrong hands and OACET took it back.

"It's kind of hopeful," Santino said, and shrugged. "Maybe if they hadn't abused you guys, you'd take what you can do for granted, I don't know. Maybe that's just me rationalizing the shit you went through. It seems like OACET is aware of what could happen if you let yourselves run wild, and you do everything you can to prevent that. You know your welfare is linked to the tech and vice versa, so you're being as smart and as careful about its use as possible."

Rachel exhaled. "It'd be nice if you were right," she said. "I'd like to think some good came out of it."

He chuckled. "Come on, OACET's a family. You wouldn't be this close if you hadn't gone through all of that together."

"You're kidding," she said. "You think being close is a good thing?"

"Yeah?" Santino was surprised by her reaction. "I've seen

how you guys are together. You... I don't know. You blend."

"You think that's a good thing?" Rachel couldn't help but repeat herself. "Oh God, I didn't explain it properly. Okay, listen. When the implant is on, we..." she said as she gestured towards her head, "...are always together. And when we're awake, the implant is never not on.

"Human beings are not meant to live like this. We shouldn't be in each others' minds all of the goddamned time! We need boundaries, limits, space to define where one person ends and another begins. If we don't have these, then we begin to think the other person is an extension of ourselves.

"We start making decisions that affect their lives. Then, when they find out we've done something that they should feel is just plain horrific—I mean, just a total violation of who they are as a person!—they don't know how they should feel about it because they also think they're part of us.

"I'm talking big things," she said, as a confused orange-yellow bloomed around him. "Not 'oh, I guess I actually did like Italian food when I thought it tasted like soggy cheese,' but issues like politics. Religion. Abortion. We screw like rabbits, Santino! Just imagine how that one played out!"

She took a breath. "Maybe the end result is homogenization, where we get rid of our personalities, I don't know. It was really bad at first, but we decided to not let it get to the point where we're nothing but cogs in the same machine. So we made rules to control how we interact with each other, and we convince ourselves we'll be okay if we follow these rules, and we try to not think about what might happen if one of us decides that the rules don't apply to him. Or her. Or...

"We work hard at keeping the walls up," she said to him. "We know it's a sham, but it's what lets us stay together, and we can't not stay together.

"Do you understand?" she asked Santino, whose confused yellows had faded down to sage. "We're not close because we've bonded against the odds. We're close because we don't have the option to be apart."

Rachel waved her drink at him as she tried to find the right words. She failed. "We're struggling," she said simply. "When we were activated, we realized we had basically lost five years of our lives. We could think and feel again, but we weren't the same people we used to be.

"Shawn was right," she said, and forced herself to look up at him. "This isn't me. I can't pick up the pieces of my old life, because who I used to be didn't extend into other bodies. So I'm… not me. I'm a completely new person with someone else's memories and parents and Social Security number, and a few hundred other appendages who just happen to walk and talk and have different memories and parents and Social Security numbers.

"It's enough to drive anyone fucking nuts," she said, and took a long drink. After a moment, she added: "I'm surprised there aren't more Shawns."

"Me too," he said quietly.

"What I'm saying is, I've got a standing reservation at a local sanatorium. Visiting hours are from ten to five."

"I'll bring snacks."

Santino finished his cider and tossed the bottle into the small recycling bin under the sink. He turned and opened the kitchen window, probably more for something to occupy his hands than the need for the night air. The sounds of busy frogs drifted in, hot and heavy.

"You're wrong, though."

"Hm?" His back was to her. Rachel wasn't sure she had heard him correctly.

"You're wrong about homogenization."

"No," she laughed wryly. "No, I'm not."

"So you lied to me back at the Mexican place?"

She coughed into her drink. "What?"

"The Mexican restaurant. The one after Edwards' press conference. You said you were all tailoring your implants to your personalities. How everyone in the Program is different."

"It's not the same."

"Really? How?"

She thought about it, then said: "I never thanked you for saving my life that night."

"No, you didn't." Santino grinned. "But we've been busy."

"Thank you," she told him, and they both knew she wasn't talking about his quick hand on a Taser.

"No problem." He took a second cider from the fridge. "Any other secrets you'd like to share?"

"Nope," she said. "We've got a few more big ones, but there's no need to get into those right now. I'm about ready to drop."

"Me too. One last thing," Santino said as he opened the new bottle. "You said someone convinced Congress to fund the Program, that he was the one who developed the PDA and the brainwashing. Do you know who that was?"

She nodded. "Definitely."

"Who?"

"Rich. Connected. Extremely powerful. And that's all I'll say because 'plausible deniability' might be a literal lifesaver here."

"Okay." He paused, and she watched his colors turn over as he moved through the possibilities. "Is he going to get away with this?" Santino finally asked.

Rachel spun her bottle in her hand and watched the last of her cider as it swirled and foamed. "No."

EIGHTEEN

The coffee shop might be her new favorite thinking spot. The expense of a cab ride was offset by the free pastries, and the cappuccino kept getting better now that the baristas knew how she liked it. The girl with the stars on her wrists had brought her a fresh cup with a clover cut into the foam, accompanied by a cupcake adorned by a tiny silver horseshoe made from spun sugar. Rachel thought about making a Lucky Charms joke before deciding that heavy tipping was the better part of valor.

"How's business?" Rachel asked the barista.

"Crazy!" the girl answered, then looked at the nearly empty room and giggled. Rachel's left eyelid twitched; the barista was close to her own age but still far too young. "Well, there'll be another rush when work lets out."

The girl smiled in yellows and scampered back behind the counter before Rachel could ask her anything else. Local hero status bought about fifteen seconds of conversation per cup.

It was rare when she had a lunch hour to herself. Santino had stayed behind at First District Station for a departmental meeting. The morning had been devoted to paperwork; she had hoped that Glazer's arrest would have shifted the bureaucracy over to the FBI, but it apparently meant that the number of forms doubled. After she had signed off on the last copy, Rachel had stepped outside, hailed a cab, and returned to the scene of the scene.

She flipped her implant to reading mode and looked back down at her notepad. It was barely three pages old, replacing the ragged wreck of a pad laid open beside it. Rachel was transcribing her case notes, feeling a little like the pigeon who believed it had to spin in a circle before tapping the pellet dispenser. Back in Afghanistan, where office supplies were few and far between, she had once cracked a murder investigation after finding a new-to-her notepad at the bottom of a box of boots. When she transferred the details of the murder from the old pad to the new, something had shaken loose in her head. This technique had only worked once, but it had worked, and she returned to it when nothing else did.

(She had told herself that returning to the coffee house might help, too, but she quickly realized she had rationalized her way into an afternoon comprised entirely of caffeine and tiramisu. Still, no regrets.)

Rachel was restructuring the timeline from scraps and little ticks, and did not recognize Edwards by his colors until he was standing by her table. She closed her new notepad and looked up at him in silence.

"May I sit?"

Her eyes moved to the middle of the room and lingered there long enough for Edwards to mentally remove the tables and replace them with three armed men. "Please," she said dryly, and kicked the chair directly across from her so it jumped towards the judge. "How did you know I'd be here?"

"I called over to First District Station. Your partner told me."

Liar. The dimples were there, but she didn't need them. Santino would have gotten in touch with her as soon as he got off of the phone with Edwards.

"No, he didn't," she said. "Try again."

"Okay," he said, and nodded towards the baristas. "They have my card. I told them to call if anything related to the other night happened."

Rachel sighed. She should have known this place was too good to be true. "What do you want?"

He pulled his chair back as far as the space between tables allowed, and sat. "I've been doing some thinking," he said. "I've been set up."

"I think my implant's buggy," she said, running a finger across the thick of her ear. "I'm hearing an echo, but it's on a two-day delay."

He flared red. "This isn't a joke," he said quietly.

"I know," Rachel replied. She began to doodle in the margins of her old notepad. "You probably were set up. You're in good company. OACET, First MPD... I guess you could argue Glazer also took a shot at the FBI when he brought them in with the kidnappings. Same applies to the three other federal agencies I saw at the shipping yard.

"And the Navy," she said, and looked straight at him. "They were there, too. So, yeah, I'm not sure what you wanted to get out of this conversation but yes, you were set up. Someone definitely used you." Rachel held up her notepad. "Now we just need to find out who it was, and why they did it."

Edwards returned her stare and his conversational colors faded to wine red at the edges. She had seen the same effect in Hill in the interview room, when he finally recognized that the Phil standing in front of him wasn't just a machine. On a whim she stuck out her right hand. "Rachel Peng, OACET," she said.

The judge blinked. She had caught him off-guard.

"Shake it. What I have isn't contagious without six hours of brain surgery."

He put on a politician's smile and his colors went to a steely professional blue as he reached towards her.

"Forget it," Rachel said, and drew her hand back. "You almost thought of me as a real person for a moment back there. Let me know when you get around to that again."

He flared with colors that she generally observed in angry convicts on their way to holding cells, but politely knitted his fingers together to keep himself still. "I wanted to know if I could help." Edwards said through his teeth. "I thought this," he said, waving his hand to take in the coffee shop, "would prove I'm sincere."

She almost laughed him off, but caught herself. The kidnapping was still headline news. OACET's dramatic aerial search-and-rescue operation had been played up to portray the Agents as modern-day superheroes, and Edwards' argument that the Agents were unaccountable to the rule of law had been thoroughly trounced after the details of the standoff between her and Bryce Knudson from Homeland were released. What did it matter if the judge was blowing with the political wind? An ally was an ally, and OACET could use Edwards' public heel-turn to their advantage.

"Thank you," she said. His surface colors went back to yellow-white with mild surprise; he had been expecting another attack. Rachel flipped her old notebook open to a clean page. Hopefully she could get some useful information before Edwards realized she was interviewing him as a suspect instead of a victim. "Tell me why you think someone would target you."

"Probably because of my position against OACET," he replied.

"Why do you think that would make you a target?"

"I don't know. I suppose if they were looking to attack you, they might have thought I could have helped."

She flipped her implant to reading mode and made sure Edwards noticed as she carefully wrote that statement out in longhand, then asked: "Has anyone approached you in the last six months to take a stand against OACET?"

"Yes. Every day. My office can put together a list if you need names."

"I mean someone with the power to make this happen. Trucks, kidnapping, manipulating security systems... This is big-ticket stuff. Your garden-variety conspiracy nutjob doesn't have the pull." Rachel counted to three, then stuck an innocently quizzical expression to her face and looked up from her notepad to Edwards. "Are you involved with anyone like that?"

"It's Washington," he evaded. "I'm involved with a lot of people like that."

"I'm asking about specific people who might be too interested in OACET," she said, and started feeding him hints from her conversation with Charley Brazee in the First District Station parking garage. "Say, for example, someone willing to fund a potential political campaign in exchange for an anti-cyborg platform."

He shook his head. "No," he said. "I'm not campaigning yet. I can't take donations."

Rachel watched his shoulders for any sign of dimpling. "As you said, this is Washington. We all know how the system really works. Has anyone offered you any incentives of any kind?"

"No," he said. "Nothing beyond a few rounds of golf at the Congressional Country Club."

Edwards still hadn't lied. *What the hell was Charley talking about when he mentioned a payoff?* Rachel growled to herself.

"Who took you to play golf?" she asked. The Congressional Country Club was where the President played. It had a ten-year waiting list and a membership fee somewhere upwards of a hundred thousand dollars. She knew Hanlon's biography better than her own; he sat on the Club's Board of Directors.

"Is that relevant?"

"Maybe," she said as she jotted three entwined Cs on her notepad.

"Two senators, a congressman, and a lobbyist. I went to Yale Law. Two of them had kids who wanted to apply. I said I'd see what I could do."

"What about the others?"

"I suppose they might have been putting out feelers," Edwards said cautiously.

"Can you be more specific?"

"No. I'm not comfortable giving out their names."

"You're positive you've never received any type of payout from these people?" Rachel pushed. Edwards used to be a lawyer; he could tell the truth without telling everything he knew.

"I said no." He was growing red again, but his shoulders stayed clean.

"Okay." She thought back to what Charley had told her. Charley had never specifically claimed it was Edwards who had accepted the payout. "Is there anyone in your office who would accept money in exchange for influencing you?"

Edwards laughed. "I like my staff, but they don't have much influence they have over me."

"We had a tip." *Sorry, Charley.* "There's evidence that someone in your office received a payout, and that it was linked to a prominent politician."

He was suddenly wary. "What evidence?"

A sticky pile of ash, she thought. "It was from a confidential informant."

"I have no idea what you're talking about," he said, and was sincere.

Rachel pushed her pen around the pad in a circle, sweeping over and under the note to check out the country club. *What the hell. Go for broke.* "Our informant linked you to a senator. I will," she said, tapping her pad, "be calling the Congressional Country Club and asking for the names of those members who invited you to play.

"I am very persuasive." She cut him off before he could interrupt. "I will know those names before the day is out. If they confirm the tip, I will keep chasing this until I learn how it goes back to Glazer. It'll better for you if you save me the effort."

Edwards flashed red; he knew there was only one reason she would pursue this line of the investigation. "Why are you treating me like a suspect?"

"Why aren't you giving me those names? And don't," she added when he took a breath, "argue the personal privacy angle. You can't come down here and ask for my help, then shut me down when you don't like my methods."

He paused, then gave a tight nod. "Randy Summerville was the lobbyist."

"The telecommunications guy?" She wasn't surprised. The Agents enjoyed free crystal-clear wireless networking, rain or shine. The telecommunications industry was paranoid that the technology could be adapted to household use.

"Yes. He implied that I could count on his support."

"Nice coup," she admitted.

"Yeah." His colors took on a silent purple-gray sigh as he watched all of that money slip through his fingers. "The senator is Richard Hanlon."

Rachel didn't bother to write Hanlon's name down.

Edwards noticed. "You already knew."

"I told you, we received a tip. The source implied you were working with him directly to overthrow OACET. If you hadn't come down here this morning, I would have been knocking on your door this afternoon." She was exaggerating; it probably would have taken her a few days to get around to it.

"I didn't know anything about this." *Truth.* "I played a round of golf with Hanlon, had a few drinks with him a week later to follow up...Agent Peng, I'm ambitious, I'm driven, but I'm not a bad guy. Whoever claimed I was a part of a conspiracy against you was wrong."

"Uh-huh." Rachel let her eyes drift over Edwards' shoulder towards the entrance with its carved wooden owl doorstop, then back to her notepad. "Sure."

"Listen..."

"You nearly got me killed," she said tersely. "You let three gun-toting men attack me. Forgive me if I don't believe you. Now," she said as she reached out to the community server and started recording. "Tell me what Hanlon wanted from you. Be specific."

Edwards sat back in frustration. "There are no specifics," he said. "That's not how politics works. We had a golf game, and later we had drinks. He never mentioned OACET, or cyborgs, or anything related to your agency."

"What was implied?" Rachel asked.

"That he approved of my opinions on law enforcement and technology." Edwards thought it over, then added: "And that if some cases ever appeared on my docket that might allow me to apply those opinions, I should hear them out."

"Instead of recusing yourself?"

The judge shrugged. "I suppose so. As I said, there are no specifics."

Interesting. She had assumed Hanlon was courting Edwards because of Edwards' political ambitions, but Hanlon might be laying the groundwork for a hearing or a trial.

Rachel scribbled notes as quickly as the ideas came to her. If Glazer had tried to frame OACET and succeeded... If the crime was local, an Agent would be brought to trial in D.C.... *It wouldn't be the first time a docket had been rearranged,* she thought. *Hanlon could have put Edwards into play and locked the verdict.*

"What are you thinking?" Edwards asked.

"Things might be falling into place," she said. "I'll keep you posted."

"Tell me," he insisted.

"Give me a few days," Rachel told him. "It's nothing but guesswork right now."

Edwards reached out and ripped her notepad out from under her hand. Rachel was so surprised she didn't bother to pick her pen up. It left a long black streak across the paper, cutting through her loose loopy script.

"Wow," she heard herself say, then bit down on her next comment. She was still recording and Mulcahy did not need to see her go after the judge. "Please give that back," she said instead.

He held up a finger as he flipped the pages. "Your handwriting is the worst I've ever seen."

I'm blind, asshole. She rarely bothered to flip frequencies when taking notes during an interview; she'd be able to make sense of them, even if no one else could.

"This," he said, and pointed to the scrawl underneath the bold heading, GLAZER. "Tell me what this says."

"Thank you for coming!" Rachel snapped at him, and started packing up her stuff. She found a plastic evidence bag in her purse, shook it out, and dropped the cupcake into it. The cappuccino was still too hot for anything but tiny sips, so she reluctantly pushed it away as she stood to leave.

Edwards called her bluff. "Tell me what this says," he

repeated, waving the notepad at her.

"Keep it," she said. Most of the relevant case notes had already been transposed to the new notepad in her jacket pocket. "Consider it an early birthday present."

"Tell me," he insisted, and he reached across the table and grabbed her wrist.

Rachel didn't bother to twist away. Instead, she spun towards the counter where the baristas were watching the confrontation with open mouths. "Call the police," she said. "Right now."

"Don't." Edwards released her as the pretty barista reached for the store phone. "It's just a misunderstanding."

"I have a lot of those with you," Rachel said, rubbing her wrist. It was the same one that Jason had grabbed the day before. She might need to start wearing thicker shirts.

"I'm sorry," he said as he slid her old notepad across the marble tabletop. "The last few days have been stressful."

Lie, she noticed. The last few days had no doubt been stressful for him, but Edwards was anything but sorry. Rachel leaned down and plucked her notepad off of the table. "I'll be in touch."

"Agent Peng? I am sorry."

Nope. She nodded curtly and pulled her purse strap over her shoulder, then dropped her connection to the OACET server.

"Is there anything you need from me?"

"That owl," she said on a whim. The door was closed against the afternoon heat but the carved antique wooden owl was pushed to the side, waiting for its opportunity to prop open the door and let in the evening air.

"What?"

"I'm walking out of here with it," Rachel said. She stood and shoved her old notepad into her purse. "Put it right."

She waved goodbye to the baristas as she crossed the coffee shop, scooping up the wooden owl on her way out.

The owl was heavier than she had expected, roughly twenty pounds of old weathered oak. It was tall enough to rest its head against her shoulder as she cradled it in the crook of her right arm. Once upon a time, it had been painted; there were flecks of blue and gray stuck in the deeper cracks. The golden rims around its eyes suggested these had been bright yellow.

Well, Madeline, she thought, the owl's new name coming to her for no obvious reason, *I sure hope you aren't someone's family heirloom.*

Mulcahy would pitch a quiet fit if he learned about her petty theft, or that she had put Edwards in the position of accomplice, but Rachel was tired of playing nice. The judge needed to learn that every time he tried to coerce her, she would respond in kind.

Although Edwards seemed a slow learner... Half a block behind her, Edwards had his checkbook out and was laughing with the baristas. It wasn't a real problem for him if he could make it go away by hurling money at it. Rachel shifted Madeline to her other arm and wondered what should come next. Vandalism? Creating a public nuisance? Indecent exposure, perhaps? So many options. She'd just have to wait for the next opportunity to present itself.

She caught a cab back to First District Station and returned to the fishbowl. The room was empty, the other members of the task force off on their own lunchtime errands. Rachel positioned Madeline on the folding table within the organized tangle of Santino's shiny new computer system. The owl peered out at her from between the two oversized monitors. She inspected the setup, then pulled a potted orchid forward to give Madeline a dapper floral hat. Perfect.

Rachel dropped down on the couch and pulled out the two notepads. Her run-in with Edwards was nagging at her, and not just because she could still feel his hand around her wrist. She flipped her implant to reading mode and struggled to read her own notes, trying to make sense of how Charley's tip and Edwards' generally honest responses might fit together.

There was a fast tapping on the glass door, and Rachel looked up, blinking. Santino jumped into focus as he entered the room. "Hey, how was lunch?"

"Unexpectedly productive," she replied, and outlined her brief encounter with Edwards.

"Huh." Santino sat down at his workstation. "Seems wrong, somehow. A judge taking the time out of his work day to track you down?"

"He's a bully," she said, shaking her head. "This wasn't the first time he's tried to get me alone to push or coerce me. I don't even think he realizes that's what he's doing."

"But you don't think he's involved?"

She mulled it over. "No," she finally said. "He's like the rest of us. Someone's been pulling his strings and he wants it to stop."

"Sure would be good for OACET if he turned out to be the bad guy."

"Now, this is why you need an implant," she said. "We don't say things like that out loud."

Santino laughed. "One of the many reasons I need an implant," he corrected her. He turned towards his computers and noticed the wooden owl hiding under his houseplants. He glanced towards Rachel as he ran a finger down the owl's beak.

"That's Madeline," Rachel told him. "She lives here now."

Santino nodded. Sometimes owls happened. He turned off the computers, then reached under the desk and started unplugging them. "Want to help me carry these up to my office?"

"Were those assigned to you?" Rachel asked. "I thought you had to give them back when the task force was disbanded."

"I will give them back when I'm asked," he said primly, and began carefully wrapping the cords so they wouldn't kink.

She chuckled and helped him move them upstairs. After the third trip, Rachel pled boredom and stayed behind in the fishbowl while he upgraded his system.

Her purse lay open beside the couch. Rachel sat and pulled her purse up beside her, then rescued the slightly squished cupcake riding on top of the mess within. She fished around inside the evidence bag until she could peel the frosting from the plastic with minimum loss of sugar. For once, she didn't feel as though she was starving. The caffeine from the cappuccinos had taken the edge off.

Rachel stretched out on the couch, the evidence bag keeping the crumbs from the cupcake off of her lap. There was a smudge of black across the bag's label. She flipped her implant to reading mode, hoping she hadn't accidentally reused a bag that had contained biological samples; she had no idea how some of the stuff that was in her purse got there.

Santino's handwriting jumped out at her. "RFID, possible Eric Witcham sigture."

Cute. Her obsessive-compulsive partner had misspelled "signature" and had used her purse as a trash bag to hide his mistake.

Rachel turned the upper part of the bag inside out and used her finger to scrape off the leftover frosting. *Eric Witcham,* she mused. They had been unable to find any connection between him and Glazer.

Too many loose ends. Zockinski and Hill were out canvassing Glazer's old neighborhood, trying to find any sign of Glazer's accomplice. Glazer himself seemed a brand-new person; they had found no evidence that Glazer even existed in any state or federal database.

She and Santino had run that one into the ground. If Glazer was a hacker whose abilities were almost on par with an Agent's, it stood to reason that his first move would be to erase himself from the system. Everyone left a trace these days. The only way Glazer could be a truly invisible man is if he wiped himself out entirely. Either that or fake his own—

Oh Jesus.

The answer hit her like a bolt of lightning. Rachel leapt up and started throwing papers. *Please please please…*

There!

Charley's shoebox, tucked between the couch and a filing cabinet, had survived the purge when the FBI had raided the task force's office. Rachel hadn't bothered to check its contents, assuming it was another pile of the same useless crap that had filled Charley's larger boxes. She slid her thumbnail under the cellophane tape sealing all four sides, then flipped it over. An avalanche of scraps cascaded down onto the floor, business cards and receipts mixed with the odd photocopied subpoena. She dropped to all fours and began pawing through the mess.

She flipped over a handmade coupon for a local dry cleaner's and found it.

The image printed in silvery ink.

Rachel turned off her implant and sat in the dark as she reviewed her last six months at the Metropolitan Police Department. There had to have been signs. Hints, at least...

When she was done berating herself, she turned her implant back on and went looking for her new autoscript. It crawled out of hiding, eager to please, and she sicced it on the passive RFID tag buried in the ink.

A name and a phone number chimed in her ears.

Rachel reached out to Mulcahy and briefed him, then kept him in her link as she placed the call.

Charley Brazee's voice greeted her with a cheerful hello. "Agent Peng! Finally."

"I see the reports of your death have been greatly exaggerated."

He chuckled. "Not really. By the time I was declared dead, I was already a footnote. No rumors to speak of, just an obituary or two."

"How did you pull it off?"

"Changed my dental records, altered the DNA on file. The hardest part was finding the right corpse."

She shivered. *"I'll bet. And then you went under the knife?"*

"Plastic surgery? Of course. Eric Witcham was fairly well known, back in his day. It'd be awkward if I bumped into an old colleague."

"So what do I call you? Are you Charley Brazee or Eric Witcham?"

The man on the other end of the phone laughed. "Neither.

They've both outlived themselves. But for you, I'll answer to either."

"That's sweet," she said. *"And Glazer?"*

"Ah," Eric Witcham almost sighed. "He was my bodyguard on a previous job. His employer thought he was just a heavy, but he had talent. I took him with me when that contract was over."

"Well, he gave you up. He's how I got this number."

Witcham laughed again. "Nice try, but you got this number from me and no one else. Glazer and I knew the risks, what would happen if one of us got caught. You're lucky if he's said five words to you."

"Can't blame a girl for trying. What is it that you and Glazer do?"

"Reputations. We make some, we break others. It's all up to the client."

"And you were told to break us."

"Brave new world, Agent Peng. Branding is everything. We do realism branding, scenarios which capture the public's attention and shape it in a specific way. It's complex, it's expensive, but we get results."

"Conspiracy theories with a marketing department."

"Something like that. Big splashy events make a better impression than any ad campaign ever could. The media loves us. If you ever see a news cycle that's dominated by a single story, there's a good chance we're involved."

Mulcahy's chartreuse avatar popped into the air above her head. "Do not," he said, "mention Hanlon. He needs to give up that name himself. Just keep fishing and see what else he tells you while we track his signal."

She nodded. Mulcahy's avatar vanished.

"Gotta say, your fallback plan was pretty good stuff. I bet your A-game would have been spectacular."

"It was one for the record books, Agent Peng." Witcham sounded wistful. "If you hadn't found that tunnel... Ach! Nearly six months of prep work ruined."

"Sorry for the inconvenience."

"No, no, I'm loving this, Agent Peng! I'm so proud of your people. I know what happened to you, those five years… What they did to you? That was an abomination. Then coming together like you did, taking my technology public and changing the entire world with it?" Witcham sighed with a small chuckle in it. "I'm just so proud. I had to tell you that before I left."

"Then why try to break us? Why not help us? Are they really paying you enough to make it worth destroying your legacy?"

Witcham was silent, then said: "Think it through, Agent Peng. You too, Agent Mulcahy."

"Hello, Doctor Witcham." Mulcahy's voice resonated through her head. It might have been a guess on Witcham's part, but Mulcahy was not about to let an opportunity slide by playing possum on the line. *"Thank you for your work on the implant."*

"You're most welcome. Thank you for what you've done with it."

"I would appreciate it if you gave me the name of your employer."

"You're recording this, I assume?" Witcham said. "I'm sure you would love to put that name into the record. But my customers appreciate confidentiality. I've got my own reputation to keep."

"What if I were to hire you?"

"I'm worth more than your fiancée has, Agent Mulcahy. Besides, money is cheap for someone like me. I'm mostly in it for the challenge." Witcham paused, then asked: "Would you consider a trade? I need access to a hardened database. One minute of your time for one name. That sounds fair to me."

"Lie!" Rachel shouted at Mulcahy across the link. *"For once in your life, just fucking lie!"*

Mulcahy didn't respond to either her or Witcham. After a few brief moments, Witcham chuckled again.

"Thought not. Had to try. It has been a real pleasure working with you, Agent Peng. And you, Agent Mulcahy. Best of luck to you and OACET."

The line went dead.

Mulcahy's avatar appeared in the task force's office. "Marketing," he said. "This was all about marketing."

"Hang on," she told him, and hurried around the glass fishbowl, lowering the blinds. The MPD did not need to catch her shouting at an empty room. When they were alone, she kicked Witcham's cunning little shoebox as hard as she could. It hit the cinderblock wall, a tornado of paper scraps in its wake.

"He used me!" Rachel paced next to Mulcahy. "He used Santino, he used the police, he used Edwards... God damn it, Mulcahy!"

"It's not the first time we've been used." Mulcahy's voice was ice. "Could you have known?"

She thought back over the last few months, each interaction she'd ever had with Charley that she could remember. "The parking garage," she said. "You saw the video. He kept flashing excitement and lies. I thought he was following a script. And before that..."

The coffee shop, she thought. Charley—Witcham—had gone brilliantly red when she walked in on Edwards' press conference. She had assumed it was a negative emotion but maybe it was something else, something she had never seen before. Was there a name for what burned in your breast when your cyborg stepchildren made good?

"No." She shook her head. "I couldn't have known. Witcham was just this annoying guy in the background. He almost never read as anything other than average, and when he did, there was always a reason to justify it."

"Then it's a non-issue," Mulcahy said.

"No, it's not," she growled. "Not for me. Did you track the call?"

"Yes, to thirty different cell towers across the D.C. area. We couldn't trace the source or triangulate the signal."

"Figures. Damn it!" Rachel kicked Witcham's box again. Mulcahy's avatar watched it sail past his head and bounce off of the blinds on the other side of the room, denting them. An officer peeked in the new hole and then quickly scurried on. "All of this was about us. He kidnapped kids because of us!"

"But we were the ones who got them back," Mulcahy said. "We've been playing as heroes in the news cycle for the last day."

"That is not my point at all!" Rachel snapped. "Those kids are still alive because it wasn't part of his master plan to kill them. A woman is dead because it was! And there were four bombs, Mulcahy! What was he going to do with those before we stopped him?

"He's getting away with murder," she said, and looked up towards the lights, then back to his avatar. "Hanlon is getting away with murder."

Mulcahy held up a cautionary finger. *"Not out loud."*

Rachel closed her eyes and nodded, then took out her service weapon and broke open the magazine. She reached into her purse and searched until her fingers closed around the waxed cardboard of a small but heavy box.

"Those might wreck your gun," Mulcahy said.

"Urban myth," she said as she replaced the MPD-issued rounds in her gun with the solid flat-nosed bullets she had bought for their last target practice session. "Unless I fire about a thousand of them, and then they might warp the barrel ever so slightly. You know that, I know you know that, so just say what you really want to say."

"Did you think this through?"

"Yes. I'm going to shoot him," she said, and drove the magazine home with the ball of her palm. "I might even kill him. It depends on my mood at the time."

"It would be better for us if you didn't kill anyone."

"My mood will certainly take that under advisement."

"Rachel."

She rounded on him, gun in hand. "Why did you put me here if you don't trust me to do my job?"

"I do," he said. "But you need to remember what your job is."

Shit. The familiar worn grip of her gun was suddenly hot in her hand. Rachel nodded again, and holstered the weapon. "Sorry."

"I am, too."

Rachel shoved a stack of files aside and leaned against a table. She was oddly attuned to her gun. Its weight was different at her hip. *"Catching and punishing Witcham should still be a priority, Mulcahy. Especially if you want me to show how valuable we can be."*

"I know," he said. *"It is, and I do. But he can't give testimony when he's dead."*

"Noted," Rachel agreed.

There was an almost-timid knock on the door, and Santino poked his head in. "Hey, Rachel? Is everything okay?"

Her partner was already slightly yellow-orange, and this deepened when she said: "No."

"Um…" Santino came inside and shut the door behind him. "What's wrong? Because there's a few people out there who are wondering about all of the yelling."

Rachel shifted her focus from Mulcahy to the exterior of the room. Dozens of officers lined the hallways, most brilliantly orange and trying to catch a glimpse of her through the blinds. She nudged Santino aside and stepped into the hallway to wave at the startled officers before slamming the door on them.

"Your congeniality is inspiring," Santino said.

"Mulcahy's here," Rachel pointed to where her boss stood. The TV in the corner came to life with the image of OACET's green seal, and Mulcahy's voice boomed a greeting at Santino from the speakers. She rushed to turn down the volume.

"Should I leave?" Santino asked.

"No, you need to hear this." Rachel sped through her conversation with Edwards and the discovery of the planted phone number, then replayed the phone call with Witcham through the TV.

"Jesus." Santino, wide-eyed, shook his head as the recording ended. "Mousy Charley Brazee's a mad social scientist. Who would have guessed? Actually..." he paused, "are you positive he's Witcham?"

Rachel and Mulcahy looked at each other. "Good question," he said.

"No, we're not," she said to Santino. "He said he was Witcham, he gave the right details... Why would he lie about that?"

"Guess it doesn't matter," Santino shrugged. "Witcham's as good a name for him as any. Get the card. We've got to brief Sturtevant."

Mulcahy left in a tiny flash of green.

Rachel and Santino rarely had cause to visit the Gold Coast, the wing of First District Station reserved for administrators and ranking officers. Rachel didn't think she had come down since she had received the perfunctory welcoming handshakes several months before. There was real tile here, not linoleum, and wood trim throughout, but each office had been diced off by carving chunks out of the school's wide hallways and stacking the extra space onto the depth of the classrooms. Long and narrow, each office was a fancy paneled tunnel lined with track lighting, broken up by drywall and doors into a smaller room with a secretary at the front who barred access to the official in the larger room at the rear.

The Chief of Detectives ignored his protesting receptionist and waved them in while he finished a conference call with a local reporter. Rachel took in a quick surface scan of the room while they waited. Her mind traveled over diplomas, service awards, the various trophies and photographs. Here was more evidence that Sturtevant did not play politics: only the occasional notable was nestled among the framed vacations and graduations. Behind her was a tall stack of media equipment, crowned by a ridiculously tiny monitor. A picture of a smiling young woman in a blue cap and gown was perched atop the DVD player.

Sturtevant was right-handed; she peeked in the lowest right-hand desk drawer and found the traditional bottle of cheap scotch.

He hung up the phone and opened that drawer, then slid two tumblers across his desk. A third tumbler and the bottle of scotch followed.

"Sit," he said. "You've got bad news. I don't want to hear it."

"Sir," Santino began.

"Oh, I will hear it," Sturtevant said as he poured a thin finger of scotch in each tumbler. "There's no doubt about that. But I've been having a fantastic day and I might as well consider it over.

"Cheers." They raised their glasses and drank; the scotch was awful.

Sturtevant tipped over his empty glass and pointed at Santino.

"We found Glazer's accomplice," Santino said.

"That should be good news," Sturtevant said. "Why isn't that good news?"

They told him. Rachel ran the phone call with Witcham through Sturtevant's fancy audiovisual system. The Chief of Detectives listened to it twice, fingers drumming on his old leather desk blotter. "Agent Peng, anybody ever tell you that you're more trouble than you're worth?"

"Frequently, sir."

"Well, prove them wrong," Sturtevant said as he paged Zockinski and Hill. "You might as well get the other two Agents back here," he said to Rachel. "I'll call the FBI and let them know someone is still playing games."

Rachel stepped out of Sturtevant's office and reached through the link to Phil and Jason. Phil was in the secure rooms in First District Station's basement, working with Sergeant Andrews and the bomb squad to dissect Glazer's machines down to their nuts and bolts. Jason was a few miles away at the Hoover Building with the FBI's tech squad, reviewing the videos for any sign of Glazer's accomplice. She told them to head to the fishbowl at double time, and played them the recording of Witcham's bragging confession as they ran.

"How did you miss this?" Jason demanded.

She broke their link without answering.

Sturtevant's receptionist was bright red as she caught him eavesdropping at the Chief's inner door. Rachel pushed past him with a raised eyebrow and made sure her jacket was pushed back just enough to expose her ugly green badge; leaks to the press were all well and good, but she wouldn't let it happen until they were closer to Witcham. Inside, Santino and Sturtevant were arguing legal process. She returned to her chair and listened to them hash out how the MPD should chase Witcham down.

"We know him as Charley Brazee," Sturtevant said. "That's the name that'll go on the warrant."

"But he confessed as Eric Witcham."

"Irrelevant. It's not the first time we've had a suspect use someone else's name. And playing dead is rare but that's happened, too. Once we get him, we'll find out who he is."

"No, we won't," Santino shook his head. "If DNA, dental, and fingerprints for the original Eric Witcham belong to a dead man, then we're just left with this guy's word. We might never know for sure."

Rachel pushed a foot flat against the front of Sturtevant's desk. It was Edward's argument against the Forensics God all over again, and she was not in the mood to wade through the metaphysics of personal identity in the digital age. In her opinion, who he was would never be as important as what he had done, or what he was capable of doing. Charley... Witcham... (*whoever!*) had provided them with little evidence but an abundance of character, and Rachel was happy to let him call himself whatever he wanted as long as he did it from the inside of a prison cell.

Sturtevant ended the discussion with a call to a judge. Rachel couldn't help herself; she listened in to the silent side of his conversation. Judge Richards shared the same floor as Edwards at the District Court, and he knew Charley Brazee by name. Richards' shock carried through the phone, and Sturtevant's conversational colors had fallen into irritated reds and yellows by the time he hung up.

"This had been such a good day." Sturtevant slammed the desk phone down into its charger so hard she heard the plastic crack. "Out," he told them, and set the example by pushing open his office door. His receptionist was lurking by the window and the door bounced off of his head. Sturtevant glared at the young man, then stalked through the tunnel and into the main hall.

"Are you okay?" Rachel asked the receptionist, who picked himself up off of the floor and pretended she wasn't there.

Behind her, Santino's conversational colors blurred to yellow as he ran his hands up the door jamb to Sturtevant's office, his fingers prodding the small hole cut into the metal. He stepped into the office to stare at the mess of electronics, then back into the hallway.

"Shit," he whispered. He ran a hand over the top of Sturtevant's television set, then went yellow-white with sudden realization.

"What?"

"Rachel?" The white had faded, replaced with a wary reddish orange. "Have you scanned this wall?"

"Why... Oh no."

As Charley Brazee, Witcham had enjoyed limited access to First District Station. Glazer had been in the building at least once that they knew of. She scrubbed at the tension lines between her eyes, then sent herself into the building.

"Yeah," she sighed as her mind brushed against a small metal device, no larger than a pack of cigarettes, hooked into the building's power grid and with a tube aimed up towards a hole cut into the door jamb. "Yeah, same setup as before. They've been here."

They started clearing the media equipment away from Sturtevant's inner wall. His receptionist peeked inside and squeaked; Santino was holding a clone of Phil's wicked folding saw.

"Where'd you get that?" Rachel asked as she scratched a cut line into the drywall with the hooked edge on her badge.

Santino hadn't been with them in Glazer's apartment and it wasn't the type of thing her partner normally carried.

"Phil gave me a spare," he said, and dug the serrated blade into the wall. "Seemed like a useful thing to have."

"You were supposed to follow me out," Sturtevant said tightly. He watched, arms crossed, as Santino pulled apart his office. "What am I missing here?"

"You remember that RFID scanner from the raid on Glazer's apartment? Looks like Witcham and Glazer were here during the renovations," Santino said, and ripped the drywall away from the studs. The small silver box glinted under a layer of dust.

The Chief of Detectives took out his cell. "This really had been such a good day."

NINETEEN

Glazer was absolutely still, and perhaps not quite by choice. He was handcuffed, a short thick chain running between the cuffs and binding him to a ring wielded to the metal table. Beneath the table, his feet were bound to an iron ring set in the floor. No chances.

The FBI has reluctantly granted temporary custody to the Metropolitan Police Department. Glazer was being held in a federal prison in Virginia prior to arraignment, but he hadn't said a single word. Moving him to First District Station was a calculated risk: he and Witcham liked to play games, and this building was where it had all begun.

"If we don't send someone in, then bringing him here was a waste of time."

Rachel had assumed that Sturtevant was another man who liked to pace, but he was almost as motionless as the man on the other side of the glass. He was intent on Glazer, never shifting his attention even as he and Gallagher fought while pretending to discuss strategy.

"It doesn't matter who you send," Gallagher said, shaking her head so slightly that only the tips of her hair moved. "We've questioned him for hours at a time. He won't talk. He barely blinks."

Glazer's head swiveled towards the one-way mirror as if pulled by Gallagher's comment. He stared at the mirror for one heartbeat, two, three, then turned back to center.

Hill leaned down towards Rachel and asked in a low voice: "Special Forces?"

"Definitely," Rachel replied. Her technical specialty as a warrant officer had been in the Special Forces. Men and women like Glazer had been everything from her best friends to her lovers to her attempted murderers. Glazer was as familiar and as deadly as a favorite gun. "Any bets?"

"No tattoos," he said. "Rules out the Marines, most of the Navy. I'd bet Army or Air Force."

She agreed. They would never know for sure. If Witcham could erase his own fingerprints and DNA from the government databases, he could do the same for his protégé. At Rachel's suggestion, Gallagher had resubmitted Glazer's face to the military and had asked them to do an old-fashioned visual comparison instead of running it through a facial recognition program. Fingers crossed the man still had his original face.

The dry cleaning coupon with Witcham's hidden message was on a table by the door, sealed in an evidence bag and resting beside a bin containing the three newly-discovered RFID devices. The one from Sturtevant's office had been joined by two others cut from the walls of the Gold Coast. Rachel had found those. She and Phil would still be searching, but they had begged a break to watch Glazer's interrogation. She was not looking forward to the next few days, how they were about to become the cyborg equivalent of drug dogs, forced to sniff up and down First District Station for anything suspicious.

Sturtevant put his palm flat on the glass and appraised Glazer for a long moment, then pointed at Hill. The other man nodded, and scooped up the plastic bin and the evidence bag as he left the room.

"Where's he going?" Jason started to ask, then stopped as he saw Hill push open the door to Interrogation. Glazer went ever so slightly yellow as he recognized the detective, but his wariness was tempered with dark professional blues as he prepared himself.

Glazer's got a job to do, Rachel thought. *Great.*

"Hill's the best interrogator we've got," Zockinski replied.

"Him?" Jason's scorn was an ugly orange.

Zockinski smirked. "The man never talks unless he has to."

On the other side of the mirror, Hill looked straight at Glazer as he placed the three devices on the table, one by one, pressing each down so it clicked as it left his fingers. Then Hill sat, slowly, his eyes never leaving the other man.

A full minute ticked by. Glazer moved his hands to cover each other, the chain on his cuffs slipping across the steel table the only sound between them.

"Your name isn't John Glazer," Hill finally said. He put an index finger on the first device in the row and slid it two inches forward. "But that doesn't matter.

"We can't find your fingerprints, or DNA, or any other record to prove who you are," Hill said, pushing the second device to align with the first. "But that doesn't matter.

"You don't have to say a damned word from now until Judgment Day." Hill pushed the last device into the new row. "You can sit there like a sphinx and pretend you've got control, that you're going to walk away from this, that maybe you've got a future outside a concrete box," he said. "But we both know better."

Hill crossed his arms and leaned back in his chair. "So tell me what matters."

"Motive," Glazer replied.

His voice was gentle, almost soft. It was the voice of a much different man. Rachel shivered and everyone in the room went a little white with chills.

Hill nodded. "Assault, kidnapping… murder. You must have had a good reason to take this that far. We want to hear it."

Glazer shrugged with one shoulder. "What do I get?"

"Depends. You give up your accomplice, lots. Maybe your room will have a view," Hill said. "Nice second-story room at a Supermax, somewhere in a city. In the spring, you can watch all the pretty girls walk by. You can tell yourself they smell sweet.

"That's the best you can expect," Hill said with a dismissive gesture, "so if he's not worth anything to you, he's worth that much to us."

Glazer said nothing.

"No?" Hill leaned forward and smiled. "Good. Thanks. I don't sleep well when I make deals with creatures like you. And since you made this personal for me, I will personally make sure they put you in a hole so deep you will never see daylight again."

The minutes ticked by, neither Hill nor Glazer moving.

Hill stood. "Good luck in your hole."

"The Agents," Glazer said, and Hill sat back down. "Those things are walking around, pretending they're human. They're corrupting us from within. They've infiltrated the government. You know this—some of them work with you. Give them a few years and they'll control the entire country."

Lie, Rachel saw, but before she could open her mouth, Hill laughed in Glazer's face.

"Bullshit," the big man said. "A guy like you doesn't waste his time on paranoid delusions. The videos, the kidnappings... Those required someone with specialized skills. And these?" Hill tapped one of the RFID devices. "These show you've been working on your master plan for months. Crazies don't have that kind of training or focus. Try again."

When Glazer didn't answer, Hill smirked. "Okay, let me take a shot at this," he said. "You know the system, you've got the resources. That puts you as either military or mercenary. Since we'd get yanked off your ass if this were an official operation, that leaves two options. One, you're military and went rogue. But that would make you a crazy, and we've already decided you aren't crazy.

"Two? You're a merc. This is all for profit."

Glazer's steel blues hardened as Hill struck close to home.

"Someone paid you to take out OACET," Hill said. "You were setting them up, making it look as though an Agent had gone rogue. Then we find your hidden tunnel, and you had to scrap that plan before you got to the part with the big explosions. So you decided to prove they're a different kind of threat. Orwellian monsters, right? You tried to play on everybody's worst fears. Show the public how they've been living in 1984 all along, and they turn against the Agents.

"That scene at the shipping yard? Clever," Hill said. "Real

clever. You couldn't incriminate them, so you tried to get them to incriminate themselves."

Glazer did his single-shoulder shrug again.

"Didn't work, though. Clever won't keep you out of prison. But you know what? If you were paid to commit murder, kidnap all of those kids? You've got an employer. You've got someone's name." Hill leaned forward and dropped his voice to just above a whisper. "You've got leverage."

The other man lifted his hands so the chains rattled across the desk. "Not from where I'm sitting."

"Ask for a lawyer," Hill said. "Get a bargain-basement public defender and tell them what they're supposed to do to keep you out of that dark hole."

Glazer gave Hill a guileless smile.

Hill slid the dry cleaning coupon from Witcham's little shoebox across the table. Unlike the three RFID devices, this seemed to catch Glazer's interest; his eyes flicked down and back up to Hill's.

"You let me believe you had figured it out on your own," Glazer said, shaking his head. "Shame on you."

"So you know what this is," Hill said. "And you probably know the Agents found it and called the number. Your boss told them everything before he signed off." The detective mimicked Glazer's innocent smile. "He abandoned you."

"We knew the risks," Glazer said.

"Some risks," Hill chuckled. "We don't even know who he is, but you get caught and you get to sit in your hole for the rest of your life."

On the other side of the glass, Rachel hissed between her teeth as Glazer's surface colors strengthened, a dark marine blue fitting him like a suit. Interrogations were a cop's equivalent of picking a lock; each pin needed to be tumbled in order, and a misstep could cause the whole process to fail. Hill was moving through the right questions, and Glazer had slumped ever so slightly, his hands folded into each other for comfort. To Hill, those tiny tells screamed the job was nearly done. But Rachel was thoroughly familiar with the dusky grays which saturated a soon-to-be-broken man, and Glazer was nowhere near to breaking.

He was preparing.

Great, Rachel thought. *Perfect. He's going to try and play Hill, get a little leeway...*

And then Glazer shocked her with the truth.

"There's a senator involved," Glazer said, straightening in his chair as though he had found inner resolve. "That's all I'm going to say until I talk to my lawyer."

Hill didn't move but his colors popped yellow-white with surprise. "U.S. or state?"

"Who gives a fuck about state senators?" Glazer said, and crossed his arms. The chains dragged across the table. "Get me my lawyer now."

Hill pushed his chair back and walked out without another word, leaving the card and the three RFID readers on the table, just out of Glazer's reach.

The interview room went mad when Hill returned, Zockinski congratulating his partner while Gallagher and Sturtevant negotiated terms for Glazer's representation. Standing apart from this, Rachel stared at Glazer while Jason and Phil burned beside her.

"What the hell is this guy playing at?" Jason hissed in their heads.

"He was supposed to do this," Rachel shot back. *"He was supposed to mention the senator."*

"Then why didn't he just tell Hill it was Hanlon?" Phil asked.

Rachel shrugged. *"Credibility? Plausibility? How should I know?"*

"Because you should!" Jason shouted. *"You're the one who's supposed to—"*

"Guys?" Phil interrupted. *"Please don't scare the normals."*

Rachel took a breath and stepped away from Jason before they started waving and pointing or, God forbid, throwing punches without having spoken a single word.

"Agent Gallagher?" Rachel stepped over to where Gallagher and Sturtevant were engaged in quiet war. "In your interviews, you asked these same questions?"

She blinked at Rachel, annoyed by the interruption. "Yes. Why?"

"And he didn't say anything while you had him?"

"No," Gallagher said. "But we didn't have that card or the readers as prompts."

"Mhm," Rachel glanced back towards Glazer. The man looked beaten but was deeply self-satisfied.

"Another hunch?" Gallagher asked her.

"Yeah," Rachel said. "Same as with the truck. None of this seems accidental or coincidental."

The SAC was not convinced, and dots and streaks of orange began to catch among the non-cyborgs in the room. "The truck had a broken axle," Gallagher said. "When we took it apart, we found nothing to suggest it was anything other than an accident."

"I might be wrong," Rachel added quickly. "I probably am. I just think there's something else at work here. We have to play it safe with these guys."

"Good advice, Agent Peng," Sturtevant said, but while he added: "What would you recommend?" his conversational colors showed nothing but irritation.

"Different questions," she stalled. Behind her, Zockinski sighed.

"Such as?" Gallagher asked.

"Let me make a call first," Rachel said.

"Take your time," Sturtevant said, and meant it.

There's a senator involved…

The door clicked behind her, sending a chill up her spine. She knew she was on edge; this was the closest they had come to third-party evidence against Hanlon. Rachel could practically feel her fingers close around Hanlon's neck. *There has to be a word for that emotion between elation and dread,* Rachel thought. Not for the first time, she wished she could read her own colors; she'd probably learn more about herself in five minutes than she would over the next five years of therapy.

Rachel searched for the closest empty office, then locked the door behind her. *"Hey,"* she reached out over the link to Mulcahy. *"You busy?"*

"Yes." He sent her a peek of oak paneling, Carrera marble floors, and a dozen furious older men with nametags and microphones in front of them. *"Can this wait?"*

"Yep. Just wanted to let you know that Glazer might give up Hanlon."

Mulcahy's avatar appeared in front of her. "You're kidding."

She covered her mouth at the look on his face. "Nope."

"You're kidding! How did that happen?"

"I'm that good."

"Rachel?" Mulcahy said with a trace of irritation.

She dropped her smile. "If he gives it up, it's because he wants to. No other reason. I think he let himself get caught so he could testify."

Mulcahy shook his head. "End this," he said. "I don't like how they're treating this like a game. Nobody lets himself go to prison. Make sure one of us is with him at all times."

Rachel unconsciously reached out to rattle Glazer's chains. He was still bound to table and floor, enduring a nervous young man who kept the table between them as he held up photographs of various crime scenes. Glazer's meek little boy of a public defender had arrived. "I'll watch him," she promised. "He'll testify."

"If he doesn't, we lose… Ach," Mulcahy muttered, his avatar fumbling slightly as he lost concentration. "I need to go. I'm in a shouting match with Hanlon."

He closed his eyes for a moment, then looked at her. "Penguin," he said, "we're losing. Josh, Mare, and I are doing all that we can, but it's just a matter of time before Hanlon gets enough momentum to break us apart. He's trying to get us shipped off to military think tanks, and you know what that means."

Dark rooms, she shivered to herself. *No sunlight, no escape. The endless, endless, streaming code.* And beyond those selfish fears lurked the big picture: the child's body lying by the side of the road; the drone screaming black rage overhead; the empty stone of broken hospitals, homes, schools... The day she had realized she was blind had been the exception to the rest of her life: she had never woken up screaming when she was in the Army, only singing, with an old Van Halen song ringing in her ears and one line of prose lifted from its video wrapped around her during the boiling days and the freezing nights in Afghanistan. *Right now, hey...*

"Yes," she whispered, then raised her head and looked him straight in the eyes. "Yes, I know what that means."

"I've got enough on him to keep him off of us if there's no other option," Mulcahy said, "but if I do, I burn our safety net. I don't want to do that unless we're trapped, and we're pretty close to that right now. Hanlon knows he's got to get rid of us before we go public. We can't do that yet; it's too important to push it ahead of schedule. If you can get Glazer to go on record that Hanlon hired him, it'll be enough to shake Hanlon's credibility for a few more months."

Right now, it's your tomorrow... She nodded quickly, hands deep in the pockets of her suit pants to keep herself from trembling. "Okay, okay."

"Buy us some time, Penguin," Mulcahy smiled sadly. "Good luck."

Rachel stared at the empty space where his avatar had stood until her heart stopped pounding in her throat.

The little animated doodle of two men pranking the third with a table top...

Right now, our government is doing things we think only other countries do...

She waited until the hall was clear before vacating the office, then rejoined the others in the observation room. Phil and Jason were gone. She searched for them and found them in the break room. Excellent. Less chance of accidental contact, of needing to explain why she had left the room with good news and had come back shaken.

She peered through the glass into the interrogation room. The public defender was terrified and shied away from Glazer if his client so much as twitched. He looked the way she felt.

"Oh, the poor thing," Rachel said to Santino.

"We've got a pool going," he said. "You want in on how long before he needs a bathroom break?"

"Nah. Wait, yeah," she caught herself. They'd know something was wrong if she didn't bet. "Seven to ten minutes."

"Peng's in under the spread," he announced to the room.

Rachel turned back to the one-way glass as the others renegotiated the pool. Glazer was answering his attorney's questions but was still professionally blue; this was part of his job.

On a whim, she flipped off the emotional spectrum and tried to view him with her old Army CID eyes. Afghanistan had been nothing but a hairy mess of Special Forces, and her job had been to sort them out when they got too tangled. Glazer had that steady confidence that she associated with Special Forces operatives, a perverted form of inner peace attainable only by those who knew how to kill everyone else in the building.

Back in her old life, interrogating these operatives had been a complicated process. The United States did not hold a monopoly on tactical bad-assery. Those who reached her holding cells were usually part of an allied military division, and knew they would be leaving as soon as the paperwork cleared. They were great fun and glad to be in American hands; Americans always had pizza and beer.

But once and a while, an orphan would show up. They claimed they didn't belong to a country, or the phone calls to their alleged homeland went unanswered. These orphans had nothing to gain by staying, and once they were sure they had been abandoned, they would simply wait for the right moment and then try to leave.

There was usually quite a lot of cleanup required after

someone with Special Forces training had decided it was time to leave.

Glazer had been Special Forces, she was absolutely sure about that, but he wasn't an orphan. He and Witcham were still working this together. The only thing that Glazer had in common with those orphans was that as soon as he was done with his job, he would try to leave First District Station.

The cleanup would be atrocious.

Oh, God, she thought. *How much of this is inevitable?*

"I think he'll talk to me," she heard herself say.

"Hm?" Sturtevant, stubby pencil in hand, looked up from a Chinese takeout menu.

"I think he'll talk to me," she said, the plan coalescing in her mind like ice crystals forming. "He's got a bug up his butt about OACET. Why not see if I can get anything else out of him before he tells his lawyer what to ask for in negotiations?"

"Conflict of interest," Sturtevant said as he passed the menu to Santino.

"You let him talk to Hill," Rachel retorted. "Let me try. Maybe I can get him to give up that senator."

"Really." It wasn't a question. Sturtevant was pushing reds in irritation, with flecks of Hill's forest green core; Sturtevant thought she couldn't do any better than his own man. "Fine."

"Can I speak to you privately?" she asked him, mostly out of habit. Rachel had always discussed strategy with her CO before an interview.

Sturtevant shook his head and took the menu back from Santino. "Peng, just do what you need to do."

"Be right back," she told them, and fled.

She was not naïve. Rachel knew she might as well have autographed some of those burned-out ruins in Afghanistan. But over there she had been one soldier in a war, and it had made all the difference. She would not spend the rest of her life as Death incarnate while locked in a basement five thousand miles away.

And today, she would not allow Glazer to cut a path out of

First District Station.

No one at the MPD would ever know, she was certain of that, but she couldn't lie to the others. Sooner or later, a stray thought or emotion would make its way into the link, and they'd realize what she had done to put Hanlon's name on the record. Josh would never forgive her. Mulcahy would burn her to ash. Phil, Mako, everyone in the Program, nobody would see this as a necessary evil.

Or maybe they'd understand. Heck, maybe they'd do it in her place. She hadn't lied to Santino: their goal never changed. *Hanlon... Hanlon... Hanlon...*

Think tanks. God, she could not shake this sour taste in her mouth.

No interrogation was conducted without props. It was part of the psychology; the bad guy who has nothing sits across the table from the good guy who has something. If the interrogator held something that intimidated the suspect, so much the better. Common knowledge, really. No one would think anything of it if she carried a folder of Glazer's handiwork in with her.

Rachel raced back to the fishbowl, found a bright blue folder, and started cramming paper into it until it was decently thick. A quick scan of the windowsills and desk drawers, the nooks by the baseboards... nothing. The renovations were too fresh. Rachel started tipping over pen cups while she ran the edges of the room, finally finding what she was searching for in a box at the bottom of a filing cabinet.

She used the first paperclip to affix a photograph of Maria Griffin to the front of the folder. The girl's smile was blurry until Rachel flipped her implant to reading mode, and then Griffin was suddenly young and bright and full of promise.

I'm going to Hell.

The flat knob to the interrogation room was cold against her hand.

Glazer recognized her, his conversational colors losing the bored grays and returning to those steely professional blues as she entered. "Out," he said to his lawyer. The young man scurried from the room.

Rachel dropped the folder down on the metal table, the paperclip banding Maria Griffin's smiling photograph to the cover making an audible click. She sat and reached into her handbag, then placed a digital recorder on the table in front of him.

"We're going to conduct this interview as though you won't be here tomorrow," Rachel told him. She lifted the corner of the folder and let it drop so the paperclip clicked against the table a second time.

"Hello Agent Peng," Glazer said in his too-soft voice. Little spots of yellow-white excitement darted through the blue. "Is this my dying declaration?"

"I'm assuming nothing with you," she said, and used her thumb to turn on the recorder. "That includes whether you'll be available to give testimony at trial."

Glazer's eyes flicked to the folder, Griffin's photograph… He nodded.

Deal proposed, she thought.

"This is Agent Rachel Peng of the Office of Adaptive and Complementary Technologies, conducting a formal interview with suspect John Glazer. This name is presumed to be an alias. Actual name of suspect is unknown, but physical and video evidence found at each scene confirms that the suspect is the likely perpetrator. The name Glazer will continue to be used throughout this interview because most of those I would prefer to use are too unsavory to put before a jury."

Sturtevant rapped on the inside of the glass. Rachel nodded to let him know she'd tone it down; they had arranged for him to call her if he had any additional questions, and she did not want to hear the Chief of Detectives reprimanding her inside her own head.

Glazer cocked his head at her like a bird of prey sighting a mouse. "Rachel Phyllis Peng," he said. "Born in Austin, Texas. Father is a U.S. native, mother immigrated from Beijing in the 'Eighties. No formal postsecondary education, but has scored in the 99th percentile on general and Psychology GREs. Entered the Army at eighteen. Served four months in basic service, twenty-four months as a MOS 31D, thirty-two months in Criminal Investigation Command as a WO1. Eighteen sanctioned missions during Operation Enduring Freedom, six off of the books. Fourteen confirmed kills."

"Public record," she said. "Mostly."

"Lapsed Catholic, last time in confession was right before you were deployed. Scared of dogs. And..." Glazer leaned forward and smiled, sitting on his secret.

For an instant, she panicked. *You can't know! There's no possible way you could know...* Then she realized what he was implying and laughed.

"If you're trying to out me, you're about a decade too late," Rachel said as she winked at him. "Just because I don't talk about it doesn't mean it's an issue. Don't ask, don't tell, don't care."

He flickered yellow.

"Oh, don't tell me that was your trump card," she said. "That's really sad."

Glazer settled back in his chair. "I know what they did to you."

"Who? What they did to OACET?"

When he nodded, she pressed her fingers to her mouth. "You poor thing," she sighed. "You actually think you've got something on us."

His conversational colors blurred: he had not expected that.

"You want to know our master plan?" Rachel whispered. She said it just loud enough to be picked up by the camera, the recorder, and those watching from behind the glass: *Spoiler alert, guys!* "The thing about going public is you accept how one day, everybody will know. We already know it'll get out. We want it to get out! We just don't want to host our own pity party. The world might tolerate a cyborg, but nobody has any time for a whiner.

"You want to tell these guys here?" She waved at the mirrored wall. "I'm fine with that. I could even get a news crew if you want, but I gotta warn you, your fifteen minutes of fame are gonna get eaten up by ours, real quick."

By their colors, the First MPD officers and the FBI in the observation room thought this was standard interrogation banter. They were barely yellow, maybe slightly curious, but she could confess to Kennedy's assassination and they'd think she was only trying to draw Glazer out. But Santino, Phil, and Jason were dumbfounded, and the cyborgs clattered in her mind until she told them that the others had no reason to suspect she was telling the truth unless they gave them a reason.

"Are you done?" Rachel asked Glazer. "Or would you like to keep playing?

"Good," Rachel said when he didn't answer. "I was the one who spoke to Witcham, and he indicated that you both specialize in manipulation. With that in mind, I am assuming you will not be here to go to trial." She drummed her fingernails on the folder. "I'm assuming you've got some fourth-quarter strategy where you try to escape, and you'll either manage it or get killed in the attempt. Either way, you're going on record with the name of the person who hired you, as well as your motives for murder, kidnapping, building bombs, and so forth. It might not hold up in court, but if something were to happen to you, we have a place to start."

Terms stated.

"Escape?" Glazer pulled his hands up so the chain pointed down at the welded ring.

"Or be killed," Rachel clarified. "Let's be blunt: escape is what I think is going to happen, but the smart money is that you'll be shanked, poisoned, or any one of the many possible outcomes for a dude who accused a senator."

"Sounds like the smart money should be on me not talking at all."

"Yeah! You'd think so!" Rachel nodded. "Except you already let it slip that you could be bought, so whoever belongs to that name you're trying to use as your bargaining chip probably won't let you get to trial. But if you're willing to bet that the news won't make its merry little way back to your senator while you're sitting in our holding cell, you could take the house for some serious cash. If you live. Fingers crossed, right?"

Glazer was so pleased with how this was going he was practically purple. She had taken the bait he had dangled in front of Hill; Glazer had willingly trapped himself, but he needed her to spring it so it would seem authentic.

"Your call. If you think you'll still be here at trial, then you don't need to say a damned word to me. But if you think you won't be around, then you lose nothing by talking."

"Revenge from beyond the grave?"

"Sure," she shrugged. "That's a little melodramatic, but I suppose the phrasing is the prerogative of the dead man."

"If I give him up, I want a walk. No charges."

"I'm sure your mewling infant of a lawyer has explained why that's not going to happen. Assault. Kidnapping. Murder."

His rough fingertip flicked against the table, striking the metal surface directly across from Rachel's blue folder.

Deal negotiated.

"You see this?" Rachel ripped Maria Griffin's photograph off of the folder and held it out at arm's length. Glazer's colors didn't change; there was no remorse. "You need to hear me, Glazer. This was a very nice woman, and she is dead. I'm sure you knew everything about her, too, and you still killed her. You owe her, and you will pay," she said. "I will make sure of that.

"And anything you might do in the future?" Rachel locked eyes with Glazer and held his with her own. He was a psychopath—a charismatic psychopath, to be sure—but after several long moments her cyborg stare caused his conversational colors to blanch. He broke first, his gaze shying down and away. "Anything you do, any harm you cause to another living person, I will make you pay for that, too."

He looked back up at her, not quite meeting her eyes. "Bill me."

Deal struck.

"Gladly," she said. "Just give me that name."

He pushed himself back in his chair and stared directly at the mirrored glass and the black ball of the video camera beside it, and said: "Joseph P. Hanlon. Four-term Senator from the state of California. Sits on almost every defense or science and technology committee out there."

Rachel hadn't realized she had been holding her breath. "And his purpose for hiring you?"

"To frame OACET for crimes that appeared to be committed by a rogue cyborg."

"Why did he want to do this?"

"Because he needs to discredit OACET before his involvement in the creation of the Program is exposed."

"How was he involved?"

"His company was one of those which collaborated on the implant. Hanlon recognized its potential but didn't have the resources to develop it on a large scale. By turning the technology over to the U.S. government, he manipulated them into funding it and supplying five hundred test subjects. He planned to reclaim control of the Program after the government declared it a loss, but OACET gained autonomy before he could do this."

Whispers of color through the glass as the humans turned to stare at the cyborgs; bright white knives of shock as they realized that Santino already knew; anger from Sturtevant and Gallagher towards Rachel as they realized they had been used.

"Do you have evidence?" she asked.

"Payments. They came through the Cayman Islands but you can backtrack to a subsidiary of Hanlon Industries. Checking account routing number starting with Four, Eight, Three, Three. You'll get the rest of the number and the dates of the transactions after my lawyer establishes terms with the District Attorney."

He stared directly ahead and refused to meet her eyes.

"I need the rest," she said. "I need proof. If I don't have

that, I'm assuming you're lying to cover your ass."

"Terms first."

"Numbers first."

There was another knock on the glass. Sturtevant was furious instead of suspicious, but Rachel knew she shouldn't push it.

"Have it your way," she snapped. She stood and slapped the folder on the desk, hard. "I'll send your childlike attorney back in. Don't eat him."

The man is a monster, she thought as she gathered up her papers and stormed out of the room. *Him and Witcham both.* Not in Mulcahy's domesticated version of evolving societal persecution, but in the original sense of the word. Stories had draped men like them in fangs; it was easier to understand them when they matched your idea of what slunk out of the dark.

And she was no better.

She slipped the second paperclip from where she had hidden it inside of her sleeve, and used it to replace the one that had secured Maria Griffin's photograph to the folder.

TWENTY

Rachel was raw. The moment she had stepped out of the interview room, Sturtevant had dragged her into the same vacant office she had used to contact Mulcahy. The Chief of Detectives had been livid and demanded to know how much of what Glazer had said about Hanlon was true.

"All of it," she had replied.

He had paused at the significance of this, then decided to go after those problems he could actually solve. "And you knew this before you went in there?"

She had nodded.

"You should never have spoken to him… Nobody from OACET should have gone anywhere near him! Everything you recorded is worthless."

Rachel had tilted her head and glanced back towards the interview room to remind him how difficult she was to fool. She could see Gallagher conducting an official version of her interview with Glazer. He was answering the SAC's questions but not deviating from the same content he had given to either Rachel or Hill. Gallagher would get nothing new out of him except an irreproachable official record. Glazer's attorney was long gone, the digital hardware swapped out, the old files erased. Nothing that had happened between Rachel and Glazer (or between Hill and Glazer, for that matter) would ever be known outside of Interrogation.

Sturtevant had followed her gaze but it didn't shake him. "We're going to reevaluate your position," he had told her coldly. "You'll probably be leaving us. I don't like to be used."

Rachel had nodded. "The feeling is mutual, sir."

His anger had softened slightly around its edges. "I'm sorry for what happened to your people," he said. "Go."

"Can I say something, sir?"

"I'm not in the mood, Peng," Sturtevant had said. "Start packing up your stuff."

Santino had met her back at the fishbowl. He was madder than Sturtevant, enraged at how she had allowed Glazer to prove OACET had an axe to grind against Hanlon.

"What the hell were you thinking?" he had said, slapping the side of the box she was using for those few belongings of hers that wouldn't fit into her purse. "You knew Sturtevant wouldn't let you run your own agenda on his watch!"

"We needed Glazer's confession." Rachel had found the last of her books under a stack of papers. Across the room, Madeline waited under the orchid. She decided to leave the owl in its new home, something for First District Station to remember her by.

"There were other ways to get it!" Santino had shouted. "But you decided the best way was to sacrifice yourself?"

Rachel had shrugged. She'd go to her grave before she let Santino know about the paperclip. "It doesn't matter what happens to me."

Santino had gaped at her. "I hope someday soon you realize how stupid you sound," he finally said, and had slammed the door as he left.

When his anger had moved down the hall, she had reached out to Phil to make sure he stuck to Santino like glue. *"Something's about to happen,"* she had told Phil. *"Keep him with you at all times. Things get rough, you knock him out, lock him up. I don't care! He's not a fighter. Your only job is to keep him out of harm's way, understand?"*

Phil did. Whatever he had felt through their link had scared him; he didn't bother to ask questions.

Then she had put Jason on Glazer. *"Watch him,"* she had ordered. *"Have your gun ready. Try and keep some distance from him, but do not let him out of your sight."*

"They're telling me to leave," he had said.

"So? Pull rank. You're an Agent."

"Why don't you do it?"

"This building is huge. Lots of exits. I need to stay where I can cover any of them if necessary."

Jason had reached out and pushed, trying to go deep. She pushed back, but he had found the guilt. *"What did you do?"* Jason had demanded. *"Tell me what you did!"*

"I got Hanlon's name!" Rachel had roared.

Jason had retreated and severed their link.

The break room was centrally located and was as good a place as any to hide in plain sight. Rachel had walked in and sat at the table closest to the door, ignoring the three officers already there. The room had cleared, the officers quietly filing out so as to not attract her attention. She had kept her back to the door and pretended to read a magazine while she watched First District Station tick on behind her.

And then she had waited.

After an hour, Rachel had hurriedly walked a nervous ten feet to the vending machines and back to her table. She was still nursing her soda when Zockinski and Hill found her. They sat across from her, mostly greens and gray, with her own turquoise core moving through their surface colors.

"Well?" Rachel finally said.

"Is it true?" Zockinski asked her.

"That I'm getting kicked out?"

"That you knew about Glazer."

"No. Sturtevant thinks I used him, maybe used everyone here at First MPD," she said. "That's not what happened. I didn't know about Witcham or Glazer until a few days ago. Everything we've gone through is as new to me as it has been to you."

"But you knew about Hanlon?"

"Yeah." There was no reason to lie. She toyed with the water droplets running down her soda can. "We knew, but there was nothing we could do. Smoking guns big enough to bring down senators are hard to come by."

"So?" Hill asked. "What made you guys stop playing along?"

"Before we went public, you mean? The short-short version is we learned we had been set up," she said. "We never did 'play along' with Hanlon. We didn't even realize he was involved until months after we found out that Congress was trying to cover up the program, and that cover-up was a big part of what drove us to go public in the first place.

"Glazer's connection to Hanlon clicked into place during your interview," she said to Hill. It was as good an explanation as any. "Once he said a senator was involved, I had a hunch it was Hanlon. Turns out I was right."

"Was that what you were trying to tell Sturtevant before you went in?" Hill asked.

She shrugged and half-nodded so Hill would think he had guessed correctly.

"Sturtevant shouldn't throw you out of the MPD because he didn't listen," Zockinski said.

"Yeah, well," Rachel said. "Few things are fair."

"Come on," Zockinski stood. "We're gonna talk to him."

"Who? Sturtevant?"

"Yes," Zockinski replied.

She looked over her shoulder at the door. "I already tried. He doesn't want to see me," she said. "It'll be better if I keep out of his way, maybe give him a chance to cool off."

"You want to stay at First District Station?" Hill asked her.

"Yeah." Rachel grinned up at him. "Yeah, I do."

"Atran and Netz, too?"

Jason would prefer the FBI, but she knew Phil had his heart set on the bomb squad. "Yes."

"Okay," Hill nodded and left.

"Where's he going?" Rachel asked Zockinski.

"He told you," Zockinski said. He got up and went to the coffee pot. "To talk to Sturtevant."

"Oh," Rachel didn't know what else to say other than offer a weak: "He doesn't have to do that."

"Shut up, Peng," Zockinski said, and sat back down with a full mug. He scowled at the taste.

She was up and cleaning out the coffee maker before she remembered she had to keep her hands free.

"It's fresh," Zockinski said as he stole her magazine.

"No, it's not. And it's disgusting. I want coffee," Rachel said. She hadn't, but she was getting jittery and needed to move. "If you don't have the sense to clean the machine first, that's your own damn fault."

He shrugged and began turning pages.

Rachel poured water into the glass carafe, then started to swirl it around and around as the dish soap foamed. Water was a problem for her, moving water especially. It ran in and out of itself, twisting back and forth in patterns she could almost but not quite understand...

Her subconscious twitched.

She rested the pot on the bottom of the sink and ran a quick scan through Glazer. He was still securely bound to table and floor in the interview room. Jason, Hill, and Sturtevant were with him; as she watched, Sturtevant left, leaving Jason and Hill alone with Glazer.

Rachel returned to her scrubbing. She knew this feeling: she was staring at something important but it hadn't yet crossed the barrier between hindbrain and conscious thought. She poured more soap in the carafe and worked at the burned-on stains, hoping the task would cause her subconscious to get bored and do something useful.

"Peng, quit humming," Zockinski said.

"Shh," she shushed him and flipped her implant to reading mode, then back to full spectrum while her subconscious started to scream.

"Snuglet the Seal?" Zockinski asked.

Rachel glanced over at the detective, her raised eyebrow asking him if he had lost his darned mind.

"My kids watch the reruns," he said, and shrugged. "Don't give me that look. You're the one humming the theme song."

Her mind slammed shut on his words like a trap. Rachel stepped back into the middle of the room and spun her sixth sense out to the edge of the building and beyond, searching through a thousand different core colors like she was trying to pick out one voice in a crowd.

There.

Eric Witcham, *né* Charley Brazee, with his distinctively bland core of Snuglet's blues and grays, bobbed and weaved through the routine activities of First District Station as he made his way towards the interrogation room.

"He's here," she whispered. Then: "He's here! Witcham's in the building!"

She was running out of the break room before she had finished shouting, Zockinski at her heels.

"Jason!" Rachel called through the link as she shook the suds off her hands. *"Put Glazer into lockdown. Witcham's coming for him."*

"Get me his cell," he said. *"A tablet, a computer… Get me something he's carrying so I can use it to track him."*

"Go," she said to the detective as she broke away and waved him on. "They're in Interrogation. I'll meet you there. I can't walk and chew gum at the same time."

Rachel leaned her forehead against the cinder block wall and followed Witcham. *"Two devices,"* she told Jason. *"A phone and a…"* It was new and unfamiliar, and it left a nasty aftertaste in her mind.

"Here." She sent him a link to Witcham's cell. *"He's got something else on him,"* she said. *"I haven't had time to pick it apart, but I don't like it at all."*

"Bomb?"

"Maybe. If it is, it's different than any I've seen before. I'm linking Phil in," she said, and pinged the wiry Agent hiding in the relative comfort of Santino's office. *"He'll know."*

Phil joined them, but before he could ask why they were hot with anxiety, Jason shouted: *"Glazer's up! He's fight—"*

Then, nothing. Jason had vanished from the link.

"Rachel?!?"

"I don't know, Phil. Here," she said, and passed him the information on Witcham's cell. *"That's Witcham's. He's in the building, and he's carrying another—"*

"Holy... It's a bomb. Rachel, he's got a live bomb!"

A live bomb and the Agent nearest to it was down. *"Jason's unconscious,"* she sent to Phil, and started running again, joining the herd of officers stampeding towards Witcham and Glazer. Four rooms away, Jason's prone body had lost its conversational colors but his core was still healthy. *"He'll be okay. Can you suppress the bomb?"*

"Already done," Phil said from two floors above her head. *"The digital detonator's useless now, don't worry about it."*

"Thanks," she told him in relief. She would have done it herself if they were down to the last few seconds on the clock, but Phil was the right choice if someone had to go spelunking around in strange explosives.

She rounded the corner as the world went white.

TWENTY-ONE

Rachel lost her balance and tripped on a body, the shock to her inner ears from the stun grenade wrecking her equilibrium. She hit the ground hard and glanced up to track movement; the first explosion had blown the Plexiglas cases over the tube lighting off of their hinges, a dozen small cylinders falling from these on thin plastic cords. She scrambled back around the corner for cover, then snapped off her visuals and got her hands over her ears as twelve more concussions ripped down the hallway, hammering the fallen officers strewn across the floor.

Rachel lurched to her feet to see Witcham and Glazer leave through the outer door of the Interrogation wing's rodeo chute, the warrens of the parking garage beyond.

"Rachel!"

"Flash-bangs," she told Phil as she went back around the corner and staggered down the corridor. Stun grenades incapacitated through flash blindness and a blast of sound loud enough to disorient; she was apparently immune to the first but not the second. It was eerily silent except for his voice in her mind; her ears had been hit so hard they'd need more time before they started to ring. *"Everyone's down but me."*

"I've still got control of Witcham's bomb," he said. *"Whatever blew, that wasn't it."*

"I know," she said, looking at the smoking tubes on the ground, those officers who were still conscious recoiling from their residual heat. *"He prepped the escape months ago, set the grenades in the lighting fixtures during the renovations... I think he tossed one and the rest were rigged to drop at the explosion."*

Zockinski had been among the first to have reached Interrogation and he had been hit full-bore by the first grenade. He had fallen next to Hill, who was down but still moving;

Hill had his arms under him and was starting to push himself upright. Rachel pulled her sleeve over her hand and bashed a grenade canister off of Zockinski's neck, then wobbled on by. It would take too long to get them to recognize her, let alone rely on them for backup.

"I'm on the first floor. Santino's with me," Phil said.

"Get a medical team in here and lock down the perimeter," she told him, then realized she had fallen back into Army lingo. Details were needed. *"They're in the parking garage. They're probably taking a car, so block off every road,"* she clarified. *"But the subway and bus lines are within walking distance so make sure those are shut down, too. Nobody enters, nobody leaves, and if you get shit about giving orders, you put Sturtevant in a headlock and you choke him until commands come out!"*

"Rachel?" Phil paused. *"I looped this conversation through Chief Sturtevant's phone. I thought it would be quicker than playing catch-up."*

She shoved the profanity deep, deep down where neither Witcham nor Sturtevant would hear.

"Sir..."

"Later, Agent Peng," Sturtevant said dryly.

"Yes, sir," she replied. *"I'm breaking communication. I need to concentrate. I'll check in every three minutes."*

She dropped the link and mentally punched the digital locks on the two chute doors so hard she crisped the circuits. "The doors are open!" Rachel felt the pressure at her jawline but couldn't hear herself shout. "Follow me out!"

She cleared the external door and tried to pick up speed, but her body wouldn't go above a fast trot. The stun grenades weren't to blame; as Rachel regained her balance and made an attempt at a run, her knees failed her. The fall in the hallway had exacerbated the days-old damage from the coffee shop and she couldn't carry her own weight.

Her hearing started to come back, the alarms on the cars closest to her cutting through the wet fog muffling her ears. The explosions in the hallway had been intense enough to rock the floors above and below, and she limped along in a sphere of automobiles all screaming for their owners.

Fifty-two alarms. Her implant had counted their frequencies for her. She didn't know it could do that; either she had been writing another script or Phil had stuck an extra into her private stash during practice.

Rachel stopped and took inventory. She had a set of busted knees and no chance in hell of catching the two men who were now almost directly below her, but she still had her gun with its solid rounds.

And her implant.

You're the scariest goddamned thing on this planet, she reminded herself. *So start acting like it.*

Fifty-two signals...   Mulcahy can do this. Her hearing had almost fully returned and the noise from the alarms was deafening. *Josh can do this. Phil can, Jason can... Hell, even Shawn can,* she thought, gathering up the cars' frequencies in her mind, tracking each back to its source, weaving the myriad threads into a single command line. *You might be the worst cyborg in OACET but you're still a cyborg. You can do this. Ready, set...*

Silence.

Through the concrete floor, underneath her own feet, she saw the two men freeze.

"Agent Peng?" The familiar friendly voice of Charley Brazee had an edge to it as it floated up from the void separating the split levels.

"Howdy, Eric!" she shouted, all happy smiles. "We've got the place surrounded. You've got rights, put your hands up, and... Aw, you boys are bright. You already know this speech."

One floor down, she saw Witcham gesture to Glazer. The younger man broke off and moved silently away. Rachel unsnapped the clasp holding her service weapon in its old leather sleeve, but instead of retracing his steps towards her, Glazer kept moving further down into the garage. She left her gun in its holster so she could keep using her hands to steady herself against the cars.

"Come on out, Eric!" Rachel called out, limping slowly towards the void and keeping her voice intentionally loud to force the echoes. Witcham must have caught a change in volume as she saw him pull out a large-caliber pistol and take aim skywards, waiting for her to poke her head over the concrete divider. "I'd love to finish our little chat!"

"I don't think we have time for that, Agent Peng," he said, going low and sneaking forward along the tire line of a late-model Tacoma for a clear shot. "I'm assuming I'm talking to Mulcahy or Sturtevant?"

"Just me." She was transmitting to the community server and to Santino's cell, but she didn't need another voice in her head. "You've got my complete attention."

Witcham said something biting but she barely heard him as she ran the angles. *Reinforced concrete, rebar...* She couldn't have asked for a better location for a shootout. If she could coax Witcham into moving closer to the void, she could use the solid rounds with no risk to herself and still practically guarantee she could send a bullet ricocheting into Witcham's skull. *God answers strange prayers.*

She shrugged out of her suit coat and tossed it over the divider. Witcham's reflexes were slow; he took several seconds to aim and fire. His shot went wide but he held his position.

"Eric!" Rachel feigned sorrow. "I thought we were friends!"

"I don't want to shoot you, Agent Peng," he said. "Stay where you are. No heroics, understand?"

"No problem, Eric! I'm not the hero type," she said, and set off the alarm of the truck he was using for shelter to rattle him.

His conversational colors barely changed, all confident blues and golds. "Sorry, Peng," Witcham laughed. "Ten years from now, you'll probably be able to drive a car straight at me. But until transmissions go digital, all you've got is noise."

"Says the man who uses flash-bangs instead of real grenades."

"You think I want to hurt people? Maybe people I know?

That's sick."

"Maria Griffin says hi," Rachel retorted.

"She was business," Witcham said, and his colors took on a mournful gray. "I hated having to do that."

Rachel blinked; he actually did regret her murder. Had circumstances been different, Rachel might have changed her mind about plotting a kill shot. "Business? There's a shitty reason to murder someone if I've ever heard one."

"New world," he said. "New opportunities. There's not a rich or a powerful man out there who doesn't have blood on his hands."

"Mercenaries don't get to pick and choose when they grow a conscience."

"Specialist-for-hire," he corrected. "I normally play with finances. This is my first job with a body count. I hope it's my last."

"You just tried to shoot me! You want me to pat you on the back for your self-control?"

Two floors below Witcham, Glazer was powering up an old electric scooter. "I'm not about to go to jail," Witcham said as the sound of the motor filled the garage. "Stay out of my way and you'll be fine."

"Hey, Charley, tell me one last thing," she said, looping his old alias into their conversation. *Dear, dear, Charley, my good friend Charley, I never thought you were a nobody, a petty annoyance, no, never...* "If you're a merc, who hired you? Your buddy told us it was Senator Hanlon. Was he right?"

His conversation colors brightened. "Can neither confirm nor deny, Agent Peng."

"Really? Because you're nodding, asshole!" Rachel shouted. "And you're nodding on camera. Thanks for the leverage."

"Nice try, Peng," he said, and pulled another couple of feet away from the void as he moved back into the garage. "But I took out all surveillance."

"Not mine," Rachel leaned against a minivan for support and took out her gun. "Not me. Why does everyone forget I can see through walls?"

Witcham's colors bled to white. She sympathized; Hanlon was a scary guy.

Please, please, please... Rachel's hands were still shaking slightly from the grenades. She steadied her weapon on the van's side view mirror and exhaled, slowly. *Come four feet towards me. That's all I need. Just four stupid feet...*

"Nothing to say, Charley?" Her window was closing and he was too far back for a head shot. Rachel decided to settle for low center mass. Stomach wounds weren't immediately fatal but she'd do her best. "I'll take that as a yes. On behalf of OACET, please accept our heartfelt appreciation for the new lead. Also? Stop or I'll shoot."

The sound of the scooter's motor grew louder as Glazer closed the distance. "Goodbye, Rachel. It's been fun," Witcham called out above its sputter. He pulled another foot away from the void and she cursed herself for procrastinating. "Don't bother looking for me. This isn't my first time going to ground. Even if we do see each other again, you won't know it's me."

And Glazer arrived, and Witcham took another step away from the void, and Rachel took squeezed off two perfect shots which moved against concrete and steel before passing through each of Eric Witcham's shins.

Then, before Witcham or gravity caught on to the fact his lower legs were gone, she put two more through his ankles, just so she and Mulcahy would have something to snicker about at parties.

"Don't be countin' on it," she muttered to herself in a mock Irish brogue.

There was screaming. Glazer grabbed Witcham in a fireman's carry, then threw him over the back seat of the scooter and swung it around so it was pointed towards the bottom of the parking garage. They took off in a sputter, Witcham's howls gradually fading as they drove down the ramp.

Rachel collapsed on the pavement. She stared at the four fresh burrs she had stamped in the concrete and idly wondered how many months of practice she would need to put in with solid rounds before she could double-bank her shots. Then she reached out through the link. *"Phil?"*

"Rachel! Thank God."

"They're on an old scooter, believe it or not. Witcham's seriously injured; he'll slow them down. Tell me you've got the ramps to the parking garage blocked off."

"They're working on it," he said. *"I think they're almost done."*

Rachel closed her eyes as she felt the cool metal of a door handle underneath Phil's fingers: her walls were weak. *"How long does it take to set up a road block at a police station? My people would have had that done in ninety seconds."*

He grinned. *"These are your people. Check your clock,"* he said. *"That's about how long you've been out of contact."*

She did: her conversation with Witcham had taken less than two minutes. *"Time flies,"* she said, and her knees throbbed as Phil knelt to help someone inside. *"I'm closing myself out until I get my reserves back. I can feel everything you're doing."*

"I know, you're open both ways. Get up off of the cold, hard ground."

"Hold my calls?"

"Done. Mulcahy's on his way," he said, and blinked out.

She heard soft-soled rubber scuff the pavement beside her and realized she had turned off visuals. "Where have you been?" she asked Santino without opening her eyes.

"Someone left a mess inside," he said. "Must have been a hell of a party."

"Yup. You missed it. There were fireworks."

"Aw." He paused. "I think you're lying in dried vomit."

"That sounds about right," she sighed, and held up her hand. Santino, the clean freak, didn't hesitate before he took it and helped her up, but she was glad she couldn't see his face when he did.

Rachel winced as her weight came down. "My knees are pooched," she said, and remembered. She turned visuals back on. Objects came first. On the lowest level of the garage,

Witcham and Glazer were trapped in a corner as officers closed in from both sides. Then she added emotions: the officers and Witcham glowed red, but theirs was from anger and his was from pain; to the side, Glazer was the calm steely-blue of professional purpose.

"They're not worried," she muttered.

"What?" Santino asked.

"Witcham and Glazer…" she answered, then reached out to Phil again. *"You still have a lock on Witcham's bomb?"*

"Of course," the other Agent replied. *"Why?"*

He would have ditched it if it were useless, she thought to herself.

Her walls were still down: Phil heard her. *"Get out of the garage!"*

He was broadcasting through the MPD's headsets. Far below, the officers turned and ran.

"Go!" She pushed Santino. "Move!"

He looped an arm under her and half-dragged, half-carried Rachel the hundred yards back to the station. He pushed them through the door and slammed it behind them, then fell face-first over one of the MPD's tactical medics. When Rachel picked herself up, she saw why there was no backup in the garage. The hallway was anarchy, with anyone in the building who had the smallest scrap of training in first aid attending to those who had been injured. There was a lot more blood than she remembered and it all smelled vaguely of cooked pork. Stun grenades weren't meant to come in contact with skin.

"How did you get through this?" Rachel asked.

"Kicking," he said. "Plenty of kicking."

The station shook ever so slightly and everyone in the hall went orange as they froze and waited to see what would come next.

"What just happened?" Santino asked as the wave of apprehension passed and normal conversational colors came back up in the crowd, curious yellows pushing out the orange.

"I don't know," Rachel said. "I've got an idea, but we need

to find Phil." Two floors down, a surge of kinetic energy and a massive cloud of dust were messing with her scans, and she didn't have the time or the composure to pick through it until she found the bodies. All she knew for sure was that there was no longer anything alive in that corner of the parking garage, and that was good enough for her.

She searched for the other Agents and found Phil in the interrogation room at the end of the hallway. Jason was still offline. She and Santino tripped and pushed themselves through the crowd, then dropped into the relative calm of a room with only six people in it. Rachel tried to shut the door behind them but its knob had been broken off at the shaft, so she nudged a chair in front of the door to hold it closed.

The ambulances were still minutes away. Zockinski and Hill were keeping Phil and another self-appointed medic busy. Hill's dress shirt was gone, the charred fabric tossed into the waste can in the corner. His arms were a mass of burns and blistered skin; at least two of the flash-bangs had fallen on him when he was prone. Phil was applying ointment to him with a sterile swab. Zockinski had a light bandage across his lower face and neck, and a thick one stuck to his back where she had knocked away the grenade canister. Both glanced up when she and Santino entered, and their colors brightened to see she was safe.

Jason was sitting up, one of the men from Andrews' bomb unit checking his vitals. The other Agent peered out at her from under the layers of gauze wrapped at his hairline. "What'd he hit you with?" she asked. She reached out to ping him as lightly as she could, but he wasn't in the link. It felt vacant without him.

"The table," he said. She raised an eyebrow and used her toe to tap the bolted plate which fixed the metal table to the floor. He shrugged. "Or, he used me to hit the table."

She found herself hugging him. "Asshole," she whispered, not sure if she meant him or Glazer.

"Yup."

The bomb unit technician detangled them and tried to give

her a fast checkup. She shrugged him off and badgered him into giving her a couple of ice packs for her knees, then claimed a spot on the polished linoleum floor as far away from Phil as she could get. Her reserves were still low and she didn't want to touch someone with an active implant until she had a few minutes to recover.

"What happened downstairs?" Rachel asked him.

"That bomb went off." Phil shook his head. "I had a lock on it, and then it was gone."

"Not your fault," she said. "Not with those two. They probably had an analog trigger as backup. Definitely not your fault."

An officer pushed the door open and ordered them to evacuate the building. Zockinski told him to fuck off. This had all of the markings of a good fight until Sturtevant followed the officer into the room.

"Sit," Sturtevant said as Rachel and Hill tried to stand for him.

"Sir?" Zockinski, his head resting against the wall, asked: "Did we get them?"

"No." Sturtevant replied. "We think they went out through the main air shaft for the ventilation system in the parking garage. It looks as though they prepped the tunnel during construction. We can't get into it yet; they detonated a bomb behind them. Took down a good part of the lowest level and sealed off the tunnel. Wherever that tunnel went, they're outside the perimeter now."

"Was anyone hurt?" Phil asked.

"We don't know," Sturtevant replied. "I left before the head count was done. But until my phone rings, I'll assume the best.

"Now. Agent Peng? Tell me what happened in the garage."

Rachel gave him the short version. She had decided Sturtevant needed to see the video for himself, so she asked him to watch that before they did a full briefing. "It won't look like normal film," she warned. "I was scanning through concrete to see Witcham and Glazer. But the audio is good, and the visuals should be enough to hold up at a hearing."

"You shot Witcham."

"Only to wound, and none in the back," she added, remembering that the police and the military had different standards for when and how it was appropriate to send a bad guy to the ground. She was suddenly glad the layout of the garage had prevented a kill shot.

"You shot him four times while standing one floor above him... Peng, I'm looking for a polite way to call you a liar."

"You can call me whatever you like, sir, but it'll be easier to explain the ballistics if you watch the video first."

Her tablet made the rounds, starting with Sturtevant and moving down the chain of command. Even the bomb unit technician took a turn. As the tablet was passed down the roster, Sturtevant contemplated her through a rolling storm of blues, reds, and oranges; Rachel couldn't spend the energy to puzzle those out, so she flipped off the emotional spectrum and turned to the man sitting on the ground beside her. "What happened in here?" she whispered to Hill.

The large man shook his head gingerly, wincing as his raw skin twisted ever so slightly under the gauze. "He was watching Jason," he said. "Your eyes change when you talk to each other. One of you said something to Jason, and Glazer just knew. I don't know how he picked his cuffs, but he took me down, then Jason. He was up and gone before I could move."

She didn't quite believe it; she would have put Hill up against Glazer in a fight. "He's that fast?"

"Yeah."

"Sorry," she said, and meant it.

"Not your fault." Hill grinned at her.

She could only meet his eyes because of a technicality.

There was some shouting from outside of the door, smoothed over by Josh's steady tenor. Mulcahy opened the door and walked into the room, an MPD officer dangling from each arm as they tried to restrain him. Mulcahy shrugged them off and went straight to Jason, while Josh headed towards Rachel.

"Penguin!" Josh grabbed her and pulled her into a hug before she could stop him. He was careful to avoid touching her skin; Phil must have warned him. "Are you okay?"

"Penguin?" Zockinski lifted his head from the wall and smirked at her.

"I *was* okay," she sighed. This was how it started. First your nickname got out, then your squad mates started leaving little items in your gear as a joke, and before you know it you're packing a bag full of toy penguins all over the Middle East. "You have problems getting in here?"

"Me? No. Pat did. I just walked behind him while he cleared a path. The place is on lockdown," Josh said, and pulled out a notepad. "I need a full report while everything is still fresh. This is about to hit the news cycle in a big way and I'm looking at a long night of interviews."

Rachel told her side of the story first, and mostly out loud for Hill's benefit, then showed Josh the video of her confrontation with Witcham in the parking garage. When she was finished, Hill filled in what had come before. Glazer was in Interrogation when Rachel had warned them to put him in lockdown. Hill and Jason had barely dropped the blinds over the windows before Glazer hit them. He had been chained to the table one instant and was loose the next. Glazer kicked Hill hard enough to knock the wind out of him, smashed Jason's head against the table, then broke the locked knob off of the door and was gone.

"Penguin?" Mulcahy, physically occupied with Jason and the arrival of the paramedics, reached out to her.

Rachel reactivated the emotional spectrum to read him. *"I'm fine,"* she assured Mulcahy. *"You can debrief me later. Just know that I gave Sturtevant the tape."*

"What's on it that shouldn't be?"

"Nothing of substance about OACET. I was running emotions while recording but those could be... I don't know, body temperature as seen through concrete, I suppose.

"Oh, and one more thing," she continued, hiding her mouth as she pretended to scratch her nose. *"He all but confessed that*

Hanlon hired him."

Mulcahy shone in purple and gold. *"On tape."*

"Yes."

"You got that on tape."

She smiled like an angel. Across from her, Phil noticed and chuckled softly.

"What are the odds it ends up online?" Mulcahy asked.

"One hundred percent," she replied, watching Sturtevant. *"I'll keep passing out the file until someone cashes it in with a network for a payout. It ends with the shooting so it'll go viral."*

Mulcahy went blue so quickly it was as though he had dipped himself in paint. *"Thanks, Penguin."*

Even if she couldn't have seen his relief, she would have felt it through the link. *"No problem,"* she replied. He looked towards the destruction in the hallway and silently laughed.

"I'm gonna go clean up," Rachel said. Every inch of her body felt crusty with stress. She wanted nothing more than to soak herself in a hot bath until she stopped trembling, but she'd settle for coffee in the break room.

She tried to stand and couldn't; her knees had frozen in place and buckled under her.

"C'mon," Santino said, and helped her up. She threw an arm across his shoulders again. He was a good foot taller than she was, and they resumed their earlier awkward stagger down the hallway.

The building had been evacuated. They encountered the odd person here and there, usually a paramedic who demanded they accompany him outside for medical assistance; Rachel and Santino ignored them and pushed on.

"I could carry you," he said.

"And my knees could magically heal themselves," she said. "Since neither of those is about to happen, we'll just make do."

He laughed.

When they reached the break room, Santino lowered her into the chair closest to the door. Rachel was relieved to find the seat was cool; everything that had happened had seemed to fall on top of each other, but it was somehow comforting to know there had been enough time for the chair to lose all trace of her body heat.

"Coffee?" Santino asked.

"Yes," she said, then saw the mess where she had dropped the coffee pot. The carafe had burst, throwing glass and water across the linoleum. "No."

There was a knock on the wall beside the open door. Sturtevant walked in before they could answer.

"Just got the call," he said. "Minor injuries, mostly, but there's no sign of Witcham or Glazer."

"There won't be," Santino sighed. "At least we know why the ventilation in the garage was crap. They had it blocked off for their escape route. They had this planned out for months."

"Yeah, I've already called the service company. They've got some explaining to do. Did you see where Witcham went?" Sturtevant asked Rachel, his hand moving towards his pocket for his phone.

"No," she said, keeping her voice steady. The inevitable giggle fit was creeping closer. "I'm so burned out right now that I can't see through an open window. Santino's right, though. Glazer let himself get taken because he knew he could walk out of here whenever he wanted."

"I brought him back to First," the Chief of Detectives said, shaking his head. "We could have interrogated him in Virginia and none of this would have happened."

"Nobody was killed, sir," Rachel reminded him. "It could have been much worse. And there was no way you could have known."

"Besides," Santino added. "Glazer would have found a way to be transferred back to First District Station. All of this was pretty much inevitable."

Rachel dropped her head to the table and used her arms to hide her face.

"Agent Peng," Sturtevant said after a long moment. "I should apologize. I had no cause to threaten you by taking away your place with us."

"S'okay," Rachel replied from inside of the hollow of her arms. Santino leaned forward and poked her, and she drew herself together and sat up. Her head started pounding. "You did what you thought was right."

"But it wasn't right. Hill and I had a long conversation about OACET. He asked me to remember how every branch of government has its own agenda. Sometimes it's convenient for me to forget you're not actually one of my officers. You were trying to tell us something before you interviewed Glazer. Was it about Hanlon?"

Rachel nodded curtly at Sturtevant. She wished she could thank Hill for giving her such a perfect excuse.

"I should have listened," Sturtevant said. "In the future, please feel free to remind me that you're a peer instead of a subordinate.

"And grow some gray hair or some wrinkles," he said, grinning. "You look too young."

"A few more days like today, sir, and I'm sure that will take care of itself."

He nodded. "You have the evening off, Agent Peng. You too, Officer Santino. The paperwork will keep."

"Thank you, sir," she said, and meant it. Then: "Sir?"

He looked back at her.

"You remember how Glazer threatened me with a secret?"

Beside her, Santino perked up warily.

"He wasn't lying," Rachel continued. "Something worse is coming. We should talk before it does."

Chief Sturtevant chuckled, and swept the pool of glass and water from the broken coffee pot around with his shoe. "One crisis at a time, Agent Peng."

Santino sighed in relief as Sturtevant closed the door behind him. "That was ballsy."

"Ball-less," she corrected. "And I needed to do it. An ounce of prevention is worth a pound of pink slips."

"You wouldn't be unemployed," he said. "You'd just go back

to OACET."

She shrugged. "But I wouldn't be here."

Her partner grinned.

There was a second knock, this one against the metal of the closed door. Santino looked at her as he got up.

"Hell if I know who it is," she said. "I'm all but shut down right now."

Santino opened the door. Jason had propped himself up against the jamb. His head was heavily bandaged in white gauze, his skin so pale it was hard to tell where the one ended and the other began.

"Can I talk to Rachel?" Jason asked.

"Uh…" Santino was lost.

"I'm offline," Jason explained, and touched the gauze wrapped around his head.

Santino glanced back at Rachel, who nodded. "Yeah," Santino said. "See you guys later."

Jason looped a hand under the backrest of the chair closest to her and tried to use his body weight to tug it away from the table. Rachel pushed it towards him; her arms felt like lead. *How many Agents does it take to move a chair?* she thought, and the first of the giggles escaped. "How are you doing?" she asked to cover it up.

"We're about to find out," Jason said, and laced his fingers together. "Make sure I shut down if I'm about to stroke out or something, okay?" He brightened as he came back online, and sighed in relief as the link welcomed him home.

"Better?"

"Yeah." He closed his eyes and let the collective wash over him.

Rachel gave him a few minutes to let him catch up with the link, then asked: *"What did you want to talk about?"*

Jason paused before he closed himself tight against the others. "I think this might be for you," he whispered.

His voice was so low that she had trouble hearing him. "What?"

"This," he said, and pressed something into her hand. "I found it in my pocket when I woke up."

She didn't bother to flip her implant to a close scan; she knew what it was by the feel of it. "I am so sorry," she whispered back. "I thought Glazer was going to cut his way out of here. I didn't know they had a real escape plan. And we needed... You know what we needed." Her voice cracked on a giggle that was too close to a sob. "I'm so sorry."

Jason already knew; she had been carrying guilt when he touched her. "It's okay," he assured her, still speaking in a whisper. He covered her hand with his own and his sincerity flooded through her. "I wanted you to know it really is okay. Mulcahy told me you just saved us from the think tanks. That's worth a concussion any day."

She wasn't as sure, but she slipped the small object into her own pocket for safekeeping.

A paperclip twisted into the shape of a heart.

TWENTY-TWO

There were late fireflies and a new baby, and the promise of barbeque after the caterers finished setting out the steam trays. This was one of OACET's civilized parties, open to friends and relatives; Shawn, almost casual in jeans and a light long-sleeved tee, had promised he would talk about nothing but fishing and would keep the conversations short.

She had stolen the baby and commandeered an overstuffed chaise lounge that had been dragged out onto the patio. Rachel lay supine with a pillow stuffed under her busted knees and Avery wrapped in a gentle bear hug on her chest, occasionally planting kisses on the baby's thin scalp. Avery was in that fleeting stage where she could sleep through a full-blown bacchanalia, which was convenient; even when they kept themselves on a short leash, the Agents would start the next day with a hunt for their clothes.

Babies are blue, she thought. *And silver and gold and cream and seafoam green, all puffing in a cloud, but mostly soft, soft blue.* Rachel might never move again.

"Any chance you'll let me hold her?" Santino plunked down beside them on an ottoman.

"Nope." Rachel snuck another kiss. "I'm not giving her up until she's hungry or I have to pee."

Her partner handed her a fresh beer with a swirly straw.

"Dirty pool, Mister Bond," she said, and swept the beer over her head in an awkward arc so the condensation wouldn't drip on the baby.

"Sturtevant called," he said.

"Is he coming?" Rachel asked.

He shook his head. "Said he had a prior commitment."

She wasn't surprised. The Chief of Detectives had avoided

her most of the week but she didn't hold it against him. Rachel was sure someone at the Metropolitan Police Department was pressuring him about their alliance with OACET, but she didn't know how, and tonight she couldn't be bothered to care. Sturtevant would probably resolve it without her help; if not, she'd wait a few more days for the dust to settle before she kicked it up again.

The whole mess had ended beautifully for OACET, with back-to-back press conferences leaving barely enough time for the pundits to nitpick each one apart. They lacked the legal language to define why the Witcham shooting wasn't a good one, the circumstances being so surreal that Rachel had been given a pass. She was federal, not police, and those four perfect shots through Glazer's legs made it impossible for Internal Affairs to argue that Rachel had intended anything other than to incapacitate. If she had killed Witcham, or if he hadn't kidnapped children? Well, things probably would have been different. But the video of her turning his legs into shards of bone made it a little easier to accept that Witcham hadn't gotten away entirely scot-free.

(That video had been viewed over eighteen million times on YouTube this week alone; Rachel had nearly achieved talking dog status. The conspiracy theorists had seized on Witcham's incrimination of Senator Hanlon and were running wild with it. Maybe, with luck, some intrepid reporter would try to fact-check those rumors and would do OACET's work for them.)

Several days after the shooting, Charlotte Gallagher had arrived on the mansion's doorstep, unannounced. Rachel had been at First District Station at the time, so Mulcahy had taken Gallagher on a tour of the upper floors, the two of them working out the details of a liaison of Agents to the FBI. Four Agents had been reassigned on temporary loan. Rachel and Phil were teaching them the finer points of looking through walls.

Edwards had cornered Rachel in the coffee shop, demanding to know why she hadn't bothered to keep him updated on the case; he had learned about Eric Witcham after he had been served the subpoena. Rachel had shrugged and played dumb until Edwards swept her cappuccino from the table, and then Rachel had lost her temper and manipulated him into a brief staring contest until he fled the store, shaken. On impulse, she had limped after him to apologize. They ended up taking shelter at a bus stop from the sheeting rain of a late summer storm, reminiscing about the man both she and Edwards had come to know as Charley Brazee. They had shaken hands before she caught a cab home.

And then Carlota had gone into labor. All of OACET had fallen silent while their first baby was born. (Mainly because they couldn't hear each other over Carlota's shouting; when Rachel had asked Mako why he hadn't blocked his wife from the link, the huge weightlifter blinked at her and walked away, shaking his head.) Jenny Davies and the rest of the medical team had concerns about the neurological implications of introducing a new mind to the world in the middle of a technological psychic maelstrom, but the kid was loved beyond belief and they all decided that nothing else mattered.

Everything had wrapped up neat and tidy, except for those last two questions.

She had walked in on Mulcahy, drawn by her own voice as she passed his office. The lights were out and he had his feet up on his desk as he listened to the audio recording of her brief phone call with Witcham. She stood in the doorway and heard herself say: *"Then why try to break us? Why not help us?"*

She and Mulcahy had locked eyes, and he shrugged. Rachel had eased herself back through his door and limped away.

Neither of them had felt the need to ask whether Witcham was just that good.

Or what it might mean that she had crippled the man who had singlehandedly altered the public's opinion of OACET.

Avery twitched, a tiny infant dream tugging at her. Rachel snuggled her chin up beside the baby's soft peach fuzz hair and listened to her breathe.

Rachel ran a quick scan through the crowd. The outsiders

marveled at the mansion. At night, lit by the faux gas lamps, it was easy to overlook how run-down the place was. There was a volleyball game and some early swimmers paddling in the pool, and enough talking and laughter outside of the link to make it a real party.

Across the patio, Josh was tending bar. The crowd was stacked three deep, most of them running a lustful red as they watched him flip bottles and pour cocktails.

There were the usual family dynamics. The gardeners were clustered by the edge of the new grass, sipping their drinks as they eyed the volleyball players with trepidation. The couples nagged and bickered sweetly. Those with quick hands or combat experience were juggling knives, lit torches, running chainsaws... The mansion provided a wealth of props for those who loved to show off.

She couldn't find either Phil or Jason, but they had brought dates from outside of OACET. They were enjoying the spoils of fame; Phil said had never been asked out more in his entire life than over the past week. If they were holed up behind a stack of boxes somewhere, she wasn't about to interrupt.

Zockinski's core of autumn orange popped at the edge of the driveway, Hill's forest green beside it. Rachel nearly sat up in surprise before the topheavy weight of the baby pushed her flat against the lounge. The detectives had come together and arrived late. Rachel hadn't thought they would come at all. Both men had declined her first invitation, but she had pushed it on them the rest of the week until they finally accepted. She had assumed they had agreed just to get her to shut up.

Avery made a tiny mewling sound, and her hands clenched on Rachel's shirt as she started to stir; Rachel pinged Mako to come and get his daughter.

Santino scooted his ottoman so his back was against a pillar. "How are the knees?"

"Fine. Davies says I need to take it slow for a few weeks, but there's no permanent damage." Rachel had been coerced into a second physical before the party started, but Jenny Davies had

had ulterior motives. The medical researcher had received a copy of Phil's adapted scanning autoscript, and was obsessed with its potential as a diagnostic instrument. Davies had all but held a gun to Rachel's head to teach her how to apply this new autoscript to deep tissue, blood, and bone. Rachel had tried her best to show Davies what she could, and fought her nausea for almost an hour until she finally threw up in the trash can.

"So..." she said, and paused to search out the end of her straw.

"I haven't seen her," her partner said in a flat voice.

"Okay," Rachel said. Santino had driven her to the mansion earlier that afternoon and had disappeared after they arrived, so she had assumed the best even though Zia was conspicuously absent from the party. Last Saturday, he had gone out to meet Zia for coffee, claiming they would work through their shared attraction like reasonable adults. He had come home an hour later in a red-white rage. Rachel had taken him straight to the OACET shooting range to let him blow off his anger with a semiautomatic tactical shotgun. He refused to say what had happened and Rachel had gathered that the conversation had not gone well, but his core colors were thoroughly and permanently saturated with Zia's and he had stopped mentioning his inevitable reunion with his ex-girlfriend. On Sunday morning, Rachel found a check taped to the coffee pot with "rent & utilities" scrawled across the bottom. They had gone shopping for furniture for the guest room that afternoon.

Mako shuffled towards them over the lawn. The man's conversational colors were layered in exhausted grays.

"Where's Carlota?" Santino asked.

"Sleeping, where else?" Mako glanced towards the mansion. "She's conked out in one of the bedrooms."

"You're not with her?" Santino asked. The dark circles under Mako's eyes made him look as though he was ready to suit up for the Superbowl.

"Pat and I were... uh..." Mako was suddenly interested in everything other than Santino. "... moving stuff for the party."

"Where'd you and Mulcahy put his car?" Rachel asked.

Santino choked on his beer. "My car? What?"

"It's your own fault for driving a hybrid," Mako sighed. "So light, so tiny."

"What did you do with my car?"

"Don't worry," Rachel shushed him as Avery began to squirm. "You'll get it back. We've got his baby."

Zockinski and Hill came out of the crowd. "Holy sh... crud," Mako said, fumbling his way through a new parent's self-censorship.

"I know," Rachel sniffed. A gorgeous brunette hung off of Zockinski's arm; his wife was stunning. "How is that fair?"

When they were close enough so she didn't have to shout, Rachel asked Zockinski, "No kids?"

"Got a sitter," he said. His conversational colors dimpled slightly as he told a white lie. "We'll probably be out past their bedtime."

Oh well, Rachel thought. He trusted them enough to bring his wife. It was a good start.

"This place is amazing," Zockinski's wife said. And it was, a fairy kingdom at twilight as long as you could overlook the cracked concrete and the areas roped off to let the seedlings grow.

"Thanks," Rachel said. "We've been renovating it since we moved in. The work is finally starting to show."

"You find the mansion okay?" Santino asked Hill.

"Got here a while ago." The tall man shrugged and took a pull from his bottle. "We would have come over sooner but there's this guy standing by the bar who really wants to talk about fish."

"Fishing?"

"No, just… fish."

"Right," Rachel said quickly. "Introductions. Mako, this is Detective Matt Hill. We worked with him on the Eric Witcham case. Matt, this is Agent Marc Hill. We call him Mako."

Zockinski looked between the two Hills and opened his

mouth, and Rachel jabbed him in the thigh with her big toe, hard.

The two men shook hands and appraised each other. I noticed their core colors had the same hints of green. handshake started as casual but their conversational co picked up speed as they shifted from casual small talk to vi red recognition.

"And Matt?" Rachel rolled forward onto her feet an pressed the drowsy baby into her father's arms before either man could speak. "This is Avery. She's your first cousin once removed, probably? I think that's how the genealogy goes."

Santino coughed, then roared with laughter. Zockinski was right behind him.

The Hills blinked and gaped, and looked down at Rachel.

Who smiled.

nearest

achel

Their

lors

id

...ledgements and Apologies

...u put up with my nonsense and give so much ...rn. I love you and I'm lucky to have you as my

... book couldn't have been written without the help of ...cond readers. Thanks to Fuzz, Gary, Tiff, Joris, Greg, ...ie, and Elizabeth, who slogged through countless drafts ...nd gave excellent critical feedback. Danny, thank you for the last-minute copy edits. As always, Dave, my friend and website administrator, helped me when I had no idea I needed help, and is apparently far more knowledgeable about gun ownership and ballistics than I had realized.

Rose Loughran of Red Moon Rising is responsible for the fantastic cover art.

Credit goes to the Foglios at Girl Genius for the lovely and inspirational phrase, "mad social scientist"—Eric Witcham will be back.

With apologies to Dante, who let me know that as a person of Irish ancestry herself, she was horrified that I credited whiskey to Tennessee. And my sincere apologies to those readers, authors, and artists I have met online and have no doubt offended in some way. Social awkwardness: it's how I roll.

I have taken some liberties with locations. The OACET mansion does not exist (although I wish it did), and while First District Station is indeed a recently remodeled elementary school, the rodeo chute off of the Interrogation wing and its attached parking garage are my own additions.

The Portsmouth Marine Terminal is in the same place but is slightly smaller than described. Directly across the harbor is its sister port, the Norfolk International Terminals, and I've combined them into a single entity. The environmental

problems associated with the dumping of shipping c
are quite real.

The Smithsonian will soon be shutting its dinosaur
while they renovate the hall. The estimated time requir
this renovation is five to seven years. Get in while you still

Finally, *Digital Divide* is set in a larger fictional unive
Patrick Mulcahy's story is free to all readers and is in grap
novel form at agirlandherfed.com. *Digital Divide*, as well as th
four upcoming novels in the Rachel Peng series, will fill in the
five-year gap between when Mulcahy discovered the purpose
of their implants and when he was finally able to establish
OACET as an independent federal organization. Please excuse
the talking koala; he has a good heart.

You can find updates on current projects and novels at
kbspangler.com and agirlandherfed.com. Thanks for reading!

Rachel Peng and Raul Santino will be back in *Maker Space*

ntainers

s away
d for
can.
rse.
nic
e